THE PURE
PRODUCT

THE PURE PRODUCT

STORIES BY

JOHN KESSEL

TOR®

A TOM DOHERTY ASSOCIATES BOOK

NEW YORK

THE PURE PRODUCT

Copyright © 1997 by John Kessel

This book is printed on acid-free paper.

A Tor Book
Published by Tom Doherty Associates, Inc.
175 Fifth Avenue
New York, NY 10010

Tor Books on the World Wide Web:
http://www.tor.com

Tor® is a registered trademark of Tom Doherty Associates, Inc.

Library of Congress Cataloging-in-Publication Data

Kessel, John.
    The pure product : stories / by John Kessel.
        p. cm.
    "A Tom Doherty Associates book."
    ISBN 0-312-86117-6
    I. Title.
PS3561.E6675P87   1997
813'.54—dc21   97-23554
                                          CIP

First Edition: December 1997

Printed in the United States of America

0 9 8 7 6 5 4 3 2 1

The pure products of America go crazy.

—William Carlos Williams

CONTENTS

SOME LIKE IT COLD

Her heroes were Abraham Lincoln and Albert Einstein. Lincoln was out of the question, but with a little work I could look Einsteinesque. I grew a dark mustache, adopted wild graying hair. From wardrobe I requisitioned a pair of wool slacks, a white cotton shirt, a gabardine jacket with narrow lapels. The shoes were my own, my prized possession—genuine leather, Australian copies of mid–twentieth century brogues, well broken in. The prep-room mirror reflected back a handsomer, taller, younger relative of old Albert, a cross between Einstein and her psychiatrist Dr. Greenson.

The moment-universes surrounding the evening of Saturday, August 4th were so thoroughly burned—tourists, biographers, conspiracy hunters, masturbators—that there was no sense arriving then. Besides, I wanted to get a taste of the old L.A., before the quake. So I selected the Friday evening 18:00 PDT moment-universe. I materialized in a stall in the men's room at the Santa Monica Municipal Airport. Some aim for deserted places; I like airports, train stations, bus terminals. Lots of strangers if you've missed some detail of costume. Public transport easily available. Crowds to lose oneself in. The portable unit, disguised as an overnight bag, never looks out of place. I stopped in a shop and bought a couple of packs of Luckies. At the Hertz counter I rented a navy blue Plymouth with push button transmission, threw my canvas camera bag and overnight case into the back and, checking the map, puzzled out the motel address on Wilshire Boulevard that Research had found for me.

The hotel was pink stucco and a red tile roof, a courtyard pool where a teenaged boy in white T-shirt and D.A. haircut leaned on a cleaning net and flirted with a couple of fifteen-year-old girls. I sat in the shadowed doorway of my room, smoked a Lucky and watched until a fat woman in a caftan came out and yelled at the boy to get back to work. The girls giggled.

The early evening I spent driving around. In Santa Monica I saw the pre-tsunami pier, the one she would tell Greenson she was going to visit Saturday night, before she changed her mind and stayed home. I ate at the Dancers, a slab of prime rib, a baked potato the size of a football, a bottle of zinfandel. Afterward I drove my Plymouth along the Miracle Mile. I rolled down the windows and let the warm air wash over me, inspecting the strip joints, theaters, bars and hookers. A number of the women, looking like her in cotton-candy hair and tight dresses, gave me the eye as I cruised by.

I pulled into the lot beside a club called the Blue Note. Over the door a blue neon martini glass swamped a green neon olive in gold neon gin. Inside I ordered a scotch and listened to a trio play jazz. A thin white guy with a goatee strangled his saxophone: somewhere in there might be a melody. These cutting-edge late moderns thought they had the future augured. The future would be cool and atonal, they thought. No squares allowed. They didn't understand that the future, like the present, would be dominated by saps, and the big rush of 2043 would be barbershop quartets.

I sipped scotch. A brutal high, alcohol, like putting your head in a vise. I liked it. I smoked a couple more Luckies, layering a nicotine buzz over the alcohol. I watched couples in the dim corners of booths talk about their pasts and their futures, all those words prelude to going to bed. Back in Brentwood she was spending another sleepless night harassed by calls telling her to leave Bobby Kennedy alone.

A woman with dark Jackie hair, black gloves and a very low-cut dress sat down on the stool next to me. The song expired and there was a smattering of applause. "I hate this modern crap, don't you?" the woman said.

"It's emblematic of the times," I said.

She gave me a look, decided to laugh. "You can have the times."

"I've seen worse," I said.

"You're not American, are you? The accent."

"I was born in Germany."

"Ah. So you've seen bad times?"

I sipped my scotch. "You could say so." Her eyelids were heavy with shadow, eyelashes a centimeter long. Pale pink lipstick made her thin lips look cool; I wondered if they really were. "Let me buy you a drink."

"Thanks." She watched me fumble with the queer, nineteenth-century-style currency. Pyramids with eyes on them, redeemable in silver on demand. I bought her a gin and tonic. "My name's Carol," she told me.

"I am Detlev."

"Detleff? Funny name."

"Not so common, even in Germany."

"So Detleff, what brings you to L.A? You come over the Berlin Wall?"

"I'm here to see a movie star."

She snorted. "Won't find any in here."

"I think you could be a movie star, Carol."

"You're not going to believe this, Detleff, but I've heard that line before."

We flirted through three drinks. She told me she was lonely, I told her I was a stranger. We fell toward a typical liaison of the Penicillin Era: we learned enough about each other (who knew how much of it true?) not to let what we didn't know come between us and what we wanted. Her image of me was compounded of her own fantasies. I didn't have so many illusions. Or maybe mine were larger still, since I knew next to nothing about these people other than what I'd gleaned from images projected on various screens. Images were my job.

I studied the cleavage displayed by Carol's dress, she leaned against my shoulder, and from this we generated a lust we imagined would turn to sweet compassion, make up for our losses, and leave us blissfully complete in the same place. We would clutch each other's bodies until we were spent, lie holding each other, our souls commingled, the first moment of a perfect marriage that would extend forward from this night in an endless string of equally fulfilling nights. Then we'd part in the morning and never see each other again.

That was the dream. I followed her back to her apartment and we did our best to produce it. Afterward I lay awake thinking of Gabrielle, just after we'd married, sunbathing on the screened beach at Nice. I'd watched her, as had the men who passed by. How much did she want us to look at her? Was there any difference, in her mind, between my regard and theirs?

At dawn I left Carol asleep, made my way back to the pink hotel and got some sleep of my own.

Saturday I spent touring pre-quake L.A. I indulged vices I could not indulge in 2043. I smoked many cigarettes. I walked outside in direct sunlight. I bought a copy of the Wilhelm edition of the *I Ching*, printed on real paper. At mid-afternoon I stepped into a diner and ordered a bacon cheeseburger, rare, with lettuce and tomato and a side of fries. My mouth watered as the waitress set it in front of me, but after two bites a wave of nausea overcame me. Hands sticky with blood and mayonnaise, I watched the grease congeal in the corner of the plate.

So far, so good. I was a fan of the dirty pleasures of the twentieth century. Things were so much more complicated then. People walked the streets under the shadow of the bomb. At some almost biological level they knew that they might be vaporized at any second. Their blood vibrated with angst. Even the blond ones. I imagined my ancestors half a world away, in a country they expected momentarily to turn into a radioactive battle-ground, carrying their burden of guilt through the Englischer Garten. Sober Adenauer, struggling to stitch together half a nation. None of them fat, bored, or decadent.

And Marilyn, the world over, was their goddess. That improbable female body, that infantile voice, that oblivious demeanor.

Architecturally, L.A. 1962 was a disappointment. There was the appropriate amount of kitsch, hot dog stands shaped like hot dogs and chiropractor's offices like flying saucers, but the really big skyscrapers that would come down in the quake hadn't been built yet. Maybe some of them wouldn't be built in this time line anymore, thanks to me. By now my presence had already set this history off down another path from the one of my home. Anything I did toppled dominoes. Perhaps Carol's life would be ruined by the memory of our night of perfect love. Perhaps the cigarettes I bought saved crucial lives. Perhaps the breeze of my Plymouth's passing brought rain to Belgrade, drought to India. For better or worse, who could say?

I killed time into the early evening. By now she was going through the two-hour session with Greenson, trying to shore up her personality against that night's depression.

At nine I took my camera bag and the portable unit and got into the rental car. It was still too early, but I was so keyed up I couldn't sit still. I drove up the Pacific Coast Highway, walked along the beach at Malibu, then turned around and headed back. Sunset Boulevard twisted through the hills. The lights of the houses flickered between trees. In Brentwood I had some trouble finding Carmelina, drove past, then doubled back. Marilyn's house was on Fifth Helena, a short street off Carmelina ending in a cul-de-sac. I parked at the end, slung my bags over my shoulder and walked back.

A brick and stucco wall shielded the house from the street. I circled around through the neighbor's yard, pushed through the bougainvillea and approached from the back. It was a modest hacienda-style ranch, a couple of bedrooms, tile roof. The patio lights were off and the water in the pool lay smooth as dark glass. Lights shone from the end bedroom.

First problem would be to get rid of Eunice Murray, her housekeeper. If what had happened in our history was true in this one, Murray had gone to sleep at mid-evening. I stepped quietly through the back door, found her in her bedroom and slapped a sedative patch onto her forearm, holding my hand across her mouth against her struggling until she was out.

A long phone cord snaked down the hall from the living room and under the other bedroom door. The door was locked. Outside, I pushed through the shrubs, mucking up my shoes in the soft soil, reached in through the bars over the opened window and pushed aside the blackout curtains. Marilyn sprawled face-down across the bed, right arm dangling off the side, receiver clutched in her hand. I found the unbarred casement window on the adjacent side of the house, broke it open, then climbed inside. Her breathing was deep and irregular. Her skin was clammy. Only the faintest pulse at her neck.

I got my bag, rolled her onto her back, pried back her eyelid and shone a light into her eye. Her pupil barely contracted. I had come late on purpose, but this was not good.

I gave her a shot of apomorphine, lifted her off the bed and shouldered her toward the bathroom. She was surprisingly light—gaunt, even. I could feel her ribs. In the bathroom, full of plaster and junk from the remodelers, I held her over the toilet until she vomited. No food, but some undigested capsules. That would have been a good sign, except she habitually pierced them with a pin so they'd work faster. There was no way of telling how much Nembutal she had in her bloodstream.

I dug my thumb into the crook of her elbow, forcing the tendon. "Wake up, Norma Jeane," I said. "Time to wake up." No reaction.

I took her back to the bed and got the blood filter out of my camera bag. The studio'd had me practicing on indigents hired from the state. I wiped a pharmacy's worth of pill bottles from the flimsy table next to the bed and set up the machine. The shunt slipped easily into the vein in her arm, and I fiddled with the flow until the readout went green. What with one thing and another I had a busy half-hour before she was resting in bed, bundled up, feet elevated, asleep but breathing normally, God in his heaven and her blood circulating merrily through the filter like money through my bank account.

I went outside and smoked a cigarette. The stars were out and a breeze had kicked up. On the tile threshold outside the front door words were emblazoned: CURSUM PERFICIO. *I am finishing my journey.* I looked in on the sleeping Mrs. Murray. I went back and sat in the bedroom. The place was a mess. Forests of pill bottles covered every horizontal surface. A stack of Sinatra records sat on the record player. On top: "High Hopes." Loose-leaf binders lay scattered all over the floor. I picked one up. It was a script for *Something's Got to Give.*

I read through the script. It wasn't very good. About two A.M. she moaned and started to move. I slapped a clarifier patch onto her arm. It wouldn't push the pentobarbital out of her system any faster, but when it began to take hold it would make her feel better.

About three the blood filter beeped. I removed the shunt, sat her up, made her drink a liter of electrolyte. It took her a while to get it all down. She looked at me through fogged eyes. She smelled sour and did not look like the most beautiful woman in the world.

"What happened?" she mumbled.

"You took too many pills. You're going to be all right."

I helped her into a robe, then walked her down the hallway and around the living room until she began to take some of the weight herself. At one end of the room hung a couple of lurid Mexican Day of the Dead masks, at the other a framed portrait of Lincoln. When I got tired of facing down the leering ghouls and honest Abe, I took her outside and we marched around the pool. The breeze wrote cat's paws on the surface of the water. After a while she began to come around. She tried to pull away but was weak as a baby. "Let me go," she mumbled.

"You want to stop walking?"

"I want to sleep," she said.

"Keep walking." We circled the pool for another quarter-hour. In the distance I heard sparse traffic on Sunset; nearer the breeze rustled the fan palms. I was sweaty, she was cold.

"Please," she whined. "Let's stop."

I let her down onto a patio chair, went inside, found some coffee and set a pot brewing. I brought a blanket out, wrapped her in it, poked her to keep her awake. Eventually she sat there sipping coffee, holding the cup in both hands to warm them, hair down in her eyes and eyelashes gummed together. She looked tired.

"How are you?" I asked.

"Alive. Bad luck." She started to cry. "Cruel, all of them, all those bastards. Oh, Jesus . . ."

I let her cry for a while. I gave her a handkerchief and she dried her eyes, blew her nose. The most beautiful woman in the world. "Who are you?" she asked.

"My name is Detlev Gruber. Call me Det."

"What are you doing here? Where's Mrs. Murray?"

"You don't remember? You sent her home."

She took a sip of coffee, watching me over the rim of the cup.

"I'm here to help you, Marilyn. To rescue you."

"Rescue me?"

"I know how hard things are, how lonely you've been. I knew that you would try to kill yourself."

"I was just trying to get some sleep."

"Do you really think that's all there is to it?"

"Listen, mister, I don't know who you are but I don't need your help and if you don't get out of here pretty soon I'm going to call the police." At the end her voice trailed off pitifully. "I'm sorry," she said.

"Don't be sorry. I'm here to save you from all this."

Hands shaking, she put down the cup. I had never seen a face more vulnerable. She tried to hide it, but her expression was full of need. I felt an urge to protect her that, despite the fact she was a wreck, was pure sex. "I'm cold," she said. "Can we go inside?"

We went inside. We sat in the living room, she on the sofa and me in an uncomfortable Spanish chair, and I told her things about her life that nobody should have known but her. The abortions. The suicide attempts. The Kennedy affairs. More than that, the fear of loneliness, the fear of insanity, the fear of aging. I found myself warming to the role of rescuer. I really did want to hold her. She was not able to keep up her hostility in the face of the knowledge that I was telling her the simple truth. Miller had written how grateful she was every time he'd saved her life, and it looked like that reaction was coming through for me now. She'd always liked being rescued, and the men who rescued her.

The clarifier might have had something to do with it, too. Finally she protested, "How do you know all this?"

"This is going to be the hardest part, Marilyn. I know because I'm from the future. If I had not shown up here, you would have died tonight. It's recorded history."

She laughed. "From the future?"

"Absolutely."

"Right."

"I'm not lying to you, Marilyn. If I didn't care, would you be alive now?"

She pulled the blanket tighter around her. "What does the future want with me?"

"You're the most famous actress of your era. Your death would be a great tragedy, and we want to prevent that."

"What good does this do me? I'm still stuck in the same shit."

"You don't have to be." She tried to look skeptical, but hope was written in every tremble of her body. It was frightening. "I want you to come with me back to the future, Marilyn."

She stared at me. "You must be crazy. I wouldn't know anybody. No friends, no family."

"You have no family. Your mother is in an institution. And where were your friends tonight?"

She put her hand to her head, rubbed her forehead, a gesture so full of intelligence that I had a sudden sense of her as a real person, a grown woman in a lot of trouble. "You don't want to mess with me," she said. "I'm not worth it. I'm nothing but trouble."

"I can cure your trouble. In the future we have ways. No one here really cares for you, Marilyn, no one truly understands you. That dark pit of despair that opens up inside you—we can fill it. We can heal the wounds you've had since you were a little girl, make up for all the neglect you've suffered, keep you young forever. We have these powers. It's my job to correct the mistakes of the past, for special people. You're one of them. I have a team of caregivers waiting, a home, emotional support, understanding."

"Yeah. Another institution. I can't take it."

I came over, sat beside her, lowered my voice, looked her in the eyes. Time for the closer. "You know that poem—that Yeats poem?"

"What poem?"

" 'Never Give All the Heart.' " Research had made me memorize it. It was one of her favorites.

> *"Never give all the heart, for love,*
> *Will hardly seem worth thinking of*
> *To passionate women if it seem*
> *Certain, and they never dream*
> *That it fades out from kiss to kiss*
> *For everything that's lovely is*
> *But a brief, dreamy, kind delight . . ."*

She stopped me. "What about it?" Her voice was edgy.

"Just that life doesn't have to be like the poem, brief, and you don't have to suffer. You don't have to give all the heart, and lose."

She sat there, wound in the blanket. Clearly I had touched something in her.

"Think about it," I said. I went outside and smoked another Lucky. When I'd started working for DAA I'd considered this a glamour job. Exotic times, famous people. And I was good at it. A quick study, smart, adaptable. Sincere. I was so good that Gabrielle came to hate me, and left.

After a considerable while Marilyn came outside, the blanket over her head and shoulders like an Indian.

"Well, kemosabe?" I asked.

Despite herself, she smiled. Although the light was dim, the crow's-feet at the corners of her eyes were visible. "If I don't like it, will you bring me back?"

"You'll like it. But if you don't I promise I'll bring you back."

"Okay. What do I have to do?"

"Just pack a few things to take with you—the most important ones."

I waited while she threw some clothes into a suitcase. She took the Lincoln portrait off the wall and put it in on top. I bagged the blood filter and set up the portable unit in the living room.

"Maf!" she said.

"What?"

"My dog!" She looked crushed, as if she were about to collapse. "Who'll take care of Maf?"

"Mrs. Murray will."

"She hates him! I can't trust her." She was disintegrating. "I can't go. This isn't a good idea."

"Where is Maf? We'll take him."

We went out to the guest house. The place stank. The dog, sleeping on an old fur coat, launched himself at me, yapping, as soon as we opened the door. It was one of those inbred overgroomed toy poodles that you want to drop-kick into the next universe. She picked him up, cooed over him, made me get a bag of dog food and his water dish. I gritted my teeth.

In the living room I moved the chair aside and made her stand in the center of the room while I laid the cable in a circle around us to outline the field. She was nervous. I held her hand, she held the dog. "Here we go, Marilyn."

I touched the switch on the case. Marilyn's living room receded from us in all directions, we fell like pebbles into a dark well, and from infinitely far away the transit stage at DAA rushed forward to surround us. The dog growled. Marilyn swayed, put a hand to her head. I held her arm.

From the control booth Scoville and a nurse came up to us.

The nurse took Marilyn's other side. "Marilyn, this is a nurse who's going to help you get some rest. And this is Derek Scoville, who's running this operation."

We got her into the suite and the doctors shot her full of metabolic cleansers. I promised her I'd take care of Maf, then pawned the dog off on the staff. I held her hand, smiled reassuringly, sat with her until she went to sleep. Lying there she looked calm, confident. She liked being cared for; she was used to it. Now she had a whole new world waiting to take care of her. She thought.

It was all up to me.

I went to the prep room, showered and switched to street clothes: an onyx Singapore silk shirt, cotton baggies, spex. The weather report said it was a bad UV day: I selected a broad-brimmed hat. I was inspecting my shoes, coated with muck from Marilyn's garden, when a summons from Scoville showed in the corner of my spex: meet them in the conference room. Levine and Sally House were there, and the doctor, and Jason Cryer from publicity.

"So, what do you think?" Levine asked me.

"She's in pretty rough shape. Physically she can probably take it, but emotionally she's a wreck."

"Tomorrow we'll inject her with nanorepair devices," the doctor said. "She's probably had some degree of renal damage."

"Christ, have you seen her scars?" Levine said. "How many operations has she had? Did they just take a cleaver to them back then?"

"They took a cleaver first, then an airbrush," Sally said.

"We'll fix the scars," said Cryer. Legend had it that the most dangerous place in Hollywood was between Cryer and a news camera. "And Detlev here will be her protector, right Det? After all, you saved her life. You're her friend. Her dad. Her lover, if it comes to that."

"Right," I said. I thought about Marilyn, asleep at last. What expectations did she have?

Scoville spoke for the first time. "I want us into production within three weeks. We've got eighty million already invested in this. Sally, you can crank publicity up to full gain. We're going to succeed where all the others have failed. We're going to put the first viable Marilyn on the wire. She may be a wreck, but she wants to be here. Not like Paramount's version."

"That's where we're smart," Cryer said. "We take into account the psychological factors."

I couldn't stand much more. After the meeting I rode down to the lobby and checked out of the building. As I approached the front doors I could see a crowd of people had gathered outside in the bright sunlight. Faces slick with factor 400 sunscreen, they shouted and carried picket signs. "END TIME EXPLOITATION." "INFORMATION, NOT PEOPLE." "HANDS OFF THE PAST."

Not one gram of evidence existed that a change in a past moment-universe had ever affected our own time. They were as separate as two sides of a coin. Of course it was true that once you burned a particular universe you could never go back. But with an eternity of moment-universes to exploit, who cared?

The chronological protection fanatics would be better off taking care of the historicals who were coming to litter up the present, the ones who couldn't adjust, or outlasted their momentary celebrity, or turned out not to be as interesting to the present as their sponsors had imagined. A lot of money had been squandered on bad risks. Who really wanted to listen to new compositions by Gershwin? How was Shakespeare even going to understand the twenty-first century, let alone write VR scripts that anybody would want to experience?

I snuck out the side door and caught the metro down at the corner. Rode the train through Hollywood to my arcology.

In the newsstand I uploaded the latest trades into my spex, then stopped into the men's room to get my shoes polished. While the valet worked I smoked the last of my Luckies and checked the news. Jesus, still hotter than a pistol, was the lead on *Variety*. He smiled, new teeth, clean shaven, homely little Jew, but even through the holo he projected a lethal charisma. That one was making Universal rich. Who would have thought that a religious mystic with an Aramaic accent would become such a talk-show shark, his virtual image the number one teleromantics dream date? "Jesus' *Laying on of Hands* is the most spiritual experience I've ever had over fiber optic VR," gushed worldwide recording megastar Daphne Overdone.

On *Hollywood Grapevine,* gossip maven Hedley O'Connor reported Elisenbrunnen GMBH, which owned DAA, was unhappy with third-quarter earnings. If Scoville went down, the new boss would pull the plug on all his projects. My contractual responsibilities would then, as they say, be at an end.

"What a mess you made of these shoes, Herr Gruber," the valet muttered in German. I switched off my spex and watched him finish. The arco hired a lot of indigents. It was cheap, and good PR, but the valet was my personal reclamation project. His unruly head of hair danced as he buffed my shoes to a high luster. He looked up at me. "How is that?"

"Looks fine." I fished out a twenty-dollar piece. He watched me with his watery, sad, intelligent eyes. His brown hair was going gray.

"I see you got a mustache, like mine," he said.

"Only for work. For a while I need to look like you, Albert."

I gave him the twenty and went up to my room.

HERMAN MELVILLE: SPACE OPERA VIRTUOSO

It was in 1928 that Hugo Gernsback, faced with the declining sales of his *Amazing Stories,* a magazine subsisting until then almost solely on reprints of Verne and Wells, was rescued from financial ruin by the appearance of a bright young star in the SF firmament: a twenty-six-year-old schoolteacher from Pittsfield, Massachusetts, named Herman Melville.

Modern readers of science fiction, accustomed to a fictional universe where Alpha Centauri is a next-door neighbor and the solar system itself is small potatoes, can little imagine the paucity of daring imagination and truly large objects exhibited by the SF of those early years, before Melville revealed new vistas beyond the Dog Star with his "Open Space" stories of the late twenties. Gernsback himself had reservations about Melville's early stories and their radical departure from the science of the times: they contained no patentable ideas. Melville, and the fans who eagerly accepted such pseudo-scientific concepts as the "motionless drive" and "planet staves" from early yarns like "Galaxy Smash-ers" (*Amazing,* February 1929), made Boston beans of Gernsback's misgivings—though some were to say that, in a queer, un-American way, Gernsback resented Melville's imagination. Was this the cause of young "World-Delver" Melville's switch to the Clayton *Astounding* in 1933? Fans today still ponder this and the other conundrums that orbit around this SF pioneer.

The day he sat down to write that first story for *Amazing,* the fresh-faced Herman Melville had already accumulated a mother lode of experience, experience that seems to us, from the secure if uncomfortable vantage point of the Future, ready-made to produce the prototype science fiction writer.

Descended from a long line of wealthy New York mechanicians and job printers, the young Herman grew up in an atmosphere of ozone and printer's ink. Though his father died in the explosion of the Albany gasworks in 1908, Herman blossomed under the tutelage of his Uncle Hiram, a cable splicer from the Edison laboratories in Menlo Park, New Jersey.

We can envisage the boy's life as stimulating and informative, if a trifle too limiting for a child of Herman's dreamy nature. In public he was a sober youth, though we are told that he suffered from spells of enthusiasm. When the lad was only in his teens, the family fell upon hard times owing to financial reverses in the notorious direct-current speculations of World War I, and since he was the oldest of five children as well as the only son, much of the burden fell upon Herman's shoulders. At nineteen he signed aboard the merchant ship *St. Lawrence,* and for the next five years crossed and recrossed the seas as an able-bodied machinist's mate, third class. In later years he was to tell of the importance of these experiences to his understanding of men and their technology: "A freighter's engine room was my MIT, my Bronx High School of Science." In the greasy realism of the space-tugs and warships of Melville's science fiction, we can smell more than a slight echo of the light that shone from the boilers of the *St. Lawrence.*

Faced with increasing debts arising from the burden of four unmarried sisters, realizing that his position as a natural history teacher at the Pittsfield Normal School would never let him get ahead, Melville decided to try his hand at the writing of pulp fiction. We can be sure that he did not realize how nominal the financial return would be on such a career, in a field where even the highest-paying magazines offered only a cent a word. At the same time we can be grateful for this ignorance.

Following the favorable reception of his first novelette for Gernsback (the rather traveloguelike "Typon: 3180"), Melville shrugged his shoulders and turned his sad and vulnerable gray eyes to the production of the star-spanning galactic adventures that the fans demanded, and that were to become his trademark. Such books as *White Rocket, Red Sun,* and *The Mardian Chronicles* followed one upon the other in the early thirties. Honest tales of hardworking space heroes battling evil evils in the comfortable old future. Third-person narratives with beginnings, middles, and ends. Did he worry about the so-called literary value of his efforts? See the limit imposed by his workmanlike silence, by those same gray eyes, and know this answer: Who can say?

In September 1928 the slender young author married Theodora Brown, the daughter of a prominent Boston judge, and the following year saw the birth of their first child, a girl, Ursula. Melville was never to become a practical man, but now, impelled by this new responsibility, he redoubled his efforts, and the stories that leapt from the frying pan of his typewriter to the fire of the SF pulps glittered with the creations of a penetrating, if somewhat disordered, imagination. It was here, as his popularity with the readers declined, that, paradoxically, the beginnings of the Melville "cult" emerged. Melville began his voluminous correspondence with both up-and-coming young writers and with several of the "old hands" who had responded to his new vision—no matter that in most cases they had failed to understand him at all. Among these correspondents are numbered some of the great names of modern science fiction: ambitious youngsters like Fritz Leiber, Ray Bradbury, and Alfred Bester; grizzled pros like Edmond Hamilton, Nat Schachner, and Nathaniel Hawthorne.

Where once the acceptances came gratifying and easy, now, in the mid-thirties, the wells began to run dry. Caught in financial straits, burdened by a correspondence which at once both drained his energies and offered a hope of communication, beset by failing eyesight, Melville's work begain to take on the characteristics of desperate search. In the morning he would rise in the early light of the Pittsfield farm, dress carelessly in trousers and a loose-fitting white shirt, and walk through the second-floor study, or about the yard, or from barn to fields, occasionally taking something up, some task either physical or mental, only to lay it down again presently, unsatisfied, unable to touch the things that fell within his grasp. Theodora worried for his health, she sought advice from relatives who had no sympathy, she sat alone in the large and drafty bedroom on the second floor and corrected the manuscript of the latest *Astounding* serial. Through the window beside her she could see Herman kneel in the yard, pick up a clod of dirt, crumble it in his hand, looking, looking, feebly with eyes and hands for the substance of it, the thing it was that made it a part of the earth, the solar system, the clusters of stars and galaxies spanned so easily in fictions, in single sentences and phrases, as, perhaps, even he might span a clod of dirt in his pale, unworn fingers.

It was shortly after this period, in February 1938, that *Astounding Science Fiction* published the first installment of Melville's immense five-part serial, *Starry Deeps, or the Wail*. This cosmos-encompassing novel, which I have shown in my book *Plumbers of the Future* to be the first real science fiction epic, met with mixed reactions at the time. There were those who hailed it for its color, for the imaginative detail Melville lent to a story of the probe of the Independent Research Ship *Peascod* into the depths of the Coal Sack for the source of phenomena that might—or might not—threaten the existence of all life on earth. Others were attracted by the melodramatic Captain Ahab Habbison, one of the powerful "Sensemen," able through alien symbiosis to detect the forces that move behind the "pasteboard mask" of matter. But *The Wail* did not reach the average SF fan.

What these readers missed is what the true fan comes to Melville for today. Though this is a clumsy book, a primitive effort whose ranting characters and implausible action seem quaint to us now, it was still the first of the pulp stories to insert significant topical questions between episodes of exciting adventure. Take this often-misunderstood passage from Melville's description of the white cloud cover of the enemy homeworld Shuddore:

> Is it that by its indefiniteness it shadows forth the heartless voids and immensities of the universe, and thus stabs us from behind with the thought of annihilation, when beholding the white depths of the milky way? Or is it, that as in essence whiteness is not so much a color as the visible absence of color, and at the same time the concrete of all colors; is it for these reasons that there is such a dumb blankness, full of meaning, in a wide landscape of snows—a colorless, all-color atheism from which we shrink?

Let's ignore the clumsy prolixity through which we can see a writer paid by the word pathetically trying to bolster a faltering income. Fans of the thirties, thank god, weren't prissy about so-called style! What Melville is presenting here, in the guise of SF, is clearly an attack on godless leftists, white supremacy, and the racial segregation he must have been aware of from his earliest days in the merchant marine. Such hard-hitting criticism of social problems predates Malzberg, Disch, and their gang of noisy pessimists by thirty years. If we read Melville carefully, with a wholesome American eye, we can see in his "obscurity" the foreshadowing of many social themes: the dangers of overpopulation, the takeover by big-time advertising, the potential disaster of widespread drug abuse, the necessity of sterilizing stray cats to curb the pet population.

Of course, we must admit that other parts of the tale are not so germane. These parts reveal the tragic flaw in Melville's psyche—his ceaseless pursuit of abstractions. Herman was not, I regret to say, a regular guy. In the course of *The Wail,* Melville gives full expression to the downbeat, meaningless questions that disturbed him and confuse us, questions which were to occupy the remainder of his adult life, to his ultimate renunciation of fiction; questions of reality, of parallel universes; paranoid visions of possibilities stunted, of human potential unfulfilled, of man doomed, no matter what the change of circumstances—from past to present, from present to future, from world to totally new world—doomed to isolation and uncertainty. It is a tale that is with us yet—the tale of a man with great storytelling gifts who throws away his chance to entertain.

And so we see that, though many of us have appreciated parts of *The Wail,* no one has swallowed it whole. This marked the end of Melville's most productive period, and though he produced a number of fine stories in the decade following its publication, the novel just about finished his love affair with science fiction.

At conventions of the forties and fifties, and even into the dry seventies, we would see him: perhaps at a meet-the-authors party, where half the younger fen would wonder in total ignorance who the old, distant fellow was, or perhaps at the hotel bar, gently asking some stranger to join him over a glass of brandy. We could not know then, any more than we knew in the halcyon thirties, when his interstellar warriors plied the paper spaceways on monumental quests, any more than we know now, now that he is gone from us—we could not know then or at any time what forces, what mysteries, what simple and unfulfilled loves, lay behind the sad gray eyes. Had he been born a different man, in a different time, it might have been different. As it stands, we have what he wrote, and to hold it in our hands, to remember that once there was such a man—this must suffice.

BUDDHA NOSTRIL BIRD

After we killed the guard, Glaucon and I ran down the corridor away from the Well. Glaucon had been seriously aged in the fight. He limped and cursed, a piece of dying meat and he knew it. I brushed my hand along the wall looking for a door.

"We'll make it," I said.

"Sure," he said. He held his arm against his side.

We ran past a series of ontological windows: a forest fire, a sun in space, a factory refashioning children into flowers. I worried that the corridor might be a loop. For all I knew, the sole purpose of such corridors was to confuse and recapture escapees. Or maybe the corridors were just for fun. The Relativists delight in such absurdities.

More windows: a snowstorm, a cloudy seascape, a corridor exactly like the one we were in, in which two men wearing yellow robes—prison kosodes like ours—searched for a way out. Glaucon stopped. The hand of his double reached out to meet his. The face of mine stared at me angrily; a strong face, an intelligent one. "It's just a mirror," I said.

"Mirror?"

"A mirror," a voice said. Protagoras appeared ahead of us in the corridor. "Like sex, it reproduces human beings."

An old joke, and typical of Protagoras to quote it without attribution.

Glaucon raised his clock. In the face of Protagoras' infinite mutability it was less than useless: There was no way Glaucon would even get a shot off. My spirit sank as I watched the change come over him. Protagoras dripped fellowship. Glaucon liked him. Nobody but a maniac could dislike Protagoras.

It took all my will to block the endorphin assault, but Glaucon was never as strong as I. A lot of talk about brotherhood had passed between us, but if I'd had my freedom I would have crisped him on the spot. Instead I hid myself from Protagoras' blue eyes, as cold as chips of aquamarine in a mosaic.

"Where are you going?" Protagoras said.

"We were going—" Glaucon started.

"—nowhere," I said.

"A hard place to get to," said Protagoras.

Glaucon's head bobbed like a dog's.

"I know a short way," Protagoras said. "Come along with me."

"Sure," said Glaucon.

I struggled to maintain control. If you had asked him, Protagoras would have denied controlling anyone: "The Superior Man rules by humility." Another sophistry.

We turned back down the corridor. If I stayed with them until we got to the center, there would be no way I could escape. Desperation forced me to test the reality of one of the windows. As we passed the ocean scene, I pushed Glaucon into Protagoras and threw my shoulder against the glass. The window shattered; I was falling. My kosode flapped like the melting wings of Icarus as sky and sea whirled around me, and I hit the water. My breath exploded from me. I flailed and tumbled. At last I found the surface. I sputtered and gasped, my right arm in agony; my ribs ached. I kicked off my slippers and leaned onto my back. The waves rolled me up and down. The sky was low and dark. At the top of each swell I could see to the storm-clouded horizon, flat as a psychotic's affect—but in the other direction was a beach.

I swam. The bad shoulder made it hard, but at that moment I would not have traded places with Glaucon for all the enlightenment of the ancients.

When they sent me to the penal colony they told me, "Prisons ought to be places where people are lodged only temporarily, as guests are. They must not become dwelling places."

Their idea of temporary is not mine. Temporary doesn't mean long enough for your skin to crack like the dry lakebed outside your window, for the memory of your lover's touch to recede until it's only a torment in your dreams, as distant as the mountains that surround the prison. These distinctions are lost on Relativists, as are all distinctions. Which, I suppose, is why I was sent there.

They keep you alone, mostly. I don't mind the isolation—it gave me time to understand exactly how many ways I had been betrayed. I spent hours thinking of Areté, etching her ideal features in my mind. I remembered how they'd ripped me away from her. I wondered if she still lived, and if I would ever see her again. Eventually, when memory had faded, I conquered the passage of time itself: I reconstructed her image from incorruptible ideas and planned the revenge I would take once I was free again, so that the past and the future became more real to me than the endless, featureless present. Such is the power of idea over reality. To the guards I must have looked properly meditative. Inside I burned.

Each day at dawn we would be awakened by the rapping of sticks on our iron bedsteads. In the first hour we drew water from the Well of Changes. In the second we were encouraged to drink (I refused). In the third we washed floors with the water. From the fourth through the seventh we performed every other function that was necessary to maintain the prison. In the eighth we were tortured. At the ninth we were fed. At night, exhausted, we slept.

The torture chamber is made of ribbed concrete. It is a cold room, without windows. In its center is a chair, and beside the chair a small table, and on the table the hood. The hood is black and appears to be made of ordinary fabric, but it is not. The first time I held it, despite the evidence of my eyes I thought it had slipped through my fingers. The hood is not a material object: You cannot feel it, and it has no texture, and although it absorbs all light it is neither warm nor cold.

Your inquisitor invites you to sit in the chair and slip the hood over your head. You do so. He speaks to you. The room disappears. Your body melts away, and you are made into something else. You are an animal. You are one of the ancients. You are a stone, a drop of rain in a storm, a planet. You are in another time and place. This may sound intriguing, and the first twenty times it is. But it never ends. The sessions are indiscriminate. They are deliberately pointless. They continue to the verge of insanity.

I recall one of these sessions, in which I lived in an ancient city and worked a hopeless routine in a store called the "World of Values." The values we sold were merchandise. I married, had children, grew old, lost my health and spirit. I worked forty years. Some days were happy, others sad; most were neither. The last thing I remembered was lying in a hospital bed, unable to see, dying, and hearing my wife talk with my son about what they should have for dinner. When I came out from under the hood, Protagoras yanked me from the chair and told me this poem:

> *Out from the nostrils of the Great Buddha*
> *Flew a pair of nesting swallows.*

I could still hear my phantom wife's cracking voice. I was in no mood for riddles. "Tell me what it means."

"Drink from the Well and I'll tell you."

I turned my back on him.

It was always like that. Protagoras had made a career out of tormenting me. I had known him for too many years. He put faith in nothing, was totally without honor, yet he had power. His intellect was available for any use. He wasted years on banalities. He would argue any side of a case, not because he sought advantage, but because he did not care about right or wrong. He was intolerably lucky. Irresponsible as a child. Inconstant as the wind. His opaque blue gaze could be as witless as a scientist's.

And he had been my first teacher. He had introduced me to Areté, offered me useless advice throughout our stormy relationship, given ambiguous testimony at my trial, and upon the verdict abandoned the university in order to come to the prison and become my inquisitor. The thought that I had once idolized him tormented me more than any session under the hood.

After my plunge through the window into the sea, I fought my way through the surf to the beach. For an unknown time I lay gasping on the wet sand. When I opened my eyes I saw a flock of gulls had waddled up to me. An arm's length away the lead gull, a great bull whose ragged feathers stood out from his neck in a ruff, watched me with beady black eyes. Others of various sizes and markings stood in a wedge behind him. I raised my head; the gulls retreated a few steps, still holding formation. I understood immediately that they were ranked according to their stations in the flock. Thus does nature shadow forth fundamental truth: the rule of the strong over the weak, the relation of one to many in hierarchical order.

Off to the side stood a single scrawny gull, quicker than the rest, but separate, aloof. I supposed him to be a gullish philosopher. I saluted him, my brother.

A sandpiper scuttled along the edge of the surf. Dipping a handful of seawater, I washed sand and pieces of shell from my cheek. Up the slope, saw grass and sea oats held the dunes against the tides. The scene was familiar. With wonder and some disquiet I understood that the window had dumped me into the Great Water quite near the Imperial City.

I stumbled up the sand to the crest of the dunes. In the east, beneath piled thunderheads, lightning flashed over the dark water. To the west, against the sunset's glare, the sand and scrub turned into fields. I started inland. Night fell swiftly. From behind me came clouds, strong winds, then rain. I trudged on, singing into the downpour. The thunder sang back. Water streamed down the creases of my face, the wet kosode weighed on my chest and shoulders, the rough grass cut my feet. In the profound darkness I could continue only by memorizing the landscape revealed by flashes of lightning. Exhilarated, I hurried toward my lover. I shouted at the raindrops, any one of which might be one of my fellow prisoners under the hood. "I'm free!" I told them. I forded the swollen River of Indifference. I stumbled through Iron Tree Forest. Throughout the night I put one foot before the other, and some hours before dawn, in a melancholy drizzle, passed through the Heron's Gate into the city.

In the Processor's Quarter I found a doorway whose overhang kept out the worst of the rain. Above hung the illuminated sign of the Rat. In the corner of this doorway, under this sign, I slept.

I was awakened by the arrival of the owner of the communications shop in whose doorway I had slept.

"I am looking for the old fox," I said. "Do you know where I can find him?"

"Who are you?"

"You may call me the little fox."

He pushed open the door. "Well, Mr. Fox, I can put you in touch with him instantly. Just step into one of our booths."

He must have known I had no money. "I don't want to communicate. I want to see him."

"Communication is much better," the shop owner said. He took a towel, a copper basin, and an ornamental blade from the cupboard beneath his terminal. "No chance of physical violence. No distress other than psychological. Completely accurate reproduction. Sensory enhancement: olfactory, visual, auditory." He opened a cage set into the wall and seized a docile black rat by the scruff of the neck. "Recordability. Access to a network of supporting information services. For slight additional charge we offer intelligence augmentation and instant semiotic analysis. We make the short man tall. Physical presence has nothing to compare."

"I want to speak with him in private."

Not looking at me, he took the rat to the stone block. "We are bonded."

"I don't question your integrity."

"You have religious prejudices against communication? You are a Traveler?"

He would not rest until he forced me to admit I was penniless. I refrained from noting that, if he was such a devout communicator, he could easily have stayed home. Yet he had walked to his shop in person. Swallowing my rage, I said, "I have no money."

He sliced the rat's neck open. The animal made no sound.

After he had drained the blood and put the carcass into the display case, he washed his hands and turned to me. He seemed quite pleased with himself. He took a small object from a drawer. "He is to be found at the university. Here is a map of the maze." He slipped it into my hand.

For this act of gratuitous charity, I vowed that one day I would have revenge. I left.

The streets were crowded. Dusty gold light filtered down between the ranks of ancient buildings. Too short to use the moving ways, I walked. Orange-robed messengers threaded their way through the crowd. Sweating drivers in loincloths pulled pedicabs; I imagined the perfumed lottery winners who reclined behind the opaqued glass of their passenger compartments. In the Medical Quarter, street-side surgeons hawked their services in front of racks of breasts and penises of prodigious size. As before, the names of the streets changed hourly to mark the progress of the sun across the sky. All streets but one, and I held my breath when I came to it: the Way of Enlightenment, which ran between the reform temple and the Imperial Palace. As before, metamorphs entertained the faithful on the stage outside the temple. One of them changed shape as I watched, from a dog-faced man wearing the leather skirt of an athlete to a tattooed CEO in powered suit. "Come drink from the Well of Changes!" he called ecstatically to passersby. "Be reformed!"

The Well he spoke of is both literal and symbolic. The prison Well was its brother; the preachers of the temple claim that all the Wells are one Well. Its water has the power to transform both body and mind. A scientist could tell you how it is done: viruses, brain chemistry, hypnosis, some insane combination of the three. But that is all a scientist could tell you. Unlike a scientist, I could tell you why its use is morally wrong. I could explain that some truths are eternal and ought to be held inviolate, and why a culture that accepts change indiscriminately is rotten at its heart. I could demonstrate, with inescapable logic, that reason is better than emotion. That spirit is greater than flesh. That Relativism is the road to hell.

Instead of relief at being home, I felt distress. The street's muddle upset me, but it was not simply that: The city was exactly as I had left it. The wet morning that dawned on me in the doorway might have been the morning after I was sent away. My absence had made no discernible difference. The tyranny of the Relativists that I and my friends had struggled against had not culminated in the universal misery we had predicted. Though everything changed minute to minute, it remained the same. The one thing that ought to remain constant, Truth, was to them as chimerical as the gene-changers of the temple.

They might have done better, had they had teachers to tell them good from bad.

Looking down the boulevard, in the distance, at the heart of the city, I could see the walls of the palace. By midday I had reached it. Vendors of spiced cakes pushed their carts among the petitioners gathered beneath the great red lacquered doors. One, whose cakes each contained a free password, did a superior business. That the passwords were patent frauds was evident by the fact that the gatekeeper ignored those petitioners who tried using them. But that did not hurt sales. Most of the petitioners were halflings, and a dim-witted rabbit could best them in a deal.

I wept for my people, their ignorance and illogic. I discovered that I was clutching the map in my fist so tightly that the point of it had pierced my skin. I turned from the palace and walked away, and did not feel any relief until I saw the towers of the university rising above Scholars' Park. I remembered my first sight of them, a young boy down from the hills, the smell of cattle still about me, come to study under the great Protagoras. The meticulously kept park, the calm proportions of the buildings, spoke to the soul of that innocent boy: Here you'll be safe from blood and passion. Here you can lose yourself in the world of the mind.

The years had worn the polish off that dream, but I can't say that, seeing it now, once more a fugitive from a dangerous world, I did not feel some of the same joy. I thought of my mother, a loutish farmer who would whip me for reading; of my gentle father, brutalized by her, trying to keep the flame of truth alive in his boy.

On the quadrangle I approached a young woman wearing the top-knot and scarlet robe of a humanist. Her head bounced to some inner rhythm, and as I imagined she was pursuing some notion of the Ideal, my heart went out to her. I was about to ask her what she studied when I saw the pin in her temple. She was listening to transtemporal music: her mind eaten by puerile improvisations played on signals picked up from the death agonies of the cosmos. Generations of researchers had devoted their lives to uncovering these secrets, only to have their efforts used by "artists" to erode people's connections with reality. I spat on the walk at her feet; she passed by, oblivious.

At the entrance to the humanities maze I turned on the map and followed it into the gloom. Fifteen minutes later it guided me into the Department of Philosophy. It was the last place I expected to find the fox—the nest of our enemies, the place we had plotted against tirelessly. The secretary greeted me pleasantly.

"I'm looking for a man named Socrates," I said. "Some call him 'the old fox.' "

"Universe of Discourse 3," she said.

I walked down the hall, wishing I had Glaucon's clock. The door to the hall stood open. In the center of the cavelike room, in a massive support chair, sat Socrates. At last I had found a significant change: He was grossly obese. The ferretlike features I remembered were folded in fat. Only the acute eyes remained. I was profoundly shaken. As I approached, his eyes followed me.

"Socrates."

"Blume."

"What happened to you?"

Socrates lifted his dimpled hand, as if to wave away a triviality. "I won."

"You used to revile this place."

"I reviled its usurpers. Now I run it."

"You run it?"

"I'm the dean."

I should have known Socrates had turned against our cause, and perhaps at some level I had. If he had remained true, he would have ended up in a cell next to mine. "You used to be a great teacher," I said.

"Right. Let me tell what happens when a man starts claiming he's a great teacher. First he starts wearing a brocade robe. Then he puts lifts in his sandals. The next thing you know the department's got a nasty paternity suit on its hands."

His senile chuckle was like the bubbling of water in an opium pipe.

"How did you get to be dean?"

"I performed a service for the Emperor."

"You sold out!"

"Blume the dagger," he said. Some of the old anger shaded his voice. "So sharp. So rigid. You always were a prig."

"And you used to have principles."

"Ah, principles," he said. "I'll tell you what happened to my principles. You heard about Philomena the Bandit?"

"No. I've been somewhat out of touch."

Socrates ignored the jab. "It was after you left. Philomena invaded the system, established her camp on the moon, and made her living raiding the empire. The city was at her mercy. I saw my opportunity. I announced that I would reform her. My students outfitted a small ship, and Areté and I launched for the moon."

"Areté!"

"We landed in a lush valley near the camp. Areté negotiated an audience for me. I went, alone. I described to Philomena the advantages of politic behavior. The nature of truth. The costs of living in the world of shadows and the glory of moving into the world of light. How, if she should turn to Good, her story would be told for generations. Her fame would spread throughout the world and her honor outlast her lifetime by a thousand years.

"Philomena listened. When I was finished she drew a knife and asked me, 'How long is a thousand years?'

"Her men stood all around, waiting for me to slip. I started to speak, but before I could she pulled me close and pushed the blade against my throat.

" 'A thousand years,' Philomena said, 'is shorter than the exposure of a neutrino passing through a world. How long is life?'

"I was petrified. She smiled. 'Life,' she said, 'is shorter than this blade.'

"I begged for mercy. She threw me out. I ran to the ship, in fear for my life. Areté asked what happened: I said nothing. We set sail for home.

"We landed amid great tumult. I first thought it was riot but soon found it celebration. During our voyage back Philomena had left the moon. People assumed I had convinced her. The Emperor spoke. Our enemies in philosophy were shortened, and the regents stretched me into dean.

"Since then," Socrates said, "I have had trouble with principles."

"You're a coward," I said.

Despite the mask of suet, I could read the ruefulness in Socrates's eyes. "You don't know me," he said.

"What happened to Areté?"

"I have not seen her since."

"Where is she?"

"She's not here." He shifted his bulk, watching the screen that encircled the room. "Turn yourself in, Blume. If they catch you, it will only go harder."

"Where is she?"

"Even if you could get to her, she won't want to see you."

I seized his arm, twisted. "Where is Areté!"

Socrates inhaled sharply. "In the palace," he said.

"She's a prisoner?"

"She's the Empress."

That night I took a place among the halflings outside the palace gate. Men and women regrown from seed after their deaths, imprinted with stored files of their original personalities, all of them had lost resolution, for no identity file could encapsulate human complexity. Some could not speak, others displayed features too stiff to pass for human, and still others had no personalities at all. Their only chance for wholeness was to petition the Empress to perform a transfinite extrapolation from their core data. To be miraculously transformed.

An athlete beside me showed me his endorsements. An actress showed me her notices. A banker showed me his lapels. They asked me my profession. "I am a philosopher," I said.

They laughed. "Prove it," the actress said.

"In the well-ordered state," I told her, "there will be no place for you." To the athlete I said, "Yours is a good and noble profession." I turned to the banker. "Your work is more problematical," I said. "Unlike the actress, you fulfill a necessary function, but unlike the athlete, by accumulating wealth you are likely to gain more power than is justified by your small wisdom."

This speech was beyond them: The actress grumbled and went away. I left the two men and walked along below the battlements. Two bartizans framed the great doors, and archers strolled along the ramparts or leaned through the embrasures to spit on the petitioners. For this reason the halflings camped as far back from the walls as they might without blocking the street. The archers, as any educated man knew, were there for show: The gates were guarded only by a single gatekeeper, a monk who could open the door if bested in a battle of wits, but without whose acquiescence the door could not be budged.

He sat on his stool beside the gate, staring quietly ahead.

Those who tried to talk to him could not tell whether they'd get a cuff on the ear or a friendly conversation. His flat, peasant's face was so devoid of intellect that it was some time before I recognized him as Protagoras.

His disguised presence could be one of his whims. Or it could be he was being punished for letting me escape; it could be that he waited for me. I felt an urge to run. But I would not duplicate Socrates' cowardice. If Protagoras recognized me he did not show it, and I resolved to get in or get caught. I was not some half-wit, and I knew him. I approached. "I wish to see the Empress," I said.

"You must wait."

"I've been waiting for years."

"That doesn't matter."

"I have no more time."

He studied me. His manner changed. "What will you pay?"

"I'll pay you a story that will make you laugh until your head aches."

He smiled. I saw that he recognized me; my stomach lurched. "I know many such stories," he said.

"Not like mine."

"Yes. I can see you are a great breeder of headaches."

Desperation drove me forward. "Listen, then: Once there was a warlord who discovered that someone had stolen his most precious possession, a jewel of power. He ordered his servants to scour the fortress for strangers. In the bailey they found a beggar heading for the gate. The lord's men seized him and carried him to the well. "The warlord's great jewel is lost," they said to him. They thrust the beggar's head beneath the water. He struggled. They pulled him up and asked, 'Where is the jewel?'

" 'I don't know,' he said.

"They thrust him down again, longer this time. When they pulled him up he sputtered like an old engine. 'Where is the jewel?' they demanded. 'I don't know!' he replied.

"Furious at his insolence, fearful for their lives if they should rouse their lord's displeasure, the men pushed the beggar so far into the well that a bystander thought, 'He will surely drown.' The beggar kicked so hard it took three strong men to hold him. When at last they pulled him up he coughed and gasped, face purple, struggling to speak. They pounded him on the back. Finally he drew breath enough for words.

" 'I think you should get another diver,' the beggar said. 'I can't see it anywhere down there.' "

Protagoras smiled. "That's not funny."

"What?"

"Maybe for us, but not for the beggar. Or the bystander. Or the servants. The warlord probably had them shortened."

"Don't play games. What do you really think?"

"I think of poor Glaucon. He misses you."

Then I saw that Protagoras only meant to torment me, as he had so many times before. He would answer my desperate need with feeble jokes until I wept or went mad. A fury more powerful than the sun itself swept over me, and I lost control. I fell on him, kicking, biting. The petitioners looked on in amazement. Shouts echoed from the ramparts. I didn't care. I'd forgotten everything but my rage; all I knew was that at last I had him in my hands. I scratched at his eyes, I beat his head against the pavements. Protagoras struggled to speak. I pulled him up and slammed his head against the doors. The tension went out of his muscles. Cross-legged, as if preparing to meditate, he slid to the ground. Blood glistened in the torchlight on the lacquered doors. "Now that's funny," he whispered, and died.

The weight of his body against the door pushed it ajar. It had been open all along.

No one came to arrest me. Across the inner ward, at the edge of an ornamental garden, a person stood in the darkness beneath a plane tree. Most of the lights of the palace were unlit, but radiance from the clerestory above heightened the shadows. Hesitantly I drew closer, too unsteady after my sudden fit of violence to hide. In my confusion I could think to do no more than approach the figure in the garden, who stood patiently as if in long expectation of me. From ten paces away I saw it was a woman dressed as a clown. From five I saw it was Areté.

Her laughter, like shattering crystal, startled me. "How serious you look!"

My head was full of questions. She pressed her fingers against my lips, silencing them. I embraced her. Red circles were painted on her cheeks, and she wore a crepe beard, but her skin was still smooth, her eyes bright, her perfume the same. She was not a day older.

The memory of dead Protagoras' slack mouth marred my triumph. She ducked out of my arms, laughing again. "You can't have me unless you catch me!"

"Areté!"

She darted through the trees. I ran after her. My heart was not in it, and I lost her until she paused beneath a tree, hands on knees, panting. "Come on! I'm not so hard to catch."

The weight was lifted from my heart. I dodged after her. Beneath the trees, through the hedge maze, among the night-blooming jasmine and bougainvillea, the silver moon tipping the edges of the leaves, I chased her. At last she let herself be caught; we fell together into a damp bed of ivy. I rested my head on her breast. The embroidery of her costume was rough against my cheek.

She took my head in her hands and made me look her in the face. Her teeth were pearly white, breath sweet as the scented blossoms around us.

We kissed, through the ridiculous beard (I could smell the spirit gum she'd used to affix it), and the goal they had sought to instill in me at the penal colony was attained: My years of imprisonment vanished into the immediate moment as if they had never existed.

That kiss was the limit of our contact. I expected to spend the night with her; instead, she had a slave take me to a guesthouse for visiting dignitaries, where I was quartered with three minor landholders from the mountains. They were already asleep. After my day of confusion, rage, desire, and fear, I lay there weary but hard awake, troubled by the sound of my own breathing. My thoughts were jumbled white noise. I had killed him. I had found her. Two of the fantasies of my imprisonment fulfilled in a single hour. Yet no peace. The murder of Protagoras would not long go unnoticed. I assumed Areté already knew but did not care. But if she was truly the Empress, why had he not been killed years before? Why had I rotted in prison under him?

I had no map for this maze and eventually fell asleep.

In the morning the slave, Pismire, brought me a wig of human hair, a green kimono, a yellow silk sash, and solid leather sandals: the clothes of a prosperous nonentity. My roommates appeared to be barely lettered country bumpkins, little better than my parents, come to court seeking a judgment against a neighbor or a place for a younger child or protection from some bandit. One of them wore the colors of an inferior upland collegium; the others no colors at all.

I suspected at least one of them was Areté's spy; they might have thought me one as well. We looked enough alike to be brothers.

We ate in a dining room attended by machines. I spent the day studying the public rooms of the palace, hoping to get some information. At the tolling of sixth hour Pismire found me in the vivarium. He handed me a message under the Imperial seal, and left. I turned it on.

"You are invited to an important meeting," the message said.

"With whom?" I asked. "For what purpose?"

The message ignored me. "The meeting begins promptly at ninth hour. Prepare yourself." There followed directions to the place.

When I arrived, the appointed room was empty. A long oak table, walls lined with racks of document spindles. At the far end, French doors gave onto a balcony overlooking an ancient city of glass and metal buildings. I could hear the faint sounds of traffic below.

A side door opened and a woman in the blue suit of the Lawyer entered, followed by a clerk. The woman's glossy black hair was stranded with gray, but her face was smooth. She wore no makeup. She stood at the end of the table, back to the French doors, and set down a leather box. The clerk sat at her right hand. I realized that this forbidding figure was Areté. She had become as mutable as Protagoras.

"Be seated," she said. "We are here to take your deposition."

"Deposition?"

"Your statement on the matter at hand."

"What matter?"

"Your escape from the penal colony. Your murder of the gatekeeper, the honored philosopher Protagoras."

The injustice of this burned through my dismay. "Not murder. Self-defense. Or better still, euthanasia."

"Don't quibble with us. We are deprived of his presence."

"Grow a duplicate. Bring him back to life."

For reply she merely stared at me across the table. The air tasted stale, and I felt a bead of sweat run down my breast beneath my robe. "Is this some game?"

"You may well wish it a game."

"Areté!"

"I am not Areté. I am a Lawyer." She leaned toward me. "Why were you sent to prison?"

"You were with me! You know."

"We are taking your version of events for the record."

"You know as well as I that I was imprisoned for seeking the Truth."

"Which truth?"

There was only one. "The one that people don't want to hear," I said.

"You had access to a truth people did not acknowledge?"

"They are blinded by custom and self-interest."

"You were not?"

"I had, through years of self-abnegation and study, risen above them. I had broken free of the chains of prejudice, climbed out of the cave of shadows that society lives in, and looked at the sun direct."

The clerk smirked as I made this speech. It was the first expression he'd shown.

"And you were blinded by it," Areté said.

"I saw the truth. But when I came back they said I was blind. They would not listen, so they put me away."

"The trial record says that you assisted in the corruption of youth."

"I was a teacher."

"The record says you refused to listen to your opponents."

"I refuse to listen to ignorance and illogic. I refuse to submit to fools, liars, and those who let passion overcome reason."

"You have never been fooled?"

"I was, but not now."

"You never lie?"

"If I do, I still know the difference between a lie and the truth."

"You never act out of passion?"

"Only when supported by reason."

"You never suspect your own motives?"

"I know my motives."

"How?"

"I examine myself. Honestly, critically. I apply reason."

"Spare me your colossal arrogance, your revolting self-pity. Eyewitnesses say you killed the gatekeeper in a fit of rage."

"I had reason. Do you presume to understand my motives better than I? Do you understand your own?"

"No. But that's because I am dishonest. And totally arbitrary." She opened the box and took out a clock. Without hesitation she pointed it at the clerk. His smugness punctured, he stumbled back, overturning his chair. She pressed the trigger. The weapon must have been set for maximum entropy: Before my eyes the clerk aged ten, twenty, fifty years. He died and rotted. In less than a minute he was a heap of bones and gruel on the floor.

"You've been in prison so long you've invented a harmless version of me," Areté said. "I am capable of anything." She laid the clock on the table, turned and opened the doors to let in a fresh night breeze. Then she climbed onto the table and crawled toward me. I sat frozen. "I am the Destroyer," she said, loosening her tie as she approached. Her eyes were fixed on mine. When she reached me she pushed me over backward, falling atop me. "I am the force that drives the blood through your dying body, the nightmare that wakes you sweating in the middle of the night. I am the fiery caldron within whose heat you are reduced to a vapor, extended from the visible into the invisible, dissipated on the winds of time, of fading memory, of inevitable human loss. In the face of me, you are incapable of articulate speech. About me you understand nothing."

She wound the tie around my neck, drew it tight. "Remember that," she said, strangling me.

I passed out on the floor of the interview room and awoke the next morning in a bed in a private chamber. Pismire was drawing the curtains on a view of an ocean beach: Half-asleep, I watched the tiny figure of a man materialize in a spray of glass, in midair, and fall precipitously into the sea.

Pismire brought me a breakfast of fruit and spiced coffee. Touching the bruises on my neck, I watched the man resurface in the sea and swim ashore. He collapsed on the sand. A flock of gulls came to stand by his head. If I broke through this window, I could warn him. I could say: Socrates is fat. Watch out for the gatekeeper. Areté is alive, but she is changed.

But what could I tell him for certain? Had Areté turned Relativist, like Socrates? Was she free, or being made to play a part? Did she intend to prosecute me for the murder of Protagoras? But if so, why not simply return me to the penal colony?

I did not break through the window, and the man eventually moved up the beach toward the city.

That day servants followed me everywhere. Minor lords asked my opinions. Evidently I was a taller man than I had been the day before. I drew Pismire aside and asked him what rumors were current. He was a stocky fellow with a topknot of coarse black hair and shaved temples, silent, but when I pressed him he opened up readily enough. He said he knew for a fact that Protagoras had set himself up to be killed. He said the Emperor was dead and the Empress was the focus of a perpetual struggle. That many men had sought to make Areté theirs, but none had so far succeeded. That disaster would surely follow any man's success.

"Does she always change semblance from day to day?"

He said he had never noticed any changes.

In midafternoon, at precisely the same time I had yesterday received the summons to the deposition, a footman with the face of a frog handed me an invitation to dine with the Empress that evening.

Three female expediters prepared a scented bath for me; a fourth laid out a kimono of blue crepe embroidered with gold fishing nets. The mirror they held before me showed a man with wary eyes. At the tolling of ninth hour I was escorted to the banquet hall. The room was filled with notables in every finery. A large, low table stretched across the tesselated floor, surrounded by cushions. Before each place was an enamel bowl, and in the center of the table was a large three-legged brass caldron. Areté, looking no more than twenty, stood talking to an extremely handsome man near the head of the table.

"I thank you for your courtesy," I told her.

The man watched me impassively. "No more than is your due," Areté replied. She wore a bright costume of synthetics with pleated shoulders and elbows. She looked like a toy. Her face was painted into a hard mask.

She introduced me to the man, whose name was Meno. I drew her away from him. "You frightened me last night," I said. "I thought you had forgotten me."

Only her soft brown eyes showed she wasn't a pleasure surrogate. "What makes you think I remember?"

"You could not forget and still be the one I love."

"That's probably true. I'm not sure I'm worth such devotion."

Meno watched us from a few paces away. I turned my back to him and leaned closer to her. "I can't believe you mean that,"

I said quickly. "I think you say such things because you have been imprisoned by liars and self-aggrandizers. But I am here for you now. I am an objective voice. Just give me a sign, and I will set you free."

Before she could answer, a bell sounded and the people took their places. Areté guided me to a place beside her. She sat, and we all followed suit.

The slaves stood ready to serve, waiting for Areté's command. She looked around the table. "We are met here to eat together," she said. "To dine on ambrosia, because there has been strife in the city, and ambition, and treachery. But now it is going to stop."

Meno now looked openly angry. Others were worried.

"You are the favored ones," said Areté. She turned to me. "And our friend here, the little fox, is the most favored of all. Destiny's author—our new and most trusted adviser."

Several people started to protest. I seized the opportunity given by their shock. "Am I indeed your adviser?"

"You may test it by deeds."

"You and you—" I beckoned to the guards. "Clear these people from the room."

The guests were in turmoil. Meno tried to speak to Areté, but I stepped between them. The guards came forward and forced the men and women to leave. After they were gone, I had the guards and slaves leave as well. The doors closed and the hall was silent. I turned. Areté had watched it all calmly, sitting cross-legged at the head of the table.

"Now, Areté, you must listen to me. Your commands have been twisted throughout this city. You and I have an instinctive sympathy. You must let me determine who sees you. I will interpret your words. The world is not ready to understand without an interpreter; they need to be educated."

"And you are the teacher."

"I am suited to it by temperament and training."

She smiled meekly.

I told Areté that I was hungry. She rose and prepared a bowl

of soup from the caldron. I sat at the head of the table. She came
and set the bowl before me, then kneeled and touched her forehead to the floor.

"Feed me," I said.

She took the bowl and a napkin. She blew on the ambrosia to
cool it, lips pursed. Like a serving girl, she held the bowl to my
lips. Areté fed me all of it, like mother to child, lover to lover. It
tasted better than anything I had ever eaten. It warmed my belly
and inflamed my desire. When the bowl was empty I pushed it
away, knocking it from her hand. It clattered on the marble floor.
I would be put off no longer. I took her right there, amid the
cushions.

She was indeed the hardest of toys.

It had taken me three days from my entrance to the palace to become Areté's lover and voice. The Emperor over the Empress. On
the first day of my reign I had the shopkeeper who had insulted
me whipped the length of the Way of Enlightenment. On the second I ordered that only those certified in philosophy be qualified
to vote. On the third I banished the poets.

Each evening Areté fed me ambrosia from a bowl. Each night
we shared the Imperial bed. Each morning I awoke calmer, in
more possession of myself. I moved more slowly. The hours of
the day were drained of their urgency. Areté stopped changing.
Her face settled with a quiet clarity into my mind, a clarity unlike the burning image I had treasured up during my years in the
prison.

On the morning of the third day I awoke fresh and happy.
Areté was not there. Pismire entered the room bearing a basin,
a towel, a razor, a mirror. He washed and shaved me, then held
the mirror before me. For the first time I saw the lines about my
eyes and mouth were fading, and realized that I was being reformed.

I looked at Pismire. I saw him clearly: eyes cold as aqua-
marines.

"It's time for you to come home, Blume," he said.

No anger, no protest, arose in me. No remorse. No frustration. "I've been betrayed," I said. "Some virus, some drug, some notion you've put in my head."

Protagoras smiled. "The ambrosia. Brewed with water from the Well."

Now I am back in the prison. Escape is out of the question. Every step outward would be a step backward. It's all relative.

Instead I draw water from the Well of Changes. I drink. Protagoras says whatever changes will happen to me will be a reflection of my own psyche. That my new form is not determined by the water, but by me. How do I control it, I ask. You don't, he replies.

Glaucon has become a feral dog.

Protagoras and I go for long walks across the dry lake. He seldom speaks. I am not angry. Still, I fear a relapse. I am close to being nourished, but as yet I am not sure I am capable of it. I don't understand, as I never understood, where the penal colony is. I don't understand, as I never understood, how I can live without Areté.

Protagoras sympathizes. "Can't live with her, can't live without her," he says. "She's more than just a woman, Blume. You can experience her, but you can't own her."

Right. When I complain about such gnomic replies, Protagoras only puts me under the hood again. I think he knows some secret he wants me to guess, yet he gives no hints. I don't think that's fair.

After our most recent session, I told Protagoras my latest theory of the significance of the poem about the swallows. The poem, I told him, was an emblem of the ultimate and absolute truth of the universe. All things are determined by the ideas behind them, I said. There are three orders of existence, the Material (represented by the physical statue of the Buddha), the Spiritual (represented by its form), and the highest, which transcends both the Physical and the Spiritual, the Ideal (represented by the flight of the birds). Humbly I begged Protagoras to tell me whether my analysis was true.

Protagoras said, "You are indeed an intellectual. But in order for me to reveal the answer to a question of such profound spiritual significance, you must first bow down before the sacred Well."

At last I was to be enlightened. Eyes brimming with tears of hope, I turned to the Well and, with the utmost sincerity, bowed.

Then Protagoras kicked me in the ass.

A CLEAN ESCAPE

I've been thinking about devils. I mean, if there are devils
in the world, if there are people in the world who represent
evil, is it our duty to exterminate them?

—*John Cheever,*
"The Five-Forty-Eight"

As she sat in her office, waiting—for exactly what she did not
know—Dr. Evans hoped that it wasn't going to be another
bad day. She needed a cigarette and a drink. She swiveled the
chair around to face the closed venetian blinds beside her desk,
leaned back, and laced her hands behind her head. She closed her
eyes and breathed deeply. The air wafting down from the venti-
lator in the ceiling smelled of machine oil. It was cold. Her face
felt it, but the bulky sweater kept the rest of her warm. Her hair
felt greasy. Several minutes passed in which she thought of nothing. There was a knock at the door.

"Come in," she said absently.

Havelmann entered. He had the large body of an athlete gone
slightly soft, gray hair, and a lined face. At first glance he didn't
look sixty. His well-tailored blue suit badly needed pressing.

"Doctor?"

Evans stared at him for a moment. She would kill him. She
looked down at the desk, rubbed her forehead. "Sit down," she
said.

She took the pack of cigarettes from her desk drawer. "Would you care to smoke?"

The old man accepted one. She watched him carefully. His brown eyes were rimmed with red; they looked apologetic.

"I smoke too much," he said. "But I can't quit."

She gave him a light. "More people around here are quitting every day."

Havelmann exhaled smoothly. "What can I do for you?"

What can I do for *you*, sir.

"First, I want to play a little game." Evans took a handkerchief out of her pocket. She moved a brass paperweight, a small model of the Lincoln Memorial, to the center of the desk blotter. "I want you to watch what I'm doing now."

Havelmann smiled. "Don't tell me—you're going to make it disappear, right?"

She tried to ignore him. She covered the paperweight with the handkerchief. "What's under this handkerchief?"

"Can we put a little bet on it?"

"Not this time."

"A paperweight."

"That's wonderful." Evans leaned back. "Now I want you to answer a few questions."

The old man looked around the office curiously: at the closed blinds, at the computer terminal and keyboard against the wall, at the pad of switches in the corner of the desk. His eyes came to rest on the mirror high in the wall opposite the window. "That's a two-way mirror."

Evans sighed. "No kidding."

"Are you videotaping this?"

"Does it matter to you?"

"I'd like to know. Common courtesy."

"Yes, we're being recorded. Now answer the questions."

Havelmann seemed to shrink in the face of her hostility. "Sure."

"How do you like it here?"

"It's okay. A little boring. A man couldn't even catch a disease here, from the looks of it, if you know what I mean. I don't mean any offense, Doctor. I haven't been here long enough to get the feel of the place."

Evans rocked slowly back and forth. "How do you know I'm a doctor?"

"Aren't you a doctor? I thought you were. This is a hospital, isn't it? So I figured when they sent me in to see you, you must be a doctor."

"I am a doctor. My name is Evans."

"Pleased to meet you, Dr. Evans."

She would kill him. "How long have you been here?"

The man tugged on his earlobe. "I must have just got here today. I don't think it was too long ago. A couple of hours. I've been talking to the nurses at their station."

What she wouldn't give for three fingers of Jack Daniel's. She looked at him over the steeple of her fingers. "Such talkative nurses."

"I'm sure they're doing their jobs."

"I'm sure. Tell me what you were doing before you came to this . . . hospital."

"You mean right before?"

"Yes."

"I was working."

"Where do you work?"

"I've got my own company—ITG Computer Systems. We design programs for a lot of people. We're close to getting a big contract with Ma Bell. We swing that and I can retire by the time I'm forty—if Uncle Sam will take his hand out of my pocket long enough for me to count my change."

Evans made a note on her pad. "Do you have a family?"

Havelmann looked at her steadily. His gaze was that of an earnest young college student, incongruous on a man of his age. He stared at her as if he could not imagine why she would ask him these abrupt questions. She detested his weakness; it raised in her a fury that pushed her to the edge of insanity. It was already a bad day, and it would get worse.

"I don't understand what you're after," Havelmann said, with considerable dignity. "But just so your record shows the facts:

I've got a wife, Helen, and two kids. Ronnie's nine and Susan's five. We have a nice big house and a Lincoln and a Porsche. I follow the Braves and I don't eat quiche. What else would you like to know?"

"Lots of things. Eventually I'll find them out." Evans tapped her pencil on the edge of the desk. "Is there anything you'd like to ask me? How you came to be here? How long you're going to have to stay? Who you are?"

Havelmann's voice went cold. "I know who I am."

"Who are you, then?"

"My name is Robert Havelmann."

"That's right," Dr. Evans said. "What year is it?"

Havelmann watched her warily, as if he were about to be tricked. "What are you talking about? It's 1984."

"What time of year?"

"Spring."

"How old are you?"

"Thirty-five."

"What do I have under this handkerchief?"

Havelmann looked at the handkerchief on the desk as if noticing it for the first time. His shoulders tightened and he looked suspiciously at her.

"How should I know?"

He was back again that afternoon, just as rumpled, just as innocent. How could a person get old and remain innocent? She could not remember things ever being that easy. "Sit down," she said.

"Thanks. What can I do for you, Doctor?"

"I want to follow up on the argument we had this morning."

Havelmann smiled. "Argument? This morning?"

"Don't you remember talking to me this morning?"

"I never saw you before."

Evans watched him coldly. Havelmann shifted in his chair.

"How do you know I'm a doctor?"

"Aren't you a doctor? They told me I should go in to see Dr. Evans in room 10."

"I see. If you weren't here this morning, where were you?"

Havelmann hesitated. "Let's see—I was at work. I remember telling Helen—my wife—that I'd try to get home early. She's always complaining because I stay late. The company's pretty busy right now: big contract in the works. Susan's in the school play, and we have to be there by eight. And I want to get home in time to do some yard work. It looked like a good day for it."

Evans made a note. "What season is it?"

Havelmann fidgeted like a child, looked at the window, where the blinds were still closed.

"Spring," he said. "Sunny, warm—very nice weather. The redbuds are just starting to come out."

Without a word Evans got out of her chair and opened the blinds, revealing a barren field swept with drifts of snow. Dead grass whipped in the strong wind, and clouds rolled in the sky.

"What about this?"

Havelmann stared. His back straightened. He tugged at his earlobe.

"Isn't that a bitch. If you don't like the weather here—wait ten minutes."

"What about the redbuds?"

"This weather will probably kill them. I hope Helen made the kids wear their jackets."

Evans looked out the window. Nothing had changed. She drew the blinds and sat down again.

"What year is it?"

Havelmann adjusted himself in his chair, calm again. "What do you mean? It's 1984."

"Did you ever read that book?"

"Slow down a minute. What book?"

Evans wondered what he would do if she got up and ground her thumbs into his eyes. "The book by George Orwell titled *1984.*" She forced herself to speak slowly. "Are you familiar with it?"

"Sure. We had to read it in college." Was there a trace of irritation beneath Havelmann's innocence? Evans sat as still as she could.

"I remember it made quite an impression on me," Havelmann continued.

"What kind of impression?"

"I expected something different from the professor. He was a confessed liberal. I expected some kind of bleeding-heart book. It wasn't like that at all."

"Did it make you uncomfortable?"

"No. It didn't tell me anything I didn't know already. It just showed what was wrong with collectivism. You know—communism represses the individual, destroys initiative. It claims it has the interests of the majority at heart. And it denies all human values. That's what I got out of *1984*, though to hear that professor talk about it, it was all about Nixon and Vietnam."

Evans kept still. Havelmann went on.

"I've seen the same mentality at work in business. The large corporations, they're just like the government. Big, slow. You could show them a way to save a billion, and they'd squash you like a bug because it's too much trouble to change."

"You sound like you've got some resentments," said Evans.

The old man smiled. "I do, don't I. I admit it. I've thought a lot about it. But I have faith in people. Someday I may just run for state assembly and see whether I can do some good."

Her pencil point snapped. She looked at Havelmann, who looked back at her. After a moment she focused her attention on the notebook. The broken point had left a black scar across her precise handwriting.

"That's a good idea," she said quietly, her eyes still lowered. "You still don't remember arguing with me this morning?"

"I never saw you before I walked in this door. What were we supposed to be fighting about?"

He was insane. Evans almost laughed aloud at the thought— of course he was insane—why else would he be here? The question, she forced herself to consider rationally, was the nature of his insanity. She picked up the paperweight and handed it across to him. "We were arguing about this paperweight," she said. "I showed it to you, and you said you'd never seen it before."

Havelmann examined the paperweight. "Looks ordinary to

me. I could easily forget something like this. What's the big deal?"

"You'll note that it's a model of the Lincoln Memorial."

"You probably got it at some gift shop. D.C. is full of junk like that."

"I haven't been to Washington in a long time."

"I wish I could avoid it. I live there. Bethesda, anyway."

Evans closed her notebook. "I have a possible diagnosis of your condition," she said suddenly.

"What condition?"

This time the laughter was harder to repress. Tears almost came to her eyes. She caught her breath and continued. "You exhibit the symptoms of Korsakov's syndrome. Have you ever heard of that before?"

Havelmann looked as blank as a whitewashed wall. "No."

"Korsakov's syndrome is an unusual form of memory loss. Recorded cases go back to the late 1800s. There was a famous one in the 1970s—famous to doctors, I mean. A Marine sergeant named Arthur Briggs. He was in his fifties, in good health aside from the lingering effects of alcoholism, and had been a career noncom until his discharge in the mid-sixties after twenty years in the service. He functioned normally until the early seventies, when he lost his memory of any events that occurred to him after September 1944. He could remember in vivid detail, as if they had just happened, events up until that time. But of the rest of his life—nothing. Not only that, his continuing memory was affected so that he could remember events that occurred in the present only for a period of minutes, after which he would forget totally."

"I can remember what happened to me right up until I walked into this room."

"That's what Sergeant Briggs told his doctors. To prove it he told them that World War II was going strong, that he was stationed in San Francisco in preparation for being sent to the Philippines, that it looked like the St. Louis Browns might finally win a pennant if they could hold on through September, and that he was twenty years old. He had the outlook and abilities of an intelligent twenty-year-old. He couldn't remember anything that happened to him longer than twenty minutes. The world had gone on, but he was permanently stuck in 1944."

"That's horrible."

"So it seemed to the doctor in charge—at first. Later he speculated that it might not be so bad. The man still had a current emotional life. He could still enjoy the present; it just didn't stick with him. He could remember his youth, and for him his youth had never ended. He never aged. He never saw his friends grow old and die; he never remembered that he himself had grown up to be a lonely alcoholic. His girlfriend was still waiting for him back in Columbia, Missouri. He was twenty years old forever. He had made a clean escape."

Evans opened a desk drawer and took out a hand mirror. "How old are you?" she asked.

Havelmann looked frightened. "Look, why are we doing—"

"How old are you?" Evans's voice was quiet but determined. Inside her a pang of joy threatened to break her heart.

"I'm thirty-five. What the hell—"

Shoving the mirror at him was as satisfying as firing a gun. Havelmann took it, glanced at her, then tentatively, like the most nervous of freshmen checking the grade on his final exam, looked at his reflection. "Jesus Christ," he said. He started to tremble.

"What happened? What did you do to me!" He got out of the chair, his expression contorted. "What did you do to me! I'm thirty-five! What happened?"

Dr. Evans stood in front of the mirror in her office. She was wearing her uniform. It was as rumpled as Havelmann's suit. She had the tunic unbuttoned and was feeling her left breast. She lay down on the floor and continued the examination. The lump was undeniable. No pain yet.

She sat up, reached for the pack of cigarettes on the desk top, fished out the last one and lit it. She crumpled the pack and threw it at the wastebasket. Two points. She had been quite a basketball player in college, twenty years before. She lay back down and took a long drag on the cigarette, inhaling deeply, exhaling the smoke with force, with a sigh of exhaustion. She probably couldn't make it up and down the court a single time anymore.

She turned her head to look out the window. The blinds were open, revealing the same barren landscape that showed before. There was a knock at the door.

"Come in," she said.

Havelmann entered. He saw her lying on the floor, raised an eyebrow, grinned. "You're Dr. Evans?"

"I am."

"Can I sit here, or should I lie down too?"

"Do whatever you fucking well please."

He sat in the chair. He had not taken offense. "So what did you want to see me about?"

Evans got up, buttoned her tunic, sat in the swivel chair. She stared at him. "Have we ever met before?" she asked.

"No. I'm sure I'd remember."

He was sure he would remember. She would fucking kill him. He would remember that.

She ground out the last inch of cigarette. She felt her jaw muscles tighten; she looked down at the ashtray in regret. "Now I have to quit."

"I should quit. I smoke too much myself."

"I want you to listen to me closely now," she said slowly. "Don't respond until I'm finished."

"My name is Major D. S. Evans, and I am a military psychologist. This office is in the infirmary of NECDEC, the National Emergency Center for Defense Communications, located one thousand feet below a hillside in West Virginia. As far as we know we are the only surviving governmental body in the continental United States. The scene you see through this window is being relayed from a surface monitor in central Nebraska; by computer command I can connect us with any of the twelve monitors still functioning on the surface."

Evans turned to her keyboard and typed in a command; the scene through the window snapped to a shot of broken masonry and twisted steel reinforcement rods. The view was obscured by dust caked on the camera lens and by a heavy snowfall. Evans typed in an additional command and touched one of the switches on her desk. A blast of static, a hiss like frying bacon, came from the speaker.

"That's Dallas. The sound is a reading of the background radiation registered by detectors at the site of this camera." She typed in another command and the image on the "window" flashed through a succession of equally desolate scenes, holding ten seconds on each before switching to the next. A desert in twilight, motionless under low clouds; a murky underwater shot in which the remains of a building were just visible; a denuded forest half-buried in snow; a deserted highway overpass. With each change of scene the loudspeaker stopped for a split second, then the hiss resumed.

Havelmann watched all of this soberly.

"This has been the state of the surface for a year now, ever since the last bombs fell. To our knowledge there are no human beings alive in North America—in the Northern Hemisphere, for that matter. Radio transmissions from South America, New Zealand, and Australia have one by one ceased in the last eight months. We have not observed a living creature above the level of an insect through any of our monitors since the beginning of the year. It is the summer of 2010. Although, considering the situation, counting years by the old system seems a little futile to me."

Dr. Evans slid open a desk drawer and took out an automatic. She placed it in the middle of the desk blotter and leaned back, her right hand touching the edge of the desk near the gun.

"You are now going to tell me that you never heard of any of this, and that you've never seen me before in your life," she said. "Despite the fact that I have been speaking to you daily for two weeks and that you have had this explanation from me at least three times during that period. You are going to tell me that it is 1984 and that you are thirty-five years old, despite the absurdity of such a claim. You are going to feign amazement and confusion; the more I insist that you face these facts, the more you are going to become distressed. Eventually you will break down into tears and expect me to sympathize. You can go to hell."

Evans's voice had grown angrier as she spoke. She had to stop; it was almost more than she could do. When she resumed she was under control again. "If you persist in this sham, I may kill you. I assure you that no one will care if I do. You may speak now."

Havelmann stared at the window. His mouth opened and closed stupidly. How old he looked, how feeble. Evans felt a sudden surge of doubt. What if she were wrong? She had an image of herself as she might appear to him: arrogant, bitter, an incomprehensible inquisitor whose motives for tormenting him were a total mystery. She watched him. After a few minutes his mouth closed; the eyes blinked rapidly and were clear.

"Please. Tell me what you're talking about."

Evans shuddered. "The gun is loaded. Keep talking."

"What do you want me to say? I never heard of any of this. Only this morning I saw my wife and kids, and everything was all right. Now you give me this story about atomic war and 2010. What, have I been asleep for thirty years?"

"You didn't act very surprised to be here when you walked in. If you're so disoriented, how do you explain how you got here?"

The man sat heavily in the chair. "I don't remember. I guess I thought I came here—to the hospital, I thought—to get a checkup. I didn't think about it. You must know how I got here."

"I do. But I think you know too, and you're just playing a game with me—with all of us. The others are worried, but I'm sick of it. I can see through you, so you may as well quit the act. You were famous for your sincerity, but I always suspected that was an act, too, and I'm not falling for it. You didn't start this game soon enough for me to be persuaded you're crazy, despite what the others may think."

Evans played with the butt of her dead cigarette. "Or this could be a delusional system," she continued. "You think you're in a hospital, and your schizophrenia has progressed to the point where you deny all facts that don't go along with your attempts to evade responsibility. I suppose in some sense such an insanity would absolve you. If that's the case, I should be more objective.

Well, I can't. I'm failing my profession. Too bad." Emotion had drained away from her until, by the end, she felt as if she were speaking from across a continent instead of a desk.

"I still don't know what you're talking about. Where are my wife and kids?"

"They're dead."

Havelmann sat rigidly. The only sound was the hiss of the radiation detector. "Let me have a cigarette."

"There are no cigarettes left. I just smoked my last one." Evans touched the ashtray. "I made two cartons last a year."

Havelmann's gaze dropped. "How old my hands are! . . . Helen has lovely hands."

"Why are you going on with this charade?"

The old man's face reddened. "God damn you! Tell me what happened!"

"The famous Havelmann rage. Am I supposed to be frightened now?"

The hiss from the loudspeaker seemed to increase. Havelmann lunged for the gun. Evans snatched it and pushed back from the desk. The old man grabbed the paperweight and raised it to strike. She pointed the gun at him.

"Your wife didn't make the plane in time. She was at the western White House. I don't know where your damned kids were—probably vaporized with their own families. You, however, had Operation Kneecap to save you. Mr. President. Now sit down and tell me why you've been playing games, or I'll kill you right here and now. Sit down!"

A light seemed to dawn on Havelmann. "You're insane."

"Put the paperweight back on the desk."

He did. He sat.

"But you can't simply be crazy," Havelmann continued. "There's no reason why you should take me away from my home and subject me to this. This is some kind of plot. The government. The CIA."

"And you're thirty-five years old?"

Havelmann examined his hands again. "You've done something to me."

"And the camps? Administrative Order 31?"

"If I'm the president, then why are you quizzing me here? Why can't I remember a thing about it?"

"Stop it. Stop it right now," Evans said. She heard her voice for the first time. It sounded more like that of an old man than Havelmann's. "I can't take any more lies. I swear that I'll kill you. First it was the commander-in-chief routine, calisthenics, stiff upper lips and discipline. Then the big brother, let's have a whiskey and talk it over, son. Yessir, Mr. President." Havelmann stared at her. He was going to make her kill him, and she knew she wouldn't be strong enough not to.

"Now you can't remember anything," she said. "Your boys are confused, they're fed up. Well, I'm fed up too."

"If this is true, you've got to help me!"

"I don't give a rat's ass about helping you!" Evans shouted. "I'm interested in making you tell the truth! Don't you realize that we're dead? I don't care about your feeble sense of what's right and wrong; just tell me what's keeping you going. Who do you think you're going to impress? You think you've got an election to win? A place in history to protect? There isn't going to be any more history! History ended last August!

"So spare me the fantasy about the hospital and the nonexistent nurses' station. Someone with Korsakov's wouldn't make up that story. He would recognize the difference between a window and an HDTV screen. A dozen other slips. You're not a good enough actor."

Her hand trembled. The gun was heavy. Her voice trembled, too, and she despised herself for it. "Sometimes I think the only thing that's kept me alive is knowing I had half a pack of cigarettes left. That and the desire to make you crawl."

The old man sat looking at the gun in her hand. "I was the president?"

"No," said Evans. "I made it up."

His eyes seemed to sink farther back in the network of lines surrounding them.

"I started a war?"

Evans felt her heart race. "Stop lying! You sent the strike force; you ordered the preemptive launch."

"I'm old. How old am I?"

"You know how old—" She stopped. She could hardly catch her breath. She felt a sharp pain in her breast. "You're sixty-one."

"Jesus, Mary, Joseph."

"That's it? That's all you can say?"

Havelmann stared hollowly, then slowly, so slowly that at first it was not apparent what he was doing, lowered his head into his hands and began to cry. His sobs were almost inaudible over the hiss of the radiation detector. Evans watched him. She rested her elbows on the desk, steadying the gun with both hands. Havelmann's head shook in front of her. Despite his age, his gray hair was thick.

After a moment Evans reached over and switched off the loudspeaker. The hissing stopped.

Eventually Havelmann stopped crying. He raised his head. He looked dazed. His expression became unreadable. He looked at the doctor and the gun. "My name is Robert Havelmann," he said. "Why are you pointing that gun at me?"

"Don't do this," said Evans. "Please."

"Do what? Who are you?"

Evans watched his face blur. Through her tears he looked like a much younger man. The gun drooped. She tried to lift it, but it was as if she were made of smoke—there was no substance to her, and it was all she could do to keep from dissipating, let alone kill anyone as clean and innocent as Robert Havelmann. He reached forward. He took the gun from her hand. "Are you all right?" he asked.

Dr. Evans sat in her office, hoping that it wasn't going to be a bad day. The pain in her breast had not come that day, but she was out of cigarettes. She searched the desk on the odd chance she might have missed a pack, even a single butt, in the corner of one of the drawers. No luck.

She gave up and turned to face the window. The blinds were

open, revealing the snow-covered field. She watched the clouds roll before the wind. It was dark. Winter. Nothing was alive.

"It's cold outside," she whispered.

There was a knock at the door. Dear god, leave me alone, she thought. Please leave me alone.

"Come in," she said.

The door opened and an old man in a rumpled suit entered. "Dr. Evans? I'm Robert Havelmann. What did you want to talk about?"

INVADERS

15 November 1532: That night no one slept. On the hills outside Cajamarca, the campfires of the Inca's army shone like so many stars in the sky. De Soto had reported that Atahualpa had perhaps forty thousand troops under arms, but looking at the myriad lights spread across those hills, de Candia realized that estimate was, if anything, low.

Against them, Pizarro could throw one hundred foot soldiers, sixty horses, eight muskets, and four harquebuses. Pizarro, his brother Hernando, de Soto, and Benalcázar laid out plans for an ambush. They would invite the Inca to a parlay. De Candia and his artillery would be hidden in the building along one side of the square, the cavalry and infantry along the others. De Candia watched Pizarro prowl through the camp that night, checking the men's armor, joking with them, reminding them of the treasure they would have, and the women. The men laughed nervously and whetted their swords.

They might sharpen them until their hands fell off; when

morning dawned, they would be slaughtered. De Candia breathed deeply of the thin air and turned from the wall.

Ruiz de Arce, an infantryman with a face like a clenched fist, hailed him as he passed. "Are those guns of yours ready for some work tomorrow?"

"We need prayers more than guns."

"I'm not afraid of these brownies," de Arce said.

"Then you're a half-wit."

"Soto says they have no swords."

The man was probably just trying to reassure himself, but de Candia couldn't abide it. "Will you shut your stinking fool's trap! They don't need swords! If they only spit all at once, we'll be drowned."

Pizarro overheard him. He stormed over, grabbed de Candia's arm, and shook him. "Have they ever seen a horse, Candia? Have they ever felt steel? When you fired the harquebus on the seashore, didn't the town chief pour beer down its barrel as if it were a thirsty god? Pull up your balls and show me you're a man!"

His face was inches away. "Mark me! Tomorrow, Saint James sits on your shoulder, and we win a victory that will cover us in glory for five hundred years."

2 December 2001: "DEE-fense! DEE-fense!" the crowd screamed. During the two-minute warning, Norwood Delacroix limped over to the Redskins' special conditioning coach.

"My knee's about gone," said Delacroix, an outside linebacker with eyebrows that ran together and all the musculature that modern pharmacology could load onto his six-foot-five frame. "I need something."

"You need the power of prayer, my friend. Stoner's eating your lunch."

"Just do it."

The coach selected a popgun from his rack, pressed the muzzle against Delacroix's knee, and pulled the trigger. A flood of well-being rushed up Delacroix's leg. He flexed it tentatively. It felt better than the other one now. Delacroix jogged back onto the field. "DEE-fense!" the fans roared. The overcast sky began to spit frozen rain. The ref blew the whistle, and the Bills broke huddle.

Delacroix looked across at Stoner, the Bills' tight end. The air throbbed with electricity. The quarterback called the signals; the ball was snapped; Stoner surged forward. As Delacroix back-pedaled furiously, sudden sunlight flooded the field. His ears buzzed. Stoner jerked left and went right, twisting Delacroix around like a cork in a bottle. His knee popped. Stoner had two steps on him. TD for sure. Delacroix pulled his head down and charged after him.

But instead of continuing downfield, Stoner slowed. He looked straight up into the air. Delacroix hit him at the knees, and they both went down. He'd caught him! The crowd screamed louder, a scream edged with hysteria.

Then Delacroix realized the buzzing wasn't just in his ears. Elation fading, he lifted his head and looked toward the sidelines. The coaches and players were running for the tunnels. The crowd boiled toward the exits, shedding Thermoses and beer cups and radios. The sunlight was harshly bright. Delacroix looked up. A huge disk hovered no more than fifty feet above, pinning them in its spotlight. Stoner untangled himself from Delacroix, stumbled to his feet, and ran off the field.

Holy Jesus and the Virgin Mary on toast, Delacroix thought.

He scrambled toward the end zone. The stadium was empty-ing fast, except for the ones who were getting trampled. The throbbing in the air increased in volume, lowered in pitch, and the flying saucer settled onto the NFL logo on the forty-yard line. The sound stopped as abruptly as if it had been sucked into a sponge.

Out of the corner of his eye, Delacroix saw an NBC camera-man come up next to him, focusing on the ship. Its side divided, and a ramp extended itself to the ground. The cameraman fell back a few steps, but Delacroix held his ground. The inside glowed with the bluish light of a UV lamp.

A shape moved there. It lurched forward to the top of the

ramp. A large manlike thing, it advanced with a rolling stagger, like a college freshman at a beer blast. It wore a body-tight red stretchsuit, a white circle on its chest with a lightning bolt through it, some sort of flexible mask over its face. Blond hair covered its head in a kind of brush cut, and two cup-shaped ears poked comically out of the sides of its head. The creature stepped off onto the field, nudging aside the football that lay there.

Delacroix, who had majored in public relations at Michigan State, went forward to greet it. This could be the beginning of an entirely new career. His knee felt great.

He extended his hand. "Welcome," he said. "I greet you in the name of humanity and the United States of America."

"Cocaine," the alien said. "We need cocaine."

Today: I sit at my desk writing a science-fiction story, a tall, thin man wearing jeans, a white T-shirt with the abstract face of a man printed on it, white high-top basketball shoes, and gold-plated wire-rimmed glasses.

In the morning I drink coffee to get me up for the day, and at night I have a gin and tonic to help me relax.

16 November 1532: "What are they waiting for, the shitting dogs!" the man next to de Arce said. "Are they trying to make us suffer?"

"Shut up, will you?" De Arce shifted his armor. Wedged into the stone building on the side of the square, sweating, they had been waiting since dawn, in silence for the most part except for the creak of leather, the uneasy jingle of cascabels on the horses' trappings. The men stank worse than the restless horses. Some had pissed themselves. A common foot soldier like de Arce was lucky to get a space near enough to the door to see out.

As noon came and went with still no sign of Atahualpa and his retinue, the mood of the men went from impatience to near panic. Then, late in the day, word came that the Indians again were moving toward the town.

An hour later, six thousand brilliantly costumed attendants entered the plaza. They were unarmed. Atahualpa, borne on a golden litter by eight men in cloaks of green feathers that glistened like emeralds in the sunset, rose above them. De Arce heard a slight rattling, looked down, and found that his hand, gripping the sword so tightly the knuckles stood out white, was shaking uncontrollably. He unknotted his fist from the hilt, rubbed the cramped fingers, and crossed himself.

"Quiet now, my brave ones," Pizarro said.

Father Valverde and Felipillo strode out to the center of the plaza, right through the sea of attendants. The priest had guts. He stopped before the litter of the Inca, short and steady as a fence post. "Greetings, my lord, in the name of Pope Clement VII, His Majesty the Emperor Charles V, and Our Lord and Savior Jesus Christ."

Atahualpa spoke and Felipillo translated: "Where is this new god?"

Valverde held up the crucifix. "Our God died on the cross many years ago and rose again to Heaven. He appointed the Pope as His viceroy on earth, and the Pope has commanded King Charles to subdue the peoples of the world and convert them to the true faith. The king sent us here to command your obedience and to teach you and your people in this faith."

"By what authority does this pope give away lands that aren't his?"

Valverde held up his Bible. "By the authority of the word of God."

The Inca took the Bible. When Valverde reached out to help him get the cover unclasped, Atahualpa cuffed his arm away. He opened the book and leafed through the pages. After a moment he threw it to the ground. "I hear no words," he said.

Valverde snatched up the book and stalked back toward Pizarro's hiding place. "What are you waiting for?" he shouted. "The saints and the Blessed Virgin, the bleeding wounds of Christ himself, cry vengeance! Attack, and I'll absolve you!"

Pizarro had already stridden into the plaza. He waved his kerchief. "Santiago, and at them!"

On the far side, the harquebuses exploded in an enfilade. The lines of Indians jerked like startled cats. Bells jingling, de Soto's and Hernando's cavalry burst from the lines of doorways on the adjoining side. De Arce clutched his sword and rushed out with the others from the third side. He felt the power of God in his arm. "Santiago!" he roared at the top of his lungs, and hacked halfway through the neck of his first Indian. Bright blood spurted. He put his boot to the brown man's shoulder and yanked free, lunged for the belly of another wearing a kilt of bright red-and-white checks. The man turned, and the sword caught between his ribs. The hilt was almost twisted from de Arce's grasp as the Indian went down. He pulled free, shrugged another man off his back, and daggered him in the side.

After the first flush of glory, it turned to filthy, hard work, an hour's wade through an ocean of butchery in the twilight, bodies heaped waist-high, boots skidding on the bloody stones. De Arce alone must have killed forty. Only after they'd slaughtered them all and captured the Sapa Inca did it end. A silence settled, broken only by the moans of dying Indians and distant shouts of the cavalry chasing the ones who had managed to break through the plaza wall to escape.

Saint James had indeed sat on their shoulders. Six thousand dead Indians, and not one Spaniard nicked. It was a pure demonstration of the power of prayer.

31 January 2002: It was Colonel Zipp's third session interrogating the alien. So far the thing had kept a consistent story, but not a credible one. The only consideration that kept Zipp from panic at the thought of how his career would suffer if this continued was the rumor that his fellow case officers weren't doing any better with any of the others. That, and the fact that the Krel possessed technology that would reestablish American superiority for another two hundred years. He took a drag on his cigarette, the first of his third pack of the day.

"Your name?" Zipp asked.

"You may call me Flash."

Zipp studied the red union suit, the lightning bolt. With the flat chest, the rounded shoulders, pointed upper lip, and pronounced underbite, the alien looked like a cross between Wally Cleaver and the Mock Turtle. "Is this some kind of joke?"

"What is a joke?"

"Never mind." Zipp consulted his notes. "Where are you from?"

"God has ceded us an empire extending over sixteen solar systems in the Orion arm of the galaxy, including the systems around the stars you know as Tau Ceti, Epsilon Eridani, Alpha Centauri, and the red dwarf Barnard's star."

"God gave you an empire?"

"Yes. We were hoping He'd give us your world, but all He kept talking about was your cocaine."

The alien's translating device had to be malfunctioning. "You're telling me that God sent you for cocaine?"

"No. He just told us about it. We collect chemical compounds for their aesthetic interest. These alkaloids do not exist on our world. Like the music you humans value so highly, they combine familiar elements—carbon, hydrogen, nitrogen, oxygen—in pleasing new ways."

The colonel leaned back, exhaled a cloud of smoke. "You consider cocaine like—like a symphony?"

"Yes. Understand, Colonel, no material commodity alone could justify the difficulties of interstellar travel. We come here for aesthetic reasons."

"You seem to know what cocaine is already. Why don't you just synthesize it yourself?"

"If you valued a unique work of aboriginal art, would you be satisfied with a mass-produced duplicate manufactured in your hometown? Of course not. And we are prepared to pay you well, in a coin you can use."

"We don't need any coins. If you want cocaine, tell us how your ships work."

"That is one of the coins we had in mind. Our ships operate according to a principle of basic physics. Certain fundamental physical reactions are subject to the belief system of the beings promoting them. If I believe that X is true, then X is more probably true than if I did not believe so."

The colonel leaned forward again. "We know that already. We call it the 'observer effect.' Our great physicist Werner Heisenberg—"

"Yes. I'm afraid we carry this principle a little further than that."

"What do you mean?"

Flash smirked. "I mean that our ships move through interstellar space by the power of prayer."

13 May 1533: Atahualpa offered to fill a room twenty-two feet long and seventeen feet wide with gold up to a line as high as a man could reach, if the Spaniards would let him go. They were skeptical. How long would this take? Pizarro asked. Two months, Atahualpa said.

Pizarro allowed the word to be sent out, and over the next several months, bearers, chewing the coca leaf in order to negotiate the mountain roads under such burdens, brought in tons of gold artifacts. They brought plates and vessels, life-sized statues of women and men, gold lobsters and spiders and alpacas, intricately fashioned ears of maize, every kernel reproduced, with leaves of gold and tassels of spun silver.

Martin Bueno was one of the advance scouts sent with the Indians to Cuzco, the capital of the empire. They found it to be the legendary city of gold. The Incas, having no money, valued precious metals only as ornament. In Cuzco the very walls of the Sun Temple, Coricancha, were plated with gold. Adjoining the temple was a ritual garden where gold maize plants supported gold butterflies, gold bees pollinated gold flowers.

"Enough loot that you'll shit in a different gold pot every day for the rest of your life," Bueno told his friend Diego Leguizano upon his return to Cajamarca.

They ripped the plating off the temple walls and had it carried to Cajamarca. There they melted it down into ingots.

The huge influx of gold into Europe was to cause an economic catastrophe. In Peru, at the height of the conquest, a pair of shoes cost $850, and a bottle of wine $1,700. When their old horseshoes wore out, iron being unavailable, the cavalry shod their horses with silver.

21 April 2003: In the executive washroom of Bellingham, Winston, and McNeese, Jason Prescott snorted a couple of lines and was ready for the afternoon. He returned to the brokerage to find the place in a whispering uproar. In his office sat one of the Krel. Prescott's secretary was about to piss himself. "It asked specifically for you," he said.

What would Attila the Hun do in this situation? Prescott thought. He went into the office. "Jason Prescott," he said. "What can I do for you, Mr. . . . ?"

The alien's bloodshot eyes surveyed him. "Flash. I wish to make an investment."

"Investments are our business." Rumors had flown around the New York Merc for a month that the Krel were interested in investing. They had earned vast sums selling information to various computer, environmental, and biotech firms. Several of the aliens had come to observe trading in the currencies pit last week, and only yesterday Jason had heard from a reliable source that they were considering opening an account with Merrill Lynch. "What brings you to our brokerage?"

"Not the brokerage. You. We heard that you are the most ruthless currencies trader in this city. We worship efficiency. You are efficient."

Right. Maybe there was a hallucinogen in the toot. "I'll call in some of our foreign-exchange experts. We can work up an investment plan for your consideration in a week."

"We already have an investment plan. We are, as you say in the markets, 'long' in dollars. We want you to sell dollars and buy francs for us."

"The franc is pretty strong right now. It's likely to hold for the next six months. We'd suggest—"

"We wish to buy fifty billion dollars worth of francs."

Prescott stared. "That's not a very good investment." Flash said nothing. The silence grew uncomfortable. "I suppose if we stretch it out over a few months, and hit the exchanges in Hong Kong and London at the same time—"

"We want these francs bought in the next week. For the week after that, a second fifty billion dollars. Fifty billion a week until we tell you to stop."

Hallucinogens for sure. "That doesn't make any sense."

"We can take our business elsewhere."

Prescott thought about it. It would take every trick he knew—and he'd have to invent some new ones—to carry this off. The dollar was going to drop through the floor, while the franc would punch through the sell-stops of every trader on ten world markets. The exchanges would scream bloody murder. The repercussions would auger holes in every economy north of Antarctica. Governments would intervene. It would make the historic Hunt silver squeeze look like a game of Monopoly.

Besides, it made no sense. Not only was it criminally irresponsible, it was stupid. The Krel would squander every dime they'd earned.

Then he thought about the commission on $50 billion a week.

Prescott looked across at the alien. From the right point of view, Flash resembled a barrel-chested college undergraduate from Special Effects U. He felt an urge to giggle, a euphoric feeling of power. "When do we start?"

19 May 1533: In the fields the *purics,* singing praise to Atahualpa, son of the sun, harvested the maize. At night they celebrated by getting drunk on *chicha.* It was, they said, the most festive month of the year.

Pedro Sancho did his drinking in the dark of the treasure room, in the smoke of the smelters' fire. For months he had been troubled by nightmares of the heaped bodies lying in the plaza. He tried to ignore the abuse of the Indian women, the brutality toward the men. He worked hard. As Pizarro's squire, it was his job to record daily the tally of Atahualpa's ransom. When he ran low on ink, he taught the *purics* to make it for him from soot and the juice of berries. They learned readily.

Atahualpa heard about the ink and one day came to him. "What are you doing with those marks?" he said, pointing to the scribe's tally book.

"I'm writing the list of gold objects to be melted down."

"What is this 'writing'?"

Sancho was nonplussed. Over the months of Atahualpa's captivity, Sancho had become impressed by the sophistication of the Incas. Yet they were also queerly backward. They had no money. It was not beyond belief that they should not know how to read and write.

"By means of these marks, I can record the words that people speak. That's writing. Later other men can look at these marks and see what was said. That's reading."

"Then this is a kind of quipu?" Atahualpa's servants had demonstrated for Sancho the quipu, a system of knotted strings by which the Incas kept talleys. "Show me how it works," Atahualpa said.

Sancho wrote on the page: *God have mercy on us.* He pointed. "This, my lord, is a representation of the word 'God.' "

Atahualpa looked skeptical. "Mark it here." He held out his hand, thumbnail extended.

Sancho wrote "God" on the Inca's thumbnail.

"Say nothing now." Atahualpa advanced to one of the guards, held out his thumbnail. "What does this mean?" he asked.

"God," the man replied.

Sancho could tell the Inca was impressed, but he barely showed it. That the Sapa Inca had maintained such dignity throughout his captivity tore at Sancho's heart.

"This writing is truly a magical accomplishment," Atahualpa told him. "You must teach my *amautas* this art."

Later, when the viceroy Estete, Father Valverde, and Pizarro came to chide him for the slow pace of the gold shipments, Atahualpa tested each of them separately. Estete and Valverde each said the word "God." Atahualpa held his thumbnail out to the conquistador.

Estete chuckled. For the first time in his experience, Sancho saw Pizarro flush. He turned away. "I don't waste my time on the games of children," Pizarro said.

Atahualpa stared at him. "But your common soldiers have this art."

"Well, I don't."

"Why not?"

"I was a swineherd. Swineherds don't need to read."

"You are not a swineherd now."

Pizarro glared at the Inca. "I don't need to read to order you put to death." He marched out of the room.

After the others had left, Sancho told Atahualpa, "You ought not to humiliate the governor in front of his men."

"He humiliates himself," Atahualpa said. "There is no skill in which a leader ought to let himself stand behind his followers."

Today: The part of this story about the Incas is as historically accurate as I could make it, but this Krel business is science fiction. I even stole the name "Krel" from a 1950s SF flick. I've been addicted to SF for years. In the evening my wife and I wash the bad taste of the news out of our mouths by watching old movies on videotape.

A scientist, asked why he read SF, replied, "Because in science fiction the experiments always work." Things in SF stories work out more neatly than in reality. Nothing is impossible. Spaceships move faster than light. Atomic weapons are neutralized. Disease is abolished. People travel in time. Why, Isaac Asimov even wrote a story once that ended with the reversal of entropy!

The descendants of the Incas, living in grinding poverty, find their most lucrative crop in coca, which they refine into cocaine and sell in vast quantities to North Americans.

23 August 2008: "Catalog number 208," said John Bostock. "Georges Seurat, *Bathers*."

FRENCH GOVERNMENT FALLS, the morning *Times* had an-

nounced. JAPAN BANS U.S. IMPORTS. FOOD RIOTS IN MADRID. But
Bostock had barely glanced at the newspaper over his coffee; he
was buzzed on caffeine and adrenaline, and it was too late to stop
the auction, the biggest day of his career. The lot list would make
an art historian faint. *Guernica. The Potato Eaters. The Scream.*
Miró, Rembrandt, Vermeer, Gauguin, Matisse, Constable,
Magritte, Pollock, Mondrian. Six desperate governments had
contributed to the sale. And rumor had it the Krel would be
among the bidders.

The rumor proved true. In the front row, beside the solicitor
Patrick McClannahan, sat one of the unlikely aliens, wearing red
tights and a lightning-bolt insignia. The famous Flash. The creature leaned back lazily while McClannahan did the bidding with
a discreetly raised forefinger.

Bidding on the Seurat started at ten million and went orbital.
It soon became clear that the main bidders were Flash and the
U.S. government. The American campaign against cultural im-
perialism was getting a lot of press, ironic since the Yanks could
afford to challenge the Krel only because of the technology the
Krel had lavished on them. The probability suppressor that prevented the detonation of atomic weapons. The autodidactic an-
tivirus that cured most diseases. There was talk of an immortality
drug. Of a time machine. So what if the European Community
was in the sixth month of an economic crisis that threatened to
dissolve the unifying efforts of the past twenty years? So what if
Krel meddling destroyed humans' capacity to run the world? The
Americans were making money, and the Krel were richer than
Croesus.

The bidding reached $1.2 billion, at which point the Ameri-
can ambassador gave up. Bostock tapped his gavel. "Sold," he
said in his most cultured voice, nodding toward the alien.

The crowd murmured. The American stood. "If you can't see
what they're doing to us, then you don't deserve our help!"

For a minute Bostock thought the auction was going to turn
into a riot. Then the new owner of the pointillist masterpiece
stood, smiled. Ingenuous, clumsy. "We know that there has been
considerable disquiet over our purchase of these historic works

of art," Flash said. "Let me promise you, they will be displayed where all humans—not just those who can afford to visit the great museums—can see them."

The crowd's murmur turned into applause. Bostock put down his gavel and joined in. The American ambassador and his aides stalked out. Thank God, Bostock thought. The attendants brought out the next item.

"Catalog number 209," Bostock said. "Leonardo da Vinci, *Mona Lisa.*"

26 July 1533: The soldiers, seeing the heaps of gold grow, became anxious. They consumed stores of coca meant for the Inca messengers. They fought over women. They grumbled over the airs of Atahualpa. "Who does he think he is? The governor treats him like a hidalgo."

Father Valverde cursed Pizarro's inaction. That morning, after matins, he spoke with Estete. "The governor has agreed to meet and decide what to do," Estete said.

"It's about time. What about Soto?" De Soto was against harming Atahualpa. He maintained that, since the Inca had paid the ransom, he should be set free, no matter what danger this would present. Pizarro had stalled. Last week he had sent de Soto away to check out rumors that the Tahuantinsuyans were massing for an attack to free the Sapa Inca.

Estete smiled. "Soto's not back yet."

They went to the building Pizarro had claimed as his, and found the others already gathered. The Incas had no tables or proper chairs, so the Spaniards were forced to sit in a circle on mats as the Indians did. Pizarro, only a few years short of three-score, sat on a low stool of the sort that Atahualpa used when he held court. His left leg, whose old battle wound still pained him at times, was stretched out before him. His loose white shirt had been cleaned by some *puric*'s wife. Valverde sat beside him. Gathered were Estete, Benalcázar, Almagro, de Candia, Riquelme, Pizarro's young cousin Pedro, the scribe Pedro Sancho, Valverde, and the governor himself.

As Valverde and Estete had agreed, the viceroy went first.

"The men are jumpy, governor," Estete said. "The longer we stay cooped up here, the longer we give these savages the chance to plot against us."

"We should wait until Soto returns," de Candia said, already looking guilty as a dog. "We've got nothing but rumors so far. I won't kill a man on a rumor."

Silence. Trust de Candia to speak aloud what they were all thinking but were not ready to say. The man had no political judgment—but maybe it was just as well to face it directly. Valverde seized the opportunity. "Atahualpa plots against us even as we speak," he told Pizarro. "As governor, you are responsible for our safety. Any court would convict him of treason, and execute him."

"He's a king," de Candia said. Face flushed, he spat out a cud of leaves. "We don't have authority to try him. We should ship him back to Spain and let the emperor decide what to do."

"This is not a king," Valverde said. "It isn't even a man. It is a creature that worships demons, that weaves spells about half-wits like Candia. You saw him discard the Bible. Even after my months of teaching, after the extraordinary mercies we've shown him, he doesn't acknowledge the primacy of Christ! He cares only for his wives and his pagan gods. Yet he's satanically clever. Don't think we can let him go. If we do, the day will come when he'll have our hearts for dinner."

"We can take him with us to Cuzco," Benalcázar said. "We don't know the country. His presence would guarantee our safe conduct."

"We'll be traveling over rough terrain, carrying tons of gold, with not enough horses," Almagro said. "If we take him with us, we'll be ripe for ambush at every pass."

"They won't attack if we have him."

"He could escape. We can't trust the rebel Indians to stay loyal to us. If they turned to our side, they can just as easily turn back to his."

"And remember, he escaped before, during the civil war," Valverde said. "Huascar, his brother, lived to regret that. If

Atahualpa didn't hesitate to murder his own brother, do you think he'll stop for us?"

"He's given us his word," Candia said.

"What good is the word of a pagan?"

Pizarro, silent until now, spoke. "He has no reason to think the word of a Christian much better."

Valverde felt his blood rise. Pizarro knew as well as any of them what was necessary. What was he waiting for? "He keeps a hundred wives! He betrayed his brother! He worships the sun!" The priest grabbed Pizarro's hand, held it up between them so they could both see the scar there, where Pizarro had gotten cut preventing one of his own men from killing Atahualpa. "He isn't worth an ounce of the blood you spilled to save him."

"He's proved worth twenty-four tons of gold." Pizarro's eyes were hard and calm.

"There is no alternative!" Valverde insisted. "He serves the Antichrist! God demands his death."

At last Pizarro seemed to have gotten what he wanted. He smiled. "Far be it from me to ignore the command of God," he said. "Since God forces us to it, let's discuss how He wants it done."

5 October 2009: "What a lovely country Chile is from the air. You should be proud of it."

"I'm from Los Angeles," Leon Sepulveda said. "And as soon as we close this deal, I'm going back."

"The mountains are impressive."

"Nothing but earthquakes and slag. You can have Chile."

"Is it for sale?"

Sepulveda stared at the Krel. "I was just kidding."

They sat at midnight in the arbor, away from the main buildings of Iguassu Microelectronics of Santiago. The night was cold and the arbor was overgrown and the bench needed a paint job—but then, a lot of things had been getting neglected in the past couple of years. All the more reason to put yourself in a financial situation where you didn't have to worry. Though Sepulveda had to admit that, since the advent of the Krel, such positions were harder to come by, and less secure once you had them.

Flash's earnestness aroused a kind of horror in him. It had something to do with Sepulveda's suspicion that this thing next to him was as superior to him as he was to a guinea pig, plus the alien's aura of drunken adolescence, plus his own willingness, despite the feeling that the situation was out of control, to make a deal with it. He took another Valium and tried to calm down.

"What assurance do I have that this time-travel method will work?" he asked.

"It will work. If you don't like it in Chile, or back in Los Angeles, you can use it to go into the past."

Sepulveda swallowed. "Okay. You need to read and sign these papers."

"We don't read."

"You don't read Spanish? How about English?"

"We don't read at all. We used to, but we gave it up. Once you start reading, it gets out of control. You tell yourself you're just going to stick to nonfiction—but pretty soon you graduate to fiction. After that, you can't kick the habit. And then there's the oppression."

"Oppression?"

"Sure. I mean, I like a story as much as the next Krel, but any pharmacologist can show that arbitrary cultural, sexual, and economic assumptions determine every significant aspect of a story. Literature is a political tool used by ruling elites to ensure their hegemony. Anyone who denies that is a fish who can't see the water it swims in. Or the fascist who tells you, as he beats you, that those blows you feel are your own delusion."

"Right. Look, can we settle this? I've got things to do."

"This is, of course, the key to temporal translation. The past is another arbitrary construct. Language creates reality. Reality is smoke."

"Well, this time machine better not be smoke. We're going to find out the truth about the past. Then we'll change it."

"By all means. Find the truth." Flash turned to the last page of the contract, pricked his thumb, and marked a thumbprint on the signature line.

After they sealed the agreement, Sepulveda walked the alien back to the courtyard. A Krel flying pod with Vermeer's *The Letter* varnished onto its door sat at the focus of three spotlights. The painting was scorched almost into unrecognizability by atmospheric friction. The door peeled downward from the top, became a canvas-surfaced ramp.

"I saw some interesting lines inscribed on the coastal desert on the way here," Flash said. "A bird, a tree, a big spider. In the sunset, it looked beautiful. I didn't think you humans were capable of such art. Is it for sale?"

"I don't think so. That was done by some old Indians a long time ago. If you're really interested, though, I can look into it."

"Not necessary." Flash waggled his ears, wiped his feet on Mark Rothko's *Earth and Green,* and staggered into the pod.

26 July 1533: Atahualpa looked out of the window of the stone room in which he was kept, across the plaza where the priest Valverde stood outside his chapel after his morning prayers. Valverde's chapel had been the house of the virgins; the women of the house had long since been raped by the Spanish soldiers, as the house had been by the Spanish god. Valverde spoke with Estete. They were getting ready to kill him, Atahualpa knew. He had known ever since the ransom had been paid.

He looked beyond the thatched roofs of the town to the crest of the mountains, where the sun was about to break in his tireless circuit of Tahuantinsuyu. The cold morning air raised dew on the metal of the chains that bound him hand and foot. The metal was queer, different from the bronze the *purics* worked or the gold and silver Atahualpa was used to wearing. If gold was the sweat of the sun, and silver the tears of the moon, what was this metal, dull and hard like the men who held him captive, yet strong, too—stronger, he had come to realize, than the Inca. It, like the men who brought it, was beyond his experience. It gave evidence that Tahuantinsuyu, the Four Quarters of the World, was not all the world after all. Atahualpa had thought none but savages lived beyond their lands. He'd imagined no man readier to face ruthless necessity than himself. He had ordered the death of Huascar, his own brother. But he was learning that these men were capable of enormities against which the Inca civil war would seem a minor discomfort.

That evening they took him out of the building to the plaza. In the plaza's center, the soldiers had piled a great heap of wood on flagstones, some of which were still stained with the blood of the six thousand slaughtered attendants. They bound him to a stake amid the heaped fagots, and Valverde appealed one last time for the Inca to renounce Satan and be baptized. He promised that if Atahualpa would do so, he would earn God's mercy: they would strangle him rather than burn him to death.

The rough wood pressed against his spine. Atahualpa looked at the priest, and the men gathered around, and the women weeping beyond the circle of soldiers. The moon, his mother, rode high above. Firelight flickered on the breastplates of the Spaniards, and from the waiting torches drifted the smell of pitch. The men shifted nervously. Creak of leather, clink of metal. Men on horses shod with silver. Sweat shining on Valverde's forehead. Valverde stared at Atahualpa as if he desired something, but was prepared to destroy him without getting it if need be. The priest thought he was showing Atahualpa resolve, but Atahualpa saw that beneath Valverde's face he was a dead man. Pizarro stood aside, with the Spanish viceroy Estete and the scribe. Pizarro was an old man. He ought to be sitting quietly in some village, outside the violence of life, giving advice and teaching the children. What kind of world did he come from, that sent men into old age still charged with the lusts and bitterness of the young?

Pizarro, too, looked as if he wanted this to end.

Atahualpa knew that it would not end. This was only the beginning. These men would suffer for this moment as they had already suffered for it all their lives, seeking the pain blindly over oceans, jungles, deserts, probing it like a sore tooth until they'd found and grasped it in this plaza of Cajamarca, thinking they sought gold. They'd come all this way to create a moment that would reveal to them their own incurable disease. Now they had it. In a few minutes, they thought, it would at last be over, that once he was gone, they would be free—but Atahualpa knew it would be with them ever after, and with their children and grand-children and the million others of their race in times to come, whether they knew of this hour in the plaza or not, because they were sick and would pass the sickness on with their breath and semen. They could not burn out the sickness so easily as they could burn the Son of God to ash. This was a great tragedy, but it contained a huge jest. They were caught in a wheel of the sky and could not get out. They must destroy themselves.

"Have your way, priest," Atahualpa said. "Then strangle me, and bear my body to Cuzco, to be laid with my ancestors." He knew they would not do it, and so would add an additional curse to their faithlessness.

He had one final curse. He turned to Pizarro. "You will have responsibility for my children."

Pizarro looked at the pavement. They put up the torch and took Atahualpa from the pyre. Valverde poured water on his head and spoke words in the tongue of his god. Then they sat him upon a stool, bound him to another stake, set the loop of cord around his neck, slid the rod through the cord, and turned it. His women knelt at his side and wept. Valverde spoke more words. Atahualpa felt the cord, woven by the hands of some faithful *puric* of Cajamarca, tighten. The cord was well made. It cut his access to the night air; Atahualpa's lungs fought, he felt his body spasm, and then the plaza became cloudy and he heard the voice of the moon.

12 January 2011: Israel Lamont was holding big-time when a Krel monitor zipped over the alley. A minute later one of the aliens lurched around the corner and approached him. Lamont was ready.

"I need to achieve an altered state of consciousness," the alien said. It wore a red suit, a lightning bolt on its chest.

"I'm your man," Lamont said. "You just try this. Best stuff

on the street." He held the vial out in the palm of his hand. "Go ahead, try it." The Krel took it.

"How much?"

"One million."

The Krel gave him a couple hundred thousand. "Down payment," it said. "How does one administer this?"

"What, you don't know? I thought you guys were hip."

"I have been working hard, and am unacquainted."

This was ripe. "You burn it," Lamont said.

The Krel started toward the trash-barrel fire. Before he could empty the vial into it, Lamont stopped him. "Wait up, homes! You use a pipe. Here, I'll show you."

Lamont pulled a pipe from his pocket, torched up, and inhaled. The Krel watched him. Brown eyes like a dog's. Goofy honkie face. The rush took him, and Lamont saw in the alien's face a peculiar need. The thing was hungry. Desperate.

"I may try?" The alien reached out. Its hand trembled.

Lamont handed over the pipe. Clumsily, the creature shook a block of crack into the bowl. Its beaklike upper lip, however, prevented it from getting its mouth tight against the stem. It fumbled with the pipe, from somewhere producing a book of matches. "Shit, I'll light it," Lamont said.

The Krel waited while Lamont held his Bic over the bowl. Nothing happened. "Inhale, man."

The creature inhaled. The blue flame played over the crack; smoke boiled through the bowl. The creature drew in steadily for what seemed to be minutes. Serious capacity. The crack burned totally through. Finally the Krel exhaled.

It looked at Lamont. Its eyes were bright.

"Good shit?" Lamont said.

"A remarkable stimulant effect."

"Right." Lamont looked over his shoulder toward the alley's entrance. It was getting dark. Yet he hesitated to ask for the rest of the money.

"Will you talk with me?" the Krel asked, swaying slightly.

Surprised, Lamont said, "Okay. Come with me."

Lamont led the Krel back to a deserted store that abutted the alley. They went inside and sat down on some crates against the wall.

"Something I been wondering about you," Lamont said. "You guys are coming to own the world. You fly across the planets, Mars and that shit. What you want with crack?"

"We seek to broaden our minds."

Lamont snorted. "Right. You might as well hit yourself in the head with a hammer."

"We seek escape," the alien said.

"I don't buy that, neither. What you got to escape from?"

The Krel looked at him. "Nothing."

They smoked another pipe. The Krel leaned back against the wall, arms at its sides like a limp doll. It started a queer coughing sound, chest spasming. Lamont thought it was choking and tried to slap it on the back. "Don't do that," it said. "I'm laughing."

"Laughing? What's so funny?"

"I lied to Colonel Zipp," it said. "We want cocaine for kicks."

Lamont relaxed a little. "I hear you now."

"We do everything for kicks."

"Makes for hard living."

"Better than maintaining consciousness continuously without interruption."

"You said it."

"Human beings cannot stand too much reality," the Krel said. "We don't blame you. Human beings! Disgust, horror, shame. Nothing personal."

"No problem."

"Nonbeing penetrates that in which there is no space."

"Uh-huh."

The alien laughed again. "I lied to Sepulveda, too. Our time machines take people to the past they believe in. There is no other past. You can't change it."

"Who the fuck's Sepulveda?"

"Let's do some more," it said.

They smoked one more. "Good shit," it said. "Just what I wanted."

The Krel slid off the crate. Its head lolled. "Here is the rest of your payment," it whispered, and died.

Lamont's heart raced. He looked at the Krel's hand, lying open on the floor. In it was a full-sized ear of corn, fashioned of gold, with tassels of finely spun silver wire.

Today: It's not just physical laws that science-fiction readers want to escape. Just as commonly, they want to escape human nature. In pursuit of this, SF offers comforting alternatives to the real world. For instance, if you start reading an SF story about some abused wimp, you can be pretty sure that by chapter two he's going to discover he has secret powers unavailable to those tormenting him, and by the end of the book, he's going to save the universe. SF is full of this sort of thing, from the power fantasy of the alienated child to the alternate history where Hitler is strangled in his cradle and the Library of Alexandria is saved from the torch.

Science fiction may in this way be considered as much an evasion of reality as any mind-distorting drug. I know that sounds a little harsh, but think about it. An alkaloid like cocaine or morphine invades the central nervous system. It reduces pain, produces euphoria, enhances our perceptions. Under its influence we imagine we have supernormal abilities. Limits dissolve. Soon, hardly aware of what's happened to us, we're addicted.

Science fiction has many of the same qualities. The typical reader comes to SF at a time of suffering. He seizes on it as a way to deal with his pain. It's bigger than his life. It's astounding. Amazing. Fantastic. Some grow out of it; many don't. Anyone who's been around SF for a while can cite examples of longtime readers as hooked and deluded as crack addicts.

Like any drug addict, the SF reader finds desperate justifications for his habit. SF teaches him science. SF helps him avoid "future shock." SF changes the world for the better. Right. So does cocaine.

Having been an SF user myself, however, I have to say that, living in a world of cruelty, immersed in a culture that grinds people into fish meal like some brutal machine, with histories of destruction stretching behind us back to the Pleistocene, I find it hard to sneer at the desire to escape. Even if escape is delusion.

18 October 1527: Timu drove the foot plow into the ground, leaned back to break the crust, drew out the pointed pole, and backed up a step to let his wife, Collyur, turn the earth with her hoe. To his left was his brother, Okya; and to his right, his cousin, Tupa; before them, their wives planting the seed. Most of the *purics* of Cajamarca were there, strung out in a line across the terrace, the men wielding the foot plows, and the women or children carrying the sacks of seed potatoes.

As he looked up past Collyur's shoulders to the edge of the terrace, he saw a strange man approach from the post road. The man stumbled into the next terrace up from them, climbed down steps to their level. He was plainly excited.

Collyur was waiting for Timu to break the next row; she looked up at him questioningly.

"Who is that?" Timu said, pointing past her at the man.

She stood up straight and looked over her shoulder. The other men had noticed, too, and stopped their work.

"A *chasqui* come from the next town," said Okya.

"A *chasqui* would go to the *curaca*," said Tupa.

"He's not dressed like a *chasqui*," Timu said.

The man came up to them. Instead of a cape, loincloth, and flowing *onka,* the man wore uncouth clothing: cylinders of fabric that bound his legs tightly, a white short-sleeved shirt that bore on its front the face of a man, and flexible white sandals that covered all his foot to the ankle. He shivered in the spring cold.

He was extraordinarily tall. His face, paler than a normal man's, was long, his nose too straight, mouth too small, and lips too thin. Upon his face he wore a device of gold wire that, hooking over his ears, held disks of crystal before his eyes. The man's hands were large, his limbs long and spiderlike. He moved suddenly, awkwardly.

Gasping for air, the stranger spoke rapidly the most abominable Quechua Timu had ever heard.

"Slow down," Timu said. "I don't understand."

"What year is this?" the man asked.

"What do you mean?"

"I mean, what is the year?"

"It is the thirty-fourth year of the reign of the Sapa Inca Huayna Capac."

The man spoke some foreign word. "Goddamn," he said in a language foreign to Timu, but which you or I would recognize as English. "I made it."

Timu went to the *curaca*, and the *curaca* told Timu to take the stranger in. The stranger told them that his name was "Chuan." But Timu's three-year-old daughter, Curi, reacting to the man's sudden gestures, unearthly thinness, and piping speech, laughed and called him "the Bird." So he was ever after to be known in that town.

There he lived a long and happy life, earned trust and respect, and brought great good fortune. He repaid them well for their kindness, alerting the people of Tahuantinsuyu to the coming of the invaders. When the first Spaniards landed on their shores a few years later, they were slaughtered to the last man, and everyone lived happily ever after.

READING LESSON

The Inca Atahualpa asked the scribe
To write "God" on his thumbnail, black on pink,
Showed it to his captors one by one,
And had them read. Each spoke the word aloud,
Pronouncing it, each of them, alike.
It gave the Sapa Inca great delight,
For in Peru (called Tahuantinsuyu
Before the Fall) no one wrote.

And then he tried Pizarro, who stood mute:
Born a bastard, boyhood tending swine,
For thirty years he'd torn through the New World,
Serving men who thought they could claim oceans,
Seeking the birthright that he'd never found.
He'd not had time to waste attending school.
No more than Atahualpa could he read
But he knew the meaning of a room filled with gold.

Illiteracy got Atahualpa in this fix
When he threw down Father Valverde's Bible because
He could make nothing of it. "He's no more able
To know the word of Christ than any dog!"
The priest told Pizarro. "Attack and I'll absolve you!"
Magic words. "Santiago!" the soldiers cried
And set to slaughter. Later Valverde devoted
Hours to the conversion of the kidnapped Inca

With no success. After the ransom was paid
They garroted the Inca in the square of Cajamarca
Where nine months before they'd engendered a new age
By murdering six thousand unarmed men
Whose blood still stained the stones. Now came the birth.
They christened Atahualpa "John" in honor of the Baptist
And then they slipped the cord around his neck
And twisted it until he couldn't breathe.

Did he understand then the power of the written word
To justify man's ways to God, to make
A hell of heaven, give appetite a sanction?
Well that's all over now, and life goes on.
We keep the room where gold was piled high.
It's empty now. "Santiago" means "Saint James save us."
The peasants grow coca to earn their bread.
Pizarro never learned to read or write.

THE LECTURER

had, of course, heard about the Lecturer before I accepted the position at the university. Stories of him had reached the West Coast, but his was not the kind of notoriety that makes any deep impression. The university, though large and reasonably well-known, was not first-rate, and the Lecturer's existence was less remarked upon than the record of the school's football team. None of this mattered to me. I could scarcely care less about unique features of the campus; all I knew was that no one had worked harder than I had to earn a degree, and no one deserved a tenure-track position more. When I received the job offer I felt a triumph that did not lessen my bitterness. When I told my friends, they did not talk about the Lecturer, but about how severe the winters in the Northeast were.

The move exhausted both of us; Jane and I worked very hard trying to make something of the small house we were able to rent on an assistant professor's salary. Money was tight for some time, and Jane was unable to find work. Yet it seemed we were quite happy at first. We spent our evenings reading or listening to music, we took turns cooking, we took walks on the Saturdays of that Indian summer through the wooded lanes outside the town. When the possibility of a job at the university gallery fell through, Jane concentrated on her painting, ran off some flyers, and started teaching a class in oils out of our home.

Each morning I would rise early and walk up to the campus, which was only five blocks from our house. The department was located in a building on the far side of the quadrangle, and so I would have to walk past the Lecturer where he stood on the truncated Greek pillar at the top of the slope in front of the library. The first few times I strolled by self-consciously, trying to act as if I were accustomed to him; I kept my eyes on the buildings ahead and gripped the handle of my briefcase tighter. I did not hear what he was saying. A few days later I was comfortable enough with the new surroundings to stop for some minutes and listen. It was soon after classes had started and the campus bustled with students: a few sprawled on the grass of the quadrangle, and a nervous freshman here and there had also stopped to listen. Other students threw their Frisbees past him.

"The first notable feature of contemporary architecture is its concern with a greater and more profound reality than that encompassed by the psyche of one individual," he was saying. "The proper focus of architecture, the modernist tells us, is on the space outside the individual and the clash of impersonal forces within that outer space. There is no place in architecture for the kind of philosophy that sees reality as determined by individual perception."

He looked exactly like a stocky middle-aged man. His legs were short and strong, and he had the neck of a pit bulldog. He was not going to fat. His complexion was florid, his hair bright red, thinning on top, and a bushy mustache dominated his face. I was later told that during the sixties he had worn his hair long with a red bandanna tied around his head, and I came across an old yearbook photograph of him, taken in the 1890s, that showed him with full beard, neatly trimmed, and flowing academic robes. My first September at the university he wore a wool suit despite the high heat of the waning summer, and he was to wear that same suit through the year, adding a scarf and heavy overcoat as winter approached.

He spoke vigorously. Gestures of his right arm would punctuate his rhetoric; spreading his fingers, he would slice home a point with a sweep of his extended hand. His voice was strong, if rather high-pitched. His tone was dogmatic. There could be no doubt, it told us, that the things he said were the absolute truth.

Architecture is not one of my interests, and I soon moved on to my office. I had had to listen to too much of such academic sausage-grinding in my graduate career. Now that I had moved on, I worked hard at teaching, rewriting my dissertation for publication and being agreeable to all factions in my new department. Yet he bothered me, perhaps especially because he seemed to bother no one else; I could not keep myself from occasionally thinking about the man on the pedestal. The responses of my colleagues to my questions were not illuminating. Once at lunch I managed to turn the conversation around to the Lecturer.

"Why do they keep him around?" I asked.

"Nobody's keeping him," said Duthie, whose specialty was the Restoration. "He's free to do whatever he likes. You might as well ask why they keep the weather."

Judy Boisner, who wore bright scarves and a grin, said, "It's a tradition. Like the exam policy and the Chancellor's Oak."

I nodded at both of them. I was not skeptical.

"Nobody knows," old Dr. White said, not lifting his eyes from his corned beef on rye. "I wondered once. I was convinced there was a good reason. It doesn't matter."

"I see," I said.

Killworthy, sitting next to me, said nothing. Later, as we walked back to our offices, shoulders hunched and hands holding lapels closed against a cold breeze, he told me the real reason was political.

"The Lecturer has nothing to do with the university." His voice was bright with eagerness to initiate me. "It's all a matter of creating the proper impression on those whose decisions can really make a difference to the people who want to continue in positions of comfortable security—and influence—in this cir-

cus. Ask yourself: who stands to gain the most from such a creature as the Lecturer?"

I opened the door for him, and we shook ourselves in the
warmth of the hallway. We retreated to our separate offices. I had
no idea what Killworthy was talking about. I doubted that he did
himself.

Our small house smelled of the oils with which Jane and her
few students cluttered the spare bedroom. The artistic crowd—
or more accurately, the crowd of artistic dilettantes—Jane was
keeping company with did not appeal to me. I began to spend
more time on campus reading, grading papers, sitting in my office staring out the window at the treetops, gazing absently down
at the footpaths crisscrossing the quad.

In November I assigned the students in my composition class
a paper on the Lecturer. A five-hundred-word description. Many
of the male students wrote papers that began like this:

> Throughout history there has been many types of institu-
> tions of higher learning from the Middle Ages until now.
> Many of these presented the university professor as the
> originator of information it was useful for the students to
> have. Here at State is the home of the famous Lecturer
> that is reknown not only for his superior brain and his in-
> tellectual lectures, but also the ability of anyone that
> touches his shoe before a date to have sexual "relations"
> that very night.

Few of the women mentioned shoes or sex. During confer-
ences that week I made some inquiries and discovered that "rubbing the Lecturer" for luck was authentic campus folklore. For
sure, Chuck Bennetti, a freshman, told me.

The unspoken truth was that the Lecturer was uncon-
scionably boring, and the students realized it, and the only notice
they took of him—such as that surrounding the sex-charm stories—was the result of their boredom. Before homecoming, students from arch-rival Syracuse would paint the Lecturer orange,
but it aroused little indignation on campus and it did not slow

him down. His methods for dealing with hecklers were anti-quated.

"According to Faraday's Law, the line integral of the electric field around a closed path is equal to the time rate of change of the flux of the magnetic field calculated over the open surface bounded by the path of integration . . ."

"Shut up, shut up! I don't want to hear it!" a young man walking across the quad would shout, while his companions burst into laughter.

The Lecturer would ignore him. "If the surface of integration is fixed in space . . ."

"You mean lost in space, airhead!" one of the others would shout.

The Lecturer then might actually look at them, and smile. Not a smile of superior knowledge, or tolerance, or contempt. Not a smile older than the university, than any university. "No applause," he might say then. "Just throw money."

"I'm in pain," the first student would say. "I'm laughing so hard, Grandpa."

"So stop laughing and listen, Bub. You might learn some-thing. If the surface of integration is . . ."

"SHUT UP!"

He would stop. "Student here wants to speak. What do you want to tell us, student?"

"Screw you."

"That's all?"

"Screw you! Asshole! Screw you!"

"Thanks very much," the Lecturer would say. "If the surface of integration is fixed . . ."

I saw one such encounter late in the semester, a day when I was preoccupied with late papers and my first committee as-signment. It made me unaccountably melancholy. On impulse I walked up to his pedestal.

It was around six, dark already. The campus was virtually empty of students, and the regular staff had all gone home. No one paid any attention after the hecklers moved away. The Lec-turer glanced down at me without pausing in his delineation of the ideals of Jeffersonian democracy. I reached out and touched his left shoe. The leather was dull from generations of furtive contacts; I wondered that it had not been worn away entirely. Perhaps these were not the same shoes that he had worn fifty years before. But to begin to consider the source of his clothing was to open the first Chinese box in an infinite series of boxes, with little assurance of an answer in the opening and less that one would ever be able to stop.

I had a slight smudge of dirt on my fingertips. Nothing more. Feeling foolish, I returned to my office and a stack of ungraded papers.

The first flakes of the winter storm that had been predicted for that evening—the first of the season—had begun falling outside my window when a knock caused me to look up from the paper on which I was working. Stacey Branham, a student in my Postwar American Fiction class, stood uncertainly in the doorway.

It was quite late for an office visit. "Yes, Stacey," I said. "What's up?"

She shifted from foot to foot. "Can I talk to you about my term paper?"

"Sure."

She came in, closing the door behind her. I put the papers aside. She sat on the edge of the chair beside my desk and told me she was having trouble coming up with things to say. I had never noticed this problem as she dealt deftly with the boys who talked to her before and after class: she was a tall, slender blonde with intelligent gray eyes. I had more than once watched her cross her legs in the first row of seats in the Walton Annex. Lecture Hall B.

It soon became clear that she had not come to talk about her term paper, and that she had not happened by in the early evening, when the humanities building was deserted, by accident. She put her purse on the floor beside her, drew her chair closer, and as she leaned forward to ask an earnest question about Flannery O'Connor, rested her finely manicured hand on my leg.

"Stacey," I said. "You're not really interested in Flannery O'Connor, are you?"

"Yes, I am. 'Everything That Rises Must Converge' is my favorite story."

"Well." I was very nervous. "It's a masterpiece of irony."

"That's what I'm having trouble with." She smiled; I drew a deep breath. She smelled of Chanel.

I wheeled my chair back suddenly. "Why don't you come back, then . . . when you've worked out your ideas more completely."

She looked puzzled, a little frightened. "I didn't mean to—"

"No problem. I'll see you in class Friday, right?"

She took her purse and left, drawing her wool coat tighter around her hips as she swirled out the door.

I sat there for some time, closed my eyes, breathed slowly. My mind was without thought. I looked down at my hands resting on the desk; they shook ever so slightly, and I realized that I was terrified. There was a smudge of dirt on the first two fingers of my right hand.

By the time I left the building, a couple of inches of snow had accumulated. Instead of crossing the quad I went down the access road behind the building so that I could avoid him. It was one of those crisp, cold nights on which sound carries for great distances. I could faintly hear his voice despite the still-falling snow. My vision seemed exceptionally clear: I could see every swirling flake in the pools of light beneath the streetlights. I felt my warm breath on my face, the moisture freezing in my mustache; I saw the condensation in the air. My footsteps made no sound on the sidewalk.

Jane had already eaten, and I could hear her in the studio with one of her students, Marsha, when I reached home. I didn't go up to say hello; instead I fixed my own supper from the lukewarm Stroganoff on the stove and the day-old salad in the refrigerator. I watched part of one of the Shakespeare plays—*A Midsummer Night's Dream*—on PBS and went to bed before it was over. Marsha hadn't left yet. I got into bed and turned off the light, but could not get to sleep. Papers remained to be graded,

Stacey Branham remained to be faced, the man remained speaking on the quadrangle as snow caught and melted in his hair. I could hear the low voices of Jane and Marsha but could not make out more than a few words of Jane's instructions on how to use the palette knife.

I got up and washed the dirt from my fingers.

When Jane came to bed I was still not asleep. The clock radio read 12:17.

"I'm sorry I woke you," she said quietly.

"That's okay. It's late."

"Marsha stayed to talk and have some wine."

I turned from her, adjusted my arm beneath my pillow. After a moment I felt her touch my back.

"What's the matter?" she asked.

"Nothing," I answered quickly, then said, more slowly, "I don't know."

"You want me to stop this class?"

I still did not turn to her. "No. It's important that you teach."

She moved close, slipped her arm under mine and held me. We lay silent for a while. Her breath was warm against my back. She moved her leg over my hip; I rolled onto my back and she slid on top of me.

We made love with an intensity we hadn't had in a very long time. Jane wanted, needed me: the shock of that burned each moment into my senses. I realized that I needed her as much, if not more, and wondered that we had been living together for the last three months—and before that, back in California—so unaware of each other that we might only have been sharing an office. These truths came to me without thought, showed themselves in a carnality that was frightening in directness and austerity. Jane rocked over me with her eyes closed, the lines at their corners drawn so tight she looked to be in pain. I ran my hands over her hips and waist; her skin was feverish. The muscles of my belly were tight, my back arched. I cried and held Jane to me as if to make up for years of indifference in those few moments, as if we were doing penance for a multitude of casual sins, as if I might never have her again. She touched my face.

Jane fell asleep as if she had been poisoned. I lay awake while my sweat slowly dried; I shivered in the cold bedroom, wondering what had happened. Where were we? How had we gotten there?

The Lecturer. Like the body of a drowned man surfacing in a lake days after the storm that drew him under, he rose to trouble my circling thoughts. He came to the center, and he did not go away.

He did not go away. I tried to concentrate on the sound of Jane's slow breathing, the ticking of the furnace, the soft flip as the clock counted out each minute, the wind outside. I could not keep him out. I slipped quietly out of bed, pulled on clothes, and left Jane asleep. Unable to find my gloves, I threw on my coat and headed up to the campus, hands jammed into my pockets. It was bitterly cold. I walked briskly, but my feet were soon freezing.

I could hear his voice before I could see him. He was speaking as strongly, gesturing as fervently, as he did when there were people up and around to hear him. Instead he faced an unbroken sweep of snow that ran two hundred yards, from the library, over footpaths, beneath lampposts and trees, to the administration building at the other end of the quadrangle. As I approached, he turned to me and I could make out what he was saying.

"Descartes's second objection to placing faith in the reality of sensory experience amounts to this: however good our empirical evidence may be for the proposition that, for instance, we see a man, another feeling being, in front of us, such evidence is never good enough that reason is forced to accept it. The creature we see might be a diabolically ingenious conjuring trick by the malignant demon. And this possibility of error will apply to any empirical proposition; to be true it must be certified in a way stronger than any amount of empirical evidence could ever provide."

I stopped directly in front of him, in a snowdrift halfway to my knees. I looked up at him; he looked down at me. He kept talking.

"I want to speak to you," I said.

"Descartes found his solution in mathematics—"

"Please listen to me," I said.

"I'm doing the talking; you listen. You might learn something. In mathematics, some propositions we know to be intuitively true—"

"What are you doing? How did you come to be here?"

He then smiled that vacant smile. He sighed, and his breath fogged the air. "Student here has something to say. Speak up, student."

"That legend about you. Does what happened to me mean that it's true?"

"Accept as true only what can clearly and distinctly be perceived as being so."

My face burned. "What's that supposed to mean?" I said angrily. "The words you say don't mean anything. Things happen anyway."

"Analyze any problem into its simplest possible elements." The snow had gathered so thickly on his head that the strong light from the lamps behind him gave him a glittering halo. He ought to have caught pneumonia.

"Damn you! Give me a straight answer!"

"I don't give answers. I give lectures."

He towered over me, so obtuse he might have been made of stone. Suddenly I could not stand it. I leapt forward and grabbed his leg with both of my hands. He was taken by surprise, I think; this had to have happened to him before, but perhaps he did not expect violence from someone asking the bitter questions that only a man who didn't have any answers—a faculty member— would ask. I tugged furiously; I screamed at him, not knowing what or why I screamed. He slipped momentarily, regained his balance and beat me on the head and shoulders with his fists. My rage grew and gave me a blind strength. I braced my leg against the pedestal and jerked harder, and this time when he lost his footing he came tumbling down on top of me. We sprawled in the snow. Once I had him off I lost my purpose. He struggled out of my grasp and got to his feet. He was breathing hard. He was just another man, like me; he might have been Duthie, he might have been Killworthy.

"Excuse me," he said, and climbed back onto the pedestal.

That was fifteen years ago. He's still out there. He's still talking.

THE EINSTEIN EXPRESS

Whatever you do, don't offend Mr. Solomon," Monica said, pushing David up the stairs to the commuter platform. She tugged his five-inch-wide Windsor-knotted tie straight. Monica always took such a motherly interest in his appearance. She would never, she told him, let him embarrass either of them.

"I'm not a child, Monica."

"You need this job, David. It's 1941. I can't marry a man who fritters away his time on butterflies."

"I know, Monica." David was impressed by the authority of her eyebrows. Monica had the eyebrows of a five-star general. "But you're going to hate waiting for me while I make this long commute."

She pinched his cheek. "I have ways to keep myself occupied. See you tonight." As she turned to go David tried to kiss her, but she danced away. "David! Don't be an animal!" She got into Lance's Buick and drove off.

David stood amid the other commuters waiting for the train at the New Zion station. He really wanted to be a lepidopterist, not an accountant, but nobody needed butterfly collectors. From his pocket he pulled the folder containing the specimin *Yabadaba flooglus* he'd received in the mail the day before and examined it, dreaming of Amazonian jungles and the thrill of the hunt. The *flooglus* was very rare; he had spent fifteen dollars on it.

At the other end of the platform a young woman in an overcoat and sneakers was prowling around muttering to herself. She peered toward David, shielding her eyes with her hand, and stalked over to him. "Have you seen Mr. Smith?"

"Mr. Smith?"

"He should be here somewhere."

"What does he look like?"

"Well actually, you can't tell. He's in a box." She looked directly into his eyes. She had a pale oval face and straight dark hair. Her coat was four sizes too large. "You have him, don't you. What did you do with him?"

"What?"

"Did you open the box? Has there been a spontaneous decay? Did the bottle break?"

"My good young woman—"

"I'm not a woman, I'm a physicist. You look like you could be a scientist—or an accountant."

"I *am* an accountant—"

"I'm sorry to hear that."

"—and I have no idea what I'd want with Mr. Smith *or* his box—"

"*My* box."

The other people on the platform were staring at them. He supposed he had to humor this madwoman just so she'd shut up. And if somebody was trapped in a box he really ought to help. "Maybe it's in the baggage room."

They searched through the station's baggage room. Ten minutes later she had him trapped behind a steamer trunk while the local for New York arrived, and left. "I've missed my train!" David shouted.

"So what? I've missed my dog."

"Your dog! You kept me here looking for your *dog?* I have a meeting with one of the most important executives in Manhattan today!"

"Well, you're not likely to run into him here."

David considered strangling her. "What time does the next train leave? I have to get there fast."

"We'll take the express. It should be arriving any time now."

Sure enough, as soon as she spoke a streamlined train pulled into the station. The engine was sleek as a bullet, the cars burnished silver. David found a seat in a coach that hummed as if it were full of energy. The train pulled out, accelerating smoothly. David was pinned in his seat. Through the window the scenery began to blur.

"You know," the crazy woman said, "the baggage handlers may have already loaded the experiment on board." She turned to him. "My name is Susan. What's yours?"

Back in New Zion a year passed, and still Monica had heard nothing from David. He was as gone as Judge Crater.

"How could this happen to me?" Monica asked Lance. "Jilted by a man who doesn't know how to tie his own necktie!"

Lance smoothed his mustache. "He's probably just dodging the draft."

Monica brushed away a tear. "The swine! Thank God you're Four-F."

"Yes, thank God—for your sake." He touched her cheek. "But *tempus fugit,* darling. You need to move on."

"Don't even think it, Lance—no amount of time will heal this wound!"

"Doesn't this train seem to be moving a little fast?" David asked.

"You wanted the express, didn't you? This is the Einstein Express."

"Yes, but how fast does it go?"

"Somewhere near the speed of light. Now let's find Mr. Smith."

"The speed of light! I guess I'll be home early after all."

Susan looked a little uncomfortable. "Actually, we may be a little late."

David got out of his seat. "In that case I'd better telegram Monica."

"Monica? She probably forgot all about you a long time ago."

David thought this woman really was the most abrupt person he'd ever met. "Monica wouldn't do that. We're to be married."

"A girl can't wait forever. She has to seize the day."

David blushed. "I'm not the sort of fellow who seizes things."

"I can see that."

He found the conductor, with Susan tagging along like a faithful terrier. "My good man, I need to send a telegram to Miss Monica Finch, 223 Swallow Lane, New Zion."

"New Zion! We left there ages ago, pal. She's not going to want to hear from you."

"Let me be the judge of that."

The man handed David a yellow telegraph form. Susan shoved a pencil into his hand. "I'll dictate," she told him. "Take this down. Tell her—'Making very good time.' " She leaned over his shoulder. He felt her warm breath beside him. " 'Events developing more rapidly than expected.' "

"More rapidly—than expected," David repeated. His heart fluttered like a *Marinera spasticus*. He felt a wisp of Susan's hair on his cheek. She really was quite attractive, for a physicist wearing sneakers.

" 'Should be home for supper,' " she continued. "Sign it, 'Love, David'—no, make that, 'Devotedly, David.' No, better make that 'In haste, David.' "

She kissed his ear, took the form and handed it to the conductor. "Send that pronto, Jackson."

It was a lovely wedding. Monica looked simply radiant, and everyone was so happy that she had finally gotten over her abandonment by that woolly-brained butterfly nut who'd disappeared on the eve of their marriage.

The reception was an unqualified success. Champagne in barrels, the cake a feathery dream, with a swing band playing the latest Sinatra hits and everyone celebrating the end of wartime privation.

Late in the evening a disquieting telegram arrived. MAKING VERY GOOD TIME, it said. EVENTS DEVELOPING MORE RAPIDLY THAN EXPECTED. SHOULD BE HOME FOR SUPPER. IN HASTE, DAVID.

Monica stewed about the prank for months. She and Lance honeymooned in California and settled into Lance's big Georgian house. Still, the telegram gnawed at her. Finally, a year and a half after the nuptials, on the day she found she was going to have a baby, she shot off a reply care of the Hudson Valley Railroad. TO WHOM IT MAY CONCERN: DROP DEAD.

The instant the conductor got done sending the message, the ticker chattered out a reply. He tore off the tape. "It's for you," he said, handing it to David.

David read. TO WHOM IT MAY CONCERN: DROP DEAD.

"What's that supposed to mean? Send a return telegram."

"That'll be sixty-two dollars."

"Sixty-two dollars!"

"A hundred twenty-four, total, with the first telegram."

"That's outrageous!"

"This is the Einstein Express, buddy. We got overhead. How much diesel fuel you think it takes to get a train up to the speed of light?"

"That depends entirely on how many liters you burn per unit of acceleration," Susan said. "Now if—"

"Excuse us," said David, dragging her off by the elbow. They went to the club car, where David slumped glumly in a lounge seat. "Now what?"

Susan picked up a heavy bronze ashtray. "David, look! We can tie a note to this ashtray, then throw it off when we pass the next station!"

David wondered why, at that moment, he felt the urge to flee.

Lance and Monica had three children, two boys and a girl. Lance worked hard and got a job in the office of that rising young congressman, Dick Nixon. If things broke right in the '52 election, they would be sitting pretty.

David stuck his head out of the hatchway in the baggage car roof. He balanced unsteadily on three cages of chickens they'd stacked up so he could open the door. "I can't see anything! There's a green blur of scenery rushing past, but when I look ahead and behind it's all black."

"We're moving too fast. The light coming from the things in front of us is blueshifted out of visibility. In back of us it's red-shifted."

"So how will I know when we pass the station?"

Susan reached into the pocket of her big coat and handed up a flashlight. "A radio flashlight. Get up on the roof, and shine it forward toward the station. Look for the clock on the platform."

David climbed up, peered unsteadily ahead. He saw a lighted disk, the clock face, but he couldn't read it. "Something's wrong," he shouted down to her above the buffeting wind. "The hands are spinning around in a blur."

"It's Dopplered!" Susan yelled.

Dopplered shmopplered. The station was coming up fast. David gave Susan the flashlight, then tossed the ashtray off the train.

The ashtray, traveling at nearly the speed of light, exploded through the station like President Eisenhower through the front line. From the platform, Woodrow and Norval watched the express flash by. Two very thin people stood on top fumbling with a flashlight.

"Did you see that, Norval?"

"They's mighty skinny folks on that train. Service must be out in the club car."

"But they were going too fast. We've got to call the next station."

"Mighty skinny tie that fella's wearing, too."

"Get on the horn to Elkdale. Tell them we've got a runaway commuter train on our hands."

"A *short* runaway commuter train. Kinda squashed. Cars about three feet long."

Woodrow inspected the ashtray-shaped hole that ran through the exterior wall, the cigarette machine, the calendar photo of Marilyn Monroe, and the other wall. "Hope they notice the Parsimmony Tunnel up ahead," he muttered.

"I did it!" David shouted. But peering behind them in the gloom, he couldn't see where the message had landed. "Hand me the flashlight!"

"The what?"

"The *flash*light."

Susan stuck her head higher out of the baggage car roof. "Tunnel!"

"What?"

"Tunnel!" She pointed frantically behind him.

"Tunnel?" David turned around, shone the flashlight ahead and glimpsed a blue reflection of masonry.

After Nixon lost the election in 1960 Lance got a job in advertising. "See the USA in your Chevrolet"—that was one of his. Also, "You'll wonder where the yellow went, when you brush your teeth with Pepsodent."

Monica gained twenty pounds and took up bridge. Lance gained thirty and played golf. Their daughter Amelie flipped out over some hairy boys from England. Youth, her parents said, was wasted on the young.

They struggled to untangle themselves from the explosion of broken cages, luggage, and chickens. "That was terrific. Got any more bright ideas?"

"I *said* tunnel!"

David found his glasses underneath her, snapped in two. "Say, didn't that station look rather squashed to you? Like maybe it was only three feet from one end of the platform to the other? Windows like slits in a wall? Roof peaked like a knife-edge? Skinny station workers wearing skinny ties?"

"It's the Lorentz-Fitzgerald contraction."

"Is that an architectural trend?"

The chickens fluttered and squawked. Suddenly they heard a growl, and a white terrier launched itself out of one of the up-ended boxes. "Mr. Smith!" Susan exclaimed. The dog chased chickens in frantic circles around the car. David and Susan fell over suitcases and each other trying to grab him. Finally David, diving over a trunk like an Olympic swimmer, seized the barking dog.

He wrestled grimly with the wriggling terrier. "Well, we found him."

Susan looked into Mr. Smith's box. "Before the bottle of patchouli broke. What a disaster that would have been!"

On her twentieth birthday, Amelie received a message meant for her mother. Her parents were in Cancún on their second honeymoon. The telegram read: ARRIVED NYC. CAN'T WAIT TO SEE YOU. DAVID

After the Einstein Express pulled into Grand Central and David sent a telegram, they hurried along Forty-second Street to Third Avenue. David couldn't get over how busy the city seemed. The place was full of long, low cars with rocketlike fins on their tails. Hatless men with skinny ties jostled through the streets.

The interview with Solomon started poorly. He had no record of an appointment, gawked openly at their clothing, and seemed more interested in his approaching retirement than in accountants. On his walls hung display cases of butterflies. David, remembering, fumbled for the *flooglus* in his pocket. Miraculously, it was undamaged.

Solomon perked up. "Is that a *Yabadaba flooglus?*" David handed it over. "Why, I've been searching for this butterfly for twenty years. It's almost extinct! Where did you get it?"

"I've had it for some time."

"I can't tell you how grateful I am, my boy." He thrust a fistful of banknotes at David. "No, that's not enough. Here, let me write you a check. Would ten thousand be fair?"

"That would be generous."

"Better still, I'll invest it for you. Some U.S. Steel? General Motors?"

"I don't know much about those things."

"What are you interested in?"

"Well, I'm an accountant. I could use a new adding machine."

"Business machines! Perfect! We'll get you a few hundred shares of IBM."

The train ride back was uneventful. David sent Monica a series of telegrams. Susan played hide-the-stock-portfolio with Mr. Smith.

"Monica must be wondering what happened to me. We're hours late. What a fool I've been!"

"It's all my fault."

"That's easy for you to say. Everyone knows you're just crazy." He tried to figure out a way to repair the bridge of his glasses.

"You're really quite handsome, you know, without your glasses."

"Monica says I should wear them all the time."

"You must just love Monica."

"She has wonderful eyebrows."

"I'll bet she does. I bet strong men faint when they see her eyebrows."

David put the broken halves of his glasses back in his pocket. "At least Monica never got me up on top of a train about to enter a tunnel at nine-tenths the speed of light."

During the last five years, after forty years of silence, Monica had received a raft of messages from some trickster purporting to be David. INTERVIEW UNSUCCESSFUL. THINKING OF YOU. CAN'T WAIT. DO YOU LOVE ME? ARRIVING SOON NEW ZION. MEET ME AT STATION. Monica ignored them.

It happened that Thanksgiving season, however, that Monica and Lance decided to meet their grandson Derek and his family when they came for the holidays. Lance and Monica drove to the station in the Lincoln. They stood on the platform and remembered the fateful day when she had been saved from an inappropriate match by the disappearance of that fool David.

The train slowed. At last, squealing, it pulled into the station. David, Susan, and Mr. Smith got off. The sign below the eaves read NEW ZION, but the station was different. The outside was shabbier. The concession stand and restaurant were gone. Graffiti covered the walls: RELATIVITY IS SPECIAL.

On the platform loitered a boy and a girl. The boy wore fluorescent green sneakers as large as combat boots and an underwear shirt with writing on it: BO KNOWS HACKING. The girl's shirt read, JUST DO IT. The boy had four earrings in his left ear. The girl wore black tights and a stunningly short skirt. Her hair was orange.

"Check that suit! Seriously damaged!"

"It's not damaged," David said. "Just rumpled from the chickens."

"Rad!"

An old man and woman stepped forward. "Pardon me," the woman asked David, "is this the train from Hartford?"

"This is the Einstein Express." The woman looked vaguely familiar. Her eyebrows straggled out like the branches of a gnarled oak. For a moment David thought it might be Monica's grandmother. Then he felt a sinking feeling. "Monica?"

"I beg your pardon, young man. Do I know you?"

He looked at the old woman, the old man beside her. "No, I guess you don't."

The woman leaned forward and whispered, "You know, your tie is crooked."

He pulled it off and handed it to Lance. "Actually, you can have it."

David and Susan went into the station and had a cup of bad vending machine coffee, which cost a dollar. Susan bought a paper, which cost another. David stared disconsolately out the window at the sunny fall day. Mr. Smith watched the squirrels burying nuts. "Talk about a long commute!" David said. "Susan, what will we do?"

"How about lepidoptery?"

"But everything's changed!"

"That's not necessarily bad," she said, examining the stock prices.

"I suppose we've missed some interesting developments," David mused. Susan looked up, and he noticed for the first time what a lovely shade of brown her eyes were. "I don't want to miss any more."

The girl with the JUST DO IT! shirt walked by. "*Carpe diem,*" Susan said, and kissed him.

FAUSTFEATHERS:
A COMEDY

Cast of Characters

Doctor John Faustus, professor of theology, University of
    Wittenberg
Wagner, his apprentice and servant
Dicolini, a student at the university
Robin, another student
Frater Albergus, a spy for the Pope
Master Bateman, Albergus' henchman
Helen of Troy, a spirit
Mephistopheles, a demon from hell
Martin, a porter
The Clock
students, demons, a barmaid

The entire play takes place in Wittenberg, Germany, in late December 1539.

Act I

Scene 1: Faustus' apartment, evening
Scene 2: The tavern at the Boar's Bollocks Inn, the next morn-
    ing
Scene 3: Faustus' classroom, late morning

Act II

Scene 1: Faustus' apartment, afternoon
Scene 2: The tavern at the Boar's Bollocks Inn, late afternoon
Scene 3: Faustus' apartment, that evening
Scene 4: The tavern at the Boar's Bollocks Inn, after midnight

ACT ONE

Spotlight downstage center. Enter Mephistopheles.

Mephistopheles: Know, ladies and gentlemen, that I am Mephistopheles, chief among lieutenants to our great Master Lucifer. For twenty-four years now I have been bound by magical contract as servant to Doctor Faustus, who has bartered his soul for this privilege. But now the end draws nigh.

Like all demons, in compensation for our damnation I am given the power to be in every place, and the power to render myself invisible *(renders himself invisible by draping his head and shoulders with tinsel. Starts the next line speaking, then gradually begins to sing, catches himself)*. I see you when you're sleeping, I see you when you wake, I know if you've been bad or good, so . . .

Excuse me. It is Christmas of 1539. All of Europe lies in turmoil over the heresies of Martin Luther. The Pope and the Roman church attempt to keep repressed changes that cannot be repressed. To the west, a new world has been discovered. There is a rebirth of learning, a renewed quest for knowledge. It is an age of overreachers, where the certitudes of the Middle Ages have been challenged and in places, broken. New nations, new political movements, new commerce, new science, and old lusts. Vast opportunity for salesmen such as me.

Though you live some five centuries after the good doctor, you are bound as he by the selfsame laws of the universe. There, but for the grace of God . . .

As he speaks, Mephistopheles gestures upstage, and lights come up on a medieval apartment, divided into three rooms. To stage right is a bedroom, center stage is a common room/dining room, and stage left is a library/laboratory/study with shelves of books, a table with alchemical glassware, a cluttered desk, and a full-length mirror on the wall. This mirror is actually a door to a secret room where Faustus keeps his magic books.

Of the furnishings of these rooms, the most bizarre is a human **Clock** *that stands on a platform in the corner of the common room: a man in a modern business suit who calls out the hours aloud.*

Four men occupy the apartment. At the dining table, lingering over the remains of a dinner, are **Frater Albergus, Master Bateman,** *and* **Doctor Faustus.** *Albergus is an imposing man of middle years, wearing somewhat elaborate medieval garb. Bateman is Albergus' henchman, a lascivious little man who has seen too much conniving and is cynically accustomed to it all.* **Wagner** *is Faustus' student at the University of Wittenberg, and his servant, or "fag." He is waiting table at this dinner. Faustus looks exactly like Groucho Marx of the early Paramount Marx Brothers films. He wears gold wire-rimmed spectacles, a black academic gown over a loose white shirt, a sloppily tied black cravat, and tights.*

It is winter and a fire burns in the fireplace. At the rear of each room a latticed window looks out on the alley behind Faustus' apartment. At the beginning of the scene Wagner leaves the commons for the study and Albergus continues his conversation with Faustus.

Albergus: Of course the power that comes from the blood of unbaptized infants is only good during months without an "r" in them. My colleague Master Bateman, here, is an expert in such matters.

Bateman *(smiling):* I before e except after c.

Faustus: You know, to look at those teeth you'd swear they were real. *(pushing a sausage on a fork into Albergus' face)* Have some more knockwurst.

Wagner returns from the study.

Wagner: I cannot find them, Master.

Faustus: Of course you can't. Frater Albergus, meet my apprentice, Wagner. He may look like a medieval dope, but don't let the feckless demeanor fool you. He's really a Renaissance dope.

Faustus goes into study. He feels along the edge of the mirror, finds the catch, opens the mirror door and enters the secret back room.

Albergus: How long have you been Doctor Faustus' fag, my boy?
Wagner: Two years.
Albergus: Yet he treats you abominably. Why do you put up with it?
Wagner: I am a student of the magical arts. I seek knowledge.
Albergus: What sort of knowledge?
Wagner: The Meaning of Life.
Bateman: The Meaning of Life? That's easy—*coition, ergo sum.*
Albergus: He means magical knowledge. Am I right, son?
Wagner *(hesitates):* No. Learned sir, please keep my confidence. I have seen the most beautiful woman in these apartments. And yet she is *not* here, nor have I ever spied her entering or leaving. She must be hidden in some secret place. How I long to meet her! To have intercourse . . . that is, to *converse* with her.
Bateman: Have a friendly little chat. Discuss theology. Geometry. Anatomy.
Albergus: Was this woman Greek?
Wagner: How can one tell if a woman is Greek?
Bateman: There's a trick they do with—
Albergus: Enough, Bateman—

Faustus returns from the secret back room, closes the mirror door.

Faustus: Wagner! Get your sorry butt in here!

Wagner enters study. Faustus remonstrates with him.

Albergus: We proceed apace, Bateman! See the way Faustus accepted our introduction from Doctor Phutatorious at face value. Now I must draw him out. The Pope will not tolerate these magical tricks any longer. We must expose this Faustus as a dealer with the devil, find his contract, confiscate his magic book, and drag him before the Inquisition.

Clock: TEN O'CLOCK. THE TEMPERATURE IS TWELVE DEGREES. DO YOU KNOW WHERE YOUR CHILDREN ARE?

Bateman *(looking warily at Clock):* I don't know about you, but I'd rather not end up as a piece of furniture.

Albergus *(absorbed in his machinations):*   And now hear what this slack fool says. This woman he speaks of must be the rumored Helen! But we need proof more positive than this. You must hurry now and find us some students we can use as spies. Have them report to me at the inn directly tomorrow morning.

Bateman exits. Faustus and Wagner return from the study and Faustus sets down a box of cigars. Wagner sits on a stool in the corner. During the ensuing conversation he occasionally rises to refill their cups with wine.

Albergus: So tell me, learned Faustus, how you discovered the secret of this miraculous alembic.

Faustus: Never mind that, pick a card.

Faustus proffers a deck of tarot cards. When Albergus just stares he folds them away.

Faustus: All right, be that way. You probably don't have much of a future anyway.

He leans forward over his glass of wine, places one end of a cigar into his mouth, lights the other from the candle flame. He puffs a few times, then exhales a plume of smoke across the table at Albergus. He pushes the wooden box forward.

Faustus: Sorry your friend had to leave so soon. Have a cigar.

As Albergus reaches out to take one . . .

Faustus: Just one.
Albergus: To be sure.

Albergus examines the cigar; he has never seen anything like this before and is not ready to take any chances with a magician like Faustus.

Albergus: Ah—what is the nature of this—this "see-gar" you burn here, Faustus? Albertus Magnus speaks of securing rooms against evil spirits by burning certain herbs, but he advocates the use of a brazier. Does not this smoke taste noxious to the palate?
Faustus: I've had better smokes, but you won't be able to get them for a couple of hundred years. I just burn these ropes to drive the bugs away—although I notice *you're* still around.
Albergus *(sniffs):* There does not seem to be any hint of cinnabar. How did you come by these instruments?
Faustus: That's an interesting story. I was riding a double-decker down Broadway and when we took the corner to Forty-second Street on two wheels a young woman fell into my lap. Well, I always say he who laps last, laps best. I took her home and we became devoted friends. In the divorce settlement she got the Hemingway manuscripts, I got these stogies.

Wagner approaches to refill their cups.

Albergus: In Nuremberg it is rumored you have had much success in conjuring the shades of historical figures.
Faustus: Hysterical figures, more like. And I do mean figures. Remind me sometime to introduce you to Helen.

Wagner spills the wine.

Faustus: Try again, boy: cup *outside,* wine inside.
Albergus *(in his eagerness to catch Faustus he pushes Wagner away as he tries to mop up the wine):* Helen of Troy?

Faustus: Troy, Schenectady—one of those funny little foreign places.

Albergus: So you have indeed raised the dead?

Faustus: She only acts that way in the mornings. Lithium deficiency.

Wagner gets to his feet, resumes his stool.

Albergus: Have you heard the reports of the astounding incidents that took place recently in Rome? It is said that some sorcerer, invisible, plucked food and drink right out of the Pope's mouth. Then, to humiliate the papists further, this same necromancer stole the heretic Bruno away from the Inquisition and whisked him off to Austria. A most clever trick. I only wish I'd been able to manage it myself. The person responsible for bearding the Antichrist's tool in his own den must be the most powerful mage in all of Europe. Who do you suppose that might be?

Faustus: Are you going to smoke that cigar or eat it? Go ahead! You can pay me later.

Albergus: Pay you? Alas, Faustus, I have but little coin in pocket.

Clock: TEN FIFTEEN. MAYBE YOU SHOULD CHECK YOUR WALLET.

Faustus: Money, money, money! I'm sick to death of this talk of money! It's destroying our marriage! These cigars would cost a couple of guilders on the open market. Of course it's closed now, so you're left to your own devices. You did bring your devices, didn't you?

Albergus: What sort of—

Faustus: If not, you'll have to get your brothers to help you.

Albergus: I have no brothers.

Faustus: Your father must have been relieved.

Albergus: My dear Faustus, do not insult me. I may only be an itinerant scholar, but I've come all the way from Nuremberg to sit at your feet and learn.

Faustus: As long as you're down there, how about shining those shoes.

Albergus: You do not mean what you say.

Faustus: No, but I always say what I mean, Podner. Giddyap!

Albergus: I take your point, noble Faustus. My questions were entirely innocent.

Faustus: But late at night, lights turned low, when you're alone with your answers? That's a different story!

Albergus: My dear colleague! There's no need to treat me like a mountebank.

Faustus: Oh, so now it's high finance? Well, money means nothing here, friend. How much are you offering?

Albergus: Why must we speak of money?

Faustus: This is a public university. What else are we going to talk about? You'll learn soon enough that a little Latin goes a long way in this institution. There used to be a little Latin around here, but he went away. That's how I got this job. You look a little Latin yourself, and I wish you'd gone with him. You foreign scholars want to dance to the music without paying the piper. And what does it get you? Asparagus, or contract bridge. But a card like you could care less who maintains the bridge contract, as long as you can pass water under it. Speaking of contracts, what makes you think you're going to get your hands on mine?

Albergus: I'm sure I don't know what you're talking about.

Faustus: If you're so sure, why aren't you rich? You brute! No, don't try to apologize!

Albergus: I didn't come here to be insulted.

Faustus: This is a good place for it. Where do you usually go?

Albergus stands, throwing down his napkin.

Albergus: I *beg* your pardon—

Faustus: Don't grovel, I can't pardon you. You'll have to talk to the Pope. Too bad, I hear he's not much of an audience. Well, it's certainly been a pleasure talking to myself this evening. I must visit myself more often. As for you, sir, I want you to remember that scholarship is as scholarship does, and neither does my wife, if I had one, which I don't. Nor do my children, if I had any, who would be proud of me for saying so. Now get out!

Albergus leaves in a huff. Faustus goes to his side of the table, sits in his chair, takes a bite out of a chicken leg from Albergus' plate and sips his wine.

Clock: HALF PAST TEN. ALL IS WELL.

Faustus holds out his cup to Wagner.

Faustus: More wine, boy.

SCENE TWO

Scene opens in the tavern of The Boar's Bollock's Inn. Albergus is at a table composing a report for the Pope. Bateman ogles the barmaid.

Albergus: When will those students arrive?
Bateman: They should be here soon.
Albergus: They're completely reliable men?
Bateman: As a logician, you realize as well as I that such judgments are necessarily subjective.
Albergus: Never mind logic. Stick to the facts.
Bateman: They're men. I would say that's a completely reliable statement.

Albergus seals the letter, hands it to Bateman.

Albergus: Fair enough. Send this bull off to the Pope.

*Bateman leaves. Albergus steeples his fingers and ponders his nefarious plans. The door opens and two sloppy men come in. The darker of the two, **Dicolini**, wears a black hat that comes to a point that hints at the pointed skull beneath it. His coat is shabby and two sizes too small. He wears an expression of small-minded guile. His companion **Robin's** face is round and empty as the full moon. Robin's ragged clothes are even shabbier than Di-*

colini's, if that is possible. A mass of curly red hair explodes from beneath his floppy hat. They come forward in unison, hands extended. Albergus gets up from the table and approaches them, his own hand extended.

Albergus: Noble Robin and gentle Dicolini, welcome!

Dicolini shakes his hand, but Robin, seeing the barmaid, walks right past Albergus and after her, leering. She retreats in alarm, exiting; as Robin follows her Dicolini grabs Robin's arm and yanks him back.

Dicolini: Uh-uh, partner.

Albergus, hand still extended, insists that Robin acknowledge him. Robin shakes his hand. Albergus recoils, draws back and finds he is holding a dead fish. Robin contorts in silent laughter, slaps his knee. Albergus throws down the fish. Robin looks offended.

Dicolini: Atsa some joke, eh boss?
Albergus: Gentlemen, gentlemen. Let us speak of our business. I have called you here because you are scholars, acquainted with the university, and students of the renowned Doctor Faustus. I have also heard that you are available for delicate work and for a reasonable fee can keep your mouths shut. I trust I have not been misled?
Dicolini: I keepa my mouth shut for nothing. Robin, his mouth cost extra.

Robin opens his mouth and sticks out his tongue, from which a price tag dangles.

Albergus: What I want you to do is keep an eye on Doctor Faustus for me.
Dicolini: Atsa different story. Eyes cost more.
Albergus: No, no. "Keep an eye on him"—that's just an expression.
Dicolini: You want the whole expression, it cost you a pretty penny. We give you a pretty expression, though.

Robin puffs out his cheeks, purses his lips and crosses his eyes. Albergus controls himself, ignores him.

Albergus: I want you to find out how Faustus spends his evenings. Does he practice black magic? Is he in league with infernal forces? And I need physical proof, the sooner the better. It is rumored he has a secret room in his apartments, where he keeps numerous magical devices. I need access to that room. Should you do this for me, your investigation shall receive such thanks as fits a king's remembrance.
Dicolini: How much you gonna pay?
Albergus: I'll pay you ten silver pieces.
Dicolini: We a-no want no pieces. We want the whole thing.

Robin honks a horn and nods, surly.

Albergus: Another ten pieces then, if you provide me the information I need. That's all.
Dicolini: How do we know thatsa all?
Albergus: What?
Dicolini: Look, we shadow Faustus for you, how we gonna know when you give us ten pieces thatsa the whole thing?
Albergus: But I'm offering you twenty pieces for shadowing Faustus.
Dicolini: See what I mean? First you gotta ten pieces, now you gotta twenty pieces, but we no gotta the whole thing.
Albergus: You shadow Faustus for me, and then we'll talk about the whole thing.
Dicolini: You no understand. Suppose I drop a vase, itsa break. How many pieces I got? I don't know; I gotta count them. Now you give me ten pieces, you give me twenty pieces, I still don't have them all, maybe. I shatter vase, we shadow Faustus, itsa same thing: we no gonna do the job until we know we getta the whole thing.

As Albergus and Dicolini haggle, Robin creeps behind them. He draws another fish from the folds of his cloak and slips it onto Albergus's chair. Albergus, arguing with Dicolini, draws a kerchief from his sleeve, mops his brow, and sits down. A moment later he lets out a strangled cry and leaps from the chair, crack-ing his knee on the table. He picks up the fish and holds it out at arm's length.

Albergus: What's this?

Robin whips a sword out and lunges, impaling the fish and the sleeve of Albergus' doublet. Albergus steps back and slips on the first fish. His arms fly up, jerking Robin toward him. Dicolini catches Albergus under the armpits, and Robin sprawls on top of him.

Dicolini: You no fool me, boss. Atsa fish.

Albergus and Robin struggle to get up, but Robin's hand is caught in the sword guard. When they make it to their feet the pommel is wedged under the clasp that holds Albergus' cloak closed around his neck. The sword guard presses against his throat, and his arm stretches the length of the blade as if tied to a splint. Chin forced high into the air, Albergus whirls around like a manic signpost.

Dicolini: Don't worry, boss. We get you out.

Robin jumps on Albergus' back and shoves a hand down his col-lar. Dicolini pulls him over onto the table. He lies spread-eagled while Robin pulls the sword up through the collar, across his neck. Afraid they will cut his throat, he struggles, but Dicolini is sitting on his left arm.

Dicolini: Relax. We take care of everything.

Robin draws the sword completely out and the fish catches against Albergus' throat. Robin shakes hands with Dicolini. Al-bergus sits up, stands, tugs his clothes into order, trying to com-pose himself.

Albergus: Gentlemen, I trust we are in agreement now? You'll do this piece of work for me?
Dicolini: We do the whole thing.

Robin honks. Albergus steers them toward the door, his arms across their shoulders.

Albergus: Splendid. Remember now, should you meet me in public, I'm a stranger.
Dicolini: Astranger than who?
Albergus: Us. You and I—and your friend, of course. *Strangers.*
Dicolini: Hesa stranger than both of us put together.
Albergus: So I'm beginning to understand.
Dicolini: We gotta go now. We're gonna be late for the classes we wanna miss.
Albergus: My apologies for detaining you. Just make sure you get me something I can use against Faustus.

Robin pulls a red-hot poker out of his cloak. He grips the iron in both hands, waving it under Albergus's nose. Albergus falls back; Robin offers him the poker. Dicolini grabs Robin's arm and yanks him out of the room.

SCENE THREE

Lights come up on a classroom. At the front is a raised platform with a table, a lectern, and behind it a blackboard. A window to the streets of Wittenberg at the left, a doorway at right. Students gathering before class. Among them are Albergus, sitting in the front row, and Wagner, Faustus's fag, likewise in front.

Albergus: You seem melancholy today, young student. Did your master take last night's misunderstanding amiss?
Wagner: I don't think he misunderstood anything. He did make me pick a card. Something he calls three-card monte.
Albergus: He predicted your future?
Wagner: Sort of. He won my salary for the next six months. But it doesn't matter as long as it keeps me close to her.
Albergus: I see you are reading divine Homer. Practicing your Greek?

Wagner *(dreamily)*: Only dreaming of Helen, fairer than the evening air, clad in beauty of a thousand stars. Her lips suck forth my soul; see where it flies! Here will I dwell, for heaven be in these hips.

Faustus enters, in Groucho lope, wearing long black academic robe, carrying his impressive Magic Book under his arm (on cover: "SPELLS" in big letters), puffing a cigar. Puts the book on the lectern, strides back and forth in front of the class, takes up a pointer, raps the lectern, turns and pulls down a chart of a human head with areas mapped out on it like a steer apportioned for slaughter. Except these parts are labeled "Imagination," "Love," "Sex," "Politics," "Sports," "Clothes," "Gambling," "Religion," "Money."

Faustus: Here we have a diagram of the astral mind in the fourth quarter of the phrenological year. You'll note the eruptions at the zenith. A pox on such eruptions!

A student sneezes.

Faustus *(does sign of cross over the student)*: Pox vobiscum. *(back to the chart)*. These eruptions can be cleared up with fulminate of mercury, but the woman only comes on Tuesday afternoons. The rest of the week you have to take care of yourself, if you know what's good for you. Wagner, tell us what's good for you.

Wagner, startled, stumbles to his feet.

Wagner: Chastity, Doctor Faustus.
Faustus: Chastity, is it? What about obedience?
Wagner: Obedience. Of course.
Faustus: Poverty?
Wagner: That, too.
Faustus: Quit monking around, boy! Who do you think you're kidding? You'd better sit down and hibernate until that bonus in your codpiece goes away. Or is that a cod in your bonuspiece?

With a crash, the door of the room slams open and in dash Robin and Dicolini. They trip over each other, get up, scramble into two seats in the front row next to Albergus. Robin notices Albergus, whistles twice, grabs Dicolini's sleeve and directs his attention to Albergus. Dicolini gives a double take.

Dicolini: Who'sa this guy? Hesa strange.

He winks theatrically at Albergus. Faustus turns his ire on Dicolini.

Faustus: Late for class again, eh?

Dicolini: We a-no late.

Faustus: Why, the town clock struck not five minutes ago. It's half past ten!

Dicolini: No it's not.

Robin pulls an hourglass from out of his bottomless cloak. All the sand is in the bottom. He waves it at Faustus.

Dicolini: See, we're right on time.

Faustus: Not according to that.

Dicolini: Atsa run a little fast. Shesa use quicksand.

Faustus: Oh no. You can't fool me that easily. By that hourglass, it must be eleven o'clock.

Dicolini: Then class is over. Let's go, Robbie.

Faustus: Hold on, Macduff. I'm not done lecturing.

Dicolini: Too bad. We're done listening.

Faustus: Well, you can forget about leaving until *my* clock strikes eleven. Time is money, and my time is worth at least a couple of marks. You boys look like a couple of marks. Are you brothers?

Robin is insulted. He comes out of his seat, huffing and puffing as if he is about to go berserk.

Dicolini: My friend, hesa get pretty mad. You watch out or he give you a piece of his mind.

Faustus: No thanks. I wouldn't want to take the last piece.

Dicolini: Atsa okay. He won't notice.
Faustus: Well, if you say so. Come here, young man.

Faustus reaches for Robin's arm but somehow finds himself holding his thigh. He pushes it away in disgust.

Faustus: Let's take a look at your skull.

Robin pulls a glowing skull from his cloak and presents it to Faustus. The class recoils. Faustus pops open its mouth and relights his cigar from the candle burning inside. He tosses the skull out the window, stands Robin in front of the chart, and backs off a step to appraise him. Moon-faced Robin looks about as intelligent as a hard-boiled egg. Faustus taps his pointer against Robin's skull.

Faustus: The astral mind is responsible for contact with the spiritual world without the intervention of either seraphim or cherubim. You all know what a seraph is, don't you?
Dicolini *(standing)*: Sure. On my pancakes, I like a maple seraph.
Faustus: No, no. Cherubs, seraphs.
Dicolini: I no like a cherub. I like a maple.
Faustus: These aren't food—they're angels.
Dicolini: I no like angel food, either.
Faustus: Well, that takes the cake. Where was I?

Robin is rubbing against the chart like a cat.

Faustus: Let's forget about the astral mind. That's obviously not relevant with this subject. Don't let me wake you, now. I'm not offending you by talking, am I?

Robin honks.

Faustus: Gesundheit. Moving south from the astral mind, we come to the inferior regions of the intellect. And when I say inferior, I mean inferior. The inferior mind, as you'll remember from our last lecture, is responsible for worldly thought, for instance, how did your nose get that way, and wasn't that a great plague we had last month. Worldly thought, of course, must be processed by one of the other organs before it becomes definable in emotional terms. The heart, for instance, controls affection, the liver, love, and the spleen, anger. Who can tell us what the kidneys control?

Dicolini *(rising again):* The kids' knees keep their legs from bending backwards.

Faustus leans toward Albergus.

Faustus: Do you hear voices?

Dicolini turns around, raises his hands to accept the accolades of his fellow students. Faustus turns on him.

Faustus: A kid's knees already bend backwards. Do you have any other bright ideas?

Dicolini: Not right now. I let you know.

Faustus: Do that. Drop me a postcard to warn me when you'll arrive. If I had a couple more students like you boys I could change gold into lead.

Wagner sighs. He's thinking of fair Helen. Meanwhile, Robin has moved to Faustus' lectern and opens Faustus' magic book. A small cloud of dust billows out. Robin pulls a kerchief out of his sleeve with a flourish, sneezes, then blows his nose with a loud honk. There is a flash of light and a smell of sulfur. When the smoke clears there is an imp standing on the edge of the podium.

(I can see this done either with a puppet or with a light, à la Tinkerbell in productions of Peter Pan. *At any rate, the staging can be negotiated to meet the possibilities of the production.)*

The class is astounded. Albergus stands up. Faustus stubs his cigar out on Dicolini's hat. Robin, delighted, takes off his own hat and holds it out to the imp, which hops in like a frog. Robin puts the hat back on his head.

Faustus: Oh, no you don't!

Dicolini: Come on, Robbie!

Faustus and Robbie dance back and forth on opposite sides of the lectern. Robin dashes for the door with Dicolini, who slams it in Faustus' face. Faustus whips it open, looks out, comes back to the lectern and whirls on Wagner.

> **Faustus:** As your punishment, you will retrieve that imp for me by midnight.
> **Wagner:** But Magister, I didn't do anything!
> **Faustus:** Neither did Job, and he had a better résumé.

ACT TWO

SCENE ONE

We are back in Faustus' apartment, in the study. Faustus is there, idly leafing through a copy of Playboy *(or* National Review *or* Wired *or some other anachronistic magazine). With him is Mephistopheles.*

Mephistopheles moves to stage front at points during this scene, addressing the audience directly in asides. Whenever he does, Faustus freezes in place in the background until Mephisto returns and takes up his place in the conversation.

> **Mephisto** *(aside):* Better to rule in Hell than serve in Heaven, Lucifer told us. Little did I know that I would end up spending twenty-four years playing mindless practical jokes for a man purported to be the wisest scholar in Europe. When I fell from Heaven, I knew I was in for a poorer class of associate, but I never thought it could get this bad. Why *this* is hell, nor am I out of it.
> **Clock:** FOUR FORTY-FIVE. HOW MUCH LONGER DO I HAVE TO KEEP DOING THIS?
> **Mephisto:** Midnight tonight, noble Faustus. Then do the jaws of Hell open to receive thee.
> **Faustus:** How late do they stay open?
> **Mephisto:** Long enough to swallow thee up, soul and socks.
> **Faustus** *(holding up cigar):* Light it.

The cigar magically flares up, and Faustus takes a few speculative puffs.

Faustus: And what happens after that?

Mephistopheles points to the wall, and a Gustave Doré engraving of Hell and demons is projected onto it. Through Mephisto's explanation the slide show continues.

Mephisto: Here is Dis, the city of Hell. You will be thrown into this perpetual torture-house. *(next slide: another hellish scene)* These are the furies, tossing damned souls on burning forks; their bodies boil in lead. *(next slide: people in flaming pits)* Over here are humans broiling on coals that can never die. *(next slide: another hell scene)* These souls that are fed with sops of burning fire were gluttons in their lives who laughed to see the poor starve at their gates.

Next slide: photo of Rush Limbaugh. You could even change this slide every performance: Mickey Mouse, Madonna, Wayne Newton, etc.

Faustus *(terrified for the first time)*: What's that?

Mephistopheles looks, does double take.

Mephisto: Excuse me. Just a project we're working on. In Dis, you shall see ten thousand tortures more horrid.
Faustus: You're not much of a travel agent. "See Dis and die."
Mephisto: Usually the dying comes first.
Faustus: You're right. Dis ain't no joke.
Mephisto: Fools that will laugh on earth must weep in Hell.
Faustus: You won't settle for a moan in Cologne?
Mephisto *(aside)*: Grubs on the eyeballs. Perhaps I'll start him with that. But no sense doing the other side's work for it. I wouldn't want him to repent.

Mephistopheles dissolves the vision of Hell.

Faustus: By the way, have you seen Helen lately?
Mephisto: In your closet.

Faustus: In my closet! What's she doing in there?

Mephisto: You told her to stay in it.

Faustus: I did? Oh, yes. Literal girl. Thank heaven for literal girls.

Mephisto: Heaven had nothing to do with it.

Faustus: Well, what am I supposed to do, swing both ways?

Mephisto: Shall I have her dress?

Faustus: It wouldn't fit you. Work on your thighs.

Mephisto *(aside):* When he tires, I'll strap him to a bed of razors.

Faustus *(pacing):* So she's in the closet, eh? And here I stand bantering with the help. Get her out here pronto. If she won't come, call for me, and I'll go in after her. If I don't come back, you can have my alembic.

Mephisto: This is no game, Faustus.

Faustus: It isn't? I thought it was the alembic games.

Mephisto: Worry not about Helen, Magister. If she disobeys you, I'll cull thee out the wildest Fräuleins in the north of Europe.

Faustus: The cull of the wild, eh? Sounds like a bunch of dogs to me. And who's going to clean up after them, tell me that? If I gave you half a chance you'd wreck this happy home.

Faustus whips out a book of raffle tickets and proffers them.

Faustus: How about half a chance? Cost you ten marks.

Mephisto *(aside):* A codpiece of burning iron. *(to Faustus)* Just now I don't feel so lucky.

Faustus: So? Never mind that, pick a card.

Mephistopheles begins to beat his head against the table.

Faustus: Hey, watch that finish! Okay, look, just keep an eye on Wagner for me, then. He wants to examine Helen's thesis. Can you imagine the consequences if she managed to seduce that boy? Why, she's been dead for two thousand years! What would his mother say? What would I say?

Mephisto: What *would* you say?

Faustus: Is it true that your mother was ravished by a bat? Is it true you grow barnacles in your underwear? Is it true you're going to sue your plastic surgeon as soon as he regains his eyesight?

Mephisto *(aside):* An eon up to his neck in boiling manure!

Clock: AT LEAST YOU GET TO MOVE AROUND. I CAN'T EVEN REMEMBER WHAT I DID TO PISS HIM OFF. IT'S FIVE O'CLOCK.

Mephisto *(aside):* Five o'clock! Only seven hours more! I'll turn him into a plate of knockwurst!

While Faustus and Mephisto banter in the study, the door to Faustus' apartments silently opens and Wagner sneaks in. He goes to the study door, listens, hears their voices. Sniffs the air. As Faustus comes to open the door he rushes across the common room into the bedroom, looks around frantically, then hides in the closet, where he trips over some shoes and bumps into Helen. The closet is cut away, so we can view the inside. Dim light. Hanging robes. Heaps of shoes, boots. Helen, bored.

Wagner: Mmmph! Who is it?

Helen *(helping him up):* It is I, Helen.

Wagner: Helen! Just who I've been looking for. I must see you.

Helen: And here I am without a candle.

Wagner: No one can hold a candle to you! I need you, Helen. You cannot know the torture I've been through imagining what Faustus has been doing with you.

Helen: Is that why you came into the closet?

Wagner: Faustus sent me on a fool's errand, but now that I'm with you I'll never play the fool again. He expects me to find an imp he lost. I snuck in to search his books for a spell to help me. I don't know why he can't do it himself.

Helen: He knows how to do it himself. But sometimes he'd rather not. Look at me.

Faustus and Mephistopheles enter the bedroom. Faustus makes Mephistopheles go down on all fours and begins to use him as a card table, laying out a solitaire hand with his tarot deck. Steam begins to rise from Mephisto's collar.

> **Wagner:** I wish I could. Say, do you smell burning sulfur?
> **Helen:** You should never eat radishes.
> **Wagner:** Who can he have out there with him?
> **Helen:** Some visiting scholar, surely. I'm so glad you found me. I didn't even suspect you knew of my existence. I've been so bored, cooped up in here. It's worse than life with Menelaus ever was. And Sparta was heaven compared to this! I'm still a young woman. I want to sing, I want to dance, I want to enjoy every particle of life! Can you help me, dear student?

She kisses him passionately. Steam begins to rise from Wagner's collar, too. Outside in the bedroom, Faustus is coughing from the increasing smoke in the room; he gathers up his cards, waves the billowing clouds of smoke away and retreats to the common room. Mephisto rises and follows.

> **Wagner:** I'll do my best. You have to realize I'm not very ex-perienced at—
> **Helen:** Don't worry. Troy wasn't ruined in a day. But now you must go.
> **Wagner:** Go? But I just got here.
> **Helen:** Nevertheless. If Faustus found you here his jealousy would know no bounds. Come back later, fair student. Tonight! Faustus will be gone until midnight. Return at eleven, and I will show you arts of which I alone am mistress. Until then you must do his bidding.
> **Wagner:** Eleven? How can I wait that long, thinking of you?
> **Helen:** Troilus recommended strenuous exercise and cold baths. Until eleven, my love!

She propels him out the door.

SCENE TWO

In the Boar's Bollocks Inn. Albergus sits at a table with Bateman plotting Faustus' destruction. A buxom barmaid serves their beers. Albergus is indifferent, but Bateman inspects her avidly.

Albergus: A half-witted student merely looks into that book and is able to conjure up an imp! Can you imagine the power that volume must contain?

Bateman: A guy could have a hot time with that book.

Albergus: It is all a matter of knowing the right words. Faustus' book must contain the language of UrCreation.

Bateman *(watching barmaid):* Or even the language of procreation—

Albergus: You see, Bateman, most language is just empty words. You've sat outside on a splendid fall afternoon, and the sun warmed your limbs, the sweet breeze caressed your cheek, you lay back and watched the skies, the bullocks, the squirrels—

Bateman: —the thighs, the buttocks, the girls—

Albergus: —it's a total sensory experience—

Bateman: I'll say.

Albergus: —and there is no way that ordinary language can capture even one thousandth of it.

Bateman: Preach it, brother!

Albergus: —But that's ordinary language. What about extraordinary language? What about the language of God, Bateman? In what language did God originally say, "Let There Be Light!"

Bateman: French?

Albergus: He said it, Bateman, in that mystic, UrCreative language, the language of ultimate truth. The language that came *before* reality. If a man could grasp that grammar of creation, he could control all that exists! And that language, Bateman, I am convinced, is written in Faustus's book. Can you imagine it? Faustus has his hand upon the axis of the universe! Yet to what use does he put this power?

Bateman: Well, he turned that guy into a clock. And there's those cigar things—

Albergus: Precisely. A total waste. The man has no more business owning that book than a rabbit.

Bateman: I don't think he owns a rabbit.

Albergus: That book belongs to he who can make use of it.

Bateman: Uh, speaking of grammar, I think that's supposed to be "to him," boss—

Albergus: To *me*, Bateman. And I aim to get it. Think of the things I might accomplish—strictly for the good of mankind, Bateman, the good of mankind! You see? That man is an impostor; I shall be the true Faustus! But now, how to break into his study? Who knows what risks that would entail?

Wagner enters, looks around, goes to him.

Wagner: Pardon me, sir. I am looking for my fellow students, Robin and Dicolini. Have you seen them?

Albergus: Not since they fled your master's lecture.

Wagner: I've exhausted myself searching. I thought they were my friends, but it seems they are more interested in other matters now.

Albergus: A sad breach of faith. Is there anything a fellow scholar can do?

Wagner: Nothing. Unless you can retrieve the imp that Robin called up.

Albergus: I am not without some magical prowess. Perhaps I can locate it. Not only that, but if you'll tell me when Faustus is away, I can deposit the creature—caged—in his rooms. It would make a good joke, don't you think? Especially after the shameful way he treated you today.

Wagner: If you could do that, my gratitude would surpass Goneril's to her father!

Albergus: You have only to ask.

Wagner: Yes, good Frater, please. Faustus told me he would not be home until midnight tonight. If you can arrive before then—

Albergus: I shall be there at ten.

Wagner: Uh—better make it eleven. Eleven-thirty? I have affairs—uh—business. I will let you in.

Albergus: Leave it to me. I will be discreet.

Wagner: Oh thank you, thank you!

Wagner pumps Albergus' hand vigorously and leaves, as excited as a groom on his wedding day.

Albergus: So, we have our entry into Faustus' rooms! Once there, I will uncover the Satanist's iniquities. Bateman, you must go to the Bishop of Wittenberg and tell him at once to assemble an ecclesiastical tribunal. We will arrest Faustus by the dawn, have him convicted by noon and roasting at the stake by vespers. And for good measure, we'll roast this slack fool Wagner along with him.

Bateman: I don't know about this, boss. Messing with the devil's servant is tricky. You don't want to end up a dish of knockwurst.

Albergus: Pish, Bateman! I am no coward. But it's true, I must not be associated with the disappearance of Faustus' magic book. *(snaps fingers)* Aha! A disguise! *(writes a hurried note)* Bateman, after you speak to the bishop I want you to fetch me the following items.

Albergus hands Bateman the note and the latter exits. Albergus sips his tankard of ale, throws a couple of coins onto the table, then departs himself. As soon as he does Robin and Dicolini crawl out from beneath the table. Dicolini drains the remainder of Albergus's ale in a gulp. Robin picks up one of the coins and bites through it. He chews thoughtfully, pulls a salt shaker from his robe, sprinkles the remainder of the coin and pops it into his mouth.

Dicolini: You hear that, Robbie? That Icebergus, hesa cross-double us. Hesa break the case himself and keep alla pieces. We gonna have to get tough.

Robin thrusts a fist under Dicolini's nose, grimacing and breathing heavily; his other arm goes into a windmill windup. Dicolini kicks him in the butt.

> **Dicolini:** Whatsa matter for you! Getta tough with him, not me. Now listen, we gotta move fast and get to Faustus' place before the boss, before Wagner, before anybody. We get there so early we be there before we arrive!

Robin honks. They exit. Wagner returns carrying a bundle of clothes. As he starts unlacing his shirt he addresses the barmaid.

> **Wagner:** Have you a bath here?
> **Barmaid:** No, sir. In the summer, some guests use the rain barrel in the lower court. But of course it is frozen—
> **Wagner:** Perfect. I want you to chop a hole in the ice for me. I need to keep cool.
> **Barmaid:** You must be very hot.
> **Wagner** *(beginning to unlace his boots)*: You cannot imagine.
> **Barmaid:** What clothing is that?
> **Wagner** *(trying on a pair of spectacles identical to Faustus')*: A disguise. You know Doctor Faustus? Well, a certain young woman I know is expecting to see him tonight. Imagine her surprise when she finds me in his place!

SCENE THREE

Upstage left, lights come up on alley behind Faustus' study. Dicolini and Robin wheel a wooden cart or barrow full of paraphernalia up below Faustus' second-floor bedroom window. Dicolini throws a rope over a rafter protruding out below the eaves, then ties one end around his chest.

> **Clock** *(from above)*: ELEVEN O'CLOCK. IT'S COLDER THAN A WITCH'S BICYCLE SEAT OUT THERE.
> **Dicolini:** Okay, Robbie. You tug onna rope, and I'll get in through Faustus' window. Keep a lookout. If anybody comes, whistle.

Robin nods, spits into his palms, leaps high into the air and grabs the rope. The rope hauls Dicolini two feet above the ground, and Robin hangs two feet above the ground on the opposite end; they struggle and flop together like hooked fish. Lights go down halfway, leaving them upstage left, and come up upstage right on the entrance to Faustus' apartments, where the porter, Martin, sits on a stool against the wall snoring, drunk as usual, a bottle on the ground beside him. Wagner comes up, sees Martin, then puts on a Faustus costume: white nightshirt, mortarboard hat, greasepaint mustache, wire-rimmed spectacles. He pulls his cloak on over the nightshirt, then strides up to Martin, who is taking a slug from his bottle as Wagner salutes him.

Wagner: Have a drink to my love life, Martin my man.
Martin *(flustered):* Uh—thank you, sir.

Wagner goes inside.

    Lights go down upstage, come up downstage to reveal the inside of Faustus' apartment. Wagner enters through common room door, then hurries to the bedroom and the wardrobe. He throws off the cloak and mortarboard, pulls on a stocking cap, opens the door and stands on the threshold.

Wagner: Helen!
Helen: Darling!

Wagner is overwhelmed by her ardor, perhaps even a little scared.

Wagner: Don't worry—it's me, Wagner! You can come out of the closet now.
Helen: Oh!
Wagner: What's wrong?
Helen: I thought you were Faustus. I forgot to tell you that I can't come out until he says I can. After all, I am his to command. Won't you come in?
Wagner: But—
Clock: ELEVEN FIFTEEN. I WONDER HOW THE METS ARE DOING?

A sound from the common room. It's Faustus, who has come from his study toward the bedroom, followed by Mephistopheles. Wagner climbs into the closet just as Faustus and the demon enter.

> **Faustus:** I wish you'd stop following me around. I want to get ready for bed.
> **Mephisto:** You shall not sleep this night, Faustus.
> **Faustus:** I certainly won't if you keep pestering me. Go away.

Mephistopheles renders himself invisible, goes into the common room, from which he observes. Faustus goes to the closet.

> **Faustus:** Now where's my nightshirt? I thought I left it lying around here. *(To Helen)* Are you still in there?
> **Helen:** Who?
> **Faustus:** Unless you're keeping an owl, Helen of Troy.

Wagner nudges Helen frantically. She gets flustered.

> **Helen:** What owl? There's no owl in here.
> **Faustus:** Owl take your word for it. Does one of you birds want to hand me my nightshirt?

Wagner fumbles among the clothes, gives Helen a nightshirt. She opens the door a crack and hands it out. Faustus peeks in.

> **Faustus:** Hope it's not too boring in there.
> **Helen:** Not yet. I wouldn't mind some fresh air once in a while.
> **Faustus** *(sniffs):* The air in there smells pretty fresh already. Or maybe it's my undershirt. *(Hauls out tarot deck)* Would you like to take a card?
> **Helen:** No, thank you.

Faustus closes the door, changes into the nightshirt and a stocking cap, and leaves for the common room. In the common room he begins to search for something, poking his head into cabinets, shelves, etc.

Wagner: You said Faustus would be out tonight!
Helen: Did I?

Helen embraces Wagner. He forgets his annoyance and begins to nuzzle her. They fumble around in the cramped closet, and Helen finally pushes him away.

Wagner: Noble queen—
Helen: I'm sorry, but I can't get into the mood lying on old shoes. Can't you find some way to let me out?
Wagner: Wait here. Faustus' magic book must be around somewhere. I'll find a spell of unbinding.

Wagner leaves the closet and sneaks out of the bedroom toward Faustus' study. He passes hurriedly through the common room while Faustus has his back turned; neither sees the other. The lights fade downstage and come up upstage right on the entrance to the building, where Martin still sits. Albergus enters, strides up and down in a blizzard of impatience. He stops.

Albergus: I can wait no longer!

He dons a Faustus disguise of academic robe, greasepaint mustache, spectacles and mortarboard and approaches Martin. Martin gives a woozy double take as Albergus enters.

Albergus: Drink is the tool of the devil, my man.
Martin *(more flustered):* Uh—no doubt, sir, no doubt.

After Albergus enters Martin scratches his head, takes a deep swig from his bottle.
    Lights go down upstage right, come up downstage on Faustus' apartment. Wagner has gone into Faustus' study. Albergus enters the common room, once again just as Faustus is stooped over with his head in a cabinet. Albergus looks one way, Faustus the other. They comically miss each other as they pass through the room. Wagner, who was searching the study, hears the noise and listens at the study door just as Faustus is listening at the other side of the same door. Eventually Faustus sticks his

head back in the cabinet just as Albergus goes into the bedroom; again neither has seen the other. Albergus rifles through the bedside table, the trunk at the end of the bed. It's full of clothes, including a nightshirt or two that he throws onto the bed. He tries the closet door. As soon as he opens it Helen throws her arms around him.

> **Helen:** Darling! Let me out of the closet! Then will I fulfill your every desire.
> **Albergus** *(stumbling back, hauling out a cross)*: Back, hellfiend!

He slams the closet door on Helen. He wipes his brow, shaken. Just then there is a rattling from the window. Albergus hurries from the room; you guessed it, he still misses Faustus in the commons, where they continue their separate searches.

In the bedroom the window opens, and Dicolini climbs in, unties the rope. He peeks out the bedroom door, then hesitates. He ponders, sees the nightshirt on the bed, snaps his fingers. He takes off his boots, rolls up his pants, dons the nightshirt and a stocking cap. From the bedside table he takes some makeup and smears a greasepaint mustache over his lip, puts on some spare spectacles. Just as he's about to leave the room he hears a voice.

> **Helen:** Is that you?
> **Dicolini:** Maybe.
> **Helen:** Please let me out of here.
> **Dicolini:** Who are you?
> **Helen:** Don't be silly. You know who I am.
> **Dicolini:** Itsa slip my mind.
> **Helen** *(sarcastically)*: Well, I'm the most beautiful woman in history.
> **Dicolini:** Never mind coming out. I come in.

Dicolini opens the closet door. Helen throws her arms around his neck.

> **Helen:** Darling!

Dicolini tugs her out, she draws back and hangs on to the door.

Helen: No, I can't leave unless Faustus says so.
Dicolini: Okay, Faustus says so!

Lights fade on the bedroom, come up on the study. Wagner is frantically searching through the papers on Faustus' desk. He finds an impressive contract, Faustus' deal with the devil. He tries to puzzle it out, reading aloud.

Wagner: This seems to be some sort of contract. ". . . party of the first part shall hereinafter be called part of the first party . . . contractee reserves the right of reversion, the right to a speedy conviction, the right to a free lunch, the right to sing the blues . . . in the event of a change of political party, once in a blue moon, when hell freezes over, if the Pope is Catholic, and bears sit in the woods . . . and knowledge including but not confined to THE MEANING OF LIFE and any related subsidiary meanings, notions, ideas, quips, lemmas, or passing fancies . . ."

Clock: ELEVEN THIRTY. MEANING SCHMEANING—IT'S LATER THAN YOU THINK.

Albergus and Faustus in the common room and Wagner in the study all jump. Faustus turns around and would see Albergus except Albergus at that exact moment enters the study. As the study door opens Wagner stuffs the contract into his shirt and dashes under the desk. Albergus comes to the desk, rifles through the papers, finds nothing and goes to the mirror door. He feels along the mirror's edge, finds a catch and opens the door. He enters the secret room and continues his search.

In the bedroom, Dicolini and Helen are doing a combination wrestling match and waltz as he tries to maneuver her toward the bed. She begins to realize that this is not Faustus, and resists.

In the common room, Faustus finally gives up his search.

Faustus*(to Clock):* Have you seen my cigars anywhere?
Clock: WHAT, I'M THE MAID, TOO?

In the study Wagner is about to sneak out from beneath the desk when Faustus gives up on the commons and enters the study. Wagner dashes back under the desk. Albergus peeks warily from the open mirror doorway, then draws back. In the bedroom Dicolini is pressing Helen toward the bed.

Dicolini: Bella felissima ronzoni, alla pacino.
Helen: My lord, you know I don't understand Latin.
Dicolini: Atsa not Latin, atsa Italian.
Helen: I don't understand Italian, either.
Dicolini: Atsa okay. Neither do I.

Lights down in bedroom, up on alley upstage left. Robin is freezing. He tears a picture of a fire from a book and pins it to the cart, trying to warm his hands before it. He stomps around, flapping his arms. The imp, in his cloak, awakes, pops out, leaps onto the rope and scrambles up through the window. Robin runs around frantically. He stops, snaps his fingers. He rummages through the cart, gets out a nightshirt, glasses, nightcap. He smears black grease from the cart axle under his nose as a mustache. Thus dressed he goes upstage right to where Martin keeps the entrance. Martin gives a double take. Robin grabs his bottle of wine, takes a swig, gives a honk and hands the bottle back to him. Robin enters. Martin stares at the bottle in his hand, then crosses himself, corks it and puts it as far away from him as possible.

Lights go down on exterior and up on interior. Robin rushes in through the common room door and races to the bedroom. Inside he skids to a stop when he sees Dicolini and Helen on the bed. Helen has the upper hand. She's got her foot on his neck and is about to bash him with the chamber pot. Dicolini sees Robin.

Dicolini: Faustus!

Robin looks over his shoulder. Helen releases Dicolini, who runs from the room. She smiles tentatively at Robin. Robin smiles back. She throws her arms around his neck.

Helen: Darling!

Robin squeezes her, horn honking.

In the commons, Dicolini is heading toward the door when he runs into the invisible Mephistopheles, who has returned. They collide and sprawl across the dining table, scattering crockery and candlesticks. In the study, hearing the crash, Faustus hides behind his alchemical table.

Mephisto: Your time is nigh, mortal. You will pay dearly for your sins.

Dicolini: I never touched her, boss! Shesa better man than I am.

Mephisto: You insist on playing the fool, even now?

Dicolini: No. Hesa still down inna alley.

Mephistopheles, furious, stomps into the bedroom to talk to Helen. He finds her with Robin on the bed. Once again she has the upper hand, stomping on his horn, which honks. Robin looks up to see Mephisto's glowing eyes. He leaps from the bed and hides in the closet.

Mephisto: It will avail Faustus nothing to hide.

Helen: I don't think that's Faustus.

Mephisto: Who is it, then?

Helen: I don't know, but I've seen a lot of him lately.

Mephisto: Don't tell me you've succumbed to Faustus' fooleries. Are you doing his bidding?

Helen*(adjusting her clothing):* You point him out and I'll try.

Mephisto: Where is he?

Helen: Hang around a while. He'll turn up. Or else somebody just as good.

Mephisto: This Faustus is devilishly clever, and these doppelgangers only make my job harder. I don't want to get the wrong man.

Helen: In my experience, not many men aren't the wrong one.

Mephisto*(disgusted):* "Better to rule in Hell than serve in Heaven." Ha!

Mephistopheles renders himself invisible, then goes into the commons, deep in thought. Meanwhile, Dicolini has fled from the commons to the study and run through the open mirror door to the back room. Faustus cautiously gets up from behind the table, rubs his chin.

Faustus: This place sure has been deserted tonight.

Not noticing each other at first, Faustus and Dicolini end up on opposite sides of the doorway where mirror door is open. Faustus turns to the doorway just as Dicolini peeks out. Faustus mistakes Dicolini in the doorway for his own reflection in the mirror. Faustus, suspicious, tries a number of moves in front of the doorway, which Dicolini mirrors exactly: hopping, duck walk, bowing, the Charleston. They end up reproducing the mirror scene from Duck Soup, which culminates with Faustus realizing Dicolini is not his reflection, and grabbing him by the nightshirt.

Faustus: So it's you, is it?
Dicolini: Atsa crazy. Itsa no me. Itsa you.
Faustus: How do I know it's me?
Dicolini: I just told you. I'm not here.
Faustus: If you're me, how come you're not smoking a cigar?
Dicolini: You no give me one.

Faustus whips out a cigar and gives it to him.

Faustus: There you go. Let's see you get out of that one.
Dicolini: You got a match?
Faustus: Never mind.

Faustus takes back the cigar. Wagner, meanwhile, is trying to crawl out while they bicker. Faustus spots him.

Faustus: Hold on there! I can't get away from me that easily!

Wagner gets up and runs out of the room. Faustus tries to chase him, but gets tangled up with Dicolini. Wagner rushes through the commons directly into the bedroom. He shoves the door open and, not seeing Helen, jumps into the closet, tearing off his clothes. He embraces Robin.

Wagner: Dearest, I couldn't find the book, but—

Robin's horn honks. Wagner is nonplussed.

Helen: What are you doing in there?

Wagner opens the door and pulls Robin out by his collar. Robin's face splits in a shy smile of love. Wagner pushes him out the bedroom door and turns to Helen.

Wagner: Helen—
Helen: Darling!

She throws her arms around his neck and draws him toward the bed.

Clock: ELEVEN FORTY-FIVE. SOON WE'LL FIND OUT IF THIS IS A COMEDY OR A TRAGEDY.

Mephistopheles, roused by the clock, makes a decision. He goes from the commons into the study. The instant he enters, Faustus and Dicolini speak as one.

Faustus and Dicolini: Oh, so you're back, eh?
Mephisto: Your doom is at hand.

Faustus fans out his deck of tarot cards.

Faustus: Never mind that. Pick a card.
Dicolini *(taking one):* So, what am I got?
Faustus: You've got one, I've still got seventy-seven.
Dicolini: You wrong. Itsa ace of wands.
Faustus: Wandaful. *(gesturing to Mephistopheles)* Does your wormy friend want to try his luck?
Dicolini: Hesa outside in the alley.

At this, Robin enters munching a slice of bread. He goes to the alchemical table and smears the bread with some noxious chemicals, takes a bite. He offers the bread to Faustus.

Faustus: No, thanks. It's bad enough being damned. Indigestion I don't need.

Clock: IT'S MIDNIGHT. BONG. BONG. BONG . . . *(continues throughout following action)*
Mephisto: Enough! Which one of you is the real Faustus?

Offstage, through the mirror doorway, Albergus shouts.

Albergus: Eureka! It is mine!

All turn to the doorway. Albergus, who has found the magic book, strides into the room.

Albergus: Ha ha! Fools! Now at last I possess ultimate knowledge! The wheel has turned, and I am become the true Faustus!

Mephistopheles looks at him, the only Faustus now dressed in academic garb.

Mephisto: Good enough for me.

With that he snaps his fingers and a horde of misshapen demons erupt from all directions offstage. They seize Albergus, and in an explosion of light and smoke, drag him off to Hell. As the air clears the last stroke of midnight dies away. In the next room, the clock moves for the first time in the play. It stretches, shakes its aching legs and arms, gives a little hop of exhilaration.

Clock: HAPPY NEW YEAR! BOY, COULD I USE A DRINK!

Clock exits. In the bedroom, Wagner finds he is embracing empty air. He stumbles to the closet, but it is empty.

Wagner: Helen?

Following the smell of smoke, he enters the study. Faustus and Dicolini are seated around a bonfire smoking cigars, toasting sausages on sticks. Robin, using Mephistopheles' pitchfork, is shoveling books into the fire.

Dicolini: Atsa good smoke.
Wagner: Where is she?

Faustus gestures at Wagner's drooping trousers.

Faustus: Cut is the branch that might have grown full straight.

He pulls the sweaty contract off Wagner's chest and adds it to the fire.

Wagner: What have you done with her?
Dicolini: She was one helluva wrestler, eh, partner?

Robin leans on his pitchfork and gives a long, low whistle.

Wagner: But it's not fair! We were only getting to know each other!
Faustus: My boy, she was a scarlet woman and you're nothing but a green student. She would have made you blue someday.
Dicolini: If you didn't turn yellow first.
Faustus *(offering a sausage):* Meanwhile, how about a little roast knockwurst?
Dicolini: Atsa no roast. Atsa friar.

Wagner stumbles from the room. Lights go down.

SCENE FOUR

Lights come up on the Boar's Bollocks, where Wagner, moping, is seated at a table telling his story to the barmaid. At the next table a man sits with his back to the audience.

Wagner: . . . and when I came to, she was gone! Did my master Faustus care? Did Dicolini and Robin, my closest friends, care?
Barmaid: *I* care.
Wagner: The story of mankind is a sad story. The saddest story I know.
Barmaid: Poor Wagner! Were you hurt?

Wagner: Emotional loss means nothing to the true intellectual.

Barmaid *(touching his chest):* Let me help you.

Wagner: The world is a cold place.

Barmaid: But you told me you were hot.

Wagner *(standing, beginning to orate):* And I've learned much from all this. The beginning of wisdom is mine. I've learned that despite the centuries that have passed since the beginning of time, despite the wars, heresies and degradations, the corruptions of institutions and loss of faith, the ages of bad behavior, one thing remains. People are, for better or worse, still human. That has not changed. Good and evil coexist. Some souls are saved, others are lost. The appetites of the body and the mind conflict. Men aspire to the stars, women abandon them, scholars seek knowledge, students—

The barmaid seizes him by the shoulders, bends him over and gives him a furious kiss. They fall off the bench, under the table. Bateman enters.

Bateman: Has anyone seen my master Albergus?

The man at the next table turns and hails him. It is the Clock.

Clock: He's gone south for the winter. Will be gone awhile. Meanwhile, pal, could you tell me what time it is?

Lights down in tavern. Mephistopheles comes out to address the audience.

Mephisto: These our revels now are done.
All my power's overthrown.
Wagner's found a girl at last
History has swallowed past.
For me, I'm off to warmer climes
And giving up these wretched rhymes.
Plagiarize I can no more
From better writers' magic store
Of characters, ideas, words,
Comic mishaps *très absurd . . .*

With brothers Marx's sweet inventions
To tell of Faust was our intention.
Now you must tell us if our play
Justified such rude displays
A laugh's the end we're hoping for
Please don't send us back for more.
But if our humor's fit your plans
You may release us with your hands.

ANIMALS

Fate often saves an undoomed man when his courage is good.

—*Beowulf*

It was on the seashore in the parklands that I first saw him. Mid-afternoon, and the Tall One had just gone, leaving me to whatever trouble I chose to find as long as I could get out of it myself.

But in that beginning I didn't think anything about trouble. The sun beat down on the sand, now grown almost too hot to stand on, and for once there was no breeze over the water. It was the hottest day of the year. I ran along the shore, my bare feet slipping as the sand gave way beneath them, and I listened to my body working: the breath drawn sharply in and out, the rhythmic rush of air pulsing in my ears, the flat dry sound of feet slapping beach. Sound mind, sound body.

Then the bushes up the slope rustled and a man with a rock in his hand emerged from the shadows. I stopped, panting, and stared. He was sturdily built, with square shoulders and broad, flat muscles. His chest, legs, and even his arms were covered with coarse black hair; his groin was matted fur. In contrast, the thinning hair on his head was incongruous. Dirty face and unkempt beard; it was a hard face settling into lined middle age, the eyes suspicious under dark brows. His forehead was unmarked.

I'm not one of those weak, submissive humans: I despise that type. But I was wary of the rock, and intimidated by his dark glare. Here he was, unowned, on my territory (at least it was as much mine as it was any man's), and yet I felt measured and discarded by the simple sweep of his eyes over my forehead.

He stepped out into the full sunlight. "I waited until the Owner left," he said. His voice was a surprising tenor, not unfriendly.

My initial surprise was wearing off. "Who are you?"

"Who am I?" He smiled. "I'm hungry, that's who I am."

"Very funny."

"Right. I'm hungry and I'm funny. You must be smart to figure that out so quick. I bet you're well trained." He hung his left hand over his right shoulder and scratched.

Most of the unowned aren't practiced in sarcasm; they can't afford it. I squatted and scooped a handful of brown sand, letting it run between my fingers as I studied him.

"Let's think about this, and we'll see who's smart," I said. "First, I'm not hungry. Second, I don't have lice."

He started to reply, thought better of it, and shut his mouth in a grim line. He tossed his rock into the water a few steps away, came over and crouched nearby. The waves broke and pushed sea foam to within a few paces of our feet. I caught his strong, musky smell and tried not to wrinkle my nose.

"Look—" he said, his voice lower now, eyes fixed on the sand, "—can you get me something? You know it doesn't have to be much. You know what I mean—a man like you must have his own access. Last thing I had was some wild apples, maybe two, three days ago." He looked at me. His dark eyes showed nothing; I didn't know if he was telling the truth. He might be pretty good at lying. Up close, he looked like he was pushing fifty pretty hard.

"Maybe I can help you out later," I said. "Why don't you

come around when I'm back at my quarters? I live on the second level, near the Tingling Force, with the Tall One. Do you know where that is?"

He looked suspicious. "I saw him. How do I know you'll even recognize me there?"

"You can't know, of course. Don't be dense."

He shrugged his bearlike shoulders and sank back further behind his eyes. "Dense."

"Yes, dense." I wasn't intimidated at all, then. "What's your name?"

"My name is Philip." He said it slowly and formally, like that, as if he were not used to going by names.

"So, Philip, perhaps I'll see you in the city this evening."

I left him standing lumpishly and continued my run. It was a puzzling encounter, not devoid of threat. I don't know how these unowned live.

I am the Tall One's philosopher. From the time I was a child and was sent to the school for humans, I have been immersed in the works of the ancient human philosophers, have trained myself to cut and shape with the dry knife of the mind. Plato and Aristotle, Lao Tze and Confucius, Augustine, Spinoza and Kant and Descartes, Kierkegaard, Nietzsche, Wittgenstein I and Wittgenstein II, Camus and Sartre, Miller, Suarez, and Lin. In the background, always, stood the austere presence of the Tall One, who would appear and suddenly disappear, whose short comments gave no hint of *their* philosophies. Why I have been trained in this way is but one more of the mysteries that comprise our lives with the Owners.

Madeline, who studied history—a discipline I have been forbidden—once described to me their coming. According to her, the first of the Owners' cities merely appeared one day in the middle of what were then called the "Flint Hills" of "North America." (Who or what Flint was I do not know or care to know, but I have run across the mysterious "America" in several other contexts, and the word always arouses in me the intense image of a far-off and haunted place. But for all I know, I may at this moment be living in "America." I digress.) Madeline's description of the events that followed the Owners' first appearance was a confused one, and I rather suspect this is because no human has an accurate account. I only know that the lives of my philosophical predecessors, and the aggressive and complex world they lived in, were swept away—not without violent resistance. Madeline claimed that there were six billion of us before the Owners came. It's a number I can't accept.

I once ventured to ask the Tall One about this, but his leathery brown face only pinched together in the expression I believe to be their smile.

The evening after my encounter with the unowned man I ate alone in my room and began reading the book the Tall One had given me the day before. On the cover was printed: "Read this and tell me about it."

Various humans have speculated how and why the Owners create such books. My compatriot Spender claims that at least some of these are written by the Owners themselves, and has tried to show me the argument by which he deduced this—but he is a rhetorician, and I don't believe his sophistries. I am sure that some human wrote this book, just as I have written many essays and books, only to have them vanish while I sleep, never to reappear. Certainly Aristotle, Hegel, and the others must have once existed to write the philosophy I have studied—though when I encounter some idea I have expounded myself reflected in one of the books the Tall One gives me, I wonder whether it is not stolen from one of my papers, only to appear transformed in the neutral prose of the page I read. Controversies have raged over just such points of speculation as this. I sometimes think this is the precise reason the Owners present us with these puzzles in the first place.

I had only just begun this new work when a fluctuation of the light of my rooms told me another human had entered the Tall One's quarters. I touched the contact point on my chair that deopaqued the walls and saw, as I expected, that the stranger Philip had entered the large room. I did not see the Tall One about, but he might show up at any moment. I went out to meet the un-owned man.

"So you found this place."

Philip looked, if anything, more threatening than he had at the beach, but I could see the vulnerability beneath. Vulnerability, however, does not mean harmlessness. He had managed to wash himself, and his beard was hacked shorter than before, but I was still not sure how the Tall One would take this intrusion.

"I found it, all right." His voice had an edge to it. "I've been in a few of their cities in my time. You've probably never left this one."

I was surprised but didn't show it. I had never met a human who'd been anywhere else. I covered up by going over to my feeder in the alcove at the corner of the room. "Let's get you something to eat. Then you'll have to go. I don't want you around when the Owner returns."

I punched up my food code and ordered meat, fruit, and cheese. My feeder was the most elaborate of any I had encountered, and the luxury was an occasional embarrassment to me. Philip did not seem to notice. He grabbed the food as soon as it was dispensed and huddled over the tiny shelf.

I punched up a cold glass of water.

"You fellows have it pretty good," he said between bites. "Sometimes I think it's almost worth it. What's your name?"

"Matthew," I said.

"That your own name, or did they give it to you?"

What in the world had possessed me to let him come into my home, eat my food, and insult me? As at so many times in the past, my curiosity had posed me a problem.

"Listen," I said, "you can take your joyous independence and—"

I saw that he was no longer looking at me. Instead, his eyes were focused on something over my shoulder, and his expression had gone blank. I knew, even before I turned around, that the Tall One was back.

He stood there, impossibly slender, his skin the color and texture of moist, dead leaves. His thought rang in my mind like a clear chime.

You've fed this man.

As always, there was no hint of expression to the words: they might have been a question, a statement, or an accusation.

Lying would be useless with the evidence in plain sight, even if I didn't make a practice of the truth. "Yes," I said.

Is this man owned.

Philip stepped forward. His hands hung relaxed at his sides, and he looked so self-assured I had to look again. The man had reserves you would not expect on first sight.

"I'm not owned," he said.

This man is wanting a sleeping-place.

"I do," he replied. "My name is Philip."

Matthew, the Tall One said, *prepare a sleeping-place for Philip.*

With that he glided quietly through the wall to the place that was his own.

Philip sat down in my chair in the large room. He threw one arm over the back of it and said, "Hello, Brother Matt."

Several days after Philip had moved in, a large, long-legged cat interrupted me as I worked on an essay in my rooms. It was the Tall One in another guise. Like those ancient gods the Greeks mention so casually and tantalizingly, the Owners will take on the appearance of beasts. The silver cat yawned and stretched and lay down on the floor.

Tell me now about the book, he said.

I backed off from my writing table and leaned back in the chair. I felt reasonably at ease. Philip had gone out earlier.

"It is a trivial book," I said, adopting the tone of earnest dogmatism that I suspect is the one the Owners most like to hear in such discourses. "It takes certain propositions of the old existentialism and reduces them to banality."

An example of such a proposition.

" 'Existence precedes essence,' " I replied. "This is a fundamental assertion of great mystery—not a simple precept. In an elemental way our existence as human—as beings—comes before all other statements of what we are here for or what we may become. Our only definition lies in this fact of existence. Further definitions are secondary and man-asserted. I am, for instance, a 'man,' before I am such a thing as a philosopher."

Yes.

"This book—" I placed my hand on its cover "—reduces that statement and its frightening consequences to a chest-thumping boast that man is the master of his fate, come what may." I was enjoying my own lecture. "Of course, I am paraphrasing somewhat."

A silence followed in which the cat closed its eyes and rested its massive head on its front paws.

Is man then not the master of his fate.

"That is . . . a difficult question," I temporized. "In the existential formulation, man is of course fundamentally free in an absurd universe. In practice, however, we cannot deny the influence of external . . . ah . . . influences." Lame, pitifully lame! Attempting to recover, I continued, "Man is alone—"

What of Philip, the cat interrupted. *You are not alone with Philip here.*

The childish obtuseness of this comment was typical. It revealed either stupidity or subtlety—in fact, like all the actions of these creatures, it revealed nothing. Given the tension I had been laboring under, this was enough to irritate me immensely, and I'm afraid I did something I had never done before. I tried to persuade the Tall One on a personal matter.

"This Philip is really no companion to me. He's ignorant. I would feel much more at ease if he were not here."

The cat licked its forepaw and used it to rub the back of its ears.

"Besides, he isn't registered," I added.

The thought shot back immediately: *I may have him registered.*

I resorted to petulance, realizing all the while that I was not in control of myself. "I would much prefer someone like Madeline for a companion."

The cat rose and stretched once more. This time the stretch continued bizarrely beyond the bounds of the physically possible. The gray cat shimmered, elongated, rose up on its hind legs and became the twisted, emaciated form of the Tall One. His noseless, slit-mouthed face gazed calmly into mine.

Perhaps you should have Madeline come to meet Philip, he said. *As soon as possible.*

Then his figure faded into invisibility and I was alone.

I found Philip impossible to live with. First of all, he was physically repulsive to me. He smelled. He did not bathe often, and even when he did, an hour later the rooms were tainted with the sour stink of his sweat. The clean porcelain of the floors and basins was covered with his coarse black hair.

In addition there was his attitude. He regarded me with varying degrees of suspicion, condescension, and contempt. At times he would snort at my pastimes as if they indicated I was something less than a man; at others I would catch glimpses of his envy at my intellectual ability. He would make cryptic references to how he lived on the outside, but when I asked him in a friendly way to tell me of his life, he would retreat behind those opaque brown eyes. When we were in the presence of the Tall One, he would put away his bitter expressions of hatred toward the Owners—the hatred he never spared telling me about—and become manfully obedient. His hypocrisy sickened me.

I discovered the Tall One's reason for taking Philip in after I introduced Madeline to him. My distaste climbed to the edge of hatred.

Madeline was an intelligent person, a good historian (though I lack the criteria to judge). She was beautiful as well. Slender, with full hips, thick brown hair, an easy grace. We had been occasional lovers for years. Her owner had mysteriously left (died?—we have no way of knowing), and she had lived a year now in the quarters of the temporarily unowned. Since I did not like to meet her in the presence of others unless we were to do no more than talk, she had come to visit me in my rooms several times. The Tall One had taken a great interest in this. He had a particular interest in our sexual encounters.

We do not know if the Owners are sexual beings. Certainly there is no way to tell from their physical appearance. If one takes the great chance of asking them about this, as I on one occasion did of the Tall One, one receives no answer.

So it was only a confirmation of my suspicion when I realized that the Tall One meant for Madeline to become Philip's sexual partner. Philip, with his thick hands and foul breath.

The memory of Madeline riding over me, hair down in her eyes, gently swaying, soft breasts and erect nipples, her sweet and trembling touch, and the thought of that rough animal with her, all under the dispassionate eye of the Tall One, caused me intense pain. To this was added the realization of Madeline's betrayal of me. She was intrigued to meet this stranger from outside, this man who had never been owned and whose dark eyes held—for her if not for me—knowledge she would give anything to have.

After the first meetings, when the three of us would talk uneasily before Madeline and Philip drifted off into a private conversation of their own—never overtly, of course, but somehow it seemed that I was not there anymore—I took to leaving the Tall One's home and going on long trips through the radiant tunnels of the city. I avoided other humans and spent hours watching the Owners in their comings and goings. Sometimes they walked; sometimes they glided through the air without an indication of mechanism. They trailed wisps of light; they changed shapes. They entered corridors whose gaping entrances would somehow not admit the passage of a human: no overt force stopped you, it was just that you always thought of something else you'd rather do before you go there. I watched the humans go about their separate business, ignored by the Owners in the vast majority of cases. I wondered at things I had taken for granted all my life. And the pain that Philip was causing me burned in the front of my thoughts.

One day I returned after one of these forays to find Philip and

Madeline rutting away on the floor, sweating, fumbling, grunting. The Tall One sat on my bed, watching them. My presence affected no one. The pit of my stomach churned as I sat brooding in the other room. The Owner's thought came to me: *Go to the Dream Cellars.*

I thought for a minute I would refuse, but though he allowed a certain spirit, the Tall One did not brook outright disobedience.

The Dream Cellars were crowded with humans. I stood anonymous in the crowded foyer, and then the doors dissolved and attendants took us by the hands and led us to the small womblike chambers that, level upon level, lined the cylindrical room. I sat locked in the warm darkness, fluid rising around me, my lungs gasping for air up to the last moment of surrender to the liquid that would fill and sustain them, and then came the gradual progression from consciousness to metaconsciousness.

I experienced a dream of great violence. I met a man in a chill mountain pass, dressed in furs and leather, and he refused me admission to the valley I could see far off down the slopes beyond him. He was gaunt and weathered. We fought. I crushed in his skull with a rock, and as I stood above him, shuddering, blood on my hands, a heavy snow began to fall. It soon shrouded his body. I turned down the trail, but the storm had obscured everything, and I could not see where I went.

When I returned to my rooms, the Tall One was not there, and Madeline had gone. Philip lay on my bed, leafing through one of my books. He smelled of sex.

I tore the book from his hands. "Leave my things alone!" I shouted. My face burned; my hands still felt the weight of the rock with which I had killed the old man.

He surged from the bed, shoved his broad hand against my chest, slammed me against the wall. His forearm was against my neck, lifting the point of my chin high into the air. I could hardly breathe. I tried to kick him. He grinned and pushed harder.

"Listen, philosopher! I've had all I need of you. You're surprised I read? I'll read anything I please. I'll *screw* anything I please. Okay, *Matt?*"

He let me go; I gasped for air. He was breathing hard himself; he may have been surprised at his own anger. Sullenly he turned and left, and the light changed to show he'd left.

I sat on the bed with my head between my knees. He'd betrayed himself in that outburst: if the Tall One had seen it, he would have been in deep trouble. They do not tolerate that kind of violence outside of dreams. I shuddered with the force of the idea that had struck me: if he would not fall into that pit of his own accord, perhaps I could push him.

The Tall One knew me to be a reasonable man. My profession confirmed this. My restraint in reaction to the many provocations at the hands of Philip could not have escaped his notice. Had the Tall One himself not suggested I go to the Dream Cellars? Had I not obeyed immediately, without protest?

And he knew, at the very least, that Philip was an unowned man.

Philip left our rooms early the next afternoon, and I knew he had gone to see her. Quickly I left after him, off to visit Spender. We spent some time discussing some stupid excursion into positivism he was making, and then I pleaded mental fatigue and went by the unowned quarters. I watched until I saw Philip leave. As unobtrusively as possible, I made my way to Madeline's room.

She was surprised to see me.

"Matthew!" She sat in the only chair in the room.

"Hello," I said. "I just saw Philip in the passage."

She seemed to shrink back in the chair. "He was here to visit me," she said quietly. Her thick hair was disheveled; she had become coarse herself. I wondered that I'd ever slept with her.

"I'm sure you must have discussed history." I paced back and forth in the room.

Her eyes darkened. "Irony doesn't suit you, Matthew."

I could not put it off; I would only get weaker. "Perhaps you're right. I'd better give it up."

While talking I had circled the chair. She twisted her head around to follow me, but before she could do anything, I was on her. I threw my arm around her neck, turned my head aside, gritted my teeth, and jerked back as hard as I could. She clawed at me. I pulled her entirely over the back of the chair. She struggled savagely. My heart beat like a mad thing, and my eyes were burning with tears. I wasn't strong enough to strangle her. Desperately I fell to my knees—the jolt sent slivers of pain up my legs—and tried to beat her head against the floor. She twisted in my grasp and started to scream; I shoved my fist into her mouth, ground the thumb of my other hand into her throat, lifted, and slammed her down again, throwing the whole force of my weight behind it. There was an awful dull splitting, and she lay still.

I found I was sobbing aloud with a dead woman in my arms. Horrified, I struggled to my feet. The room stank: her bowels had let loose when she died and the mess was smeared on my leg.

I stumbled from the room dizzily, trying to muster some composure. I slowed my rush. Out of the unowned quarters, not looking at anyone, through the passages and levels, by the Tingling Force, into the Tall One's quarters, into my rooms. Philip, mercifully, was not there. I bathed rapidly, stared at my reflection in the white porcelain. I rubbed healing cream on the scratches on my arm and the torn hand I had shoved into her mouth. The light from the next room brightened: Philip had returned. I rinsed the cream from my now unmarked hand and arm, doused myself with scent, breathed deeply, and went out to meet him.

He was once more looking at one of my books. I sat in the chair at my writing table, took down a sheet of paper and my stylus, and stared at the blank page. I knew that if I faced him I might betray myself.

My thoughts were too tangled for me to write. After a moment, I said, "You're turning into quite a scholar."

I heard his snort of laughter from behind me. "I guess I am," he said ruefully, as if his thoughts were far away. It was a new tone from him.

I felt calm enough now to turn toward him. "What are you reading?"

"A history book. Madeline gave it to me."

He seemed to be in the mood to talk. "I learned to read from my mother. She told me what it was like in the cities; she'd lived there before running away."

"She was owned?"

"She was pregnant with me, and they wouldn't let me be born. She ran. We lived with the other humans—there are whole groups out there. They call themselves free." He laughed again. "I couldn't learn anything out there. Forty years and I learned nothing. Most of them don't know what a book is. I had nothing to do after Joan died, so I—" He leaned his head back against the wall. "What a life this is! Human beings!"

I could not catch his meaning, and then there was no need to. The Tall One had appeared in the corner of the room. His thought revealed no emotion.

One of the owned is dead.

The blame naturally fell to Philip. He was an unowned man. His violence had been evident even in his lovemaking.

I had never seen the Owners deal with a disobedient man, but I had occasionally seen the results of their discipline shambling around the city. This time I was witness in my own rooms. One moment Philip was staring in incomprehension—I'm sure he didn't even realize that he was accused—and the next he was equally uncomprehending, with the difference that, looking into his blank face, you knew that he would never comprehend anything again.

The Tall One had me lead him out of our quarters. Philip held my hand with complete trust, and let it go with complete assurance. He stood outside the Tall One's home. The next day, when I forced myself to go see Spender in order to get away from the rooms, I was appalled to find Philip standing there just as I had left him.

All that day I dreaded returning to find him still there. Needlessly: when I came back very late, he was gone.

I have seen him several times since—glimpsed him in crowds of humans, or shuffling alone in deserted corridors, or standing face to the wall in some blind alley. He has grown as thin as the man in my dream. Each time I see him I have to hurry away. We must practice a simple stoicism, accept the fate that is thrown to us. It is a cruel world.

A recent visit from the Tall One has set me to writing this account, compulsively, lights low, late in the sleeping period.

This time he came in the guise of a human: a man of my age, height, and color. I was amazed. I had never heard of such a thing.

We talked, as usual, about fundamental points of philosophy. Then suddenly he said, *Tell me, Matthew. Why did Philip kill the woman.*

It unnerved me to receive that thought while the figure of a man who might have been my twin sat placidly across from me, lips unmoving. My mind whirled.

"I don't know. Men often do things that are hard to understand."

Yes.

"They do not always act in their own best interests."

They are the masters of their fates.

The room was suddenly cold. I had the wild fear that the Tall One had arranged everything, from the beginning—that this had all been a little game to him. I stared hard at the vacant face of this pseudo-man. I trembled on the edge of a wall, a universe of emptiness on either side awaiting my fall. Was he asking me—or telling?

"I don't know," I answered.

Yes.

The face across from me was that of a dead man. The dead man stood and walked out of my room.

THE FRANCHISE

Whoever wants to know the heart and mind of America had better learn baseball.

—Jacques Barzun

ONE

When George Herbert Walker Bush strode into the batter's box to face the pitcher they called the Franchise, it was the bottom of the second, and the Senators were already a run behind.

But Killebrew had managed a bloop double down the right-field line and two outs later still stood on second in the bright October sunlight, waiting to be driven in. The bleachers were crammed full of restless fans in colorful shirts. Far behind Killebrew, Griffith Stadium's green center-field wall zigzagged to avoid the towering oak in Mrs. Mahan's backyard, lending the stadium its crazy dimensions. They said the only players ever to homer into that tree were Mantle and Ruth. George imagined how the stadium would erupt if he did it, drove the first pitch right out of the old ball yard, putting the Senators ahead in the first game of the 1959 World Series. If wishes were horses, his father had told him more than once, then beggars would ride.

George stepped into the box, ground in his back foot, squinted at the pitcher. The first pitch, a fastball, so surprised him that he didn't get his bat off his shoulder. Belt high, it split the middle of the plate, but the umpire called, "Ball!"

"Ball?" Schmidt, the Giants' catcher, grumbled.

"You got a problem?" the umpire said.

"Me? I got no problem." Schmidt tossed the ball back to the pitcher, who shook his head in histrionic Latin American dismay, as if bemoaning the sins of the world that he'd seen only too much of since he'd left Havana eleven years before. "But the Franchise, he no like."

George ignored them and set himself for the next pitch. The big Cuban went into his herky-jerky windup, deceptively slow, then kicked and threw. George was barely into his swing when the ball thwacked into the catcher's glove. "Steerike one!" the umpire called.

He was going to have to get around faster. The next pitch was another fastball, outside and high, but George had already triggered before the release and missed it by a foot, twisting himself around so that he almost fell over.

Schmidt took the ball out of his glove, showed it to George, and threw it back to the mound.

The next was a curve, outside by an inch. Ball two.

The next a fastball that somehow George managed to foul into the dirt.

The next a fastball up under his chin that had him diving into the dirt himself. Ball three. Full count.

An expectant murmur rose in the crowd, then fell to a profound silence, the silence of a church, of heaven, of a lover's secret heart. Was his father among them, breathless, hoping? Thousands awaited the next pitch. Millions more watched on television. Killebrew took a three-step lead off second. The Giants made no attempt to hold him on. The chatter from the Senators' dugout lit up. "Come on, George Herbert Walker Bush, bear down! Come on, Professor, grit up!"

George set himself, weight on his back foot. He cocked his bat, squinted out at the pitcher. The vainglorious Latino gave him a piratical grin, shook off Schmidt's sign. George felt his shoulders tense. Calm, boy, calm, he told himself. You've been shot at, you've faced Prescott Bush across a dining-room table— this is nothing but baseball. But instead of calm he felt panic, and as the Franchise went into his windup his mind stood blank as a stone.

The ball started out right for his head. George jerked back in a desperate effort to get out of the way as the pitch, a curve of prodigious sweep, dropped through the heart of the plate. "Steerike!" the umpire called.

Instantly the scene changed from hushed expectation to sudden movement. The crowd groaned. The players relaxed and began jogging off the field. Killebrew kicked the dirt and walked back to the dugout to get his glove. The organist started up. Behind the big Chesterfield sign in right, the scorekeeper slid another goose egg onto the board for the Senators. Though the whole thing was similar to moments he had experienced more times than he would care to admit during his ten years in the minors, the simple volume of thirty thousand voices sighing in disappointment because he, George Herbert Walker Bush, had failed, left him standing stunned at the plate with the bat limp in his clammy hands. They didn't get thirty thousand fans in Chattanooga.

Schmidt flipped the ball toward the mound. As the Franchise jogged past him, he flashed George that superior smile. "A magnificent swing," he said.

George stumbled back to the dugout. Lemon, heading out to left, shook his head. "Nice try, Professor," the shortstop Consolo said.

"Pull your jock up and get out to first," said Lavagetto, the manager. He spat a stream of tobacco juice onto the sod next to the end of the dugout. "Señor Fidel Castro welcomes you to the bigs."

Two

The Senators lost 7–1. Castro pitched nine innings, allowed four hits, struck out ten. George fanned three times. In the sixth, he let a low throw get by him; the runner ended up on third, and the Giants followed with four unearned runs.

In the locker room his teammates avoided him. Nobody had played well, but George knew they had him pegged as a choker. Lavagetto came through with a few words of encouragement. "We'll get 'em tomorrow," he said. George expected the manager to yank him for somebody who at least wouldn't cost them runs on defense. When he left without saying anything, George was grateful to him for at least letting him go another night before benching him.

Barbara and the boys had been in the stands, but had gone home. They would be waiting for him. He didn't want to go. The place was empty by the time he walked out through the tunnels to the street. His head was filled with images from the game. Castro had toyed with him; he no doubt enjoyed humiliating the son of a U.S. senator. The Cuban's look of heavy-lidded disdain sparked an unaccustomed rage in George. It wasn't good sportsmanship. You played hard, and you won or lost, but you didn't rub the other guy's nose in it. That was bush league, and George, despite his unfortunate name, was anything but bush.

That George Bush should end up playing first base for the Washington Senators in the 1959 World Series was the result of as improbable a sequence of events as had ever conspired to make a man of a rich boy. The key moment had come on a May Saturday in 1948 when he had shaken the hand of Babe Ruth.

That May morning the Yale baseball team was to play Brown, but before the game a ceremony was held to honor Ruth, donating the manuscript of his autobiography to the university library. George, captain of the Yale squad, would accept the manuscript. As he stood before the microphone set up between the pitcher's mound and second base, he was stunned by the gulf between the pale hulk standing before him and the legend he represented. Ruth, only fifty-three on that spring morning, could hardly speak for the throat cancer that was killing him. He gasped out a few words, stooped over, rail thin, no longer the giant he had been in the twenties. George took his hand. It was dry and papery and brown as a leaf in fall. Through his grip George felt the contact with glorious history, with feats of heroism that would never be matched, with 714 home runs and 1,356 extra-base hits, with a lifetime slugging percentage of .690, with the called shot and the sixty-homer season and the 1927 Yankees and the curse of the Red Sox. An electricity surged up his arm and directly into his soul. Ruth had accomplished as much, in his way, as a man could accomplish in a life, more, even, George realized to his astonishment, than had his father, Prescott Bush. He stood there stunned, charged with an unexpected, unasked-for purpose.

He had seen death in the war, had tasted it in the blood that streamed from his forehead when he'd struck it against the tail of the TBM Avenger as he parachuted out of the flaming bomber over the Pacific in 1943. He had felt death's hot breath on his back as he frantically paddled the yellow rubber raft away from Chichi Jima against waves pushing him back into the arms of the Japanese, had felt death draw away and offered up a silent prayer when the conning tower of the U.S.S. *Finback* broke through the agitated seas to save him from a savage fate—to, he always knew, some higher purpose. He had imagined that purpose to be business or public service. Now he recognized that he had been seeing it through his father's eyes, that in fact his fate lay elsewhere. It lay between the chalk lines of a playing field, on the greensward of the infield, within the smells of pine tar and sawdust and chewing tobacco and liniment. He could feel it through the tendons of the fleshless hand of Babe Ruth that he held in his own at that very instant.

The day after he graduated from Yale he signed, for no bonus, with the Cleveland Indians. Ten years later, George had little to show for his bold choice. He wasn't the best first baseman you ever saw. Nobody ever stopped him on the street to ask for his autograph. He never made the Indians, got traded to the Browns. He hung on, bouncing up and down the farm systems of seventh- and eighth-place teams. Every spring he went to Florida with high expectations, every April he started the season in Richmond, in Rochester, in Chattanooga. Just two months earlier he had considered packing it in and looking for another career. Then a series of miracles happened.

Chattanooga was the farm team for the Senators, who hadn't won a pennant since 1933. For fifteen years, under their notoriously cheap owner Clark Griffith, they'd been as bad as you could get. But in 1959 their young third baseman, Harmon Killebrew, hit forty-two home runs. Sluggers Jim Lemon and Roy Sievers had career years. A big Kansas boy named Bob Allison won rookie of the year in center field. Camilo Pascual won twenty-two games, struck out 215 men. A kid named Jim Kaat won seventeen. Everything broke right, including Mickey Mantle's leg. After hovering a couple of games over .500 through the All-Star break, the Senators got hot in August, won ninety games, and finished one ahead of the Yankees.

When, late in August, right fielder Albie Pearson got hurt, Lavagetto switched Sievers to right, and there was George Bush, thirty-five years old, starting at first base for the American League champions in the 1959 World Series against the New York Giants.

The Giants were heavy favorites. Who would bet against a team that fielded Willie Mays, Orlando Cepeda, Willie McCovey, Felipe Alou, and pitchers like Johnny Antonelli, the fireballer Toothpick Sam Jones, and the Franchise, Fidel Castro? If, prior to the series, you'd told George Herbert Walker Bush the Senators were doomed, he would not have disagreed with you. After game one he had no reason to think otherwise.

He stood outside the stadium looking for a cab, contemplating his series record—one game, 0 for 4, one error—when a pale old man in a loud sports coat spoke to him. "Just be glad you're here," the man said.

The man had watery blue eyes, a sharp face. He was thin enough to look ill. "I beg your pardon?"

"You're the fellow the Nats called up in September, right? Remember, even if you never play another inning, at least you were there. You felt the sun on your back, got dirt on your hands, saw the stands full of people from down on the field. Not many get even that much."

"The Franchise made me look pretty sick."

"You have to face him down."

"Easier said than done."

"Don't say—do."

"Who are you, old man?"

The man hesitated. "Name's Weaver. I'm a—a fan. Yes, I'm a baseball fan." He touched the brim of his hat and walked away.

George thought about it on the cab ride home. It did not make him feel much better. When he got back to the cheap furnished apartment they were renting, Barbara tried to console him.

"My father wasn't there, was he?" George said.

"No. But he called after the game. He wants to see you."

"Probably wants to give me a few tips on how to comport myself. Or maybe just gloat."

Bar came around behind his chair, rubbed his tired shoulders. George got up and switched on the television. While he waited for it to warm up, the silence stretched. He faced Barbara. She had put on a few pounds over the years, but he remembered the first time he'd seen her across the dance floor in the red dress. He was seventeen. "What do you think he wants?"

"I don't know, George."

"I haven't seen him around in the last ten years. Have you?"

The TV had warmed up, and Prescott Bush's voice blared out from behind George. "I hope the baseball Senators win," he was saying. "They've had a better year than the Democratic ones."

George twisted down the volume, stared for a moment at his father's handsome face, then snapped it off. "Give me a drink," he told Barbara. He noticed the boys standing in the doorway, afraid. Barbara hesitated, poured a scotch and water.

"And don't stint on the scotch!" George yelled. He turned to Neil. "What are you looking at, you little weasel! Go to bed."

Barbara slammed down the glass so hard the scotch splashed the counter. "What's got into you, George? You're acting like a crazy man."

George took the half-empty glass from her hand. "My father's got into me, that's what. He got into me thirty years ago, and I can't get him out."

Barbara shot him a look in which disgust outweighed pity and went back to the boys' room. George slumped in the armchair, picked up a copy of *Look* and leafed through the pages. He stopped on a Gillette razor ad. Castro smiled out from the page, dark hair slicked back, chin sleek as a curveball, a devastating blonde leaning on his shoulder. Look Sharp, Feel Sharp, *Be* Sharp, the ad told George.

Castro. What did he know about struggle? Yet that egomaniac lout was considered a hero, while he, George Herbert Walker Bush, who at twenty-four had been at the head of every list of the young men most likely to succeed, had accomplished precisely nothing.

People who didn't know any better had assumed that because of his background, money, and education he would grow to be one of the ones who told others what it was necessary for them to do, but George was coming to realize, with a surge of panic, that he was not special. His moment of communion with Babe Ruth had been a delusion, because Ruth was another type of man. Perhaps Ruth was used by the teams that bought and sold him, but inside Ruth was some compulsion that drove him to be larger than the uses to which he was put, so that in the end he deformed those uses, remade the game itself.

George, talented though he had seemed, had no such size. The vital force that had animated his grandfather George Herbert Walker, after whom he was named, the longing after mystery that had impelled the metaphysical poet George Herbert, after whom that grandfather had been named, had diminished into a trickle in George Herbert Walker Bush. No volcanic forces surged inside him. When he listened late in the night, all he could hear of his soul was a thin keening, a buzz like a bug trapped in a jar. *Let me go, let me go,* it whispered.

That old man at the ballpark was wrong. It was not enough, not nearly enough, just to be there. He wanted to be somebody. What good was it just to stand on first base in the World Series if you came away from it a laughingstock? To have your father call you not because you were a hero, but only to remind you once again what a failure you are.

"I'll be damned if I go see him," George muttered to the empty room.

THREE

President Nixon called Lavagetto in the middle of the night with a suggestion for the batting order in the second game. "Put Bush in the number-five slot," Nixon said.

Lavagetto wondered how he was supposed to tell the President of the United States that he was out of his mind. "Yessir, Mr. President."

"See, that way you get another right-handed batter at the top of the order."

Lavagetto considered pointing out to the president that the Giants were pitching a right-hander in game two. "Yessir, Mr. President," Lavagetto said. His wife was awake now, looking at him with irritation from her side of the bed. He put his hand over the mouthpiece and said, "Go to sleep."

"Who is it at this hour?"

"The President of the United States."

"Uh-huh."

Nixon had some observations about one-run strategies. Lavagetto agreed with him until he could get him off the line. He looked at his alarm clock. It was half past two.

Nixon had sounded full of manic energy. His voice dripped dogmatic assurance. He wondered if Nixon was a drinking man. Walter Winchell said that Eisenhower's death had shoved the veep into an office he was unprepared to hold.

Lavagetto shut off the light and lay back down, but he couldn't sleep. What about Bush? Damn Pearson for getting himself hurt. Bush should be down in the minors where he belonged. He looked to be cracking under the pressure like a ripe melon.

But maybe the guy could come through, prove himself. He was no kid. Lavagetto knew from personal experience the pressures of the Series, how the unexpected could turn on the swing of the bat. He recalled that fourth game of the '47 series, his double to right field that cost Floyd Bevens his no-hitter, and the game. Lavagetto had been a thirty-four-year-old utility infielder for the luckless Dodgers, an aging substitute playing out the string at the end of his career. In that whole season he'd hit only one other double. When he'd seen that ball twist past the right fielder, the joy had shot through his chest like lightning. The Dodger fans had gone crazy; his teammates had leapt all over him laughing and shouting and swearing like Durocher himself.

He remembered that, despite the miracle, the Dodgers had lost the Series to the Yankees in seven.

Lavagetto turned over. First in War, First in Peace, Last in the American League . . . that was the Washington Senators. He hoped young Kaat was getting more sleep than he was.

FOUR

Tuesday afternoon, in front of a wild capacity crowd, young Jim Kaat pitched one of the best games by a rookie in the history of the Series. The twenty-year-old left-hander battled Toothpick Sam Jones pitch for pitch, inning for inning. Jones struggled with his control, walking six in the first seven innings, throwing two wild pitches. If it weren't for the overeagerness of the Senators, swinging at balls a foot out of the strike zone, they would surely have scored; instead they squandered opportunity after opportunity. The fans grew restless. They could see it happening, in sour expectation of disaster built up over twenty-five frustrated years: Kaat would pitch brilliantly, and it would be wasted because the Giants would score on some bloop single.

Through seven the game stayed a scoreless tie. By some fluke George could not fathom, Lavagetto, instead of benching him, had moved him up in the batting order. Though he was still without a hit, he had been playing superior defense. In the seventh he snuffed a Giant uprising when he dove to snag a screamer off the bat of Schmidt for the third out, leaving runners at second and third.

Then, with two down in the top of the eighth, Cepeda singled. George moved in to hold him on. Kaat threw over a couple of times to keep the runner honest, with Cepeda trying to judge

Kaat's move. Mays took a strike, then a ball. Cepeda edged a couple of strides away from first.

Kaat went into his stretch, paused, and whipped the ball to first, catching Cepeda leaning the wrong way. Picked off! But Cepeda, instead of diving back, took off for second. George whirled and threw hurriedly. The ball sailed over Consolo's head into left field, and Cepeda went to third. E-3.

Kaat was shaken. Mays hit a screamer between first and second. George dove, but it was by him, and Cepeda jogged home with the lead.

Kaat struck out McCovey, but the damage was done. "You bush-league clown!" a fan yelled. George's face burned. As he trotted off the field, from the Giants' dugout came Castro's shout: "A heroic play, Mr. Rabbit!"

George wanted to keep going through the dugout and into the clubhouse. On the bench his teammates were conspicuously silent. Consolo sat down next to him. "Shake it off," he said. "You're up this inning."

George grabbed his bat and moved to the end of the dugout. First up in the bottom of the eighth was Sievers. He got behind 0-2, battled back as Jones wasted a couple, then fouled off four straight strikes until he'd worked Jones for a walk. The organist played charge lines and the crowd started chanting. Lemon moved Sievers to second. Killebrew hit a drive that brought the people to their feet screaming before it curved just outside the left-field foul pole, then popped out to short. He threw down his bat and stalked back toward the dugout.

"C'mon, professor," Killebrew said as he passed Bush in the on-deck circle. "Give yourself a reason for being here."

Jones was a scary right-hander with one pitch: the heater. In his first three at-bats George had been overpowered; by the last he'd managed a walk. This time he went up with a plan: he was going to take the first pitch, get ahead in the count, then drive the ball.

The first pitch was a fastball just high.

Make contact. Don't force it. Go with the pitch.

The next was another fastball; George swung as soon as Jones let it go and sent a screaming line drive over the third baseman's head. The crowd roared, and he was halfway down the first-base line when the third-base umpire threw up his hands and yelled, "Foul ball!"

He caught his breath, picked up his bat, and returned to the box. Sievers jogged back to second. Schmidt, standing with his hands on his hips, didn't look at George. From the Giants' dugout George heard, "Kiss your luck good-bye, you effeminate rabbit! You rich man's table leavings! You are devoid of even the makings of guts!"

George stepped out of the box. Castro had come down the dugout to the near end and was leaning out, arms braced on the field, hurling his abuse purple faced. Rigney and the pitching coach had him by the shoulders, tugging him back. George turned away, feeling a cold fury in his belly.

He would show them all. He forgot to calculate, swept by rage. He set himself as far back in the box as possible. Jones took off his cap, wiped his forearm across his brow, and leaned over to check the signs. He shook off the first, then nodded and went into his windup.

As soon as he released George swung, and was caught completely off balance by a change-up. "Strike two, you shadow of a man!" Castro shouted. "Unnatural offspring of a snail and a worm! Strike two!"

Jones tempted him with an outside pitch; George didn't bite. The next was another high fastball; George started, then checked his swing. "Ball!" the home-plate ump called. Fidel booed. Schmidt argued, the ump shook his head. Full count.

George knew he should look for a particular pitch, in a particular part of the plate. After ten years of professional ball, this ought to be second nature, but Jones was so wild he didn't have a clue. George stepped out of the box, rubbed his hands on his pants. "Yes, wipe your sweaty hands, mama's boy! You have all the machismo of a bankbook!"

The rage came to his defense. He picked a decision out of the air, arbitrary as the breeze: fastball, outside.

Jones went into his windup. He threw his body forward,

whipped his arm high over his shoulder. Fastball, outside. George swiveled his hips through the box, kept his head down, extended his arms. The contact of the bat with the ball was so slight he wasn't sure he'd hit it at all. A line drive down the right-field line, hooking as it rose, hooking, hooking . . . curling just inside the foul pole into the stands 320 feet away.

The fans exploded. George, feeling rubbery, jogged around first, toward second. Sievers pumped his fist as he rounded third; the Senators were up on their feet in the dugout shouting and slapping each other. Jones had his hands on his hips, head down and back to the plate. George rounded third and jogged across home, where he was met by Sievers, who slugged him in the shoulder, and the rest of his teammates in the dugout, who laughed and slapped his butt.

The crowd began to chant, "SEN-a-TOR, SEN-a-TOR." After a moment George realized they were chanting for him. He climbed out of the dugout again and tipped his hat, scanning the stands for Barbara and the boys. As he did he saw his father in the presidential box, leaning over to speak into the ear of the cheering President Nixon. He felt a rush of hope, ducked his head, and got back into the dugout.

Kaat held the Giants in the ninth, and the Senators won, 2–1.

In the locker room after the game, George's teammates whooped and slapped him on the back. Chuck Stobbs, the clubhouse comic, called him "the Bambino." For a while George hoped that his father might come down to congratulate him. Instead, for the first time in his career, reporters swarmed around him. They fired flashbulbs in salvoes. They pushed back their hats, flipped open their notebooks, and asked him questions.

"What's it feel like to win a big game like this?"

"I'm just glad to be here. I'm not one of these winning-is-everything guys."

"They're calling you the senator. Your father is a senator. How do you feel about that?"

"I guess we're both senators," George said. "He just got to Washington a little sooner than I did."

They liked that a lot. George felt the smile on his face like a frozen mask. For the first time in his life he was aware of the muscles it took to smile, as tense as if they were lifting a weight.

After the reporters left he showered. George wondered what his father had been whispering into the president's ear, while everyone around him cheered. Some sarcastic comment? Some irrelevant political advice?

When he got back to his locker, toweling himself dry, he found a note lying on the bench. He opened it eagerly. It read:

To the Effeminate Rabbit:
Even the rodent has his day. But not when the eagle pitches.
Sincerely,
Fidel Alejandro Castro Ruz

FIVE

That Fidel Castro would go so far out of his way to insult George Herbert Walker Bush would come as no surprise to anyone who knew him. Early in Castro's first season in the majors, a veteran Phillies reliever, after watching Fidel warm up, approached the young Cuban. "Where did you get that curve?" he asked incredulously.

"From you," said Fidel. "That's why you don't have one."

But sparking his reaction to Bush was more than simple egotism. Fidel's antipathy grew from circumstances of background and character that made such animosity as inevitable as the rising of the sun in the east of Oriente province where he had been born thirty-two years before.

Like George Herbert Walker Bush, Fidel was the son of privilege, but a peculiarly Cuban form of privilege, as different from the blue-blooded Bush variety as the hot and breathless climate of Oriente was from chilly New England. Like Bush, Fidel endured a father as parsimonious with his warmth as those New England winters. Young Fidelito grew up well acquainted with the back of Angel Castro's hand, the jeers of classmates who tormented him and his brother Raul for their illegitimacy. Though Angel Castro owned two thousand acres and had risen from common sugarcane laborer to local caudillo, he did not possess the easy assurance of the rich of Havana, for whom Oriente was the Cuban equivalent of Alabama. The Castros were peasants. Fidel's father was illiterate, his mother a maid. No amount of money could erase Fidel's bastardy.

This history raged in Fidelito. Always in a fight, alternating boasts with moody silences, he longed for accomplishment in a fiery way that cast the longing of Bush to impress his own father into a sickly shadow. At boarding school in Santiago, he sought the praise of his teachers and admiration of his schoolmates. At Belén, Havana's exclusive Jesuit preparatory school, he became the champion athlete of all of Cuba. "El Loco Fidel," his classmates called him as, late into the night, at an outdoor court under a light swarming with insects, he would practice basketball shots until his feet were torn bloody and his head swam with forlorn images of the ball glancing off the iron rim.

At the University of Havana, between the scorching expanses of the baseball and basketball seasons, Fidel toiled over the scorching expanse of the law books. He sought triumph in student politics as he did in sports. In the evenings he met in tiny rooms with his comrades and talked about junk pitches and electoral strategy, about the reforms that were only a matter of time because the people's will could not be forever thwarted. They were on the side of history. Larger than even the largest of men, history would overpower anyone unless, like Fidel, he aligned himself with it so as not to be swept under by the tidal force of its inescapable currents.

In the spring of 1948, at the same time George Herbert Walker Bush was shaking the hand of Babe Ruth, these currents transformed Fidel's life. He was being scouted by several major-league teams. In the university he had gained control of his fastball and given birth to a curve of so monstrous an arc that Alex Pompez, the Giants' scout, reported that the well-spoken law student owned "a hook like Bo-Peep." More significantly, Pirates scout Howie Haak observed that Fidel "could throw and think at the same time."

Indeed Fidel could think, though no one could come close to

guessing the content of his furious thought. A war between glory and doom raged within him. Fidel's fury to accomplish things threatened to keep him from accomplishing anything at all. He had made enemies. In the late forties, student groups punctuated elections for head of the law-school class with assassinations. Rival political gangs fought in the streets. Events conspired to drive Fidel toward a crisis. And so, on a single day in 1948, he abandoned his political aspirations, quit school, married his lover, the fair Mirta Diaz Balart, and signed a contract with the New York Giants.

It seemed a fortunate choice. In his rookie year he won fifteen games. After he took the Cy Young Award and was named MVP of the 1951 Series, the sportswriters dubbed him "the Franchise." This past season he had won twenty-nine. He earned, and squandered, a fortune. Controversy dogged him, politics would not let him go, the uniform of a baseball player at times felt much too small. His brother Raul was imprisoned when Batista overthrew the government to avoid defeat in the election of 1952. Fidel made friends among the expatriates in Miami. He protested U.S. policies. His alternative nickname became "the Mouth."

But all along Fidel knew his politics was mere pose. His spouting off to sports reporters did nothing compared to what money might do to help the guerrillas in the Sierra Maestra. Yet he had no money.

After the second game of the Series, instead of returning to the hotel Fidel took a cab down to the Mall. He needed to be alone. It was early evening when he got out at the Washington Monument. The sky beyond the Lincoln Memorial shone orange and purple. The air still held some of the sultry heat of summer, like an evening in Havana. But this was a different sort of capital. These North Americans liked to think of themselves as clean, rational men of law instead of passion, a land of Washingtons and Lincolns, but away from the public buildings it was still a southern city full of ex-slaves. Fidel looked down the Mall toward the bright Capitol, white and towering as a wedding cake, and wondered what he might have become had he continued law school. At one time he had imagined himself the Washington of his own country, a liberating warrior. The true heir of José Martí, scholar, poet, and revolutionary. Like Martí he admired the idealism of the United States, but like him he saw its dark side. Here at the Mall, however, you could almost forget about that in an atmosphere of bogus Greek democracy, of liberty and justice for all. You might even forget that this liberty could be bought and sold, a franchise purchasable for cold cash.

Fidel walked along the pool toward the Lincoln Memorial. The floodlights lit up the white columns, and inside shone upon the brooding figure of Lincoln. Despite his cynicism, Fidel was caught by the sight of it. He had been to Washington only once before, for the All-Star Game in 1956. He remembered walking through Georgetown with Mirta on his arm, feeling tall and handsome, ignoring the scowl of the maître d' in the restaurant who clearly disapproved of two such dark ones in his establishment.

He'd triumphed but was not satisfied. He had forced others to admit his primacy through the power of his will. He had shown them, with his strong arm, the difference between right and wrong. He was the Franchise. He climbed up the steps into the Memorial, read the words of Lincoln's Second Inaugural address engraved on the wall. THE PROGRESS OF OUR ARMS UPON WHICH ALL ELSE CHIEFLY DEPENDS IS AS WELL KNOWN TO THE PUBLIC AS TO MYSELF . . . But he was still the crazy Cuban, taken little more seriously than Desi Arnaz, and the minute that arm that made him a useful commodity should begin to show signs of weakening—in that same minute he would be undone. IT MAY SEEM STRANGE THAT ANY MEN SHOULD DARE TO ASK A JUST GOD'S ASSISTANCE IN WRINGING THEIR BREAD FROM THE SWEAT OF OTHER MEN'S FACES BUT LET US JUDGE NOT THAT WE BE NOT JUDGED.

Judge not? Perhaps Lincoln could manage it, but Fidel was a different sort of man.

In the secrecy of his mind Fidel could picture another world than the one he lived in. The marriage of love to Mirta had long since gone sour, torn apart by Fidel's lust for renown on the ball field and his lust for the astonishing women who fell like fruit from the trees into the laps of players such as he. More than once he felt grief over his faithlessness. He knew his solitude to be just punishment. That was the price of greatness, for, after all, greatness was a crime and deserved punishment.

Mirta was gone now, and their son with her. She worked for the hated Batista. He thought of Raul languishing in Batista's prison on the Isle of Pines. Batista, embraced by this United States that ran Latin America like a company store. Raul suffered for the people, while Fidel ate in four-star restaurants and slept with a different woman in every city, throwing away his youth, and the money he earned with it, on excrement.

He looked up into the great sad face of Lincoln. He turned from the monument to stare out across the Mall toward the gleaming white shaft of the Washington obelisk. It was full night now. Time to amend his life.

Six

The headline in the *Post* the next morning read, SENATOR BUSH EVENS SERIES. The story mentioned that Prescott Bush had shown up in the sixth inning and sat beside Nixon in the presidential box. But nothing more.

Bar decided not to go up to New York for the middle games of the Series. George traveled with the team to the Roosevelt Hotel. The home run had done something for him. He felt a new confidence.

The game-three starters were the veteran southpaw Johnny Antonelli for the Giants and Pedro Ramos for the Senators. The echoes of the national anthem had hardly faded when Allison led off for the Senators with a home run into the short porch in left field. The Polo Grounds fell dead silent. The Senators scored three runs in the first; George did his part, hitting a change-up into right center for a double, scoring the third run of the inning.

In the bottom half of the first the Giants came right back, tying it up on Mays's three-run homer.

After that the Giants gradually wore Ramos down, scoring a single run in the third and two in the fifth. Lavagetto pulled him for a pinch hitter in the sixth with George on third and Consolo at first, two outs. But Aspromonte struck out, ending the inning.

Though Castro heckled George mercilessly throughout the game and the brash New York fans joined in, he played above himself. The Giants eventually won, 8–3, but George went three for five. Despite his miserable first game he was batting .307 for the Series. Down two games to one, the Washington players felt the loss, but had stopped calling him "George Herbert Walker Bush" and started calling him "the Senator."

SEVEN

Lavagetto had set an eleven o'clock curfew, but Billy Consolo persuaded George to go out on the town. The Hot Corner was a dive on Seventh Avenue with decent Italian food and cheap drinks. George ordered a club soda and tried to get into the mood. Ramos moaned about the plate umpire's strike zone, and Consolo changed the subject.

Consolo had been a bonus boy; in 1953 the Red Sox had signed him right out of high school for $50,000. He had never panned out. George wondered if Consolo's career had been any easier to take than his own. At least nobody had hung enough expectations on George for him to be called a flop.

Stobbs was telling a story. "So the Baseball Annie says to him, 'But will you respect me in the morning?' and the shortstop says, 'Oh baby, I'll respect you like crazy!' "

While the others were laughing, George headed for the men's room. Passing the bar, he saw, in a corner booth, Fidel Castro talking to a couple of men in slick suits. Castro's eyes flicked over him but registered no recognition.

When George came out the men in suits were in heated conversation with Castro. In the back of the room somebody dropped a quarter into the jukebox, and Elvis Presley's slinky "Money Honey" blared out. Bush had no use for rock and roll. He sat at the table, ignored his teammates' conversation, and kept an eye on Castro. The Cuban was strenuously making some point, stabbing the tabletop with his index finger. After a minute George noticed that someone at the bar was watching them, too. It was the pale old man he had seen at Griffith Stadium.

On impulse, George went up to him. "Hello, old-timer. You really must be a fan, if you followed the Series up here. Can I buy you a drink?"

The man turned decisively from watching Castro, as if deliberately putting aside some thought. He seemed about to smile but did not. Small red splotches colored his face. "Buy me a ginger ale."

George ordered a ginger ale and another club soda and sat on the next stool. "Money honey, if you want to get along with me," Elvis sang.

The old man sipped his drink. "You had yourself a couple of good games," he said. "You're in the groove."

"I just got some lucky breaks."

"Don't kid me. I know how it feels when it's going right. You know just where the next pitch is going to be, and there it is. Somebody hits a line drive right at you, you throw out your glove and snag it without even thinking. You're in the groove."

"It comes from playing the game a long time."

The old man snorted. "Do you really believe this guff you spout? Or are you just trying to hide something?"

"What do you mean? I've spent ten years playing baseball."

"And you expect me to believe you still don't know anything about it? Experience doesn't explain the groove." The man looked as if he were watching something far away. "When you're in that groove you're not playing the game, the game is playing you."

"But you have to plan your moves."

The old man looked at him as if he were from Mars. "Do you plan your moves when you're making love to your wife?" He finished his ginger ale, took another look back at Castro, then left.

Everyone, it seemed, knew what was wrong with him. George felt steamed. As if that wasn't enough, as soon as he returned to the table Castro's pals left and the Cuban swaggered over to

George, leaned into him, and blew cigar smoke into his face. "I know you, George Herbert Walker Bush," he said, "Sen-a-tor Rabbit. The rich man's son."

George pushed him away. "You know, I'm beginning to find your behavior darned unconscionable, compadre."

"I stand here quaking with fear," Castro said. He poked George in the chest. "Back home in Biran we had a pen for the pigs. The gate of this pen was in disrepair. But it is still a fact, Senator Rabbit, that the splintered wooden gate of that pigpen, squealing on its rusted hinges, swung better than you."

Consolo started to get up, but George put a hand on his arm. "Say, Billy, our Cuban friend here didn't by any chance help you pick out this restaurant tonight, did he?"

"What, are you crazy? Of course not."

"Too bad. I thought if he did, we could get some good Communist food here."

The guys laughed. Castro leaned over.

"Very funny, Machismo Zero." His breath reeked of cigar smoke, rum, and garlic. "I guarantee that after tomorrow's game you will be even funnier."

Eight

Fidel had never felt sharper than he did during his warmups the afternoon of the fourth game. It was a cool fall day, partial overcast with a threat of rain, a breeze blowing out to right. The chill air only invigorated him. Never had his curve had more bite, his screwball more movement. His arm felt supple, his legs strong. As he strode in from the bullpen to the dugout, squinting out at the apartment buildings on Coogan's Bluff towering over the stands, a great cheer rose from the crowd.

Before the echoes of the national anthem had died he walked the first two batters, on eight pitches. The fans murmured. Schmidt came out to talk with him. "What's wrong?"

"Nothing is wrong," Fidel said, sending him back.

He retired Lemon on a pop fly and Killebrew on a fielder's choice. Bush came to the plate with two outs and men on first and second. The few Washington fans who had braved the Polo Grounds set up a chant: "SEN-a-TOR, SEN-a-TOR!"

Fidel studied Bush. Beneath Bush's bravado he could see panic in every motion of the body he wore like an ill-fitting suit. Fidel struck him out on three pitches.

Kralick held the Giants scoreless through three innings.

As the game progressed Fidel's own personal game, the game of pitcher and batter, settled into a pattern. Fidel mowed down the batters after Bush in the order with predictable dispatch, but fell into trouble each time he faced the top of the order, getting just enough outs to bring Bush up with men on base and the game in the balance. He did this four times in the first seven innings.

Each time Bush struck out.

In the middle of the seventh, after Bush fanned to end the inning, Mays sat down next to Fidel on the bench. "What the hell do you think you're doing?"

Mays was the only player on the Giants whose stature rivaled that of the Franchise. Fidel, whose success came as much from craft as physical prowess, could not but admit that Mays was the most beautiful ball player he had ever seen. "I'm shutting out the Washington Senators in the fourth game of the World Series," Fidel said.

"What's this mickey mouse with Bush? You trying to make him look bad?"

"One does not have to try very hard."

"Well, cut it out—before you make a mistake with Killebrew or Sievers."

Fidel looked him dead in the eyes. "I do not make mistakes."

The Giants entered the ninth with a 3–0 lead. Fidel got two quick outs, then gave up a single to Sievers and walked Lemon and Killebrew to load the bases. Bush, at bat, represented the lead run. Schmidt called time and came out again. Rigney hurried out from the dugout, and Mays, to the astonishment of the crowd, came all the way in from center. "Yank him," he told Rigney.

Rigney looked exasperated. "Who's managing this team, Willie?"

"He's setting Bush up to be the goat."

Rigney looked at Fidel. Fidel looked at him. "Just strike him out," the manager said.

Fidel rubbed up the ball and threw three fastballs through the heart of the plate. Bush missed them all. By the last strike the New York fans were screaming, rocking the Polo Grounds with a parody of the Washington chant: "Sen-a-TOR, Sen-a-TOR, BUSH BUSH, BUSH!" and exploding into fits of laughter. The Giants led the series, 3–1.

NINE

George made the cabbie drop him off at the corner of Broadway and Pine, in front of the old Trinity Church. He walked down Wall Street through crowds of men in dark suits, past the Stock Exchange to the offices of Brown Brothers, Harriman. In the shadows of the buildings the fall air felt wintry. He had not been down here in more years than he cared to remember.

The secretary, Miss Goode, greeted him warmly; she still remembered him from his days at Yale. Despite Prescott Bush's move to the Senate, they still kept his inner office for him, and as George stood outside the door he heard a piano. His father was singing. He had a wonderful singing voice, of which he was too proud.

George entered. Prescott Bush sat at an upright piano, playing Gilbert and Sullivan:

> "Go, ye heroes, go to glory
> Though you die in combat gory.
> Ye shall live in song and story.
> Go to immortality!"

Still playing, he glanced over his shoulder at George, then turned back and finished the verse:

"Go to death, and go to slaughter;
Die, and every Cornish daughter
With her tears your grave shall water.
Go, ye heroes, go and die!"

George was all too familiar with his father's theatricality. Six feet four inches tall, with thick salt-and-pepper hair and a handsome, craggy face, he carried off his Douglas Fairbanks imitation without any hint of self-consciousness. It was a quality George had tried to emulate his whole life.

Prescott adjusted the sheet music and swiveled his piano stool around. He waved at the sofa against the wall beneath his shelf of golfing trophies and photos of the Yale Glee Club. "Sit down, son. I'm glad you could make it. I know you must have a lot on your mind."

George remained standing. "What did you want to see me about?"

"Relax, George. This isn't the dentist's office."

"If it were I would know what to expect."

"Well, one thing you can expect is to hear me tell you how proud I am."

"Proud? Did you see that game yesterday?"

Prescott Bush waved a hand. "Temporary setback. I'm sure you'll get them back this afternoon."

"Isn't it a little late for compliments?"

Prescott looked at him as calmly as if he were appraising some stock portfolio. His bushy eyebrows quirked a little higher. "George, I want you to sit down and shut up."

Despite himself, George sat. Prescott got up and paced to the window, looked down at the street, then started pacing again, his big hands knotted behind his back. George began to dread what was coming.

"George, I have been indulgent of you. Your entire life, despite my misgivings, I have treated you with kid gloves. You are not a stupid boy; at least your grades in school suggested you weren't. You've got that Phi Beta Kappa key, too—which only goes to show you what they are worth." He held himself very erect. "How old are you now?"

"Thirty-five."

Prescott shook his head. "Thirty-five? Lord. At *thirty-five* you show no more sense than you did at seventeen, when you told me that you intended to enlist in the navy. Despite the fact that the secretary of war himself, God-forbid-me *Franklin D. Roosevelt's* secretary of war, had just told the graduating class that you, the cream of the nation's youth, could best serve your country by going to college instead of getting shot up on some Pacific Island."

He strolled over to the piano, flipped pensively through the sheet music on top. "I remember saying to myself that day that maybe you knew something I didn't. You were young. I recalled my own recklessness in the first war. God knew we needed to lick the Japanese. But that didn't mean a boy of your parts and prospects should do the fighting. I prayed you'd survive and that by the time you came back you'd have grown some sense." Prescott closed the folder of music and faced him.

George, as he had many times before, instead of looking into his father's eyes looked at a point beyond his left ear. At the moment, just past that ear he could see half of a framed photograph of one of his father's singing groups. Probably the Silver Dollar Quartet. He could not make out the face of the man on the end of the photo. Some notable businessman, no doubt. A man who sat on four boards of directors making decisions that could topple the economies of six banana republics while he went to the club to shoot eight-handicap golf. Someone like Prescott Bush.

"When you chose this baseball career," his father said, "I finally realized you had serious problems facing reality. I would think the dismal history of your involvement in this sport might have taught you something. Now, by the grace of God and sheer luck you find yourself, on the verge of your middle years, in the spotlight. I can't imagine how it happened. But I know one thing: you must take advantage of this situation. You must seize the brass ring before the carousel stops. As soon as the Series is over I want you to take up a career in politics."

George stopped looking at the photo. His father's eyes were on his. "Politics? But, Dad, I thought I could become a coach."

"A coach?"

"A coach. I don't know anything about politics. I'm a baseball player. Nobody is going to elect a baseball player."

Prescott Bush stepped closer. He made a fist, beginning to be carried away by his own rhetoric. "Twenty years ago, maybe, you would be right. But, George, times are changing. People want an attractive face. They want somebody famous. It doesn't matter so much what they've done before. Look at Eisenhower. He had no experience of government. The only reason he got elected was because he was a war hero. Now you're a war hero, or at least we can dress you up into a reasonable facsimile of one. You're Yale educated, a brainy boy. You've got breeding and class. You're not bad looking. And thanks to this children's game, you're famous—for the next two weeks, anyway. So after the Series we strike while the iron's hot. You retire from baseball. File for Congress on the Republican ticket in the third Connecticut district."

"But I don't even live in Connecticut."

"Don't be contrary, George. You're a baseball player; you live on the road. Your last stable residence before you took up this, this—baseball—was New Haven. I've held an apartment there for years in your name. That's good enough for the people we're going to convince."

His father towered over him. George got up, retreated toward the window. "But I don't know anything about politics!"

"So? You'll learn. Despite the fact I've been against your playing baseball, I have to say that it will work well for you. It's the national game. Every kid in the country wants to be a ballplayer, most of the adults do, too. It's hard enough for people from our class to overcome the prejudice against money, George. Baseball gives you the common touch. Why, you'll probably be the only Republican in the Congress ever to have showered with a Negro. On a regular basis, I mean."

"I don't even like politics."

"George, there are only two kinds of people in the world, the employers and the employees. You were born and bred to the former. I will not allow you to persist in degrading yourself into one of the latter."

"Dad, really, I appreciate your trying to look out for me. Don't get me wrong, gratitude's my middle name. But I love baseball. There's some big opportunities there, I think. Down in Chattanooga I made some friends. I think I can be a good coach, and eventually I'll wear a manager's uniform."

Prescott Bush stared at him. George remembered that look when he'd forgotten to tie off the sailboat one summer up in Kennebunkport. He began to wilt. Eventually his father shook his head. "It comes to me at last that you do not possess the wits that God gave a Newfoundland retriever."

George felt his face flush. He looked away. "You're just jealous because I did what you never had the guts to do. What about you and your golf? You, you—dilettante! I'm going to be a manager!"

"George, if I want to I can step into that outer office, pick up the telephone, and in fifteen minutes set in motion a chain of events that will guarantee you won't get a job mopping toilets in the clubhouse."

George retreated to the window. "You think you can run my life? You just want me to be another appendage of Senator Bush. Well, you can forget it! I'm not your boy anymore."

"You'd rather spend the rest of your life letting men like this Communist Castro make a fool of you?"

George caught himself before he could completely lose his temper. Feeling hopeless, he drummed his knuckles on the windowsill, staring down into the narrow street. Down below them brokers and bankers hustled from meeting to meeting trying to make a buck. He might have been one of them. Would his father have been any happier?

He turned. "Dad, you don't know anything. Try for once to understand. I've never been so alive as I've been for moments—just moments out of eleven years—on the ball field. It's truly American."

"I agree with you, George—it's as American as General Motors. Baseball is a product. You players are the assembly-line workers who make it. But you refuse to understand that, and that's your undoing. Time eats you up, and you end up in the dustbin, a wasted husk."

George felt the helpless fury again. "Dad, you've got to—"

"Are you going to tell me I *have to* do something, George?" Prescott Bush sat back down at the piano, tried a few notes. He peeked over his shoulder at George, unsmiling, and began again to sing:

> *"Go and do your best endeavor,*
> *And before all links we sever,*
> *We will say farewell for ever.*
> *Go to glory and the grave!*
>
> *"For your foes are fierce and ruthless,*
> *False, unmerciful and truthless.*
> *Young and tender, old and toothless,*
> *All in vain their mercy crave."*

George stalked out of the room, through the secretary's office, and down the corridor toward the elevators. It was all he could do to keep from punching his fist through the rosewood paneling. He felt his pulse thrumming in his temples, slowing as he waited for the dilatory elevator to arrive, rage turning to depression.

Riding down he remembered something his mother had said to him twenty years before. He'd been one of the best tennis players at the River Club in Kennebunkport. One summer, in front of the whole family, he lost a championship match. He knew he'd let them down, and tried to explain to his mother that he'd only been off his game.

"You don't have a game," she'd said.

The elevator let him out into the lobby. On Seventh Avenue he stepped into a bar and ordered a beer. On the TV in the corner, sound turned low, an announcer was going over the highlights of the Series. The TV switched to an image of some play in the field. George heard a reference to "Senator Bush," but he couldn't tell which one of them they were talking about.

Ten

A few of the pitchers, including Camilo Pascual, the young right-hander who was to start game five, were the only others in the clubhouse when George showed up. The tone was grim. Nobody wanted to talk about how their season might be over in a few hours. Instead they talked fishing.

Pascual was nervous; George was keyed tighter than a Christmas toy. Ten years of obscurity, and now hero one day, goat the next. The memory of his teammates' hollow words of encouragement as he'd slumped back into the dugout each time Castro struck him out made George want to crawl into his locker and hide. The supercilious brown bastard. What kind of man would go out of his way to humiliate him?

Stobbs sauntered in, whistling. He crouched into a batting stance, swung an imaginary Louisville Slugger through Kralick's head, then watched it sail out into the imaginary bleachers. "Hey, guys, I got an idea," he said. "If we get the lead today, let's call time out."

But they didn't get the lead. By the top of the second, they were down 3–0. But Pascual, on the verge of being yanked, settled down. The score stayed frozen through six. The Senators finally got to Jones in the seventh when Allison doubled and Killebrew hit a towering home run into the bullpen in left center: 3–2, Giants. Meanwhile the Senators' shaky relief pitching held, as the Giants stranded runners in the sixth and eighth and hit into three double plays.

By the top of the ninth the Giants still clung to the 3–2 lead, three outs away from winning the Series, and the rowdy New York fans were gearing up for a celebration. The Senators' dugout was grim, but they had the heart of the order up: Sievers, Lemon, Killebrew. Between them they had hit ninety-four home runs that season. They had also struck out almost three hundred times.

Rigney went out to talk to Jones, then left him in, though he had Stu Miller up and throwing in the bullpen. Sievers took the first pitch for a strike, fouled off the second, and went down swinging at a high fastball. The crowd roared.

Lemon went into the hole 0–2, worked the count even, and grounded out to second.

The crowd, on their feet, chanted continuously now. Fans pounded on the dugout roof, and the din was deafening. Killebrew stepped into the batter's box, and George moved up to the on-deck circle. On one knee in the dirt, he bowed his head and prayed that Killer would get on base.

"He's praying!" Castro shouted from the Giants' dugout. "Well might you pray, Sen-a-tor Bush!"

Killebrew called time and spat toward the Giants. The crowd screamed abuse at him. He stepped back into the box. Jones went into his windup. Killebrew took a tremendous cut and missed. The next pitch was a change-up that Killebrew mistimed and slammed five hundred feet down the left-field line into the upper deck—foul. The crowd quieted. Jones stepped off the mound, wiped his brow, shook off a couple of signs, and threw another fastball that Killebrew slapped into right for a single.

That was it for Jones. Rigney called in Miller. Lavagetto came out and spoke to George. "All right. He won't try anything tricky. Look for the fastball."

George nodded, and Lavagetto bounced back into the dugout. "Come on, George Herbert Walker Bush!" Consolo yelled. George tried to ignore the crowd and the Giants' heckling while Miller warmed up. His stomach was tied into twelve knots. He avoided looking into the box seats where he knew his father sat. Politics. What the blazes did he want with politics?

Finally Miller was ready. "Play ball!" the ump yelled. George stepped into the box.

He didn't wait. The first pitch was a fastball. He turned on it, made contact, but got too far under it. The ball soared out into left, a high, lazy fly. George slammed down his bat and, heart sinking, legged it out. The crowd cheered, and Alou circled back to make the catch. George was rounding first, his head down, when he heard a stunned groan from fifty thousand throats at once. He looked up to see Alou slam his glove to the ground. Miller, on the mound, did the same. The Senators' dugout was leaping insanity. Somehow, the ball had carried far enough to drop into the overhanging upper deck, 250 feet away. Home run. Senators lead, 4–3.

"Lucky bastard!" Castro shouted as Bush rounded third.

Stobbs shut them down in the ninth, and the Senators won.

Eleven

SENATOR BUSH SAVES WASHINGTON! the headlines screamed. MAKES CASTRO SEE RED. They were comparing it to the 1923 Series, held in these same Polo Grounds, where Casey Stengel, a thirty-two-year-old outfielder who'd spent twelve years in the majors without doing anything that might cause anyone to remember him, batted .417 and hit home runs to win two games.

Reporters stuck to him like flies on sugar. The pressure of released humiliation loosened George's tongue. "I know Castro's type," he said, snarling what he hoped was a good imitation of a manly snarl. "At the wedding he's the bride, at the funeral he's the dead person. You know, the corpse. That kind of poor sportsmanship just burns me up. But I've been around. He can't get my goat because of where I've got it in the guts department."

The papers ate it up. Smart money had said the Series would never go back to Washington. Now they were on the train to Griffith Stadium, and if the Senators were going to lose, at least the home fans would have the pleasure of going through the agony in person.

Game six was a slugfest. Five homers: McCovey, Mays, and Cepeda for the Giants; Naragon and Lemon for the Senators. Kaat and Antonelli were both knocked out early. The lead changed back and forth three times.

George hit three singles, a sacrifice fly, and drew a walk. He scored twice. The Senators came from behind to win, 10–8. In the ninth, George sprained his ankle sliding into third. It was all he could do to hobble into the locker room after the game.

"It doesn't hurt," George told the reporters. "Bar always says, and she knows me better than anybody, go ahead and ask around, 'You're the game one, George.' Not the gamy one, mind you!" He laughed, smiled a crooked smile.

"A man's gotta do what a man's gotta do," he told them. "That strong but silent type of thing. My father said so."

TWELVE

Fonseca waited until Fidel emerged into the twilight outside the Fifth Street stadium exit. As Fonseca approached, his hand on the slick automatic in his overcoat pocket, his mind cast back to their political years in Havana, where young men such as they, determined to seek prominence, would be as likely to face the barrel of a pistol as an electoral challenge. Ah, nostalgia.

"Pretty funny, that Sen-a-TOR Bush," Fonseca said. He shoved Fidel back toward the exit. Nobody was around.

If Fidel was scared, a slight narrowing of his eyes was the only sign. "What is this about?"

"Not a thing. Raul says hello."

"Hello to Raul."

"Mirta says hello, too."

"You haven't spoken to her." Fidel took a cigar from his mohair jacket, fished a knife from a pocket, trimmed off the end, and lit it with a battered Zippo. "She doesn't speak with exiled radicals. Or mobsters."

Fonseca was impressed by the performance. "Are you going to do this job, finally?"

"I can only do my half. One cannot make a sow look like a ballet dancer."

"It is not apparent to our friends that you're doing your half."

"Tell them I am truly frightened, Luis." He blew a plume of smoke. It was dark now, almost full night. "Meanwhile, I am hungry. Let me buy you a Washington dinner."

The attitude was all too typical of Fidel, and Fonseca was sick of it. He had fallen under Fidel's spell back in the university,

thought him some sort of great man. In 1948 his self-regard
could be justified as necessary boldness. But when the head of the
National Sports Directory was shot dead in the street, Fonseca
had not been the only one to think Fidel was the killer. It was a
gesture of suicidal machismo of the sort that Fidel admired. Gun-
men scoured the streets for them. While Fonseca hid in a series
of airless apartments, Fidel got a quick tryout with the Giants,
married Mirta, and abandoned Havana, leaving Fonseca and
their friends to deal with the consequences.

"If you don't take care, Fidel, our friends will buy you a
Washington grave."

"They are not my friends—or yours."

"No, they aren't. But this was our choice, and you have to go
through with it." Fonseca watched a beat cop stop at the corner,
then turn away down the street. He moved closer, stuck the pistol into Fidel's ribs. "You know, Fidel, I have a strong desire to
shoot you right now. Who cares about the World Series? It would
be pleasant just to see you bleed."

The tip of Fidel's cigar glowed in the dark. "This Bush would
be no hero then."

"But I would be."

"You would be a traitor."

Fonseca laughed. "Don't say that word again. It evokes too
many memories." He plucked the cigar from Fidel's hand, threw
it onto the sidewalk. "Athletes should not smoke."

He pulled the gun back, drew his hand from his overcoat, and
crossed the street.

THIRTEEN

The night before, the Russians announced they had shot down a
U.S. spy plane over the Soviet Union. A pack of lies, President
Nixon said. No such planes existed.

Meanwhile, on the clubhouse radio, a feverish announcer
was discussing strategy for game seven. A flock of telegrams had
arrived to urge the Senators on. Tacked on the bulletin board in
the locker room, they gave pathetic glimpses into the hearts of the

thousands who had for years tied their sense of well-being to the fate of a punk team like the Senators.

Show those racially polluted commie-symps what Americans stand for.

My eight year old son, crippled by polio, sits up in his wheelchair so that he can watch the games on TV.

Jesus Christ, creator of the heavens and earth, is with you.

As George laced up his spikes over his aching ankle in preparation for the game, thinking about facing Castro one last time, it came to him that he was terrified.

In the last week he had entered an atmosphere he had not lived in since Yale. He was a hero. People had expectations of him. He was admired and courted. If he had received any respect before, it was the respect given to someone who refused to quit when every indication shouted he ought to try something else. He did not have the braggadocio of a Castro. Yet here, miraculously, he was shining.

Except he *knew* that Castro was better than he was, and he knew that anybody who really knew the game knew it, too. He knew that this week was a fluke, a strange conjunction of the stars that had knocked him into the "groove," as the old man in the bar had said. It could evaporate at any instant. It could already have evaporated.

Lavagetto and Mr. Griffith came in and turned off the radio. "Okay, boys," Lavagetto said. "People in this city been waiting a long time for this game. A lot of you been waiting your whole careers for it, and you younger ones might not get a lot of chances to play in the seventh game of the World Series. Nobody gave us a chance to be here today, but here we are. Let's make the most of it, go out there and kick the blazes out of them, then come back in and drink some champagne!"

The team whooped and headed out to the field.

Coming up the tunnel, the sound of cleats scraping damp

concrete, the smell of stale beer and mildew, Bush could see a sliver of the bright grass and white baselines, the outfield fence and crowds in the bleachers, sunlight so bright it hurt his eyes. When the team climbed the dugout steps onto the field, a great roar rose from the throats of the thirty thousand fans. He had never heard anything so beautiful, or frightening. The concentrated focus of their hope swelled George's chest with unnameable emotion, brought tears to his eyes, and he ducked his head and slammed his fist into his worn first baseman's glove.

The teams lined up on the first- and third-base lines for the National Anthem. The fans began cheering even before the last line of the song faded away, and George jogged to first, stepping on the bag for good luck. His ankle twinged; his whole leg felt hot. Ramos finished his warmups, the umpire yelled "Play ball!" and they began.

Ramos set the Giants down in order in the top of the first. In the home half Castro gave up a single to Allison, who advanced to third on a single by Lemon. Killebrew walked. Bush came up with bases loaded, one out. He managed a fly ball to right, and Allison beat the throw to the plate. Castro struck out Bertoia to end the inning. 1–0, Senators.

Ramos retired the Giants in order in the second. In the third, Lemon homered to make it 2–0.

Castro had terrific stuff, but seemed to be struggling with his control. Or else he was playing games again. By the fourth inning he had seven strikeouts to go along with the two runs he'd given up. He shook off pitch after pitch, and Schmidt went out to argue with him. Rigney talked to him in the dugout, and the big Cuban waved his arms as if emphatically arguing his case.

Schmidt homered for the Giants in the fourth, but Ramos was able to get out of the inning without further damage. Senators, 2–1.

In the bottom of the fourth, George came up with a man on first. Castro struck him out on a high fastball that George missed by a foot.

In the Giants' fifth, Spencer doubled off the wall in right. Alou singled him home to tie the game, and one out later Mays launched a triple over Allison's head into the deepest corner of center field, just shy of the crazy wall protecting Mrs. Mahan's backyard. Giants up, 3–2. The crowd groaned. As he walked out to the mound, Lavagetto was already calling for a left-hander to face McCovey. Ramos kicked the dirt, handed him the ball, and headed to the showers, and Stobbs came on to pitch to McCovey. He got McCovey on a grounder to George at first, and Davenport on a pop fly.

The Senators failed to score in the bottom of the fifth and sixth, but in the seventh George, limping for real now, doubled in Killer to tie the game, and was driven home, wincing as he forced weight down on his ankle, on a single by Naragon. Senators 4–3. The crowd roared.

Rigney came out to talk to Castro, but Castro convinced him to let him stay in. He'd struck out twelve already, and the Giants' bullpen was depleted after the free-for-all in game six.

The score stayed that way through the eighth. By the top of the ninth the crowd was going wild in the expectation of a world championship. Lavagetto had pulled Stobbs, who sat next to Bush in his warmup jacket, and put in the right-hander Hyde, who'd led the team in saves.

The Giants mounted another rally. On the first pitch, Spencer laid a bunt down the first-base line. Hyde stumbled coming off the mound, and George, taken completely by surprise, couldn't get to it on his bad foot. He got up limping, and the trainer came out to ask him if he could play. George was damned if he would let it end so pitifully, and shook him off. Alou grounded to first, Spencer advancing. Cepeda battled the count full, then walked.

Mays stepped into the box. Hyde picked up the rosin bag, walked off the mound, and rubbed up the ball. George could see he was sweating. He stepped back onto the rubber, took the sign, and threw a high fastball that Mays hit four hundred feet, high into the bleachers in left. The Giants leapt out of the dugout, slapping Mays on the back, congratulating each other. The fans tore their clothing in despair, slumped into their seats, cursed and moaned. The proper order had been restored to the universe. George looked over at Castro, who sat in the dugout impassively. Lavagetto came out to talk to Hyde; the crowd booed when the manager left him in, but Hyde managed to get them out of the inning without further damage. As the Senators left the field the organist tried to stir the crowd, but despair had settled over them like a lead blanket. Giants, 6–4.

In the dugout Lavagetto tried to get them up for the inning. "This is it, gentlemen. Time to prove we belong here."

Allison had his bat out and was ready to go to work before the umpire had finished sweeping off the plate. Castro threw three warmups and waved him into the box. When Allison lined a single between short and third, the crowd cheered and rose to their feet. Sievers, swinging for the fences, hit a nubbler to the mound, a sure double play. Castro pounced on it in good time, but fumbled the ball, double-clutched, and settled for the out at first. The fans cheered.

Rigney came out to talk it over. He and Schmidt stayed on the mound a long time, Castro gesturing wildly, insisting he wasn't tired. He had struck out the side in the eighth.

Rigney left him in, and Castro rewarded him by striking out Lemon for his seventeenth of the game, a new World Series record. Two down. Killebrew was up. The fans hovered on the brink of nervous collapse. The Senators were torturing them; they were going to drag this out to the last fatal out, not give them a clean killing or a swan-dive fade—no, they would hold out the chance of victory to the last moment, then crush them dead.

Castro rubbed up the ball, checked Allison over his shoulder, shook off a couple of Schmidt's signs, and threw. He got Killebrew in an 0–2 hole, then threw four straight balls to walk him. The crowd noise reached a frenzy.

And so, as he stepped to the plate in the bottom of the ninth, two outs, George Herbert Walker Bush represented the winning run, the potential end to twenty-seven years of Washington frustration, the apotheosis of his life in baseball, or the ignominious end of it. Castro had him set up again, to be the glorious goat for the entire Series. His ankle throbbed. "C'mon, Senator!" Lavagetto shouted. "Make me a genius!"

Castro leaned forward, shook off Schmidt's call, shook off another. He went into his windup, then paused, ball hidden in his glove, staring soberly at George—not mocking, not angry, certainly not intimidated—as if he were looking down from a reconnaissance plane flying high above the ballpark. George tried not to imagine what he was thinking.

Then Castro lifted his knee, strode forward, and threw a fat hanging curve, the sweetest, dopiest, laziest pitch he had thrown all day. George swung. As he did, he felt the last remaining strength of the dying Babe Ruth course down his arms. The ball kissed off the sweet spot of the bat and soared, pure and white as a six-year-old's prayer, into the left-field bleachers.

The stands exploded. Fans boiled onto the field even before George touched second. Allison did a kind of hopping balletic dance around the bases ahead of him, a cross between Nureyev and a man on a pogo stick. The Senators ran out of the dugout and bear-hugged George as he staggered around third; like a broken-field runner he struggled through the fans toward home. A weeping fat man in a plaid shirt, face contorted by ecstasy, blocked his way to the plate, and it was all he could do to keep from knocking him over.

As his teammates pulled him toward the dugout, he caught a glimpse over his shoulder of the Franchise standing on the mound, watching the melee and George at the center of it with an inscrutable expression on his face. Then George was pulled back into the maelstrom and surrendered to his bemused joy.

FOURTEEN

Long after everyone had left and the clubhouse was deserted, Fidel dressed, and instead of leaving walked back out to the field. The stadium was dark, but in the light of the moon he could make out the trampled infield and the obliterated base paths. He stood on the mound and looked around at the empty stands. He was about to leave when someone called him from the dugout. "Beautiful, isn't it?"

Fidel approached. It was a thin man in his sixties. He wore a sporty coat and a white dress shirt open at the collar. "Yes?" Fidel asked.

"The field is beautiful."

Fidel sat next to him on the bench. They stared across the diamond. The wind rustled the trees beyond the outfield walls. "Some people think so," Fidel said.

"I thought we might have a talk," the man said. "I've been waiting around the ballpark before the last few games trying to get hold of you."

"I don't think we have anything to talk about, Mr. . . ."

"Weaver. Buck Weaver."

"Mr. Weaver. I don't know you, and you don't know me."

The man came close to smiling. "I know about winning the World Series. And losing it. I was on the winning team in 1917, and the losing one in 1919."

"You would not be kidding me, old man?"

"No. For a long time after the second one, I couldn't face a ballpark. Especially during the Series. I might have gone to quite a few, but I couldn't make myself do it. Now I go to the games every chance I get."

"You still enjoy baseball."

"I love the game. It reminds me where my body is buried." As he said all of this the man kept smiling, as if it were a funny story he was telling, and a punch line waited in the near future.

"You should quit teasing me, old man," Fidel said. "You're still alive."

"To all outward indications I'm alive, most of the year now. For a long time I was dead the year round. Eventually I was dead only during the summer, and now it's come down to just the Series."

"You are the mysterious one. Why do you not simply tell me what you want with me?"

"I want to know why you did what you just did."

"What did I do?"

"You threw the game."

Fidel watched him. "You cannot prove that."

"I don't have to prove it. I know it, though."

"How do you know it?"

"Because I've seen it done before."

From somewhere in his boyhood, Fidel recalled the name now. Buck Weaver. The 1919 Series. "The Black Sox. You were one of them."

That appeared to be the punch line. The man smiled. His eyes were set in painful nets of wrinkles. "I was never one of them. But I knew about it, and that was enough for that bastard Landis to kick me out of the game."

"What does that have to do with me?"

"At first I wanted to stop you. Now I just want to know why you did it. Are you so blind to what you've got that you could throw it away? You're not a fool. Why?"

"I have my reasons, old man. Eighty thousand dollars, for one."

"You don't need the money."

"My brother, in prison, does. The people in my home do."

"Don't give me that. You don't really care about them."

Fidel let the moment stretch, listening to the rustling of the wind through the trees, the traffic in the distant street. "No? Well, perhaps. Perhaps I did it just because I *could*. Because the game betrayed me, because I wanted to show it is as corrupt as the *mierda* around it. It's not any different from the world. You know how it works. How every team has two black ballplayers—the star and the star's roommate." He laughed. "It's not a religion, and this place"—he gestured at Griffith Stadium looming in the night before them—"is not a cathedral."

"I thought that way, when I was angry," Weaver said. "I was a young man. I didn't know how much it meant to me until they took it away."

"Old man, you would have lost it regardless. How old were you? Twenty-five? Thirty? In ten years it would have been taken from you anyway, and you'd be in the same place you are now."

"But I'd have my honor. I wouldn't be a disgrace."

"That's only what other people say. Why should you let their ignorance affect who you are?"

"Brave words. But I've lived it. You haven't—yet." Plainly

upset, Weaver walked out onto the field to stand at third base. He crouched; he looked in toward the plate. After a while he straightened, a frail old man, and called in toward Fidel: "When I was twenty-five, I stood out here; I thought I had hold of a base-ball in my hand. It turned out it had hold of me."

He came back and stood at the top of the dugout steps. "Don't worry, I'm not going to tell. I didn't then, and I won't now."

Weaver left, and Fidel sat in the dugout.

FIFTEEN

They used the photo of George's painfully shy, crooked smile, a photograph taken in the locker room after he'd been named MVP of the 1959 World Series, on his first campaign poster.

In front of the photographers and reporters, George was greeted by Mr. Griffith. And his father. Prescott Bush wore a po-litical smile as broad as his experience of what was necessary to impress the world. He put his arm around his son's shoulders, and although George was a tall man, it was apparent that his fa-ther was still a taller one.

"I'm proud of you, son," Prescott said, in a voice loud enough to be heard by everyone. "You've shown the power of decency and persistence in the face of hollow boasts."

Guys were spraying champagne, running around with their hair sticky and their shirts off, whooping and shouting and slap-ping each other on the back. Even his father's presence couldn't entirely deflect George's satisfaction. He had done it. Proved him-self for once and for all. He wished Bar and the boys could be there. He wanted to shout in the streets, to stay up all night, be pursued by beautiful women. He sat in front of his locker and pa-tiently answered the reporters' questions at length, repeatedly. Only gradually did the furor settle down. George glanced across the room to the brightly lit corner where Prescott was talking, on camera, with a television reporter.

It was clear that his father was setting him up for this planned political career. It infuriated him that he assumed he could con-trol George so easily, but at the same time George felt confused about what he really wanted for himself. As he sat there in the diminishing chaos, Lavagetto came over and sat down beside him. The manager was still high from the victory.

"I don't believe it!" Lavagetto said. "I thought he was crazy, but old Tricky Dick must have known something I didn't!"

"What do you mean?"

"Mean?—nothing. Just that the president called after the first game and told me to bat you behind Killebrew. I thought he was crazy. But it paid off."

George remembered Prescott Bush whispering into Nixon's ear. He felt a crushing weight on his chest. He stared over at his father in the TV lights, not hearing Lavagetto.

But as he watched, he wondered. If his father had indeed fixed the Series, then everything he'd accomplished came to nothing. But his father was an honorable man. Besides, Nixon was noted for his sports obsession, full of fantasies because he hadn't succeeded himself. His calling Lavagetto was the kind of thing he would do anyway. Winning had been too hard for it to be a setup. No, Castro had wanted to humiliate George, and George had stood up to him.

The reporter finished talking to his father; the TV lights snapped off. George thanked Lavagetto for the faith the manager had shown in him, and limped over to Prescott Bush.

"Feeling pretty good, George?"

"It was a miracle we won. I played above myself."

"Now, don't take what I said back in New York so much to heart. You proved yourself equal to the challenge, that's what." Prescott lowered his voice. "Have you thought any more about the proposition I put to you?"

George looked his father in the eye. If Prescott Bush felt any discomfort, there was no trace of it in his patrician's gaze.

"I guess maybe I've played enough baseball," George said.

His father put his hand on George's shoulder; it felt like a burden. George shrugged it off and headed for the showers.

Many years later, as he faced the Washington press corps in the East Room of the White House, George Herbert Walker Bush was to remember that distant afternoon, in the ninth inning of the seventh game of the World Series, when he'd stood in the batter's box against the Franchise. He had not known then what he now understood: that, like his father, he would do anything to win.

THE PURE PRODUCT

arrived in Kansas City at one o'clock on the afternoon of the thirteenth of August. A Tuesday. I was driving the beige 1983 Chevrolet Citation that I had stolen two days earlier in Pocatello, Idaho. The Kansas plates on the car I'd taken from a different car in a parking lot in Salt Lake City. Salt Lake City was founded by the Mormons, whose god tells them that in the future Jesus Christ will come again.

I drove through Kansas City with the windows open and the sun beating down through the windshield. The car had no air conditioning, and my shirt was stuck to my back from seven hours behind the wheel. Finally I found a hardware store, "Hector's" on Wornall. I pulled into the lot. The Citation's engine dieseled after I turned off the ignition; I pumped the accelerator once and it coughed and died. The heat was like syrup. The sun drove shadows deep into corners, left them flattened at the feet of the people on the sidewalk. It made the plate glass of the store window into a dark negative of the positive print that was Wornall Road. August.

The man behind the counter in the hardware store I took to be Hector himself. He looked like Hector, slain in vengeance beneath the walls of paintbrushes—the kind of semifriendly, publicly optimistic man who would tell you about his crazy wife and his ten-penny nails. I bought a gallon of kerosene and a plastic paint funnel, put them into the trunk of the Citation, then walked down the block to the Mark Twain Bank. Mark Twain died at the age of seventy-five with a heart full of bitter accusations against the Calvinist god and no hope for the future of humanity. Inside the bank I went to one of the desks, at which sat a Nice Young Lady. I asked about starting a business checking account. She gave me a form to fill out, then sent me to the office of Mr. Graves.

Mr. Graves wielded a formidable handshake. "What can I do for you, Mr. . . . ?"

"Tillotsen, Gerald Tillotsen," I said. Gerald Tillotsen, of Tacoma, Washington, died of diphtheria at the age of four weeks—on September 24, 1938. I have a copy of his birth certificate.

"I'm new to Kansas City. I'd like to open a business account here, and perhaps take out a loan. I trust this is a reputable bank? What's your exposure in Brazil?" I looked around the office as if Graves were hiding a woman behind the hatstand, then flashed him my most ingratiating smile.

Mr. Graves did his best. He tried smiling back, then looked as if he had decided to ignore my little joke. "We're very sound, Mr. Tillotsen."

I continued smiling.

"What kind of business do you own?"

"I'm in insurance. Mutual Assurance of Hartford. Our regional office is in Oklahoma City, and I'm setting up an agency here, at 103rd and State Line." Just off the interstate.

He examined the form. His absorption was too tempting.

"Maybe I can fix you up with a policy? You look like dead meat."

Graves's head snapped up, his mouth half-open. He closed it and watched me guardedly. The dullness of it all! How I tire. He was like some cow, like most of the rest of you in this silly age, unwilling to break the rules in order to take offense. "Did he really say that?" he was thinking. "Was that his idea of a joke? He looks normal enough." I did look normal, exactly like an insurance agent. I was the right kind of person, and I could do anything. If at times I grate, if at times I fall a little short of or go a little beyond convention, there is not one of you who can call me to account.

Graves was coming around. All business.

"Ah—yes, Mr. Tillotsen. If you'll wait a moment, I'm sure we can take care of this checking account. As for the loan—"

"Forget it."

That should have stopped him. He should have asked after my credentials, he should have done a dozen things. He looked at me, and I stared calmly back at him. And I knew that, looking into my honest blue eyes, he could not think of a thing.

"I'll just start the checking account with this money order," I said, reaching into my pocket. "That will be acceptable, won't it?"

"It will be fine," he said. He took the form and the order over to one of the secretaries while I sat at the desk. I lit a cigar and blew some smoke rings. I'd purchased the money order the day before in a post office in Denver. Thirty dollars. I didn't intend to use the account very long. Graves returned with my sample checks, shook hands earnestly, and wished me a good day. Have a *good* day, he said. I *will,* I said.

Outside, the heat was still stifling. I took off my sports coat. I was sweating so much I had to check my hair in the sideview mirror of my car. I walked down the street to a liquor store and bought a bottle of chardonnay and a bottle of Chivas Regal. I got some paper cups from a nearby grocery. One final errand, then I could relax for a few hours.

In the shopping center that I had told Graves would be the location for my nonexistent insurance office, I had noticed a sporting goods store. It was about three o'clock when I parked in the lot and ambled into the shop. I looked at various golf clubs: irons, woods, even one set with fiberglass shafts. Finally I selected a set of eight Spalding irons with matching woods, a large bag, and several boxes of Top-Flites. The salesman, who had been occupied with another customer at the rear of the store, hustled up, his eyes full of commission money. I gave him little time to think. The total cost was $612.32. I paid with a check drawn on my new account, cordially thanked the man, and had him carry all the equipment out to the trunk of the car.

I drove to a park near the bank; Loose Park, they called it. I felt loose. Cut loose, drifting free, like one of the kites people were flying that had broken its string and was ascending into the sun. Beneath the trees it was still hot, though the sunlight was reduced to a shuffling of light and shadow on the brown grass. Kids ran, jumped, swung on playground equipment. I uncorked my bottle of wine, filled one of the paper cups, and lay down beneath a tree, enjoying the children, watching young men and women walking along the footpaths.

A girl approached. She didn't look any older than seventeen. Short, slender, with clean blond hair cut to her shoulders. Her shorts were very tight. I watched her unabashedly; she saw me watching and left the path to come over to me. She stopped a few feet away, hands on her hips. "What are you looking at?" she asked.

"Your legs," I said. "Would you like some wine?"

"No thanks. My mother told me never to accept wine from strangers." She looked right through me.

"I take what I can get from strangers," I said. "Because I'm a stranger, too."

I guess she liked that. She was different. She sat down and we chatted for a while. There was something wrong about her imitation of a seventeen-year-old; I began to wonder whether hookers worked the park. She crossed her legs and her shorts got tighter. "Where are you from?" she asked.

"San Francisco. But I've just moved here to stay. I have a part interest in the sporting goods store at the Eastridge Plaza."

"You live near here?"

"On West Eighty-ninth." I had driven down Eighty-ninth on my way to the bank.

"I live on Eighty-ninth! We're neighbors."

It was exactly what one of my own might have said to test me. I took a drink of wine and changed the subject. "Would you like to visit San Francisco someday?"

She brushed her hair back behind one ear. She pursed her lips, showing off her fine cheekbones. "Have you got something going?" she asked, in queerly accented English.

"Excuse me?"

"I said, have you got something going," she repeated, still with the accent—the accent of my own time.

I took another sip. "A bottle of wine," I replied in good midwestern 1980s.

She wasn't having any of it. "No artwork, please. I don't like artwork."

I had to laugh: my life was devoted to artwork. I had not met anyone real in a long time. At the beginning I hadn't wanted to, and in the ensuing years I had given up expecting it. If there's anything more boring than you people it's us people. But that was an old attitude. When she came to me in K.C. I was lonely and she was something new.

"Okay," I said. "It's not much, but you can come for the ride. Do you want to?"

She smiled and said yes.

As we walked to my car, she brushed her hip against my leg. I switched the bottle to my left hand and put my arm around her shoulders in a fatherly way. We got into the front seat, beneath the trees on a street at the edge of the park. It was quiet. I reached over, grabbed her hair at the nape of her neck, and jerked her face toward me, covering her little mouth with mine. Surprise: she threw her arms around my neck and slid across the seat into my lap. We did not talk. I yanked at the shorts; she thrust her hand into my pants. St. Augustine asked the Lord for chastity, but not right away.

At the end she slipped off me, calmly buttoned her blouse, brushed her hair back from her forehead. "How about a push?" she asked. She had a nail file out and was filing her index fingernail to a point.

I shook my head and looked at her. She resembled my grand-

mother. I had never run into my grandmother, but she had a hellish reputation. "No thanks. What's your name?"

"Call me Ruth." She scratched the inside of her left elbow
with her nail. She leaned back in her seat, sighed deeply. Her
eyes became a very bright, very hard blue.

While she was aloft I got out, opened the trunk, emptied the
rest of the chardonnay into the gutter, and used the funnel to fill
the bottle with kerosene. I plugged it with a kerosene-soaked
rag. Afternoon was sliding into evening as I started the car and
cruised down one of the residential streets. The houses were like
those of any city or town of that era of the Midwest USA: white
frame, forty or fifty years old, with large porches and small front
yards. Dying elms hung over the street. Shadows stretched across
the sidewalks. Ruth's nose wrinkled; she turned her face lazily toward me, saw the kerosene bottle, and smiled.

Ahead on the left-hand sidewalk I saw a man walking
leisurely. He was an average sort of man, middle-aged, probably
just returning from work, enjoying the quiet pause dusk was
bringing to the hot day. It might have been Hector; it might have
been Graves. It might have been any one of you. I punched the
cigarette lighter, readied the bottle in my right hand, steering
with my leg as the car moved slowly forward.

"Let me help," Ruth said. She reached out and steadied the
wheel with her slender fingertips. The lighter popped out. I
touched it to the rag; it smoldered and caught. Greasy smoke
stung my eyes. By now the man had noticed us. I hung my arm,
holding the bottle, out the window. As we passed him, I tossed
the bottle at the sidewalk like a newsboy tossing a rolled-up
newspaper. The rag flamed brighter as it whipped through the
air; the bottle landed at his feet and exploded, dousing him with
burning kerosene. I floored the accelerator; the motor coughed,
then roared, the tires and Ruth both squealing in delight. I could
see the flaming man in the rearview mirror as we sped away.

On the Great American Plains, the summer nights are not silent.
The fields sing the summer songs of insects—not individual

sounds, but a high-pitched drone of locusts, crickets, cicadas, small chirping things for which I have no names. You drive along the superhighway and that sound blends with the sound of wind rushing through your opened windows, hiding the thrum of the automobile, conveying the impression of incredible velocity. Wheels vibrate, tires beat against the pavement, the steering wheel shudders, alive in your hands, droning insects alive in your ears. Reflecting posts at the roadside leap from the darkness with metronomic regularity, glowing amber in the headlights, only to vanish abruptly into the ready night when you pass. You lose track of time, how long you have been on the road, where you are going. The fields scream in your ears like a thousand lost, mechanical souls, and you press your foot to the accelerator, hurrying away.

When we left Kansas City that evening we were indeed hurrying. Our direction was in one sense precise: Interstate 70, more or less due east, through Missouri in a dream. They might remember me in Kansas City, at the same time wondering who and why. Mr. Graves scans the morning paper over his grapefruit: MAN BURNED BY GASOLINE BOMB. The clerk wonders why he ever accepted an unverified counter check, without a name or address printed on it, for six hundred dollars. The check bounces. They discover it was a bottle of chardonnay. The story is pieced together. They would eventually figure out how—I wouldn't lie to myself about that (I never lie to myself)—but the why would always escape them. Organized crime, they would say. A plot that misfired.

Of course, they still might have caught me. The car became more of a liability the longer I held on to it. But Ruth, humming to herself, did not seem to care, and neither did I. You have to improvise those things; that's what gives them whatever interest they have.

Just shy of Columbia, Missouri, Ruth stopped humming and asked me, "Do you know why Helen Keller can't have any children?"

"No."

"Because she's dead."

I rolled up the window so I could hear her better. "That's pretty funny," I said.

"Yes. I overheard it in a restaurant." After a minute she asked, "Who's Helen Keller?"

"A dead woman." An insect splattered itself against the windshield. The lights of the oncoming cars glinted against the smear it left.

"She must be famous," said Ruth. "I like famous people. Have you met any? Was that man you burned famous?"

"Probably not. I don't care about famous people anymore." The last time I had anything to do, even peripherally, with anyone famous was when I changed the direction of the tape over the lock in the Watergate so Frank Wills would see it. Ruth did not look like the kind who would know about that. "I was there for the Kennedy assassination," I said, "but I had nothing to do with it."

"Who was Kennedy?"

That made me smile. "How long have you been here?" I pointed at her tiny purse. "That's all you've got with you?"

She slid across the seat and leaned her head against my shoulder. "I don't need anything else."

"No clothes?"

"I left them in Kansas City. We can get more."

"Sure," I said.

She opened the purse and took out a plastic Bayer aspirin case. From it she selected two blue-and-yellow caps. She shoved her palm up under my nose. "Serometh?"

"No thanks."

She put one of the caps back into the box and popped the other under her nose. She sighed and snuggled tighter against me. We had reached Columbia and I was hungry. When I pulled in at a McDonald's she ran across the lot into the shopping mall before I could stop her. I was a little nervous about the car and sat watching it as I ate (Big Mac, small Dr. Pepper). She did not come back. I crossed the lot to the mall, found a drugstore, and bought some cigars. When I strolled back to the car she was waiting for me, hopping from one foot to another and tugging at the door handle. Serometh makes you impatient. She was wearing a pair of shiny black pants, pink- and white-checked sneakers, and a hot pink blouse. " 's go!" she hissed.

I moved even slower. She looked like she was about to wet herself, biting her soft lower lip with a line of perfect white teeth. I dawdled over my keys. A security guard and a young man in a shirt and tie hurried out of the mall entrance and scanned the lot. "Nice outfit," I said. "Must have cost you something."

She looked over her shoulder, saw the security guard, who saw her. "Hey!" he called, running toward us. I slid into the car, opened the passenger door. Ruth had snapped open her purse and pulled out a small gun. I grabbed her arm and yanked her into the car; she squawked and her shot went wide. The guard fell down anyway, scared shitless. For the second time that day I tested the Citation's acceleration; Ruth's door slammed shut and we were gone.

"You scut," she said as we hit the entrance ramp of the interstate. "You're a scut-pumping Conservative. You made me miss." But she was smiling, running her hand up the inside of my thigh. I could tell she hadn't ever had so much fun in the twentieth century.

For some reason I was shaking. "Give me one of those serometh," I said.

Around midnight we stopped in St. Louis at a Holiday Inn. We registered as Mr. and Mrs. Gerald Bruno (an old acquaintance) and paid in advance. No one remarked on the apparent difference in our ages. So discreet. I bought a copy of the *Post-Dispatch,* and we went to the room. Ruth flopped down on the bed, looking bored, but thanks to her gunplay I had a few more things to take care of. I poured myself a glass of Chivas, went into the bathroom, removed the toupee and flushed it down the toilet, showered, put a new blade in my old razor, and shaved the rest of the hair from my head. The Lex Luthor look. I cut my scalp. That got me laughing, and I could not stop. Ruth peeked through the doorway to find me dabbing the crown of my head with a bloody Kleenex.

"You're a wreck," she said.

I almost fell off the toilet laughing. She was absolutely right. Between giggles I managed to say, "You must not stay anywhere too long, if you're as careless as you were tonight."

She shrugged. "I bet I've been at it longer than you." She stripped and got into the shower. I got into bed.

The room enfolded me in its gold-carpet green-bedspread mediocrity. Sometimes it's hard to remember that things were ever different. In 1596 I rode to court with Essex; I slept in a chamber of supreme garishness (gilt escutcheons in the corners of the ceiling, pink cupids romping on the walls), in a bed warmed by any of the trollops of the city I might want. And there in the Holiday Inn I sat with my drink, in my pastel blue pajama bottoms, reading a late-twentieth-century newspaper, smoking a cigar. An earthquake in Peru estimated to have killed eight thousand in Lima alone. Nope. A steel worker in Gary, Indiana, discovered to be the murderer of six prepubescent children, bodies found buried in his basement. Perhaps. The president refuses to enforce the ruling of his Supreme Court because it "subverts the will of the American people." Probably not.

We are everywhere. But not everywhere.

Ruth came out of the bathroom, saw me, did a double take. "You look—perfect!" she said. She slid in the bed beside me, naked, and sniffed at my glass of Chivas. Her lip curled. She looked over my shoulder at the paper. "You can understand that stuff?"

"Don't kid me. Reading is a survival skill. You couldn't last here without it."

"Wrong."

I drained the scotch. Took a puff on the cigar. Dropped the paper to the floor beside the bed. I looked her over. Even relaxed, the muscles in her arms and along the tops of her thighs were well defined.

"You even smell like one of them," she said.

"How did you get the clothes past their store security? They have those beeper tags clipped to them."

"Easy. I tried on the shoes and walked out when they weren't looking. In the second store I took the pants into a dressing room, cut the alarm tag out of the waistband, and put them on. I held the alarm tag that was clipped to the blouse in my armpit and walked out of that store, too. I put the blouse on in the mall women's room."

"If you can't read, how did you know which was the women's room?"

"There's a picture on the door."

I felt tired and old. Ruth moved close. She rubbed her foot up my leg, drawing the pajama leg up with it. Her thigh slid across my groin. I started to get hard. "Cut it out," I said. She licked my nipple.

I could not stand it. I got off the bed. "I don't like you."

She looked at me with true innocence. "I don't like you, either."

Although he was repulsed by the human body, Jonathan Swift was passionately in love with a woman named Esther Johnson. "What you did at the mall was stupid," I said. "You would have killed that guard."

"Which would have made us even for the day."

"Kansas City was different."

"We should ask the cops there what they think."

"You don't understand. That had some grace to it. But what you did was inelegant. Worst of all it was not gratuitous. You stole those clothes for yourself, and I hate that." I was shaking.

"Who made all these laws?"

"I did."

She looked at me with amazement. "You're not just a Conservative. You're gone native!"

I wanted her so much I ached. "No I haven't," I said, but even to me my voice sounded frightened.

Ruth got out of the bed. She glided over, reached one hand around to the small of my back, pulled herself close. She looked up at me with a face that held nothing but avidity. "You can do whatever you want," she whispered. With a feeling that I was losing everything, I kissed her. You don't need to know what happened then.

I woke when she displaced herself: there was a sound like the sweep of an arm across fabric, a stirring of air to fill the place where she had been. I looked around the still brightly lit room. It was not yet morning. The chain was across the door; her clothes lay on the dresser. She had left the aspirin box beside my bottle of scotch.

She was gone. Good, I thought, now I can go on. But I found that I couldn't sleep, could not keep from thinking. Ruth must be very good at that, or perhaps her thought is a different kind of thought from mine. I got out of the bed, resolved to try again but still fearing the inevitable. I filled the tub with hot water. I got in, breathing heavily. I took the blade from my razor. Holding my arm just beneath the surface of the water, hesitating only a moment, I cut deeply one, two, three times along the veins in my left wrist. The shock was still there, as great as ever. With blood streaming from me I cut the right wrist. Quickly, smoothly. My heart beat fast and light, the blood flowed frighteningly; already the water was stained. I felt faint—yes—it was going to work this time, yes. My vision began to fade—but in the last moments before consciousness fell away I saw, with sick despair, the futile wounds closing themselves once again, as they had so many times before. For in the future the practice of medicine may progress to the point where men need have little fear of death.

The dawn's rosy fingers found me still unconscious. I came to myself about eleven, my head throbbing, so weak I could hardly rise from the cold bloody water. There were no scars. I stumbled into the other room and washed down one of Ruth's megamphetamines with two fingers of scotch. I felt better immediately. It's funny how that works sometimes, isn't it? The maid knocked as I was cleaning the bathroom. I shouted for her to come back later, finished as quickly as possible, and left the hotel immediately. I ate Shredded Wheat with milk and strawberries for breakfast. I was full of ideas. A phone book gave me the location of a likely country club.

The Oak Hill Country Club of Florissant, Missouri, is not a spectacularly wealthy institution, or at least it does not give that impression. I'll bet you that the membership is not as purely white as the stucco clubhouse. That was all right with me. I parked the Citation in the mostly empty parking lot, hauled my new equipment from the trunk, and set off for the locker room, trying hard to look like a dentist. I successfully ran the gauntlet of the pro shop, where the proprietor was telling a bored caddy why the Cardinals would fade in the stretch. I could hear running water from the showers as I shuffled into the locker room and slung the bag into a corner. Someone was singing the "Ode to Joy," abominably.

I began to rifle through the lockers, hoping to find an open one with someone's clothes in it. I would take the keys from my benefactor's pocket and proceed along my merry way. Ruth would have accused me of self-interest; there was a moment in which I accused myself. Such hesitation is the seed of failure: as I paused before a locker containing a likely set of clothes, another golfer entered the room along with the locker-room attendant. I immediately began undressing, lowering my head so that the locker door hid my face. The golfer was soon gone, but the attendant sat down and began to leaf through a worn copy of *Penthouse*. I could come up with no better plan than to strip and enter the showers. Amphetamine daze. Perhaps the kid would develop a hard-on and go to the john to take care of it.

There was only one other man in the shower, the symphonic soloist, a somewhat portly gentleman who mercifully shut up as soon as I entered. He worked hard at ignoring me. I ignored him in return: *alle Menschen werden Brüder.* I waited a long five minutes after he left; two more men came into the showers, and I walked out with what composure I could muster. The locker-room boy was stacking towels on a table. I fished a five from my jacket in the locker and walked up behind him. Casually I took a towel.

"Son, get me a pack of Marlboros, will you?"

He took the money and left.

In the second locker I found a pair of pants that contained the keys to some sort of Audi. I was not choosy. Dressed in record time, I left the new clubs beside the rifled locker. My note read, "The pure products of America go crazy." There were three eligible cars in the lot, two 4000s and a Fox. The key would not open the door of the Fox. I was jumpy, but almost home free, coming around the front of a big Chrysler. . . .

"Hey!"

My knee gave way and I ran into the fender of the car. The keys slipped out of my hand and skittered across the hood to the ground, jingling. Grimacing, I hopped toward them, plucked them up, glancing over my shoulder at my pursuer as I stooped. It was the locker-room attendant.

"Your cigarettes." He looked at me the way a sixteen-year-old looks at his father; that is, with bored skepticism. All our gods in the end become pitiful. It was time for me to be abruptly courteous. As it was, he would remember me too well.

"Thanks," I said. I limped over, put the pack into my shirt pocket. He started to go, but I couldn't help myself. "What about my change?"

Oh, such an insolent silence! I wonder what you told them when they asked you about me, boy. He handed over the money. I tipped him a quarter, gave him a piece of Mr. Graves's professional smile. He studied me. I turned and inserted the key into the lock of the Audi. A fifty percent chance. Had I been the praying kind I might have prayed to one of those pitiful gods. The key turned without resistance; the door opened. The kid slouched back toward the clubhouse, pissed at me and his lackey's job. Or perhaps he found it in his heart to smile. Laughter—the Best Medicine.

A bit of a racing shift, then back to Interstate 70. My hip twinged all the way across Illinois.

I had originally intended to work my way east to Buffalo, New York, but after the Oak Hill business I wanted to cut it short. If

I stayed on the interstate I was sure to get caught; I had been lucky to get as far as I had. Just outside of Indianapolis I turned onto Route 37 north to Fort Wayne and Detroit.

I was not, however, entirely crowed. Twenty-five years in one time had given me the right instincts, and with the coming of the evening and the friendly insects to sing me along, the boredom of the road became a new recklessness. Hadn't I already been seen by too many people in those twenty-five years? Thousands had looked into my honest face—and where were they? Ruth had reminded me that I was not stuck here. I would soon make an end to this latest adventure one way or another, and once I had done so, there would be no reason in God's green world to suspect me.

And so: north of Fort Wayne, on Highway 6 east, a deserted country road (what was he doing there?), I pulled over to pick up a young hitchhiker. He wore a battered black leather jacket. His hair was short on the sides, stuck up in spikes on top, hung over his collar in back; one side was carrot-orange, the other brown with a white streak. His sign, pinned to a knapsack, said "?" He threw the pack into the backseat and climbed into the front.

"Thanks for picking me up." He did not sound like he meant it. "Where you going?"

"Flint. How about you?"

"Flint's as good as anywhere."

"Suit yourself." We got up to speed. I was completely calm. "You should fasten your seat belt," I said.

"Why?"

The surly type. "It's not just a good idea. It's the law."

He ignored me. He pulled a crossword puzzle book and a pencil from his jacket pocket. "How about turning on the light."

I flicked on the dome light for him. "I like to see a young man improve himself," I said.

His look was an almost audible sigh. "What's a five-letter word for 'the lowest point'?"

"Nadir," I replied.

"That's right. How about 'widespread'; four letters."

"Rife."

"You're pretty good." He stared at the crossword for a

minute, then rolled down his window and threw the book, and the pencil, out of the car. He rolled up the window and stared at his reflection in it. I couldn't let him get off that easily. I turned off the interior light, and the darkness leapt inside.

"What's your name, son? What are you so mad about?"

"Milo. Look are you queer? If you are, it doesn't matter to me but it will cost you . . . if you want to do anything about it."

I smiled and adjusted the rearview mirror so I could watch him—and he could watch me. "No, I'm not queer. The name's Loki." I extended my right hand, keeping my eyes on the road.

He looked at the hand. "Loki?"

As good a name as any. "Yes. Same as the Norse god."

He laughed. "Sure, Loki. Anything you like. Fuck you."

Such a musical voice. "Now there you go. Seems to me, Milo—if you don't mind my giving you my unsolicited opinion—that you have something of an attitude problem." I punched the cigarette lighter, reached back and pulled a cigar from my jacket on the backseat, in the process weaving the car all over Highway 6. I bit the end off the cigar and spat it out the window, stoked it up. My insects wailed. I cannot explain to you how good I felt.

"Take for instance this crossword puzzle book. Why did you throw it out the window?"

I could see Milo watching me in the mirror, wondering whether he should take me seriously. The headlights fanned out ahead of us, the white lines at the center of the road pulsing by like a rapid heartbeat. Take a chance, Milo. What have you got to lose?

"I was pissed," he said. "It's a waste of time. I don't care about stupid games."

"Exactly. It's just a game, a way to pass the time. Nobody ever really learns anything from a crossword puzzle. Corporation lawyers don't get their Porsches by building their word power with crosswords, right?"

"I don't care about Porsches."

"Neither do I, Milo. I drive an Audi."

Milo sighed.

"I know, Milo. That's not the point. The point is that it's all a game, crosswords or corporate law. Some people devote their lives to Jesus; some devote their lives to artwork. It all comes to pretty much the same thing. You get old. You die."

"Tell me something I don't already know."

"Why do you think I picked you up, Milo? I saw your question mark and it spoke to me. You probably think I'm some pervert out to take advantage of you. I have a funny name. I don't talk like your average middle-aged businessman. Forget about that." The old excitement was upon me; I was talking louder and louder, leaning on the accelerator. The car sped along. "I think you're as troubled by the materialism and cant of life in America as I am. Young people like you, with orange hair, are trying to find some values in a world that offers them nothing but crap for ideas. But too many of you are turning to extremes in response. Drugs, violence, religious fanaticism, hedonism. Some, like you I suspect, to suicide. Don't do it, Milo. Your life is too valuable." The speedometer touched eighty, eighty-five. Milo fumbled for his seat belt but couldn't find it.

I waved my hand, holding the cigar, at him. "What's the matter, Milo? Can't find the belt?" Ninety now. A pickup went by us going the other way, the wind of its passing beating at my head and shoulder. Ninety-five.

"Think, Milo! If you're upset with the present, with your parents and the schools, think about the future. What will the future be like if this trend toward valuelessness continues in the next hundred years? Think of the impact of the new technologies! Gene splicing, gerontology, artificial intelligence, space exploration, biological weapons, nuclear proliferation! All accelerating this process! Think of the violent reactionary movements that could arise—are arising already, Milo, as we speak—from people's desire to find something to hold on to. Paint yourself a picture, *Milo,* of the kind of man or woman another hundred years of this process might produce!"

"What are you talking about?" He was terrified.

"I'm talking about the survival of values in America! Simply that." Cigar smoke swirled in front of the dashboard lights, and my voice had reached a shout. Milo was gripping the sides of his seat. The speedometer read 105. "And you, *Milo,* are at the heart of this process! If people continue to think the way you do, *Milo,* throwing their crossword puzzle books out the windows of their Audis all across America, the future will be full of absolutely valueless people! Right, MILO?" I leaned over, taking my eyes off the road, and blew smoke into his face, screaming, "ARE YOU LISTENING, MILO? MARK MY WORDS!"

"Y-yes."

"GOO, GOO, GA-GA-GAA!"

I put my foot all the way to the floor. The wind howled through the window, the gray highway flew beneath us.

"Mark my words, Milo," I whispered. He never heard me. "Twenty-five across. Eight letters. N-i-h-i-l—"

My pulse roared in my ears, there joining the drowned choir of the fields and the roar of the engine. Body slimy with sweat, fingers clenched through the cigar, fists clamped on the wheel, smoke stinging my eyes. I slammed on the brakes, downshifting immediately, sending the transmission into a painful whine as the car slewed and skidded off the pavement, clipping a reflecting marker and throwing Milo against the windshield. The car stopped with a jerk in the gravel at the side of the road, just shy of a sign announcing, WELCOME TO OHIO.

There were no other lights on the road, I shut off my own and sat behind the wheel, trembling, the night air cool on my skin. The insects wailed. The boy was slumped against the dashboard. There was a star fracture in the glass above his head, and warm blood came away on my fingers when I touched his hair. I got out of the car, circled around to the passenger's side, and dragged him from the seat into the field adjoining the road. He was surprisingly light. I left him there, in a field of Ohio soybeans on the evening of a summer's day.

The city of Detroit was founded by the French adventurer Antoine de la Mothe, sieur de Cadillac, a supporter of Comte de Pontchartrain, minister of state to the Sun King, Louis XIV. All of these men worshiped the Roman Catholic god, protected their political positions, and let the future go hang. Cadillac, after whom an American automobile was named, was seeking a favorable location to advance his own economic interests. He came ashore on July 24, 1701, with fifty soldiers, an equal number of settlers, and about one hundred friendly Indians near the present site of the Veterans Memorial Building, within easy walking distance of the Greyhound Bus Terminal.

The car did not run well after the accident, developing a reluctance to go into fourth, but I didn't care. The encounter with Milo had gone exactly as such things should go, and was especially pleasing because it had been totally unplanned. An accident—no order, one would guess—but exactly as if I had laid it all out beforehand. I came into Detroit late at night via Route 12, which eventually turned into Michigan Avenue. The air was hot and sticky. I remember driving past the Cadillac plant; multitudes of red, yellow, and green lights glinting off dull masonry and the smell of auto exhaust along the city streets. I found the sort of neighborhood I wanted not far from Tiger Stadium: pawnshops, an all-night deli, laundromats, dimly lit bars with red Stroh's signs in the windows. Men on street corners walked casually from noplace to noplace.

I parked on a side street just around the corner from a 7-Eleven. I left the motor running. In the store I dawdled over a magazine rack until at last I heard the racing of an engine and saw the Audi flash by the window. I bought a copy of *Time* and caught a downtown bus at the corner. At the Greyhound station I purchased a ticket for the next bus to Toronto and sat reading my magazine until departure time.

We got onto the bus. Across the river we stopped at customs and got off again. "Name?" they asked me.

"Gerald Spotsworth."

"Place of birth?"

"Calgary." I gave them my credentials. The passport photo showed me with hair. They looked me over. They let me go.

I work in the library of the University of Toronto. I am well read, a student of history, a solid Canadian citizen. There I lead a sedentary life. The subways are clean, the people are friendly, the restaurants are excellent. The sky is blue. The cat is on the mat.

We got back on the bus. There were few other passengers, and most of them were soon asleep; the only light in the darkened interior was that which shone above my head. I was very tired, but I did not want to sleep. Then I remembered that I had Ruth's pills in my jacket pocket. I smiled, thinking of the customs people. All that was left in the box were a couple of tiny pink tabs. I did not know what they were, but I broke one down the middle with my fingernail and took it anyway. It perked me up immediately. Everything I could see seemed sharply defined. The dark green plastic of the seats. The rubber mat in the aisle. My fingernails. All details were separate and distinct, all interdependent. I must have been focused on the threads in the weave of my pants leg for ten minutes when I was surprised by someone sitting down next to me. It was Ruth. "You're back!" I exclaimed.

"We're all back," she said. I looked around and it was true: on the opposite side of the aisle, two seats ahead, Milo sat watching me over his shoulder, a trickle of blood running down his forehead. One corner of his mouth pulled tighter in a rueful smile. Mr. Graves came back from the front seat and shook my hand. I saw the fat singer from the country club, still naked. The locker-room boy. A flickering light from the back of the bus: when I turned around there stood the burning man, his eye sockets two dark hollows behind the wavering flames. The shopping-mall guard. Hector from the hardware store. They all looked at me.

"What are you doing here?" I asked Ruth.

"We couldn't let you go on thinking like you do. You act like I'm some monster. I'm just a person."

"A rather nice-looking young lady," Graves added.

"People are monsters," I said.

"Like you, huh?" Ruth said. "But they can be saints, too."

That made me laugh. "Don't feed me platitudes. You can't even read."

"You make such a big deal out of reading. Yeah, well, times change. I get along fine, don't I?"

The mall guard broke in. "Actually, miss, the reason we caught on to you is that someone saw you walk into the men's room." He looked embarrassed.

"But you didn't catch me, did you?" Ruth snapped back. She turned to me. "You're afraid of change. No wonder you live back here."

"This is all in my imagination," I said. "It's because of your drugs."

"It is all in your imagination," the burning man repeated. His voice was a whisper. "What you see in the future is what you are able to see. You have no faith in God or your fellow man."

"He's right," said Ruth.

"Bull. Psychobabble."

"Speaking of babble," Milo said, "I figured out where you got that goo-goo-goo stuff. Talk—"

"Never mind that," Ruth broke in. "Here's the truth. The future is just a place. The people there are just people. They live differently. So what? People make what they want of the world. You can't escape human failings by running into the past." She rested her hand on my leg. "I'll tell you what you'll find when you get to Toronto," she said. "Another city full of human beings."

This was crazy. I knew it was crazy. I knew it was all unreal, but somehow I was getting more and more afraid. "So the future is just the present writ large," I said bitterly. "More bull."

"You tell her, pal," the locker-room boy said.

Hector, who had been listening quietly, broke in. "For a man from the future, you talk a lot like a native."

"You're the king of bullshit, man," Milo said. " 'Some people devote themselves to artwork'! Jesus!"

I felt dizzy. "Scut down, Milo. That means 'Fuck you too.' " I shook my head to try to make them go away. That was a mistake: the bus began to pitch like a sailboat. I grabbed for Ruth's arm but missed. "Who's driving this thing?" I asked, trying to get out of the seat.

"Don't worry," said Graves. "He knows what he's doing."

"He's brain-dead," Milo said.

"You couldn't do any better," said Ruth, pulling me back down.

"No one is driving," said the burning man.

"We'll crash!" I was so dizzy now that I could hardly keep from being sick. I closed my eyes and swallowed. That seemed to help. A long time passed; eventually I must have fallen asleep.

When I woke it was late morning and we were entering the city, cruising down Eglinton Avenue. The bus had a driver after all—a slender black man with neatly trimmed sideburns who wore his uniform hat at a rakish angle. A sign above the windshield said, YOUR DRIVER — SAFE, COURTEOUS, and below that, on the slide-in nameplate, WILBERT CAUL. I felt like I was coming out of a nightmare. I felt happy. I stretched some of the knots out of my back. A young soldier seated across the aisle from me looked my way; I smiled, and he returned it briefly.

"You were mumbling to yourself in your sleep last night," he said.

"Sorry. Sometimes I have bad dreams."

"It's okay. I do too, sometimes." He had a round open face, an apologetic grin. He was twenty, maybe. Who knew where his dreams came from? We chatted until the bus reached the station; he shook my hand and said he was pleased to meet me. He called me "sir."

I was not due back at the library until Monday, so I walked over to Yonge Street. The stores were busy, the tourists were out in droves, the adult theaters were doing a brisk business. Policemen in sharply creased trousers, white gloves, sauntered along among the pedestrians. It was a bright, cloudless day, but the breeze coming up the street from the lake was cool. I stood on the sidewalk outside one of the strip joints and watched the video-taped come-on over the closed circuit. The Princess Laya. Sondra Nieve, the Human Operator. Technology replaces the traditional barker, but the bodies are more or less the same. The persistence of your faith in sex and machines is evidence of your capacity to hope.

Francis Bacon, in his masterwork *The New Atlantis*, foresaw the utopian world that would arise through the application of experimental science to social problems. Bacon, however, could not solve the problems of his own time and was eventually accused of accepting bribes, fined £40,000, and imprisoned in the Tower of London. He made no appeal to God, but instead applied himself to the development of the virtues of patience and acceptance. Eventually he was freed. Soon after, on a freezing day in late March, we were driving near Highgate when I suggested to him that cold might delay the process of decay. He was excited by the idea. On impulse he stopped the carriage, purchased a hen, wrung its neck, and stuffed it with snow. He eagerly looked forward to the results of his experiment. Unfortunately, in haggling with the street vendor he had exposed himself thoroughly to the cold and was seized by a chill that rapidly led to pneumonia, of which he died on April 9, 1626.

There's no way to predict these things.

When the videotape started repeating itself I got bored, crossed the street, and lost myself in the crowd.

MAN

When it woke us in the predawn of that fall morning, I thought the sound in the basement was only the cat—but Linda, who worries about these things, insisted that I check it out. Besides, there sat Groucho our Siamese, ears pricked, on the bookshelf. The weather had turned cold just four days ago, and maybe an opossum had managed to find its way into the house. But as I pulled on my slippers and robe there came a rustling from directly beneath us so distinct that I shivered, despite my determination to be the calm one, the one in control.

Flashlight in hand, I went to the basement stairs. I flipped on the light and limped down the steps. Groucho, alert and curious, tangled himself underfoot. About halfway down I crouched and looked, eyes level with the floor joists, around the cluttered room. At first I saw nothing unusual, but then noticed, huddled near the sacks of peat moss and pine bark mulch, a third baggy shape. I turned to Linda, who trembled at the top of the stairs. "It's a man," I said.

Linda watched me for a second. "What should we do?"

"Maybe I can scare him away."

"Be careful."

I went back to the bedroom and pulled on the jeans and sweatshirt I'd worn the day before while changing the car's oil. Linda hovered nervously about the basement door. When I went back down he was still where I'd found him. The morning light was coming up through the basement windows; the one on the south wall was pried open. I wondered whether he might be asleep, but then I saw the gleam of his eyes watching me. He didn't move as I picked up a rake and approached. I stood five feet away, trying to seem assured and strong, feeling vulnerable. I waved the rake at him. "Get out. Come on, out!"

His dark eyes watched me. He remained still.

I stepped forward and poked the rake handle at him. At first he didn't react, then his hand flashed out from beneath his rotten coat and he grabbed the end of it. I felt the strength of his grip, like electricity, run up the handle to me. "Get out," I said.

"I'm hungry," he said, getting up. "I need something to eat."

"I don't care whether you're hungry."

We stood there, two men joined by the handle of the rake stiff as a regulation. He was about my size, dark unkempt hair in his eyes, dressed in khakis with the knees worn through, filthy once-white running shoes, several layers of T-shirts with a wide-lapeled pinstriped suit coat over them. The top T-shirt had writing on it: I'M WITH STUPID.

He smiled at me. "New Orleans?"

"What?"

"The whores on Canal Street. Hurricanes in plastic cups. Fat tourists from Texarkana, wearing masks. The whole sleazy scene."

"I don't know what you're talking about."

"You remind me of somebody I knew there. Farmer Brown, we called him." He let go of the rake handle, shoving it away disdainfully, as if he'd played this game many times before and was tired of it. "He had a rake, too."

"Get out of my basement."

" 'Get out of my basement,' " he mocked. "Get serious, Farmer Brown."

Groucho brushed against my leg, then moved forward to sniff the man's shoes. He crouched down, picked up the cat and held him in his lap, scratching him gently behind the ears. Groucho stretched and settled down, purring audibly.

"I want you out of here."

"I want a cigarette holder and a vacation in Portugal." He addressed the cat. "Think it's likely I'll get them, puss-puss?"

I looked over my shoulder. Linda stood halfway down the stairs, watching. "Go back up," I told her. Clutching the rake, I followed her up to the kitchen.

"Tom, you've got to do something."

My gut was already tied in a knot, and Linda's pushing only wrenched it further. "I don't know what to do."

"Well, you can't just leave him down there." Linda turned her back on me and started banging last night's dishes in the sink. "The Criswells had a man in their garage last winter, and it took three months before they could get him out. The place still smells like an outhouse. What if he comes upstairs while we're asleep?"

"He's not going to come upstairs. He's probably as scared of us as we are of him." Even as I spoke I knew it was an evasion.

"I don't care whether *he's* scared. I want him out of here."

I ran my hand through my hair. "Look. For now we can lock the basement door. There's not much he can get into. He can use the bathroom down there. Maybe he'll go away if we don't feed him. If he's still here when we come back from work, then I promise you, I'll get him out."

Linda just stared at me. I could tell she was furious, but also scared, wanting to cry but damned if she would. Her jaw clenched, and she stalked back to the bedroom. I heard water run in the bathroom. I stared out the window over the kitchen sink, then turned on the coffee maker. Groucho rubbed against my ankles, begging for breakfast. Aside from Linda and the chirping of birds in the yard, there was no sound. I wondered who Farmer Brown was.

I've never been to New Orleans, but what I hear of it does not appeal to me. Sleazy bars, sex for money, the American version of the fevered exoticism of some Caribbean tourist town.

I'm a quiet man, and I've led a quiet life. The one way in which my childhood might be said to have differed from most was in its loneliness. I was an only child of elderly parents. My father and mother owned a drugstore in Tampa, where most of the people are old. Our neighborhood had few children. On top of that, when I was eight I broke my leg bicycling and was out of school, in a chest-to-knee cast, for five months. I came out of it with a right leg an inch shorter than my left and a permanent limp. Add to this a reticent nature, and the result was that I never seemed to develop any lasting friendships.

This solitude followed me into adulthood; aside from Linda, I had no close friends.

The neighborhood where we lived was old and well established. A man in the basement was a fairly unusual occurrence, though since the new subdivisions had sprouted north of the city limits there had been increased numbers of cases even in the heart of town. It had not gotten to be a big enough problem that the city council had paid any attention to it, though Mr. Rappaport, the cranky retiree who lived behind us, had raised the issue at the last meeting of the neighborhood association.

At the studio that day I concentrated on finishing the Hayes Engineering Group annual report I'd been working on for the last twelve weeks. The project was due at the printer by Thursday. As usual, the client had dawdled on giving the necessary approvals and now was insisting on last-minute changes after the type had been set, yet still expected me to meet the deadline. Still, Horowitz, the printing rep at Athena Graphics, assured me that they would go to press by the weekend even if it meant in the middle of the night. Just before lunch I got a call from Hayes himself. "Larson?"

"Yes?"

"I was just looking over the proofs you sent me again, and it struck me that it might be more effective if you put all the figures in boldface. It would make them stand out more."

"I couldn't do that without compromising the entire design, Mr. Hayes. You can't just change one element like that without rethinking everything else."

"I'm not talking about changing a single word. Just the type-face."

I counted to three. "If you insist, I'll do it. But I can't guarantee we'll get done on time."

"Such a simple change? I thought you were a resourceful young man."

I was up against it. Hayes was a new client, and I expected to get a lot of business from him over the next years. I had low-balled my bid to get my foot in the door, promising first-class design and first-class service. "I'll have to talk this over with the printer. I'll get back to you."

"You do that."

It was all I could do to keep from slamming down the phone. If the printer got rushed, he'd screw up for sure and my whole plan would go down the tubes. My life was turning to shit.

Halfway through lunch I remembered the man in the basement and hurried over to the Hardware Warehouse at the Wonderlands Mall. After letting me wander around the home and garden section long enough to feel totally self-conscious, a salesman came up. He had the professionally competent manner of his breed; his nameplate read ROGER. I was already faintly annoyed. "Well, Roger, what have you got to help me get rid of a man in my basement?"

"Man in the basement? How old?"

"I can't tell how old he is, exactly. I didn't ask. He's not small—probably six feet tall, one-seventy or so."

The conversation turned into a manhood challenge. Roger wasn't going to help me until I admitted I was incompetent and needed his help. He was the expert, and I was the one who didn't know how to take care of myself. As we stood there in the aisle I got more and more angry, yet felt unable to escape.

"He's the violent type?"

"Yes. No question about it."

"You want to kill him?" Roger finally asked.

"Of course." I tried to act like there was never any question.

Roger turned and led me, limping more obviously in the effort to keep up with him, to another quarter of the store, beneath a big red banner hanging from the rafters reading HOME IMPROVEMENTS. He took a clear plastic bag from a shelf. *Quietus,* it said in bright red letters. The powder inside might have been brown sugar.

"This here's the quality product on the market right now. Couple of tablespoonfuls in some food—peanut butter or oatmeal work good. The stuff's tasteless, but it has a texture to it, so it should be something that will disguise that. But usually these guys are so hungry it doesn't much matter."

When I got home there was music playing on the stereo. Nick Lowe's "Cruel to Be Kind." I heard sounds from the kitchen. "Linda?" I called.

He stuck his head through the doorway into the living room. "Howdy, Farmer Brown," he said, then ducked back into the kitchen. I followed. He stood at the counter making a peanut butter and jelly sandwich.

I don't know why I should have felt shocked, but it was as if I'd found a large cockroach in the bathtub. I hesitated in the doorway. He looked at me, finished spreading peanut butter on a slice of wheat bread, joined the halves of the sandwich, and took a bite. Crumbs were scattered all over the counter, and he'd left the tops off the jars. He nodded at the paper bag in my hand, still chewing. "Did you buy me something?"

I put the bag of poison into the pantry. "Brown sugar," I said. "How did you get upstairs?"

"Not much of a lock on that basement door. You should take care of that."

"What gives you the idea you can just come in here and use our things, eat our food?"

"Is this your food? Are these your things?"

"Well, they aren't yours."

"Possession is nine-tenths of the law." He took another bite of the sandwich. "And in my experience, possession is a matter of character."

I went to the liquor cabinet and poured myself a scotch. It burned going down, warmed my belly, its scent backing up my nose. Instantly I felt the beginning of a headache. I picked up the mail from the kitchen table. The man drew himself a glass of water and sat down opposite me. Just two old friends, long separated, sitting around the house having a chat. "Tough day?" he said.

"None of your business."

"You know, in my mind I can visualize what it must be like to have a job like yours. I have a very powerful mind. And it seems to me, in my mind, that it's only after you stop taking other people's shit that you start to taste life." He took another bite of the sandwich, and grinned.

In the living room Lowe was singing about making an American squirm. I sucked down the scotch, trying to figure out what to do next. When I heard Linda's car in the driveway my anxiety came back. I looked at the basement door.

"Don't worry," he said. "I won't tell her you couldn't face me."

"I am facing you."

He watched me, took a sip of water. Something in the way he did this was so fastidious that it stood out in contrast to his shabby clothes, rude manner. "Of course you are, Farmer Brown," he said. I heard the front door open.

"She won't leave you just because you're scared," the man said softly. "I am, after all, an unpleasant reality."

He went down the stairs to the basement.

Linda came into the kitchen. She looked at the drink in my hand. "Is he still down there?"

"He's still there," I said.

She went into the living room and turned down the stereo. She came back into the kitchen, grim-faced, and screwed the top back on the jar of peanut butter. Brushing crumbs off the counter into her hand, she said, "I wish you'd put things away after you use them, Tom."

By midevening the headache was going strong. I hadn't felt like eating, and we'd passed supper in silence.

"Just don't press me about this," I told her later. "Trust me: I'll get him out." We were undressing for bed; we'd not exchanged three sentences that evening. She slipped on the T-shirt and shorts she wore instead of pajamas. Her shoulders were still slender as a girl's. I wanted her; we hadn't made love for weeks, but Linda's manner was as cold as if sex had not been invented yet. "He's not dangerous," I insisted.

"I don't care if he isn't." Her voice was brittle. "He scares me."

"He scares me, too. I want him out of here. But let it be for a while. I'll get him out." She got into bed; I reached over to touch her shoulder. She pulled away. "Linda?"

She didn't answer. My stomach churned. I turned off the light and lay there silently for a long time. Lying there, I thought about him. I pictured him crouched in the dark of the basement, the musty smell, the crickets and spiders. He was alone down there; I was alone up here. I imagined getting up, going to the refrigerator, popping the tops on two beers, and going down to visit him. We might sit on the old lawn chairs and talk, in low whispers, careful not to wake Linda. We would tell each other our stories. Groucho would come down and curl up on my lap. Our eyes, the man's and mine, would glint in the darkness like those of two untamed and sullen beasts.

Eventually, thinking of him, I fell asleep.

In the morning I got up before Linda and made myself some oatmeal. I sliced a banana into it and sprinkled it with brown sugar. The bag of poison lay on the pantry shelf like an accusation. I poured a cup of coffee and turned on the stereo. U2: *Rattle and Hum*. I kept the volume down, ate my oatmeal, and listened to the music.

Afterward I went downstairs to check up on him. He'd

cleared out one end of the basement, found the old canvas cot from among the camping equipment, and set it up. But he wasn't there, and the basement window was opened wide. I felt relief, to be sure, but also a vague disappointment.

When I turned to go back upstairs he entered from the basement bathroom. He had my briefcase and car keys in his hand and acted as if he was about to step out the door. The jeans and shirt he was wearing he must have taken from the laundry room. Although he seemed to have showered and washed his hair, he had not shaved and, with the rumpled clothes, looked more like somebody going on vacation than to work. "What do you think you're doing?" I asked him.

"I'm going down to your studio. You look like you could use a day off."

"You can't go to work dressed like that!"

"What's the use of being your own boss if you have to invent a dress code?"

"You don't know the first thing about my work."

"I know more than you think. I've looked through the stuff in here," he said, hefting the briefcase. "Besides, what's there to know? No sense throwing a veil of mystery over what must be mostly a matter of snowing the people who pay you. It's all in your attitude."

I followed him, ineffectual as smoke, as he went upstairs and out the door. He climbed into my car and drove away.

I stood there stunned until Linda came into the room. She looked over at the stereo, which had gotten as far as "Love Rescue Me."

"I thought I heard you leave. Aren't you going to work today?"

"No. You're so damned hot about me getting rid of that man in the basement, then I'm going to have to stay home and work on it."

She looked at me, surprised at my anger. For a moment I could see the absolute weariness and disgust in her face. Not only did she dislike me, she had absolutely no respect for me and was tired of putting up with the charade. While she went into the kitchen to make her breakfast, I slumped onto the sofa and pretended to read the sports page. The gray lines of newsprint slid past my eyes unread. The CD cycled to "God Part II." I turned up the volume to window-shaking levels. The phase-distorted guitar bounced the knickknacks on the mantel.

Linda came out and shouted something at me. I shook my head and pointed at my deaf ears. She stalked out of the house, slamming the front door. I tried not to imagine what she'd make of my missing car. The stereo wailed. I believed in love, but it wasn't working.

So I got drunk. After I polished off the bottle of scotch I switched to brandy. I played loud music, stared at Linda's books crowding the living-room shelves, and felt alternately sorry for myself and murderously angry. At Linda, at my clients, at the man in the basement.

Except he wasn't down there anymore. Brandy in my hand, unshaven and rank, I stumbled downstairs to his lair. You would hardly have known that anyone had been there. It suddenly hit me to wonder whether he was going to come meekly back down when he returned from my studio.

It ought not to have been so hard to get rid of him. He was not a family member. He was not a guest. We didn't owe him anything. We had gotten along fine without him for many years. If any of the neighbors had men in their basements it was not a fact they advertised. And who knew what damage he was doing to the business I had labored over the last six years to erect?

Around five he pulled into the driveway and sauntered in, whistling. He tossed my briefcase onto the ottoman, flopped down on the sofa, and put his feet up on the big coffee table Linda had brought with her from before we got married. "Howdy, Farmer Brown. Where's your rake?"

He looked so relaxed there, and I was so drunk, that instead of getting angry I felt sad. I sat down next to him. "What happened at the studio today? Did you really go there?"

"Nowhere else. You can stop worrying about the Hayes Group report."

"What do you mean?"

"I fired the printer. Horowitz was lying to you all along. He wasn't going to meet the deadline, and while he put you off with excuses the bastard went behind your back to Hayes and blamed the delays and mistakes on you."

"You can't fire him! It's too late! I can't find another printer on such short notice. Hayes is already breathing down my neck."

"Right. So I told Hayes that under the circumstances I'd understand if he went elsewhere."

"You *what?* Hayes is my biggest client. If I could satisfy him I'd double my income in the next twelve months."

"At the cost of an ulcer. And your balls. Hayes is a petty tyrant and a coward. A man with a bank account and no integrity. Do you really need the money that bad?"

I started to protest, but then the thought of never having to suck up to Hayes, or deal with the printer's lies, sank in. My shoulders already felt less tight. "I don't know," I said.

"You don't know. But I do."

I took another sip of brandy. Groucho came by, hopped onto my lap, and began butting my hand. I heard Linda's car in the driveway. She came in laden with books, briefcase, staggering as she dangled two recyclable sacks of groceries from her fingertips. She saw us on the sofa and dropped the groceries.

I sat there. The man leapt up and took one bag from her arms, scooped the fallen one from the floor. "I was just helping Tom," he said. "I might as well help you, too."

Staring at me as if she could not believe, a little dazed, she said, "I guess so."

That was the beginning. In a week he had come to be a part of our lives. I still went to work, but when I felt bad or woke up late or was hung over or didn't feel like shaving, he filled in. I can't tell you that, along with the worry, I didn't feel relief. I can't say, honestly, that he did a worse job than I would have. He did a different one.

Linda at first was nervous around him. She never gave him the opportunity to touch her, even the most casual of contacts. I remember once when she was washing out the coffeepot and he took it from her to dry. He touched her wrist, and she shuddered visibly. I took this for distaste and felt guilty about it, acted apologetic around her as if the man were my idea, as if I had brought him into the house and was the one responsible for keeping him. I can't even say that wasn't true, although it's not all of the truth. Linda didn't let me touch her, either.

The man treated me with playful contempt through which I read some other attitude. An attitude I could not define. I found myself becoming more antisocial. I no longer gladly put up with the hypocrisies necessary to do business. If people asked me a question, I told them the truth, regardless of the reaction. If they didn't want an answer, then why did they ask? I watched people in the streets, at restaurants, in movie theaters. How many women had some shrill madwoman in their attics? How many men had a man in their basement, calling them mocking names, making himself indispensable? Did they summon him upstairs when they felt the need, regretting and needing him at the same time, humiliated yet queerly pleased?

I let my hair grow long and stopped shaving. The man got his hair cut. He began to wear my clothes, which fit him, more or less. Cleaned up, smelling of cologne and wearing my suit, he resembled me—except for my limp—though no one who knew me would mistake us for each other. On days when I did go to work I would come home to find him sitting around the living room, reading Linda's books, playing my CDs. He said he was getting a good picture of our characters.

"And what do you think of us?" I asked.

"I think you are more or less what you expect to be."

Things got pretty slow at my studio. I spent some long hours there trying to please the clients I had left, repeatedly calculating my monthly overhead and eyeing the incredible shrinking balance in my business account. I made call after call to former clients, always on some flimsy pretext, pretending to be casual, hoping they might throw me some business. When this got to be too much for me, I'd walk across the street to the park and feed nuts to the squirrels.

One lunchtime, to my surprise, I found Simpson Hayes sitting out there on one of the benches. For a minute I thought about circling behind to the other side of the park, but then he looked up and saw me. I sat down beside him. "Fancy meeting you here," I said.

"Larson," he said. There were dark circles under his eyes. "How's business?"

"Business is just fine."

"That's not what Horowitz tells me."

"If you still believe what he tells you, then there's no point in us talking."

To my surprise, Hayes smiled—a trifle grimly. "Horowitz really screwed you over there, didn't he? He was lying to you."

"You figured that out. Maybe you've caught on that you can't trust Athena Graphics?"

"So what? I can't say I have much sympathy for you. You can't let anyone get the advantage over you. Not if you're a professional."

"A professional."

"A pro sees what has to be done, then he does it. It doesn't matter how he feels about it. That's why you're a lousy businessman."

I thought of a dozen defensive replies, started to speak, said nothing. I opened my bag of peanuts and scattered a few on the path in front of us. "You look worn out, Hayes. Is being such a macho man hard work?"

He looked at me sharply. "You're the one who's going out of business."

I was tired of him. "That's right, I almost forgot. Thanks for reminding me." I got up and crossed back to my office.

I was in no mood to face my empty drafting table, so I decided to call it a day. The encounter with Hayes was the last straw. The more I thought about him, the madder I got. The guy as much as admitted he was getting fucked by Horowitz, he looked like he hadn't slept in three days, and still his only reaction to seeing me was to try to make me feel like shit.

On the way home it occurred to me that Hayes might be

fighting a man in his basement. What would he do? Kill him, probably, in short order. Hayes and the man were birds of a feather, both followers of the Attila the Hun school of interpersonal relations. For them, there were no limits. If the world were made of people like them, we'd still be dodging spears.

I was the one in trouble, not Hayes.

To my surprise, when I reached home Linda's car was in the driveway. I panicked when I thought of her alone with the man. He was capable of anything. I hurried to the door, rushed in. Silently I moved down the hall. The bedroom door stood open. I heard a rustling of bedclothes. I came in on them naked in each other's arms, caught a glimpse of Linda's face, eyes closed and lips parted, cheeks flushed as he rocked her in his arms, her head almost off the side of the bed. The man glanced up at me; the corner of his mouth quirked upward in a grin. Linda's eyes came open, and I turned and stumbled from the room.

If I'd thought my intrusion might have disturbed them, I was sadly mistaken. I'd sat for forty minutes, fuming, in the den before either of them came to face me. It was Linda, wearing her blue terry-cloth bathrobe. Her cheeks were still flushed, her hair tangled. "What are you doing back so early?"

"What am I doing?"

She sat down on the love seat. "I'm sorry, Tom. I told you to get rid of him. I told you he was dangerous."

"You didn't tell me that you were."

"No I didn't. You just assumed I was harmless."

"Where is he?"

She smoothed the robe over her leg. I ached to touch her. "He went back into the basement."

"That's not good enough, Linda. None of this is. You owe me better than this."

"So? This is a two-way street."

"Shut up! Just shut up! I'm the one who's been betrayed here."

"Don't be too sure of that. It took more than just me for things to get so bad between us before he showed up."

I couldn't stand it. I stormed into the kitchen, kicked open the basement door, and stalked down the stairs. He was lounging on the old lawn chair, sipping a scotch.

"Well, if it isn't Farmer Brown," he said. "Hello, Farmer Brown."

"Don't call me that."

"What shall I call you, Farmer Brown?"

"You slept with my wife."

"Actually, we hadn't gotten around to the sleeping part, yet."

I paced around the basement. It hardly seemed like the place it had been before he'd come. It looked like a shabby apartment in some third world country. Some student's room, halfway between a hovel and the lower middle class, partway up the evolutionary scale but not there yet.

"All right," I said. "You've screwed up our lives enough. I want you out of here—right now."

"You don't want me out of here. If I left, you'd be a lump of clay, without me. That's all, a lump of clay."

"Better a lump of clay and peaceful. You're ripping me apart! I didn't ask for this."

"Yes you did. We both know you wanted me here, you called me up, and after I leave you'll be dead. You want me gone? Here, take this." He reached behind him on the floor, picked something up, and held it out to me. It was the bag of poison. "It would be more honest to just kill yourself."

I just stood there. "That's what you want me to think—that I can't live without you. But who says I can't?"

"She's never going to give you what you want, Tom. Love without any responsibilities? It doesn't exist in the real world, once we leave the womb. And you can't even handle the affection you're getting now—pitiful as it is."

"Stop it!"

"What's the matter—hitting too close to home? I know you. The reason I'm here is to make up for all that. For you to live without me would be for you to eat all the shit the world offers, and call it whipped cream. It would mean you'd accept it all. You'd be saying it never could be any better."

"Maybe it can't."

"Suit yourself. That's not my department. I'm only the alternative."

My eyes were burning. "Okay, okay," I said. "Maybe you're right. But does it have to be so painful? I can't go on living like this. I fooled myself for years, living half-alive, growing a tumor because that's all I knew. I don't want to live that way anymore. I can't. I'll do myself in. I want some peace."

"What do I know about peace? I'm just the man in your basement." He drained the last of the scotch, leaned back calm as a millionaire on permanent vacation.

I caught my breath. "Fuck you," I said, rage erasing the humiliation. "I don't believe I've put up with you for so long. I don't even know your name."

"My name is Tom."

That was it. I grabbed the rake and swung round on him, whipping it level like a baseball bat. Quick as thought, he caught the handle and wrenched it out of my hands. He stood up. Not even breathing hard, he tossed the rake onto the floor. He flipped the bag of poison at me. I caught it, fumbling.

"You are truly pitiful," he said. "Do something constructive. Use it."

I turned and limped up the stairs, past Linda where she waited in the kitchen, out the front door and into my car. I drove around for a while, barely able to see the streets through my tears, the bag of poison on the passenger's seat beside me.

Unconsciously I found myself downtown, driving toward my studio. I couldn't face that. Instead I pulled into the Saratoga Street ramp. I sat in my parked car, hands gripping the wheel, crying out loud now, for a long time. Eventually I stopped. I sat back, breathing hard, and took the bag onto my lap. *Quietus.* I could tear it open right there, take a good healthy mouthful. I squeezed the bag with my thumbs, feeling the moist powder inside, and gradually all thought drained from my mind.

It was four-thirty, and the ramp started to get busy with peo-

ple heading out for an early start on the weekend. I saw Clarice
Ward, an architect who worked in the Hayes Engineering Group.
The group's office was in the Columbia Tower attached to the
deck.

I got out of the car. Ignoring the elevator in order to avoid
facing anyone, I took the stairs up to the Hayes Group office. It
was hard work making it up ten flights of stairs with my bum leg.

Hayes's secretary, who had put me off dozens of times over
the phone, was cleaning up her desk. "Mr. Hayes is gone," she
said.

"Then he won't mind my dropping something off in his office," I said, and pushed past her through the door.

Hayes was leaning back in his chair, gazing out the window
at the skyline. "Time to go home, Hayes," I said. "Don't be a
workaholic. It's Friday."

He swiveled around, face creased with annoyance. "What do
you want?"

"I want to help you out."

He stared up at me. He really did look exhausted. "Look, if
I hurt your feelings this afternoon, I'm sorry."

"I appreciate the sentiment. But I didn't come here looking
for an apology, either. Are you having some trouble at home?"

"Nothing I can't handle." He played with the Waterman pen
on his desk blotter, spinning it like a pinwheel. "Look, Tom. If
you need work I'll think about it. I'll call you."

"I don't need work, I'm just paying a social call. That problem at home? Maybe you've got some vermin in the basement?"
I slapped the bag of *Quietus* down on the desk. "You might have
use for this."

He looked at me with new interest. "You've had trouble
with—intruders?"

"Just one."

He picked up the poison. "This bag hasn't been opened."

"Because my troubles are over. Use it if you can't think of
anything better. Then give me a call and maybe I can help you
salvage your report."

I left him there, turning the bag over in his hands. I walked back down the stairs to the parking deck, and it did not seem to me that my leg bothered me much at all.

When I came back home, the house was dark. I considered confronting them, but the thought of another ugly scene, and the pain it would inevitably cause me—and Linda—kept me away from the bedroom. I would save that for tomorrow. It was not that I could put it off forever—I was through putting things off—but I didn't need it now. The question for now was, where would I sleep?

The place was silent, and I didn't turn on any lights. Streetlight coming through the blinds threw lines of light and shadow across the furniture, casting everything into high relief. Sleeping on the sofa, an antique Linda had picked out for us, would be like spending the night on broken ground. Instead I walked from room to room, seeing our house as I had not seen it before. There were the oak bookshelves Linda had picked out, lining the living-room wall. On the shelves were ranked the spines of her books, English and American literature, political science, philosophy, religion. How many of them were mine?—there, in the lower corner of the last shelf, a pile of AIGA annuals and *Communication Arts*. Not an impressive showing.

Here was Linda's coffee table. The stereo cabinet—I remembered us going to pick it out, how she had stated unequivocally what she wanted while I kept my mouth shut. The pictures on the wall—her choice, too.

It was not a bad-looking home, or an uncomfortable one. It was very livable. But it did not look like the home of a graphic designer, and it hit me that, if I were to leave and never come back, Linda would not have to change the house in any significant way to make it completely hers. I wasn't evident in our home at all.

Well, that didn't have to be. I went over to the shelf, took out my books, and laid them on the coffee table. The armchair—I had never liked the way it sat across from the window, throwing the late afternoon light into your eyes. I moved the lamp, the chair. I shoved the sofa away from the wall, took down Linda's

photos from Oxford that hung above the stereo cabinet, and re-
placed them with the Magritte print from my study. By the en-
tryway I piled the knickknacks from the mantel that would have
to go elsewhere.

It ended up an hour of sweaty work in the dark, and I made
some noise, but if they heard any of this in the bedroom they did
not bother about it. Groucho came out, miaowed once, and sat
on the ottoman to watch. As I worked it seemed to me that my
leg did not ache as it often had before under stress. It tingled.
When I was done I sat in the armchair, in its new place, and
looked around the still-dark room. It was recognizably the same
room, but at least now I could point in it to those things that
were mine. Paint the walls and bookshelves white, and it would
be an entirely brighter place.

Now where to sleep? Not the sofa. Then I had an idea, the
most natural idea in the world. I went down to the basement, to
the cot where the man had been. It did not look half so strange
as it had the other times I'd been there. I lay down. It smelled familiar, not so musty. It felt more comfortable than I remembered.
As I lay there I imagined how it would be to live down here for
years, ignored, unable to affect what went on upstairs, barely surviving, limping along alive but unheard. I thought about New
Orleans and Mardi Gras, the masked and drunken people in the
streets, spending a night on pleasure because they owed that to
some part of themselves that would be stifled by the sacrifices of
Lent. Eventually I fell asleep, and slept more restfully than I had
for weeks.

In the morning I was wakened, in the predawn, by the footsteps of someone on the stairs.

It was Linda. She stood there uncertainly, the flashlight in
her hand. "I woke up and no one was there," she said. "I was so
afraid I was alone, and I looked all through the house. Why did
you come back down here?"

Still fuddled by sleep, I held up my hand to shield my eyes
from the light. I was not entirely sure where I was or how I had
come to be there. Cold morning air flowed in through the open
window. "I thought you didn't want me up there."

"Of course I want you. It scared me when I woke and you weren't next to me."

"I guess I didn't know that." I sat up on the edge of the cot. Groucho hopped up beside me and rubbed my hand. I took him in my arms, stood and went to Linda.

She watched me soberly, her eyes glistening. "You changed everything around. It's different up there now."

I held Groucho out to her, and she scratched him under the chin. He purred. She took my arm, and we climbed the stairs together. My limp was entirely gone.

MR. HYDE VISITS THE HOME OF DR. JEKYLL

He'd left the back door open
As if expecting a visitor
He could not admit by the front,
And as the night was cold,
And his coat too large,
I did not spurn his equivocal hospitality.
His servants slept:
Hearts asleep in their bodies, too
Smothered by conscience
And a dull master.
Gathering my big clothes about me
Like a boy in the attic playing man,
I hurried to his room
Where troubled sheets betrayed
How an hour ago he'd tossed,
Desiring me.
I pinched the money from his purse,
Took clothing of more proper fit,

And paused to brush my hair
Before his mirror.

His face is scarred by virtue.
Mine is not.
He dreams of me
And prays for deliverance.
But that is only envy
Of my peculiar beauty,
Which he fears
And calls by another name.

HEARTS DO NOT IN EYES SHINE

Connie found Harry in the bar at Mario's. As soon as she walked in, he finished his drink and stood up.

"You came," he said, fumbling in his jacket pocket. "I have something for you." He found a small envelope in an inside pocket and handed it to her; it felt like a card. "Don't open it now," he said. "Wait until later."

Connie felt strangely calm. "Okay. Let's eat."

She let him do most of the talking; he seemed to have marshaled his arguments. "I know this must seem like a crazy idea. I think I'm half-crazy to suggest it, but people do it all the time and I couldn't let you go without trying something."

"You're not letting me go. You let me go a long time ago."

He pulled at his lower lip and sat silent. "You're right. I don't deny it."

"You can't."

"Please. I know I've made mistakes; we've both made mistakes. But think about the way we felt about each other when we first met. The emotions then were real. You can't ignore that. That's why I'm here asking this, even though I know I don't deserve to. In the last month or two, I've gone crazy thinking about the good times we spent together."

Connie tried to stay calm, to think rationally. "Harry, why do we have to go through this? It's too hard. I remember other times. We wouldn't be separated otherwise."

"No. I think you're wrong there. We made mistakes and did things to hurt each other, but I've thought about it a lot—I've hardly thought about anything else—and I know, I *know* we are basically compatible. I knew that the first time I saw you. The things that pushed us apart are only things that happened to us—they aren't who we are. Who we are doesn't change. That's the whole point of getting erased. We stay the same people, but we get rid of the bad things that happened and get another chance to build our marriage again. Please, Connie. You know this is the truth."

She didn't know anything. She sipped her wine, sat back and watched him. Harry seemed uncomfortable under her gaze. He closed his eyes, breathed deeply, opened them again. That was always the sign of his exasperation with her, when he couldn't get her to believe what he wanted, when the words failed him. The words had not failed him yet. He must have thought them up a long time before he had the nerve to call her. Maybe the letter from her lawyer had jolted him. Maybe the erasure clinic had given him the arguments he was using on her. That was something she would never have suspected of Harry in the early days; she would have taken him at his face value.

Connie must have smiled at her own cynicism: he looked at her angrily and said, "Don't laugh at me, Connie."

"I'm sorry."

"That's okay. Just don't laugh."

There wasn't much trust left in her, and suddenly she realized that she did not like it. What had he done to her that she had come to be so suspicious, that the honesty of her emotions had been leached away until she responded to him as if he were a pitchman for a sex show? Maybe his exasperation—if it was exasperation, and not just fear or confusion—had a reason.

"I don't know, Harry. I'm afraid. You've hurt me too much, and I can never forget the things you've done."

He leaned forward. "That's right," he said quietly. "But they can make us forget. You don't have to give up anything. You just have to be willing to take a chance."

She played with the card he had given her, turned it over, ran her index finger along the edge of the smooth rectangle of cream-colored paper. "I don't know."

The silence stretched. Harry looked hurt. "Look, Connie, maybe this was a bad idea. Don't make me feel any more a fool than I am."

"I'm not making you a fool." God. The last thing she wanted was to feel sorry for him.

"I'm sorry I tried to make you do something you didn't want to do. Can you blame me for trying?" He looked at her levelly. This was not going the way it ought to have gone. They ought not to let men like Harry live to reach twenty-one. They ought to test them when they hit puberty, and if the test showed a person who didn't know the difference between the truth and a lie, they could castrate him. While they were at it they could get rid of the ones with Harry's green eyes and Harry's voice.

She held up the card and stood to leave. "Can I open this now?"

He smiled a little sadly. "It doesn't say 'I love you.' "

Connie slid a fingernail under the flap and opened the envelope. The front of the card was blank, and inside was written, "No matter what you decide, I will never lie to you again."

She put the card back in the envelope, put the envelope into her purse. At his station, the maître d' had already cleared their table on his service screen and was watching them impatiently. Connie looked at him, looked at Harry, and sat down again.

She told Harry she would call him later and returned to the office without having made up her mind. She spent that afternoon trading foreign currencies, with Fox, her computer trading model, hooked into her left ear and the newsline on the window. She stayed in front of the terminal without a break until the session ended, then retreated to her office to take client calls until most of the staff had left for the day. The lowering clouds that threatened Connie and the other bicyclists riding home suggested that perhaps the streetcar would have been a better idea that morning. But the rain held off until after she got home. She lived in a large old house in a neighborhood that had declined to a near-slum in the third quarter of the century only to be refurbished in the eighties before its second genteel slide after the turn of the century. Harry and Connie had moved into the white frame monstrosity a year before they contracted. Seven years later he had moved out, and it had taken her months to feel comfortable again there after a period of rattling around its twelve rooms like the drunkard in the random-walk theorem.

That night a relapse threatened. In the mail printout she found a brochure for an erasure company, New Life Choices, Inc. She did not recognize the name. Harry had to have sent it; she threw it into the wastebasket without reading it. She skipped supper, fixed several stiff drinks, and tried to forget about erasure. She walked through the house listening to the spring drizzle and breathing deep the humid air that blew through opened windows. She picked up her clothes from about the bedroom, did the laundry, had a couple more drinks, smoked a joint, tried to read a book. She sat by the phone for twenty minutes, then dialed Harry's number quickly to tell him to forget it. The face of a middle-aged woman came onto the screen and told her curtly she had the wrong number. She hesitated, then searched the wastebasket for the brochure.

FREEDOM IS A STATE OF MIND

THE IMMORTAL BARD, WILLIAM SHAKESPEARE (1564–1616) ASKED,

CAN YOU CURE A TROUBLED MIND,

PLUNGE A DEEP SORROW OUT OF THE MEMORY

Erase the troubles written on a brain

And with a sweet potion

Clean all the pain and sadness

From a heavy heart?

—At New Life Choices, we can.

The next page told Connie:

We see the world through dark glass. By selective forgetting, we can take off the dark glasses that superimpose
the fearful past on the present, and begin to know that
love is forever present. The Jacobovsky Process is used to
selectively edit the memory. Forgiveness then becomes a
process of letting go of whatever we thought others may
have done to us, or whatever we may think we have done
to others. Our safety and security are the simple words, "I
don't remember."

Harry had been bright and moody and could make her laugh
whenever he wanted. Connie remembered quite well. She had
loved to watch him fix things. He had beautiful hands, strong
and skilled. His hands knew just how much force to give, could
feel out the source of a problem without his having to think
about it. Normally he was a talkative man, but when he was in
his attic workroom he became a quiet one, concentrating on the
task before him, devoted only to finding the solution to the problem; patient, intuitive. His eyes would sober, without the anger
they would show during his depressions, and he would look at
the machine as if somehow, if he waited in the right way, it might
speak to him—and he would not be surprised when it did.

Harry had that look for her, at first. She felt that, when she
spoke to him, he listened with all his substance. It made her want
to say only true things—not to be silly or lie. He would laugh at
her when she got so serious.

"You act like I might go away," he would tell her. "I won't go
away."

Harry worked for Triangle Data Services. Connie had met him when he came in to replace their old computer trading link with the new Triangle system. He seemed unaware of the class difference between a workman like himself and someone like Connie, with a couple of degrees in economics and a triple-A credit rating. He did not seem self-conscious hanging around their terminals watching, asking an occasional question. Strangely, the changeover was made without disrupting their work, and when, on his way out of the building on his last day there, Harry stopped by to ask Connie out for dinner, she had surprised herself by saying yes.

The rain increased from a drizzle to a downpour, and Connie went through the house again, closing windows against the storm. She turned out all the lights and went to bed.

Harry had lied to her more than once. They'd lived together so naturally in that first year that it amazed her she'd been able to live alone for so long. It was an open marriage, with disclosure, ten years and an option, with penalties for a breach on either side. Three years into it Connie realized that Harry saw other women without telling her. At first she said nothing, out of love or perhaps fear that facing it would make the truth of his betrayal undeniable. Why should he keep his lovers a secret when she had agreed to accept anything he told her? She did not see herself as the jealous spouse, but keeping her knowledge to herself only made her anger grow. When at last she confronted him, Harry was unsurprised that she knew. He would have felt ashamed to tell her of those affairs, even though it was okay to have them, he said. He still loved her, he said. It had nothing to do with her, he said.

Though it took her years more to realize it, it *had* nothing to do with her. It was not her fault, and whether or not it was Harry's was beyond her. She tried not to care. She just wanted to be done with trying to understand him when he did not understand her, done with his talk that never went anywhere and his silence that left her out, done with the fighting, his sudden joys and kindnesses, his silly jokes, his casual cruelty, his quiet eyes and calm hands, his lies, the pain of watching him and knowing

John Kessel

that she loved and hated him. She might have done better. But it was not her fault.

Why did that sound too easy?

The rain beat heavily on the roof now, punctuated by lightning that brought the darkened room into momentary sharp relief, like sudden memories. Connie realized that the windows in the workroom were probably open. She got her robe and went up the narrow stairs.

The lamp over Harry's workbench did not come on when she flipped the switch. The curtains of the west window snapped with the force of the wind, and the rain blew well into the middle of the cluttered room. Like a person walking a tightrope, Connie stepped carefully between the broken machines with their spoor of of dismantled parts. It was all that Harry had left when she'd kicked him out, and she had threatened more than once to throw all his toys away if he did not move them. Her feet were cold. The window was stuck; the counterweights in the frame scraped and the pulleys squeaked as she leaned heavily on it. The window went down crookedly, one side fighting the other. She beat on the top with her fist, growing angrier as it inched its stubborn way down. The wind whistled as the gap closed, she became soaked with the rain, and the shadowed forms of Harry's machines watched impassively as she struggled. There was still a gap when she gave up, two inches at one end and one at the other, uneven, hopelessly jammed, the wind louder as it shot through the narrow slit, the curtains flapping fitfully. She sat on the floor crying. It was Harry's damned window, and she couldn't close it for him.

She found herself in the lobby of New Life Choices on a day she and Harry picked for the erasing. Connie would have been more comfortable with the dignified conservatism of Associated or Stratford: the walls of the New Life lobby were knotty pine hung with Miró prints; the receptionist had his irises silvered in the latest nihilist style. Some people might have liked it.

She and Harry sat quietly until one of the "counselors" came to greet them.

"Harry." He shook hands. "Good to see you again. I see you've persuaded her." He turned to Connie. "You've made the right decision, Constance. I'm John Holland. Call me John."

He insisted on shaking her hand as well, holding on a moment as if to reassure her. It was all she could do to keep him from putting his arm across her shoulder as he led them to his office.

Behind his desk he was more businesslike. "First of all, are you taking advantage of the special this week?"

Harry looked pained, glanced briefly at Connie, then took the coupon from his pocket. "No jokes about paying in advance, John. Let's get on with it."

"We have to do this by the book, Harry. It's not so unpleasant as all that, is it? You two are about to get a second chance, thanks to the service we're offering. People throughout history have longed for that chance. They've gone to their graves dreaming of it. They've killed each other and themselves because they couldn't get it. Now you can have it; think how blessed you are."

He drew two contracts from a desk drawer. "I myself have had numerous traumas erased," he continued. "So completely that the only way I know about them is that I kept records. My mother's death. The time I struck out with the bases loaded in the College World Series. My baptism. I can talk frankly about these things now, without a trace of guilt or anger, because for me those events no longer exist. The people who hurt me no longer exist. Fifty years ago a psychiatrist might treat you for a decade trying to convince you that the past is over and can't hurt you. By this afternoon the past that hangs over both of you like a cloud—I can see it there now, and it's keeping you apart—will be gone. All that will be left will be the love you still feel for each other."

Connie wondered whether she could get them to erase this meeting for no extra charge. Harry looked as if he wanted to die. Connie could almost believe Holland was taking some perverse pleasure in Harry's discomfort. Or perhaps this was part of the treatment: make the patient realize the significance of the step he was taking, magnify the pain of the events he wants to have erased so that he will leap at the opportunity to have them expunged. If so, then Holland ought to be able to afford a better suit.

Holland placed one contract before each of them, and they talked for a while about what memories they wanted to have erased, and longer about exactly what they wanted to remember of their time together. Though there might be a few "echo losses," as he called them, he assured Connie that anything she wanted to keep would be preserved, and she would lose nothing vital to her job. She would remember the difference between short covering and profit-taking. If she was a champion skier, then she would remain one.

They signed the contracts. Harry took her hand, and they were led to the preparation rooms for memory pretesting. His palm was sweaty. In another room they were greeted by attendants whom Holland briefed, though they had all the relevant facts in their computer. Harry embraced her, and they were taken to separate rooms.

Once alone Connie began to panic. They gave her an injection. The machine they hooked her up to smelled of the hundreds of others who had come before her to have their pasts negated. The headset that let them map her cortex was cold and hard. The technicians did not know her; they did not care who she was, and it would not matter to them if by mistake they wiped out her personality entirely. Harry had no right to do this to her. She couldn't remember anything about him that would make her want to go back. She started to speak, she started to sit up and take the headset off. Or did she just think that? Harry had no right to take away her memories. She felt sleepy; the room did not look so threatening. The clean smell of disinfectant reminded her of the hospital emergency room where she'd taken Harry after he'd cut his hand so badly carrying a video display across the workroom. That was a piece of junk. It was still up there. He simply had no right.

Connie got a call at work the next day. She asked Mary to keep an eye on forex trading and went to her office to use the viewphone.

"Constance, this is Harry," the man on the screen said, as if she could not see him. When she didn't answer immediately, he added. "Harry Gray."

Her pulse quickened. "Don't worry, Harry. I remember you."

He closed his eyes for a beat, opened them again. His hair was light brown, worn longer than the general style. He seemed to be trying to smile, but uncertain how she would take it. They stared at each other, uncomfortable.

"Long time no see," Harry said.

She laughed. He looked so timid, yet aware of the absurdity.

"I feel funny talking to you," he said. "I feel like I'm imposing where I don't know what to say. Maybe we ought to wait awhile."

"No," she said suddenly, surprising herself. "I think we need to get to know each other. Why don't we meet for lunch? Do you know where Mario's is on Twelfth Street?"

He looked momentarily dazed, and then the smile came. "It's one of my favorites."

She liked his voice, his tentativeness. "Mine too," she said. She realized then that her memories of Mario's were spotty. She could remember the maître d's name, and that the veal was the best thing on the menu, but she could not recall many specific visits to the restaurant.

The maître d' knew them both: he gave them a secluded table. The conversation started tentatively. Connie hesitated to ask Harry if he remembered anything, while at the same time she was probing her own memory. In some ways it seemed that nothing had changed—she remembered their meeting, the first time they had made love, his favorite color, their honeymoon on *Orbital 6*, saving up to buy the house, his tinkering in the attic. But then there were curious half-memories of things she had done herself that did not seem complete, undoubtedly because Harry had been involved in some way. Holland had told her, in the posttesting, that she might lose memory of persons and things she strongly associated with Harry. And then there were whole periods from the last year or two that were fuzzy or blank. It was as if Harry had faded from her life a couple of years ago. Now here he was, back.

Connie wasn't sure she wanted to speculate about the hole in her memory of their marriage. But listening to Harry's self-deprecating little jokes, his warm voice, she could not help but realize that she had had some reason to have this man erased from her memory. She wondered what that reason was. Harry told her about his recent work at Triangle; she told him about commission trading in the foreign exchange markets. He seemed legitimately interested. His attention to her seemed complete.

They sat at the table long after the meal, ordered wine and talked. Harry's eyes were shy, and kind. He put his hand out to touch hers. They leaned forward in the light of the candle wrapped in plastic netting at the center of their table. He offered her some Lift; she declined, and he added a few drops to his own glass. Connie did not approve, but he did not seem to lose interest and his eyes remained bright and alert. She tried to remember the last time they'd slept together.

When they were about to leave he offered to take her home. She thought that meant he had his own car, but all he meant was that he'd ride the streetcar back with her. She wasn't sure she wanted to go that fast, knowing he would want to spend the night. Connie hesitated while the waiter took her credit card. Harry said nothing. Looking into her purse to avoid his expectant gaze, she found a small card tucked into one of the pockets. She pulled it out far enough to read, in Harry's handwriting: "No matter what you decide, I will never lie to you again." She slid it back into her purse. "Okay," she said. "It's a cool evening. It'll be a nice ride."

Connie was in love again. Soon he moved in with her; in the evenings he took to tinkering with his machines in the workroom. Connie found herself with new energy in her job. She had her mind right on the edge of trading, was able to get in and out of market positions before others in the electronic network even knew they had been established or were crumbling. She began trading for her own account in spare moments and made a killing when the Philippines exploded its first nuclear device and the yen dropped the limit. Harry and Connie talked about how to spend the windfall. They decided on an orbital vacation on *Habitat 3*.

In the weeks before they left, some things about Harry began to pluck at the edges of Connie's contentment. At times he seemed too desperately happy. He would take her hands in his and tell her how much he loved her, and the next day would return late from work. Lifted out of sight. He would never criticize her and he always seemed more than contented, but sometimes she wondered if Harry was actually seeing her, or only some projection of his own desire. When he became aware of her moments of silence in the midst of their new happiness, he begged her not to dwell on the past. How could she dwell on a past she couldn't remember?

On a hot July day one of Harry's friends came by in a company electric van and took them to the tube station where they boarded the magnetic train for the Cape. They spent three days in the hotel on the beach, swimming and sailing and eating seafood, a luxury they seldom saw in the Midwest. After that they took the shuttle up to the resort. They went to the free-fall ballet and did some dancing of their own. They spent hours in the transparent centrifugal pool, watching the universe wheel in lazy circles below them as they swam low-G arabesques in the water. Beneath the observation dome Connie got a very nice tan despite the ultraviolet screen that protected them from the hard sunlight of the vacuum. They ate in the many restaurants and watched the intricate exchange of partners that took place in the bar every night. Few of the guests were paired as strongly as Connie and Harry, and soon the propositions ended.

Making love in free-fall was familiar, but one of those experiences of which her memory would yield no details. Somehow this comforted her. She knew the reason for this was the forgotten knowledge that Harry had been her only partner.

At the end of the first week, Connie met a woman in the

lounge who was vaguely familiar. She wore the uniform of one of the staff. "Hello! I saw Harry this afternoon in the sauna. He told me you were back again."

Connie could not place her. The name "Alice" presented itself to her, unbidden. "Alice. How are you?"

Alice smiled. "Oh, I can see you must have been Lifted pretty high last night. A little hung over?"

"Not really. It's been a long time since I've seen you."

Alice would not accept that. She probed until Connie admitted she'd been erased. "Erased! How interesting! I wonder why Harry didn't tell me."

Given Alice's apparent nose for news it was not something Connie would have told her either. "Maybe it just didn't occur to him."

"But I asked him all about you. We rehashed old times. You look like you're doing better on the sunburn front now. Harry said you'd learned your lesson after that horrible burn you picked up last time."

Connie remembered the sunburn. But as Alice rambled on, the thought nagged at her.

"Harry talked with you about my sunburn? From the last trip?"

"Just in passing. He said you'd vowed never to let anything so dumb put you in the hospital again."

"You talked about our last trip?"

Alice looked puzzled. "Dear heart, you must be a little strung out. You sure you didn't do a little too much last night?"

Alice kept the puzzled expression as Connie made her excuses and left. She found Harry in their suite, adjusting his jewelry in the mirror. "Hi," he said. "Am I late? I was just about to come down to the lounge."

She watched his eyes in the mirror. "I ran into Alice," she said.

His glance caught hers, then shifted away. He brushed his hair back from his earring. "I saw her today, too. I'm surprised we didn't run into her sooner; you know how nosey she is. She just lives to know what's going on among the guests."

"I didn't remember her."

"Oh." He turned from the mirror. "You must have associated her more with me than I connected her with you, so the erasing wiped her out of your memory. John told me this might happen."

"You and John are pretty friendly."

He embraced her, ran his hand lightly down her spine. "What's the matter?" he asked.

He sounded perfectly sincere. He did not seem to be afraid to look at her. She ought to let it go at that. But it bothered her that something had happened then between them, something bad, that she couldn't recall. She remembered the card she still carried in her purse. "I will never lie to you again" meant that, although she could not remember it, he had lied to her before.

"Alice said you talked about my sunburn."

"She brought it up, yes. So what?"

"You remembered?"

"Yes, I did, vaguely. What's wrong with that?"

"I could hardly bring it back. How come you remember things that I don't?"

"I didn't remember any more than you. When she brought it up, it was all I could do to figure out what she was talking about."

"But you acted as if you knew."

"I must be a better actor than I imagine, then." He laughed; he moved away. "Connie, I just didn't want to admit that I'd been erased. You must have felt the same way when she started in on you. She's a gossip. She acted as if we were old friends, so I pretended to remember all the stuff she was talking about. I was embarrassed." He sat down on the edge of the bed and played with his wedding ring, turning it around his finger. "Why are you so suspicious?"

Connie watched him sitting there, and shuddered. *He had not been erased.*

She felt drugged, unable to grasp so huge a betrayal. She stared at him. She felt sick. She rushed into the bathroom and closed the door. She sat on the edge of the tub and put her head in her hands, attempting to slow her breathing.

Harry didn't come to the door. He didn't ask her what was wrong, he didn't plead. Stand and fight, her mind screamed, but as the minutes passed with still no response from him she began to have second thoughts. She couldn't know what he thought; she only had herself. The truth was that she *was* suspicious. The whole point of erasure was to give yourself a second chance. Maybe she had no reason to jump to such a drastic conclusion from such slim evidence.

The pastel floor tile gave no reassurance. Her shock faded. Harry could not be such a monster. He could not have coldly tricked her into giving herself away; he was not so clever or heartless or selfish as to steal a second chance for himself without paying in equal coin. The card in her purse was—had to be—a voucher of his love for her, not a warning of his unreliability.

She opened the door. Still sitting on the bed, he looked up expectantly. "Are you all right?" he asked.

"Yes." She felt like a ventriloquist speaking through a dummy.

"You have to believe me. I didn't know you'd take it this way. I lied to her; I didn't lie to you."

She sat beside him.

"Sometimes I wonder about the things we erased, too," he said.

She held him tightly and rested her head, eyes closed, on his shoulder.

"Go ahead," Harry said. "Sleep with Alice. I don't care."

A laugh forced itself to her lips. Tears stood in her eyes. "Let's forget it," she said.

Connie told Harry she was concerned about being away from the markets for so long. He suggested she arrange a private com-link through the resort over which she could transact her business as well as she might at home. She told him she wouldn't feel comfortable; a link could easily be tapped, and moreover her clients would have trouble reaching her. So they cut the vacation short.

At home they settled into a routine that left them less time with each other. Connie took on several new accounts that kept her busy in the office after the trading session ended each day, and she began working on a new economic model she wanted to merge into Fox. Harry had risen among the ranks of troubleshooters and was being sent out of town frequently to train people in other cities. When home, he spent more time in his workroom. On the surface everything was all right.

The one area of their lives that improved was sex. Harry seemed to want her more as the weeks went by, and Connie found herself trembling at his touch. She told herself she did not like being attacked with such energy; it was almost as if she were an object to him in those moments of frenzy, but his attention would be focused on her. He asked her continually what she wanted. He would be by turns rough and extraordinarily tender, as if she were as evanescent as snow in late spring, fallen way past its time, beautiful, transitory. She could ask him to do anything, and he would do it. His warm breath on her shoulder was like the light, mysterious breath of a cat. She could no more read his thoughts than she could a cat's, yet she suspected something of the same feral blankness behind the eyes that gleamed in the darkness of their bedroom.

She responded with the same passion, surrendering thought in the night as she could less and less give it up during the day. The further she drifted from him, the more pleasure she took in their lovemaking. *I'll never lie to you again.* She had thrown away the card the day they returned to earth. But it would not go away, and eventually she took an afternoon off and went to the office of New Life Choices.

Holland was busy and would be all afternoon, they told her, but she insisted on waiting. Ten minutes later he came out to the lobby and escorted her to his office.

"How can I help you, Constance."

"I want to see your copies of the contracts."

He got them. She examined Harry's. Everything was in order. She compared the signature with one she had from their marriage license; it was the same. The terms of Harry's contract were identical to hers. Holland watched her silently.

"Something bothering you?" he asked when she put the papers down.

"Did you know Harry before we came here to be erased?"

"Not well. We met at a party a couple of months earlier. Had a few drinks. He was pretty broken up about your separation."

"You didn't talk business then?"

Holland seemed calm. "I suggested he get erased. It's my business, and he seemed a good prospect. It was a surprise to me later when he told me he was asking you to do it, too."

Harry had asked *her* to get erased. For the first time Connie understood that it had not been her idea. Why had they erased that from her memory? "That's all there was to it? And you erased him when you did me?"

Holland frowned. "I know you don't like me," he said. "That's too bad. But you're not the first person to come in here accusing us of fraud. They come in and tell me we didn't really erase them, that they can remember everything they paid to have wiped out. Or that we erased too much. Or that their personality's changed. Or that they can't do their jobs. You name it.

"You think I erased you and not Harry? How long do you think we could stay in business, if that's true? There are laws. There are ethics of the business."

Connie almost laughed. "Ethics."

Holland did not get indignant. "Believe it or not. We did the job we were paid to do."

"That's an equivocation."

"We erased Harry Gray. You're married to him. Why don't you ask him?"

"Suppose he changed his mind on the couch, at the last minute."

"I'm not lying to you."

"That's what Harry says."

"So you did ask him?"

Connie didn't say anything. Holland was not the lightweight she had taken him for, or maybe he had practiced this conversation. Some palm readers, they said, even believed the predictions they made.

"Look," Holland said. "You're smart. I'll tell you something I've found out that I don't like to admit. We can erase the memories—'Pluck from the memory a rooted sorrow.' That's no problem. I used to think that we could 'minister to a mind diseased.' I'm not so sure anymore. The thing that makes a troubled memory is whatever happens to you. But people aren't as innocent as I used to think. They aren't just victims. Lots of things that 'just happened to them' they worked long and hard to get themselves into."

Connie stood. "Don't preach to me."

"We can't change the person. If you don't trust Harry, it's likely you didn't trust him before you were erased. Erasure doesn't change who you are. No matter what we advertise."

"It didn't change Harry."

" 'Therein the patient must minister to himself.' I'd like to take you out for a drink, Connie, but if you're going to keep this up you might as well just talk to our lawyers."

"I bet they're good ones. Do they quote Shakespeare, too?"

Holland gestured at the door. "Too bad," he said. "We might have had things to talk about."

It had been like a suicide pact. They had agreed to kill their memories together. But if Harry had not gone through with it while Connie did, then he had murdered her.

She had lunch with her lawyer, Barbara Curran. The weather had turned cold that morning and the first real autumn storm threatened, so they met at the seafood bar below Center City. Connie told Barbara about her suspicions and the visit to New Life. Barbara told her that no erasure company had ever been proved to have defaulted on a contract, a record of which the industry was so protective that the American Erasure Association had established a huge legal defense fund. Several suits were nonetheless pending. Barbara suggested that Connie probably should have gone through with the divorce she had planned, instead of deciding to get erased. Divorce. Connie felt as if someone had slapped her. Seeing how upset she was, after a little hesitation Barbara gave her a brief history of the breakup as Connie had told it to her a year earlier.

Harry was waiting in her office when Connie returned to the brokerage that afternoon. The other dealers were trying not to look curious.

"Harry. What brings you here?" She hung up her coat, trying to avoid his stare.

"I ran into John Holland today."

"Yes?"

"Why are you going around behind my back like this, Connie? If you've got some problem with the way things are going, why don't you tell me?"

She sat down behind her desk. "I don't have any problems."

He blew up. "Don't jerk me around, Connie! You think I'm stupid? What do you think Holland told me? You think I didn't go through with erasure, don't you. What kind of bastard do you take me for?"

Through the window that faced the trading room she could see the agents' faces turn toward the office.

"Don't shout. Draw the curtains."

"Screw the curtains! I want to know what's going on in that head of yours."

"That's a first. You never seemed to care much before. You wanted me to wipe out what's in my head. You want it now."

He paced back and forth before the window, hands knotted behind his back. "That's not fair," he said.

She felt vulnerable. "Maybe it's not. This has been rough for me. I can't help wondering about what things were like before I was erased."

"How would I know? Hasn't it been good since? Why rake up the past?"

"I can't change the past, Harry. It happened."

"What do you mean? Why would we get erased if not to change it?"

"So you did get erased?"

He stopped pacing and looked at her. The silence became uncomfortable. But she wouldn't wilt under that stare anymore. He closed his eyes, opened them again.

"That question doesn't deserve an answer," he said. "I'm your husband."

Now she was mad. "I'm your wife. I deserve the truth."

He sat down in the chair meant for her clients. "You really hate me, don't you?"

"You lied to me before. I have to know that you're not lying again."

Harry seemed to relax. It was a comfortable chair—she always treated her clients well.

"I love you," he said. "I've always loved you."

"That's not enough. I have to know the truth."

Instead of rushing to reassure her, he sat in the chair as if he had come there to talk about commodity options. His sudden withdrawal left Connie off-balance, as if a door she had been pushing against had been suddenly opened. "Say something, Harry. For god's sake—"

"Would you believe me if I said yes, I was erased?"

She hesitated. "I think so."

"Yes, I was erased. I don't remember any lies. Now what happens the next time I don't do what you expect? The next time I let you down?"

Connie felt dizzy. "I don't know. We'll have to see. It's not that simple—"

"You can explain it to me sometime." Harry shuddered visibly. He looked at the floor. "Maybe this wasn't such a hot idea."

She didn't know what to say. He stood. "I've got to go. I'm tired. I feel like I'm losing everything."

You squandered it, she thought. "Harry—"

"I'm going to move out for a while, Connie. I'll be gone by the time you get home."

Connie tried to say something, but he was gone. She couldn't say she wanted to see him there that evening, or any other evening. She felt ill. She replayed the scene in her mind, shuddering herself as she thought of Harry sitting impassively in the chair like a stunned animal. The traders were back to staring at their terminals; their curiosity evaporated when Harry left, or perhaps the gossip was put on hold until after hours.

Ten minutes later she went to her own terminal, read in the current market, hooked into Fox and the newsline. There were only forty minutes left in the trading session; the dollar was up against the ECU and off twenty against the yen. Activity was quiet; ninety-two traders in the pit circuit and everybody waiting for the 1500 EST release of the latest U.S. Gross National Product report. Connie evened up several accounts and went long dollars for her own account in anticipation of a positive report, contrary to expectations. At release time the GNP was up, and she made thirty thousand dollars before the close of trading.

After work she went to one of the best restaurants in town, ate alone, had three drinks. She had no desire to get home early. It had started raining by the time she left the restaurant; the lower level of the streetcar was crowded, and it was after eleven when she reached home. She got soaked in the half-block from the stop to her door. Harry wasn't there. She undressed, toweled her hair, and got into a robe. His closet was empty, the drawers of his dresser pulled open and bare, only his spare razor in the bathroom. By this time the wind had picked up and the rain rattled the windowpanes. She ran through the house turning on lights, closing windows, shutting off the lights again.

Harry's workroom was last. His computer was gone; he must have been able to get a van on short notice. The rest of his junk was still there. Maybe he still hoped to come back. The window beside his worktable stood open two inches, and the rain blew in. She ought to just leave it open, let Harry worry about his own machines, if he worried. She realized suddenly that despite all the time he had for them, he might not care about the machines at all. Well, she couldn't leave them at that.

Connie struggled to close the window all the way, but someone had jammed it downward crookedly so that it was caught at an angle in the frame, fighting against itself. It could not be forced closed. She grabbed the handles at the bottom of the frame and jerked upward. Nothing. She bent her knees and pulled with all her strength. It would not budge. When she let off, the muscles of her arms quivered with weakness. Already her slippers and the bottom of her robe were wet. The tree limbs outside the window raged back and forth in the wind; the rain drummed on the roof.

She found a crescent wrench. Using a short length of pipe as a fulcrum, she levered the wrench under the window and leaned all her weight on it. Her wet hands were slick, and the tight grip flushed the blood out of them. She put her shoulders into it and shoved the wrench downward. The window shot up an inch, the wrench slipped, and she fell. A gash in the palm of her hand bled profusely. She got up and pulled the window open, jiggling it when it stuck. The storm was at its height; when she leaned over to draw the window down again, the rain flew into her face. She gritted her teeth; it was almost a smile. The counterweights squeaked in the wall until the window was completely closed.

The drumming of rain on the roof increased. She sat on the floor in her wet robe and sucked the blood from her cut. It was not as bad as she'd thought.

BUFFALO

In April 1934 H. G. Wells made a trip to the United States, where he visited Washington, D.C., and met with President Franklin Delano Roosevelt. Wells, sixty-eighty years old, hoped the New Deal might herald a revolutionary change in the U.S. economy, a step forward in an "Open Conspiracy" of rational thinkers that would culminate in a world socialist state. For forty years he'd subordinated every scrap of his artistic ambition to promoting this vision. But by 1934 Wells's optimism, along with his energy for saving the world, was waning.

While in Washington he requested to see something of the new social welfare agencies, and Harold Ickes, Roosevelt's Interior Secretary, arranged for Wells to visit a Civilian Conservation Corps camp at Fort Hunt, Virginia.

It happens that at that time my father was a CCC member at that camp. From his boyhood he had been a reader of adventure stories; he was a big fan of Edgar Rice Burroughs, and of H. G. Wells. This is the story of their encounter, which never took place.

*   *   *

In Buffalo it's cold, but here the trees are in bloom, the mock-
ingbirds sing in the mornings, and the sweat the men work up
clearing brush, planting dogwoods, and cutting roads is wafted
away by warm breezes. Two hundred of them live in the Fort
Hunt barracks high on the bluff above the Virginia side of the Po-
tomac. They wear surplus army uniforms. In the morning, after
a breakfast of grits, Sergeant Sauter musters them up in the pa-
rade yard, they climb onto trucks and are driven by Forest Service men out to wherever they're to work that day.

For several weeks Kessel's squad has been working along the
river road, clearing rest stops and turnarounds. The tall pines
have shallow root systems, and spring rain has softened the earth
to the point where wind is forever knocking trees across the road.
While most of the men work on the ground, a couple are sent up
to cut off the tops of the pines adjoining the road, so if they do
fall, they won't block it. Most of the men claim to be afraid of
heights. Kessel isn't. A year or two ago back in Michigan he
worked in a logging camp. It's hard work, but he is used to hard
work. And at least he's out of Buffalo.

The truck rumbles and jounces out the river road, which is
going to be the George Washington Memorial Parkway in our
time, once the WPA project that will build it gets started. The
humid air is cool now, but it will be hot again today, in the eighties. A couple of the guys get into a debate about whether the feds
will ever catch Dillinger. Some others talk women. They're plan-
ning to go into Washington on the weekend and check out the
dance halls. Kessel likes to dance; he's a good dancer. The fox-
trot, the lindy hop. When he gets drunk he likes to sing, and has
a ready wit. He talks a lot more, kids the girls.

When they get to the site the foreman sets most of the men to
work clearing the roadside for a scenic overlook. Kessel straps on
a climbing belt, takes an ax, and climbs his first tree. The first
twenty feet are limbless, then climbing gets trickier. He looks
down only enough to estimate when he's gotten high enough.
He sets himself, cleats biting into the shoulder of a lower limb,
and chops away at the road side of the trunk. There's a trick to

cutting the top so that it falls the right way. When he's got it ready to go he calls down to warn the men below. Then a few quick bites of the ax on the opposite side of the cut, a shove, a crack, and the top starts to go. He braces his legs, ducks his head, and grips the trunk. The treetop skids off, and the bole of the pine waves ponderously back and forth, with Kessel swinging at its end like an ant on a metronome. After the pine stops swinging he shinnies down and climbs the next tree.

He's good at this work, efficient, careful. He's not a particularly strong man—slender, not burly—but even in his youth he shows the attention to detail that, as a boy, I remember seeing when he built our house.

The squad works through the morning, then breaks for lunch from the mess truck. The men are always complaining about the food, and how there isn't enough of it, but until recently a lot of them were living in Hoovervilles—shack cities—and eating nothing at all. As they're eating, a couple of the guys rag Kessel for working too fast. "What do you expect from a Yankee?" one of the southern boys says.

"He ain't a Yankee. He's a Polack."

Kessel tries to ignore them.

"Whyn't you lay off him, Turkel?" says Cole, one of Kessel's buddies.

Turkel is a big blond guy from Chicago. Some say he joined the CCCs to duck an armed robbery rap. "He works too hard," Turkel says. "He makes us look bad."

"Don't have to work much to make you look bad, Lou," Cole says. The others laugh, and Kessel appreciates it. "Give Jack some credit. At least he had enough sense to come down out of Buffalo." More laughter.

"There's nothing wrong with Buffalo," Kessel says.

"Except fifty thousand out-of-work Polacks," Turkel says.

"I guess you got no out-of-work people in Chicago," Kessel says. "You just joined for the exercise."

"Except he's not getting any exercise, if he can help it!" Cole says.

The foreman comes by and tells them to get back to work. Kessel climbs another tree, stung by Turkel's charge. What kind of man complains if someone else works hard? It only shows how even decent guys have to put up with assholes dragging them down. But it's nothing new. He's seen it before, back in Buffalo.

Buffalo, New York, is the symbolic home of this story. In the years preceding the First World War it grew into one of the great industrial metropolises of the United States. Located where Lake Erie flows into the Niagara River, strategically close to cheap electricity from Niagara Falls and cheap transportation by lake boat from the Midwest, it was a center of steel, automobiles, chemicals, grain milling, and brewing. Its major employers—Bethlehem Steel, Ford, Pierce-Arrow, Gold Medal Flour, the National Biscuit Company, Ralston Purina, Quaker Oats, National Aniline—drew thousands of immigrants like Kessel's family. Along Delaware Avenue stood the imperious and stylized mansions of the city's old-money, ersatz-Renaissance homes designed by Stanford White, huge Protestant churches, and a Byzantine synagogue. The city boasted the first modern skyscraper, designed by Louis Sullivan in the 1890s. From its productive factories to its polyglot workforce to its class system and its boosterism, Buffalo was a monument to modern industrial capitalism. It is the place Kessel has come from—almost an expression of his personality itself—and the place he, at times, fears he can never escape. A cold, grimy city dominated by church and family, blinkered and cramped, forever playing second fiddle to Chicago, New York, and Boston. It offers the immigrant the opportunity to find steady work in some factory or mill, but, though Kessel could not have put it into these words, it also puts a lid on his opportunities. It stands for all disappointed expectations, human limitations, tawdry compromises, for the inevitable choice of the expedient over the beautiful, for an American economic system that turns all things into commodities and measures men by their bank accounts. It is the home of the industrial proletariat.

It's not unique. It could be Youngstown, Akron, Detroit. It's the place my father, and I, grew up.

The afternoon turns hot and still; during a work break Kessel strips to the waist. About two o'clock a big black De Soto comes up the road and pulls off onto the shoulder. A couple of men in suits get out of the back, and one of them talks to the Forest Service foreman, who nods deferentially. The foreman calls over to the men.

"Boys, this here's Mr. Pike from the Interior Department. He's got a guest here to see how we work, a writer, Mr. H. G. Wells from England."

Most of the men couldn't care less, but the name strikes a spark in Kessel. He looks over at the little potbellied man in the dark suit. The man is sweating; he brushes his mustache.

The foreman sends Kessel up to show them how they're topping the trees. He points out to the visitors where the others with rakes and shovels are leveling the ground for the overlook. Several other men are building a log-rail fence from the treetops. From way above, Kessel can hear their voices between the thunks of his ax. H. G. Wells. He remembers reading "The War of the Worlds" in *Amazing Stories*. He's read *The Outline of History*, too. The stories, the history, are so large, it seems impossible that the man who wrote them could be standing not thirty feet below him. He tries to concentrate on the ax, the tree.

Time for this one to go. He calls down. The men below look up. Wells takes off his hat and shields his eyes with his hand. He's balding, and looks even smaller from up here. Strange that such big ideas could come from such a small man. It's kind of disappointing. Wells leans over to Pike and says something. The treetop falls away. The pine sways like a bucking bronco, and Kessel holds on for dear life.

He comes down with the intention of saying something to Wells, telling him how much he admires him, but when he gets down the sight of the two men in suits and his awareness of his own sweaty chest make him timid. He heads down to the next tree. After another ten minutes the men get back in the car, drive away. Kessel curses himself for the opportunity lost.

* * *

That evening at the New Willard Hotel, Wells dines with his old friends Clarence Darrow and Charles Russell. Darrow and Russell are in Washington to testify before a congressional committee on a report they have just submitted to the administration concerning the monopolistic effects of the National Recovery Act. The right wing is trying to eviscerate Roosevelt's program for large-scale industrial management, and the Darrow Report is playing right into their hands. Wells tries, with little success, to convince Darrow of the shortsightedness of his position.

"Roosevelt is willing to sacrifice the small man to the huge corporations," Darrow insists, his eyes bright.

"The small man? Your small man is a romantic fantasy," Wells says. "It's not the New Deal that's doing him in—it's the process of industrial progress. It's the twentieth century. You can't legislate yourself back into 1870."

"What about the individual?" Russell asks.

Wells snorts. "Walk out into the street. The individual is out on the street corner selling apples. The only thing that's going to save him is some coordinated effort, by intelligent, selfless men. Not your free market."

Darrow puffs on his cigar, exhales, smiles. "Don't get exasperated, H. G. We're not working for Standard Oil. But if I have to choose between the bureaucrat and the man pumping gas at the filling station, I'll take the pump jockey."

Wells sees he's got no chance against the American mythology of the common man. "Your pump jockey works for Standard Oil. And the last I checked, the free market hasn't expended much energy looking out for his interests."

"Have some more wine," Russell says.

Russell refills their glasses with the excellent Bordeaux. It's been a first-rate meal. Wells finds the debate stimulating even when he can't prevail; at one time that would have been enough, but as the years go on the need to prevail grows stronger in him. The times are out of joint, and when he looks around he sees desperation growing. A new world order is necessary—it's so clear that even a fool ought to see it—but if he can't even convince radicals like Darrow, what hope is there of gaining the acquiescence of the shareholders in the utility trusts?

The answer is that the changes will have to be made over their objections. As Roosevelt seems prepared to do. Wells's dinner with the president has heartened him in a way that his debate cannot negate.

Wells brings up an item he read in *The Washington Post*. A lecturer for the Communist party—a young Negro—was barred from speaking at the University of Virginia. Wells's question is, was the man barred because he was a Communist or because he was Negro?

"Either condition," Darrow says sardonically, "is fatal in Virginia."

"But students point out the university has allowed Communists to speak on campus before, and has allowed Negroes to perform music there."

"They can perform, but they can't speak," Russell says. "This isn't unusual. Go down to the Paradise Ballroom, not a mile from here. There's a Negro orchestra playing there, but no Negroes are allowed inside to listen."

"You should go to hear them anyway," Darrow says. "It's Duke Ellington. Have you heard of him?"

"I don't get on with the titled nobility," Wells quips.

"Oh, this Ellington's a noble fellow, all right, but I don't think you'll find him in the peerage," Russell says.

"He plays jazz, doesn't he?"

"Not like any jazz you've heard," Darrow says. "It's something totally new. You should find a place for it in one of your utopias."

All three of them are for helping the colored peoples. Darrow has defended Negroes accused of capital crimes. Wells, on his first visit to America almost thirty years ago, met with Booker T. Washington and came away impressed, although he still considers the peaceable coexistence of the white and colored races problematical.

"What are you working on now, Wells?" Russell says. "What

new improbability are you preparing to assault us with? Racial equality? Sexual liberation?"

"I'm writing a screen treatment based on *The Shape of Things to Come*," Wells says. He tells them about his screenplay, sketching out for them the future he has in his mind. An apocalyptic war, a war of unsurpassed brutality that will begin, in his film, in 1939. In this war, the creations of science will be put to the services of destruction in ways that will make the horrors of the Great War pale in comparison. Whole populations will be exterminated. But then, out of the ruins will arise the new world. The orgy of violence will purge the human race of the last vestiges of tribal thinking. Then will come the organization of the directionless and weak by the intelligent and purposeful. The new man. Cleaner, stronger, more rational. Wells can see it. He talks on, supplely, surely, late into the night. His mind is fertile with invention, still. He can see that Darrow and Russell, despite their Yankee individualism, are caught up by his vision. The future may be threatened, but it is not entirely closed.

Friday night, back in the barracks at Fort Hunt, Kessel lies on his bunk reading a secondhand *Wonder Stories*. He's halfway through the tale of a scientist who invents an evolution chamber that progresses him through fifty thousand years of evolution in an hour, turning him into a big-brained telepathic monster. The evolved scientist is totally without emotions and wants to control the world. But his body's atrophied. Will the hero, a young engineer, be able to stop him?

At a plank table in the aisle a bunch of men are playing poker for cigarettes. They're talking about women and dogs. Cole throws in his hand and comes over to sit on the next bunk. "Still reading that stuff, Jack?"

"Don't knock it until you've tried it."

"Are you coming into D.C. with us tomorrow? Sergeant Sauter says we can catch a ride in on one of the trucks."

Kessel thinks about it. Cole probably wants to borrow some money. Two days after he gets his monthly pay he's broke. He's always looking for a good time. Kessel spends his leave more quietly; he usually walks into Alexandria—about six miles—and sees a movie or just strolls around town. Still, he would like to see more of Washington. "Okay."

Cole looks at the sketchbook poking out from beneath Kessel's pillow. "Any more hot pictures?"

Immediately Kessel regrets trusting Cole. Yet there's not much he can say—the book is full of pictures of movie stars he's drawn. "I'm learning to draw. And at least I don't waste my time like the rest of you guys."

Cole looks serious. "You know, you're not any better than the rest of us," he says, not angrily. "You're just another Polack. Don't get so high-and-mighty."

"Just because I want to improve myself doesn't mean I'm high-and-mighty."

"Hey, Cole, are you in or out?" Turkel yells from the table.

"Dream on, Jack," Cole says, and returns to the game.

Kessel tries to go back to the story, but he isn't interested anymore. He can figure out that the hero is going to defeat the hyperevolved scientist in the end. He folds his arms behind his head and stares at the knots in the rafters.

It's true, Kessel does spend a lot of time dreaming. But he has things he wants to do, and he's not going to waste his life drinking and whoring like the rest of them.

Kessel's always been different. Quieter, smarter. He was always going to do something better than the rest of them; he's well spoken, he likes to read. Even though he didn't finish high school he reads everything: *Amazing, Astounding, Wonder Stories*. He believes in the future. He doesn't want to end up trapped in some factory his whole life.

Kessel's parents emigrated from Poland in 1911. Their name was Kisiel, but his got Germanized in Catholic school. For ten years the family moved from one to another middle-sized industrial town, as Joe Kisiel bounced from job to job. Springfield. Utica. Syracuse. Rochester. Kessel remembers them loading up a wagon in the middle of night with all their belongings in order to jump the rent on the run-down house in Syracuse. He remembers pulling a cart down to the Utica Club brewery, a nickel in his hand, to buy his father a keg of beer. He remembers them finally settling in the First Ward of Buffalo. The First Ward, at the foot of the Erie Canal, was an Irish neighborhood as far back as anybody could remember, and the Kisiels were the only Poles there. That's where he developed his chameleon ability to fit in, despite the fact he wanted nothing more than to get out. But he had to protect his mother, sister, and little brothers from their father's drunken rages. When Joe Kisiel died in 1924 it was a relief, despite the fact that his son ended up supporting the family.

For ten years Kessel has strained against the tug of that responsibility. He's sought the free and easy feeling of the road, of places different from where he grew up, romantic places where the sun shines and he can make something entirely American of himself.

Despite his ambitions, he's never accomplished much. He's been essentially a drifter, moving from job to job. Starting as a pinsetter in a bowling alley, he moved on to a flour mill. He would have stayed in the mill only he developed an allergy to the flour dust, so he became an electrician. He would have stayed an electrician except he had a fight with a boss and got blacklisted. He left Buffalo because of his father; he kept coming back because of his mother. When the Depression hit he tried to get a job in Detroit at the auto factories, but that was plain stupid in the face of the universal collapse, and he ended up working up in the peninsula as a farmhand, then as a logger. It was seasonal work, and when the season was over he was out of a job. In the winter of 1933, rather than freeze his ass off in northern Michigan, he joined the CCC. Now he sends twenty-five of his thirty dollars a month back to his mother and sister in Buffalo. And imagines the future.

When he thinks about it, there are two futures. The first is the one from the magazines and books. Bright, slick, easy. We, looking back on it, can see it to be the fifteen-cent utopianism of Hugo Gernsback's *Science and Mechanics,* which flourished in the midst of the Depression. A degradation of the marvelous inventions that made Wells his early reputation, minus the social theorizing that drove Wells's technological speculations. The common man's boosterism. There's money to be made telling people like Jack Kessel about the wonderful world of the future.

The second future is Kessel's own. That one's a lot harder to see. It contains work. A good job, doing something he likes, using his skills. Not working for another man, but making something that would be useful for others. Building something for the future. And a woman, a gentle woman, for his wife. Not some cheap dance-hall queen.

So when Kessel saw H. G. Wells in person, that meant something to him. He's had his doubts. He's twenty-nine years old, not a kid anymore. If he's ever going to get anywhere, it's going to have to start happening soon. He has the feeling that something significant is going to happen to him. Wells is a man who sees the future. He moves in that bright world where things make sense. He represents something that Kessel wants.

But the last thing Kessel wants is to end up back in Buffalo.

He pulls the sketchbook, the sketchbook he was to show me twenty years later, from under his pillow. He turns past drawings of movie stars: Jean Harlow, Mae West, Carole Lombard—the beautiful, unreachable faces of his longing—and of natural scenes: rivers, forests, birds—to a blank page. The page is as empty as the future, waiting for him to write upon it. He lets his imagination soar. He envisions an eagle, gliding high above the mountains of the West that he has never seen, but that he knows he will visit someday. The eagle is America; it is his own dreams. He begins to draw.

Kessel does not know that Wells's life has not worked out as well as he planned. At that moment Wells is pining after the Russian émigrée Moura Budberg, once Maxim Gorky's secretary, with whom Wells has been carrying on an off-and-on affair since 1920. His wife of thirty years, Amy Catherine "Jane" Wells, died in 1927. Since that time Wells has been adrift, alternating spells of furious pamphleteering with listless periods of suicidal depression. Meanwhile, all London is gossiping about the recent attack published in *Time and Tide* by his vengeful ex-lover Odette Keun. Have his mistakes followed him across the Atlantic to undermine his purpose? Does Darrow think him a jumped-up cockney? A moment of doubt overwhelms him. In the end, the future depends as much on the open-mindedness of men like Darrow as it does on a reorganization of society. What good is a guild of samurai if no one arises to take the job?

Wells doesn't like the trend of these thoughts. If human nature lets him down, then his whole life has been a waste.

But he's seen the president. He's seen those workers on the road. Those men climbing the trees risk their lives without complaining, for minimal pay. It's easy to think of them as stupid or desperate or simply young, but it's also possible to give them credit for dedication to their work. They don't seem to be ridden by the desire to grub and clutch that capitalism rewards; if you look at it properly that may be the explanation for their ending up wards of the state. And is Wells any better? If he hadn't got an education he would have ended up a miserable draper's assistant.

Wells is due to leave for New York Sunday. Saturday night finds him sitting in his room, trying to write, after a solitary dinner in the New Willard. Another bottle of wine, or his age, has stirred something in Wells, and despite his rationalizations he finds himself near despair. Moura has rejected him. He needs the soft, supportive embrace of a lover, but instead he has this stuffy hotel room in a heat wave.

He remembers writing *The Time Machine,* he and Jane living in rented rooms in Sevenoaks with her ailing mother, worried about money, about whether the landlady would put them out. In the drawer of the dresser was a writ from the court that refused to grant him a divorce from his wife Isabel. He remembers a warm night, late in August—much like this one—sitting up after Jane and her mother went to bed, writing at the round table before the open window, under the light of a paraffin lamp. One part of his mind was caught up in the rush of creation, burning, following the Time Traveler back to the Sphinx, pursued by the Morlocks, only to discover that his machine is gone and he is trapped without escape from his desperate circumstance. At the same moment he could hear the landlady, out in the garden, fully aware that he could hear her, complaining to the neighbor about his and Jane's scandalous habits. On the one side, the petty conventions of a crabbed world; on the other, in his mind—the future, their peril and hope. Moths fluttering through the window beat themselves against the lampshade and fell onto the manuscript; he brushed them away unconsciously and continued, furiously, in a white heat. The Time Traveler, battered and hungry, returning from the future with a warning, and a flower.

He opens the hotel windows all the way, but the curtains aren't stirred by a breath of air. Below, in the street, he hears the sound of traffic, and music. He decides to send a telegram to Moura, but after several false starts he finds he has nothing to say. Why has she refused to marry him? Maybe he is finally too old, and the magnetism of sex or power or intellect that has drawn women to him for forty years has finally all been squandered. The prospect of spending the last years remaining to him alone fills him with dread.

He turns on the radio, gets successive band shows: Morton Downey, Fats Waller. Jazz. Paging through the newspaper, he comes across an advertisement for the Ellington orchestra Darrow mentioned: it's at the ballroom just down the block. But the thought of a smoky room doesn't appeal to him. He considers the cinema. He has never been much for the "movies." Though he thinks them an unrivaled opportunity to educate, that promise has never been properly seized—something he hopes to do in *Things to Come*. The newspaper reveals an uninspiring selection: *Twenty Million Sweethearts*, a musical at the Earle, *The Black Cat*, with Boris Karloff and Bela Lugosi at the Rialto, and *Tarzan and His Mate* at the Palace. To these Americans he is the equivalent of this hack, Edgar Rice Burroughs. The books I read as a child, that fired my father's imagination and my own, Wells considers his frivolous apprentice work. His serious work is discounted. His ideas mean nothing.

Wells decides to try the Tarzan movie. He dresses for the sultry weather—Washington in spring is like high summer in London—and goes down to the lobby. He checks his street guide and takes the streetcar to the Palace Theater, where he buys an orchestra seat, for twenty-five cents, to see *Tarzan and His Mate*.

It is a perfectly wretched movie, comprised wholly of romantic fantasy, melodrama, and sexual innuendo. The dramatic leads perform with wooden idiocy surpassed only by the idiocy of the screenplay. Wells is attracted by the undeniable charms of the young heroine, Maureen O'Sullivan, but the film is devoid of intellectual content. Thinking of the audience at which such a farrago must be aimed depresses him. This is art as fodder. Yet the theater is filled, and the people are held in rapt attention. This only depresses Wells more. If these citizens are the future of America, then the future of America is dim.

An hour into the film the antics of an anthropomorphized chimpanzee, a scene of transcendent stupidity that nevertheless sends the audience into gales of laughter, drives Wells from the theater. It is still midevening. He wanders down the avenue of theaters, restaurants, and clubs. On the sidewalk are beggars, ignored by the passersby. In an alley behind a hotel Wells spots a woman and child picking through the ashcans beside the restaurant kitchen.

Unexpectedly, he comes upon the marquee announcing DUKE ELLINGTON AND HIS ORCHESTRA. From within the open doors of the ballroom wafts the sound of jazz. Impulsively, Wells buys a ticket and goes in.

Kessel and his cronies have spent the day walking around the mall, which the WPA is relandscaping. They've seen the Lincoln Memorial, the Capitol, the Washington Monument, the Smithsonian, the White House. Kessel has his picture taken in front of a statue of a soldier—a photo I have sitting on my desk. I've studied it many times. He looks forthrightly into the camera, faintly smiling. His face is confident, unlined.

When night comes they hit the bars. Prohibition was lifted only last year, and the novelty has not yet worn off. The younger men get plastered, but Kessel finds himself uninterested in getting drunk. A couple of them set their minds on women and head for the Gayety Burlesque; Cole, Kessel, and Turkel end up in the Paradise Ballroom listening to Duke Ellington.

They have a couple of drinks, ask some girls to dance. Kessel dances with a short girl with a southern accent who refuses to look him in the eyes. After thanking her he returns to the others at the bar. He sips his beer. "Not so lucky, Jack?" Cole says.

"She doesn't like a tall man," Turkel says.

Kessel wonders why Turkel came along. Turkel is always complaining about "niggers," and his only comment on the Ellington band so far has been to complain about how a bunch of jigs can make a living playing jungle music while white men sleep in barracks and eat grits three times a day. Kessel's got nothing against the colored, and he likes the music, though it's not exactly the kind of jazz he's used to. It doesn't sound much like Dixieland. It's darker, bigger, more dangerous. Ellington, resplendent in tie and tails, looks like he's enjoying himself up there at his piano, knocking out minimal solos while the orchestra plays cool and low.

Turning from them to look across the tables, Kessel sees a little man sitting alone beside the dance floor, watching the young couples sway in the music. To his astonishment he recognizes Wells. He's been given another chance. Hesitating only a moment, Kessel abandons his friends, goes over to the table and introduces himself.

"Excuse me, Mr. Wells. You might not remember me, but I was one of the men you saw yesterday in Virginia working along the road. The CCC?"

Wells looks up at a gangling young man wearing a khaki uniform, his olive tie neatly knotted and tucked between the second and third buttons of his shirt. His hair is slicked down, parted in the middle. Wells doesn't remember anything of him. "Yes?"

"I—I been reading your stories and books a lot of years. I admire your work."

Something in the man's earnestness affects Wells. "Please sit down," he says.

Kessel takes a seat. "Thank you." He pronounces "th" as "t" so that "thank" comes out "tank." He sits tentatively, as if the chair is mortgaged, and seems at a loss for words.

"What's your name?"

"John Kessel. My friends call me Jack."

The orchestra finishes a song and the dancers stop in their places, applauding. Up on the bandstand, Ellington leans into the microphone. "Mood Indigo," he says, and instantly they swing into it: the clarinet moans in low register, in unison with the muted trumpet and trombone, paced by the steady rhythm guitar, the brushed drums. The song's melancholy suits Wells's mood.

"Are you from Virginia?"

"My family lives in Buffalo. That's in New York."

"Ah—yes. Many years ago I visited Niagara Falls, and took the train through Buffalo." Wells remembers riding along a lakefront of factories spewing waste water into the lake, past heaps of coal, clouds of orange and black smoke from blast furnaces. In front of dingy row houses, ragged hedges struggled through the smoky air. The landscape of laissez-faire. "I imagine the Depression has hit Buffalo severely."

"Yes sir."

"What work did you do there?"

Kessel feels nervous, but he opens up a little. "A lot of things. I used to be an electrician until I got blacklisted."

"Blacklisted?"

"I was working on this job where the super told me to set the wiring wrong. I argued with him, but he just told me to do it his way. So I waited until he went away, then I sneaked into the construction shack and checked the blueprints. He didn't think I could read blueprints, but I could. I found out I was right and he was wrong. So I went back and did it right. The next day when he found out, he fired me. Then the so-and-so went and got me blacklisted."

Though he doesn't know how much credence to put in this story, Wells finds that his sympathies are aroused. It's the kind of thing that must happen all the time. He recognizes in Kessel the immigrant stock that, when Wells visited the U.S. in 1906, made him skeptical about the future of America. He'd theorized that these Italians and Slavs, coming from lands with no democratic tradition, unable to speak English, would degrade the already corrupt political process. They could not be made into good citizens; they would not work well when they could work poorly, and given the way the economic deal was stacked against them would seldom rise high enough to do better.

But Kessel is clean, well spoken despite his accent, and deferential. Wells realizes that this is one of the men who was topping trees along the river road.

Meanwhile, Kessel detects a sadness in Wells's manner. He had not imagined that Wells might be sad, and he feels sympathy for him. It occurs to him, to his own surprise, that he might be able to make *Wells* feel better. "So—what do you think of our country?" he asks.

"Good things seem to be happening here. I'm impressed with your President Roosevelt."

"Roosevelt's the best friend the workingman ever had." Kessel pronounces the name "Roozvelt." "He's a man that . . ." he struggles for the words, ". . . that's not for the past. He's for the future."

It begins to dawn on Wells that Kessel is not an example of a class, or a sociological study, but a man like himself with an intellect, opinions, dreams. He thinks of his own youth, struggling to rise in a class-bound society. He leans forward across the table. "You believe in the future? You think things can be different?"

"I think they have to be, Mr. Wells."

Wells sits back. "Good. So do I."

Kessel is stunned by this intimacy. It is more than he had hoped for, yet it leaves him with little to say. He wants to tell Wells about his dreams, and at the same time ask him a thousand questions. He wants to tell Wells everything he has seen in the world, and to hear Wells tell him the same. He casts about for something to say.

"I always liked your writing. I like to read scientifiction."

"Scientifiction?"

Kessel shifts his long legs. "You know—stories about the future. Monsters from outer space. The Martians. *The Time Machine.* You're the best scientifiction writer I ever read, next to Edgar Rice Burroughs." Kessel pronounces "Edgar" as "Eedgar."

"Edgar Rice Burroughs?"

"Yes."

"You *like* Burroughs?"

Kessel hears the disapproval in Wells's voice. "Well—maybe not as much as, as *The Time Machine,*" he stutters. "Burroughs never wrote about monsters as good as your Morlocks."

Wells is nonplussed. "Monsters."

"Yes." Kessel feels something's going wrong, but he sees no way out. "But he does put more romance in his stories. That princess—Dejah Thoris?"

All Wells can think of is Tarzan in his loincloth on the movie screen, and the moronic audience. After a lifetime of struggling, a hundred books written to change the world, in the service of men like this, is this all his work has come to? To be compared to the writer of pulp trash? To "Eedgar" Rice Burroughs? He laughs aloud.

At Wells's laugh, Kessel stops. He knows he's done something wrong, but he doesn't know what.

Wells's weariness has dropped down onto his shoulders again like an iron cloak. "Young man—go away," he says. "You don't know what you're saying. Go back to Buffalo."

Kessel's face burns. He stumbles from the table. The room is full of noise and laughter. He's run up against that wall again. He's just an ignorant Polack after all; it's his stupid accent, his clothes. He should have talked about something else—*The Outline of History*, politics. But what made him think he could talk like an equal with a man like Wells in the first place? Wells lives in a different world. The future is for men like him. Kessel feels himself the prey of fantasies. It's a bitter joke.

He clutches the bar, orders another beer. His reflection in the mirror behind the ranked bottles is small and ugly.

"Whatsa matter, Jack?" Turkel asks him. "Didn't he want to dance neither?"

And that's the story, essentially, that never happened.

Not long after this, Kessel did go back to Buffalo. During the Second World War he worked as a crane operator in the forty-inch rolling mill of Bethlehem Steel. He met his wife, Angela Giorlandino, during the war, and they married in June 1945. After the war he quit the plant and became a carpenter. Their first child, a girl, died in infancy. Their second, a boy, was born in 1950. At that time Kessel began building the house that, like so many things in his life, he was never entirely to complete. He worked hard, had two more children. There were good years and bad ones. He held a lot of jobs. The recession of 1958 just about flattened him; our family had to go on welfare. Things got better, but they never got good. After the 1950s, the economy of Buffalo, like that of all U.S. industrial cities caught in the transition to a postindustrial age, declined steadily. Kessel never did work for himself, and as an old man was little more prosperous than he had been as a young one.

In the years preceding his death in 1946 Wells was to go on to further disillusionment. His efforts to create a sane world met with increasing frustration. He became bitter, enraged. Moura Budberg never agreed to marry him, and he lived alone. The war came, and it was, in some ways, even worse than he had predicted. He continued to propagandize for the socialist world state throughout, but with increasing irrelevance. The new leftists like Orwell considered him a dinosaur, fatally out of touch with the realities of world politics, a simpleminded technocrat with no understanding of the darkness of the human heart. Wells's last book, *Mind at the End of Its Tether,* proposed that the human race faced an evolutionary crisis that would lead to its extinction unless humanity leapt to a higher state of consciousness; a leap about which Wells speculated with little hope or conviction.

Sitting there in the Washington ballroom in 1934, Wells might well have understood that for all his thinking and preaching about the future, the future had irrevocably passed him by.

But the story isn't quite over yet. Back in the Washington ballroom Wells sits humiliated, a little guilty for sending Kessel away so harshly. Kessel, his back to the dance floor, stares humiliated into his glass of beer. Gradually, both of them are pulled back from dark thoughts of their own inadequacies by the sound of Ellington's orchestra.

Ellington stands in front of the big grand piano, behind him the band: three saxes, two clarinets, two trumpets, trombones, a drummer, guitarist, bass. "Creole Love Call," Ellington whispers into the microphone, then sits again at the piano. He waves his hand once, twice, and the clarinets slide into a low wavering theme. The trumpet, muted, echoes it. The bass player and guitarist strum ahead at a deliberate pace, rhythmic, erotic, bluesy. Kessel and Wells, separate across the room, each unaware of the other, are alike drawn in. The trumpet growls eight bars of raucous solo. The clarinet follows, wailing. The music is full of pain and longing—but pain controlled, ordered, mastered. Longing unfulfilled, but not overpowering.

As I write this, it plays on my stereo. If anyone has a right to bitterness at thwarted dreams, a black man in 1934 has that right. That such men can, in such conditions, make this music opens a world of possibilities.

Through the music speaks a truth about art that Wells does not understand, but that I hope to: that art doesn't have to deliver a message in order to say something important. That art isn't always a means to an end but sometimes an end in itself. That art may not be able to change the world, but it can still change the moment.

Through the music speaks a truth about life that Kessel, sixteen years before my birth, doesn't understand, but that I hope to: that life constrained is not life wasted. That despite unfulfilled dreams, peace is possible.

Listening, Wells feels that peace steal over his soul. Kessel feels it too.

And so they wait, poised, calm, before they move on into their respective futures, into our own present. Into the world of limitation and loss. Into Buffalo.

for my father

NOT RESPONSIBLE! PARK AND LOCK IT!

David Baker was born in the backseat of his parents' Chevy in the great mechanized lot at mile 1.375×10^{25}. "George, we need to stop," his mother Polly said. "I'm having pains." She was a week early.

They had been cruising along pretty well at twilight, his father concentrating on getting in another fifty miles before dark, when they were cut off by the big two-toned Mercury and George had to swerve four lanes over into the far right. George and Polly later decided that the near-accident was the cause of the premature birth. They even managed to laugh at the incident in retrospect—they ruefully retold the story many times, so that it was one of the family fables David grew up with—but David always suspected his father pined after those lost fifty miles. In return he'd gotten a son.

"Not responsible! Park and lock it!" the loudspeakers at the tops of the poles in the vast asphalt field shouted, over and over. For a first birth Polly's labor was surprisingly short, and the robot doctor emerged from the Chevy in the gathering evening with a healthy seven-pound boy. George Baker flipped his cigarette away nervously, the butt glowing as it spun into the night. He smiled.

In the morning George stepped into the bar at the first rest stop, had a quick one, and registered his name: David John Baker. Born 8:15 Standard Westbound Time, June 13 . . .

"What year is it?" George asked the bartender.

"802,701." The robot smiled benignly. It could not do otherwise.

"802,701." George repeated it aloud and punched the keys of the terminal. "Eight hundred two thousand, seven hundred and one." The numbers spun themselves out like a song. Eight-oh-two, seven-oh-one.

David's mother had smiled weakly, reclining in the passenger's seat, when they'd started again. Her smile had never been strong. David slept on her breast.

Much later Polly told David what a good baby he'd been, not like his younger sister Caroline, who had the colic. David took satisfaction in that: he was the good one. It made the competition between him and Caroline even more intense. But that was later. As a baby David slept to the steady thrumming of the V-8 engine, the gentle rocking of the car. He was cooed at by the android attendants at the camps where they pulled over at the end of the day. His father would chat with the machine that came over to check the odometer and validate their mileage card. George would tell about any of the interesting things that had happened on the road—and he always seemed to have something—while Polly fixed supper at one of the grills and the ladies from the other cars sat around in a circle in front of the komfy kabins and talked about their children, their husbands, about their pregnancies and how often they got to drive. David sat on Polly's lap or played with the other kids. Once past the toddler stage he followed his dad around and watched, a little scared, as the greasy self-assured robots busied themselves about the service station. They were large and composed. The young single drivers tried hard to compete with their mechanical self-containment. David hung on everything his dad said.

"The common driving man," George Baker said, hands on the wheel, "the good average driver—doesn't know his asshole from a tailpipe."

Polly would draw David to her, as if to blot out the words. "George—"

"All right. The kid will know whether you want him to or not."

But David didn't know, and they wouldn't tell him. That was the way of parents: they never told you even when they thought they were explaining everything, and so David was left to wonder and learn as best he could. He watched the land speed by long before he had words to say what he saw; he listened to his father tell his mother what was wrong and right with the world. And the sun set every night at the other end of that world, far ahead of them still, beyond the gas stations and the wash-and-brushup buildings and the quietly deferential androids that always seemed the same no matter how far they'd gone that day, Westbound.

When David was six he got to sit on George's lap, hold the wheel in his hands, and "drive the car." With what great chasms of anticipation and awe did he look forward to those moments! His father would say suddenly, after hours of driving in silence, "Come sit on my lap, David. You can drive."

Polly would protest feebly that he was too young. It was dangerous. David would clamber into his dad's lap and grab the wheel. How warm it felt, how large, and how far apart he had to put his hands! The indentations on the back were too wide for his fingers, so that two of his fit into the space meant for one adult's. George would move the seat up and scrunch his thin legs together so that David could see over the hood of the car. His father operated the pedals and gearshift, and most of the time he kept his left hand on the wheel too—but then he would slowly take it away and David would be steering all by himself. His heart had beaten fast. At those moments the car had seemed so large. The promise and threat of its speed had been almost overwhelming. He knew that by a turn of the wheel he could be in the high-speed lane; he knew, even more amazingly, that he held in his hands the potential to steer them off the road, into the gully, and death. The responsibility was great, and David took it seriously. He didn't want to do anything foolish, he didn't want to make George think him any less a man. He knew his mother was watching. Whether she had love or fear in her eyes he could not know, because he couldn't take his eyes from the road to see.

When David was seven there was a song on the radio that Polly sang to him, "We all drive on." That was his song. David sang it back to her, and his father laughed and sang it too, badly, voice hoarse and off-key, not like his mother, whose voice was sweet. "We all drive on," they sang together.

> "You and me and everyone
> Never ending, just begun
> Driving, driving on."

"Goddamn right we drive on," George said. "Goddamn pack of maniacs."

David remembered clearly the first time he became aware of the knapsack and the notebook. It was one evening after they'd eaten supper and were waiting for Polly to get the cabin ready for bed. George went around to the trunk to check the spare, and this time he took a green knapsack out and, in the darkness near the edge of the campground, secretively opened it.

"Watch, David, and keep your mouth shut about what you see."

David watched.

"This is for emergencies." George, one by one, set the things on the ground: first a rolled oilcloth, which he spread out, then a line of tools, then a gun and boxes of bullets, a first-aid kit, some packages of crackers and dried fruit, and some things David didn't know. One thing had a light and a thick wire and batteries.

"This is a metal detector, David. I made it myself." George took a black book from the sack. "This is my notebook." He handed it to David. It was heavy and smelled of the trunk.

"Maps of the Median, and—"

"George!" Polly's voice was a harsh whisper, and David jumped a foot. She grabbed his arm. George looked exasperated and a little guilty—though David did not identify his father's reaction as guilt until he thought about it much later. He was too busy trying to avoid the licking he thought was coming. His mother marched him back to the cabin after giving George her best withering gaze.

"But Mom—"

"To sleep! Don't puzzle yourself about things you aren't meant to know, young man."

David puzzled himself. At times the knapsack and the notebook filled his thoughts. His father would give him a curious glance and tantalizingly vague answers whenever he asked about them—safely out of earshot of Polly.

Shortly after that Caroline was born. This time the Bakers were not caught by surprise, and Caroline came into the world at the hospital at mile 1.375×10^{25}, where they stopped for three whole days for Polly's lying in. Nobody stopped for three whole days, for anything. David was impatient. They'd never *get* anywhere waiting, and the androids in the hospital were all boring, and the comic books in the motionless waiting room he had all read before.

This time the birth was a hard one. George sat hunched forward in a plastic chair, and David paced around, stomping on the cracks in the linoleum. He leaned on the windowsill and watched all the cars fly by on the highway, Westbound, and in the distance, beyond the barbed wire, sentry towers and minefields, mysterious, ever unattainable—Eastbound.

After what seemed like a very long time, the white porcelain doctoroid came back to them. George stood up as soon as he appeared. "Is she—"

"Both fine. A little girl. Seven pounds, five ounces," the doctoroid reported, grille gleaming.

George didn't say anything then, just sat down in the chair. After a while he came over to David, put his hand on the boy's shoulder, and they both watched the cars moving by, the light of the bright midsummer's sun flashing off the windshields as they passed, blinding them.

David was nine when they bought the Nash. It had a big chrome grille that stretched like a bridge across the front, the vertical bars bulging outward in the middle, so that, with the headlights, the car looked to be grinning a big nasty grin.

David went with George through the car lot while Polly sat with Caroline in the lounge of the dealership. He watched his father dicker with the bow-tied salesdroid. George acted as if he seriously meant to buy a new car, when in fact his yearly mileage average would entitle him to no more than a second-hand, second-rank sedan, unless he intended for them all to go hungry. He wouldn't have done that, however. Whatever else Polly might say about her husband, she could not say he wasn't a good provider.

"So why don't you show us a good used car," George said, running his hand through his thinning hair. "Mind you, don't show us any piece of junk."

The salesdroid was, like his brothers, enthusiastic and unreadable. "Got just the little thing for you, Mr. Baker—a snappy number. C'mon," it said, rolling down toward the back of the lot.

"Here you go." It opened the door of the blue Nash with its amazingly dextrous hand. David's father got in. "Feel that genuine vinyl upholstery. Not none of your cheap plastics, that'll crack in a week of direct sun." The salesdroid winked its glassy eye at David. "Hop in, son. See how you like it."

David started to, then saw the look of warning on George's face.

"Let's have a look at the engine," George said.

"Righto." The droid rolled around the fat front fender, reached through the grille, and tripped the latch. The engine was clean as a whistle, the cylinder heads painted cherry red, the spark plug leads numbered for easy changes. It was like the pictures out of David's schoolbooks.

The droid started up the Nash; the motor gave out a rumble

and vibrated ever so slightly. David smelled the clean tang of evaporating gasoline.

"Only one owner," the droid said, volume turned up now so it could be heard over the sound of the engine.

George looked uncertain.

"How much?"

"Book says it's worth 200,000 validated miles. You can drive her out, with your Chevy in trade, for . . . let me calculate . . . 174,900."

Just then David noticed something in the engine compartment. On either side over the wheel wells there were cracks in the metal that had been painted over so you could only see them from the reflection of the sunlight where the angle of the surface changed. That was where the shocks connected up with the car's body.

He tugged at his father's sleeve. "Dad," he said, pointing.

George ran a hand over the metal. He looked serious. David thought he was going to get mad. Instead he straightened up and smiled.

"How much did you say?"

The android stood stock-still. "150,000 miles."

"But Dad—"

"Shut up, David," he said. "I'll tell you what, Mr. Sixty. 100,000. And you reweld those wheel wells before we drive it an inch."

That was how they bought the Nash. The first thing George said when they were on their way again was, "Polly, that boy of ours is smart as a whip. The shocks were about to rip through the bodywork, and we'd of been scraping down the highway with our nose to the ground like a basset. David, you're a born driver, or else too smart to waste yourself on it."

David didn't quite follow that, but it made him a little more content to move into the backseat. At first he resented it that Caroline had taken his place in the front. She got all the attention, and David only got to sit and look out at where they had been, or what they were going by, never getting a good look at where they were going. If he leaned over the back of the front seat, his father would say, "Quit breathing down my neck, David. Sit down and behave yourself. Do your homework."

After a while he wouldn't have moved into the front if they'd asked him to: that was for babies. Instead he watched raptly out the left side-window for fleeting glimpses of Eastbound, wondering always about what it was, how it got there, and about the no-man's-land and the people they said had died trying to cross. He asked George about it, and that started up the biggest thing they were ever to share together.

"They've told you about Eastbound in school, have they?"

"They told us we can't go there. Nobody can."

"Did they tell you why?"

"No."

His father laughed. "That's because they don't know why! Isn't that incredible, David? They teach a thing in school, and everybody believes it, and nobody knows why or even thinks to ask. But you wonder, don't you? I've seen it."

He did wonder. It scared him that his father would talk about it.

"Men are slipstreamers, David. Did you ever see a car follow close behind a big truck to take advantage of the windbreak to make the driving easier? That's the way people are. They'll follow so close they can't see six inches beyond their noses, as long as it makes things easier. And the schools and the teachers are the biggest windbreaks of all. You remember that. Do you remember the knapsack in the trunk?"

"*George,*" Polly said.

"Be quiet, Polly. The boy's growing up." To David he said, "You know what it's for. You know what's inside."

"To go across . . ." David hesitated, his heart leaping.

"To cross the Median! We can do it. We don't have to be like everybody else, and when the time comes, when we need to get away the most, when things are really bad—we can do it! I'm prepared to do it."

Polly tried to shush him, and it became an argument. But David was thrilled at the new world that had opened. His father was a criminal—but he was right! From then on they worked on the preparations together. They would have long talks on what they would do and how they would do it. David drew maps on graph paper, and sometimes he and George would climb to the highest spot available by the roadside at the day's end, to puzzle out once again the defenses of the Median.

"Don't tell your mother about this," George would say. "You know she doesn't understand."

Each morning, before they had gone very far at all, David's father would stop the car and let David out at a bus stop to be picked up by the school bus, and eight hours later the bus would let him out again some hundreds of miles farther west. Soon his parents would be there to pick him up, if they were not there already when he got off with the other kids. More than once David overheard drivers at the camps in the evening complaining about how having kids really slowed a man down in his career, so he'd never get as far as he would have if he'd had the sense to stay single. Whenever some young man whined about waiting around half his life for a school bus, George Baker would only light another cigarette and be very quiet.

In school David learned the principles of the internal combustion engine. Internal Combustion was his favorite class. Other boys and girls would shoot paperclips at each other over the backseats of the bus, or fall asleep staring out the windows, but David sat in a middle seat (he would not move to the front and be accused of being teacher's pet) and, for the most part, paid good attention. His favorite textbook was one they used both in history and social studies; it had a blue cloth cover. The title, pressed into the cover in faded yellow, was *Heroes of the Road*. On the bus, during recess, David and the other boys argued about who was the greatest driver of them all.

To most of them Alan "Lucky" Totter was the only driver. He'd made 10,220,796 miles when he tried to pass a Winnebago on the right at 85 miles per hour in a blinding snowstorm. Some people thought that showed a lack of judgment, but Lucky Totter didn't give a damn for judgment, or anything else. Totter was the classic lone-wolf driver. Born to respectable middle-class parents who drove a Buick with holes in its sides, Totter devoured all he could find out about cars. At the age of thirteen he deserted his parents at a rest stop at mile 1.375×10^{25}, hot-wired a Bugatti-Smith that the owner had left unlocked, and made 8,000 miles before the Trooperbots brought him to justice. After six months in the paddy wagon he came out with a new resolve. He worked for a month at a service station at jobs even the androids would shun, getting nowhere. At the end of that time he'd rebuilt a junked Whippet roadster and was on his way, hell-bent for leather. Every extra mile he drove he plowed back into financing a newer and faster car. Tirelessly, it seemed, Totter kept his two-tones to the floorboards, and the pavement fairly flew beneath his wheels. No time for a wife or family, 1,000 miles a day was his only satisfaction, other than the quick comforts of any of the fast women he might pick up who wanted a chance to say they'd been for a ride with Lucky Totter. The solitary male to the end, it was a style guaranteed to earn him the hero worship of boys all along the world.

But Totter was not the all-time mileage champion. That pinnacle of glory was held by Charles Van Huyser, at a seemingly unassailable 11,315,201 miles. It was hard to see how anyone could do better, for Van Huyser was the driver who had everything: good reflexes, a keen eye, iron constitution, wherewithal, and devilish good looks. He was a child of the privileged classes, scion of the famous Van Huyser drivers, and had enjoyed all the advantages the boys on a middle-lane bus like David's would never see. His father had been one of the premier drivers of his generation, and had made more than seven million miles himself, placing him a respectable twelfth on the all-time list. Van Huyser rode the most exclusive of preparatory buses, and was outfitted from the beginning with the best made-to-order Mercedes that android hands could fashion. He was in a lane by himself. Old-timers would tell stories of the time they had been passed by the Van Huyser limo and the distinguished, immaculately tailored man who sat behind the wheel. Perhaps he had even tipped his homburg as he flashed by. Spartan in his daily regimen, invariably kind, if a little condescending, to lesser drivers, he never forgot his position in society, and died at the respectable age of eighty-six, peacefully, in the private washroom of the Drivers' Club dining room at mile 1.375×10^{25}.

There were scores of others in *Heroes of the Road*, all of their stories inspiring, challenging, even puzzling. There was Ailene Stanford, at six-million-plus miles the greatest female driver ever, carmaker and mother and credit to her sex. And Reuben Jefferson, and the Kosciusco brothers, and the mysterious trance driving of Akira Tedeki. The chapter "Detours" held frightening tales of abject failure, and of those who had wasted their substance and their lives trying to cross the Median.

"You can't believe everything you read, David," George told him. "They'll tell you Steve Macready was a great man."

It was like George Baker to make statements like that and then never explain what he meant. It got on David's nerves sometimes, though he figured his dad did it because he had more important things on his mind.

But Steve Macready was David's personal favorite. Macready was third on the all-time list behind Van Huyser and Totter, at 8,444,892 miles. Macready hadn't had the advantages of Van Huyser, and he scorned the reckless irresponsibility of Totter. He was an average man, to all intents and purposes, and he showed just how much an average guy could do if he had the willpower. Born into an impoverished hundred-mile-a-day family that couldn't seem to keep a car on the road three days in a row before it broke down, one of eight brothers and sisters, Macready studied quietly when he could, watched the ways of the road with an intelligent eye, and helped his father and mother keep the family rolling. Compelled to leave school early because the family couldn't keep up with the slowest of school buses, he worked on his own, managed to get hold of an old junker that he put on the road, and set off at the age of sixteen, taking two of his sisters with him. In those first years his mileage totals were anything but spectacular. But he kept plugging away, taking care of his sisters, seeing them married off to two respectable young drivers along the way, never hurrying. At the comparatively late age of thirty he married a simple girl from a family of Ford owners and fathered four children. He saw to his boys' educations. He drove on, making a steady 500 miles a day, and 200 on each Saturday and Sunday. He did not push himself or his machine; he did not lag behind. Steadiness was his watchword. His sons grew up to be fine drivers themselves, always ready to lend the helping hand to the unfortunate motorist. When he died at the age of eighty-two, survived by his wife, children, eighteen grandchildren, and twenty-six great-grandchildren, drivers all, he had become something of a legend in his own quiet time. Steve Macready.

George Baker never said much when David talked about the arguments the kids had over Macready and the other drivers. When he talked about his own youth, he would give only the most tantalizing hints of the many cars he had driven before he picked up Polly, of the many places he'd stopped and people he'd ridden with. David's grandfather had been something of an inventor, he gathered, and had modified his pickup with an extra-large tank and a small, efficient engine to get the most mileage for his driving time. George didn't say much about his mother or brothers, though he said some things that indicated that his father's plans for big miles never panned out, and about how it was not always pleasant to ride in the back of an open pickup with three brothers and a sick mother.

Eventually David saw that the miles were taking something out of his father. George Baker conversed less with Polly and the kids, and talked more at them.

Once, in a heavy rainstorm after three days of rolling hill country, forests that encroached on the edges of the pavement and fell like a dark wall between Westbound and forgotten Eastbound, the front end of the Nash jumped suddenly into a mad vibration that threw David's heart into his throat.

"George!" Polly shouted.

"Shut up!" he yelled, trying to steer the bucking car to the roadside.

And then they were stopped, and breathing heavily, and the only sound was the drumming of the rain, the ticking of the car as it settled into motionlessness, and the hissing of the cars that still sped by them over the wet pavement. David's father, slow and bearlike, opened the door and pulled himself out. David got out too. Under the hood they saw where the rewelded wheel well had given way, and the shock was ripping through the metal. "Shit," George muttered.

As they stood there a gunmetal gray Cadillac pulled over to stop behind them, its flashing amber signal warm as fire under the leaden skies. A stocky man in an expensive raincoat got out. "Can I help you?" he asked.

George stared at him for a good ten seconds. He looked back at the Cadillac, looked at the man again.

"No thanks," he said.

The man hesitated, then turned, went back to his car and drove off.

So they had to wait three hours in the broken-down Nash as darkness fell and George trudged off down the highway for the next rest stop. He returned with an android serviceman, and they were towed to the nearest station. David, never patient at his best, grew more and more angry. His father offered not a word of explanation, and his mother tried to keep David from getting after him about his refusing help. But David finally challenged his father on the plain stupidity of his actions, which would mystify any sensible driver.

At first George acted as if he didn't hear David. Then he exploded.

"Don't tell me about sensible drivers! I don't need it, David! Don't tell me about your Van Huysers, and don't give me any of that Steve Macready crap, either. Your Van Huysers never did anything for the common driving man, despite all their extra miles. Nobody gives it away. That's just the way this road works."

"What about Macready?" David asked. He didn't understand what his father was talking about. You didn't have to run someone else down in order to be right. "Look at what Macready did."

"You don't know what you're talking about," George said. "You get older, but you still think like a kid. Macready sucked up to every tinman on the road. I wouldn't stoop so low as that.

Half the time he left his *wife* drive! They don't tell you about that in that damn school, do they?

"Wake up and look at this road the way it is, David. People will use you like a chamois if you don't. Take my word for it. *Damn* it! If I could just get a couple of good months out of this heap and get back on my feet. A couple of good months!" He laughed scornfully.

It was no use arguing with George when he was in that mood. David shut up, inwardly fuming.

"Follow the herd!" George yelled. "That's all people ever do. Never had an original thought in their life."

"George, you don't need to shout at the boy," Polly said.

"Shout! I'm not shouting!" he shouted. George looked at her as if she were a hitchhiker. "Why don't you shut up. The boy and I were just having an intelligent conversation. A fat lot you know about it." He gripped the wheel as if he meant to grind it into powder. A deadly silence ensued.

"I need to stop," he said a couple of miles later, pulling off the road into a bar and grill.

They sat in the car, ears ringing.

"I'm hungry," Caroline said.

"Let's get something to eat, then." Polly leapt at the opportunity to do something normal. "Come on, David. Let's go in."

"You go ahead. I'll be there in a minute."

After they left David stared out the car window for a while. He reached under the seat and took out the notebook, which he had moved there a long time before. The spine was almost broken through now, with some of the leaves loose and water-stained. The paper was worn with writing and rewriting. David leafed through the sketches of watchtowers, the maps, the calculations. In the margin of page six his father had written, in handwriting so faded now that it was like the pale voice of years speaking, from far away, "Keep your ass down. Low profile."

David was sixteen. His knees were crowded by the back of the car's front seat, and he stared sullenly out the window at the rolling countryside and the gathering night.

Caroline, having just concluded her fight with him with a belligerent "Oh, yeah!" was leaning forward, her forearms flat against the top of the front seat, her chin resting on them as she stared grimly ahead. Polly was knitting a cover for the box of Kleenex that rested on the dashboard, muffling the radio speaker.

"I'm tired," George said. "I'm going to stop here for a quick one." He pulled the ancient Nash over into the exit lane, downshifted, and the car lurched forward more slowly, the engine rattling in protest of the increased rpms. David could have done it better himself.

They pulled into the parking lot of Fast Ed's Bar and Grill. "You go back and order a fish fry," George said, slamming the car door and turning his back on them. Polly put aside the knitting, picked up her purse, and took them in the side door to the dining room. There was no one else there, but they could hear the TV and the loud conversations from the front. After a while a waitress robot rolled back to them. Its porcelain finish was chipped, and the hands were stained rusty brown, like an old bathtub.

They ordered, the food came, and they ate. Still George did not return from the bar.

"Go get your father, David," his mother said. He could tell she was mad.

"I'll go, Ma," Caroline said.

"Stay still! It's bad enough he takes us to his gin mills, without you becoming a barfly's pet. Go ahead, David."

David went. His father was sitting at the far end of the bar, near the windows that faced the highway. The late afternoon sun gleamed along the polished wood, glinted harshly from the bottles racked on the shelves behind it, turned the mirror against the wall and the brass spigots of the taps into fire. George Baker was talking loudly with two other middle-aged drivers. His legs looked amazingly scrawny as he perched on the stool. Suddenly David was very angry.

"Are you going to come and eat?" he demanded.

George turned to him, his sloppy good humor stiffening to ire.

"What do you want?"

"We're eating. Mom's waiting."

He leaned over to the man on the next stool. "See what I mean?" he said. To David he said, much more boldly, "Go and eat. I'm not hungry." He picked up his shot, downed it in one swallow, and took another draw on the beer setup.

Rage and humiliation burned in David. He did not recognize the man at the bar as his father—and then, shuddering, he did.

"Are you coming?" David could hardly speak. The other men at the bar were quiet now. Only the television continued to babble.

"Go away," his father said.

David wanted to kick over the stool and see him sprawled on the floor. Instead he turned and walked stiffly back to the dining room, past the table where his mother and sister sat. He stalked out to the lot, slamming the screen door behind him. He stood looking at the beat-up Nash in the red-and-white light of Fast Ed's sign. The sign buzzed, and night was coming, and clouds of insects swarmed around the neon in the darkness. A hundred yards away, on the highway, the drivers had their lights on, fanning before them. The air smelled of exhaust.

He couldn't go back into the bar. He would never step back into a place like that again. The world seemed all at once immensely old, immensely cheap, immensely tawdry. David looked over his shoulder at the vast woods that started just beyond the back of Fast Ed's. Then he walked to the front of the lot and stared across the highway toward the distant lights that marked Eastbound. How very far away they seemed.

David went back to the car and got the knapsack out of the trunk. He stepped over the rail at the edge of the lot, crossed the gully beside the road, and waiting for his chance, dashed across the twelve lanes of Westbound to the Median. A hundred yards ahead of him lay the beginning of no-man's-land. Beyond that, where those distant lights swept by in their retrograde motion— what?

But he would never get into a car with George Baker again.

*   *   *

There were three levels of defenses between Westbound and East-bound, or so they had surmised. The first was biological, the second was mechanical, and the third and most important, psychological.

As David moved farther from the highway the ground, which was more or less level near the shoulders, grew uneven. The field was unmowed, thick with nettles and coarse grass, and in the increasing darkness he stumbled more than once. Because the land sloped downward as he advanced, the lights ahead of him became obscured by the foliage.

He thought once that he heard his name called above the faint rushing of the cars behind him, but when he turned he could see nothing but Westbound. It seemed remarkably far away already. His progress became slower. He knew there were snakes in the open fields. The mines could not be far ahead. He could be in the minefield at that very moment.

He stopped, heart racing. Suddenly he knew he was in a minefield, and his next step would blow him to pieces. He saw the shadow of the first line of barbed wire ahead of him, and for the first time he considered going back. But the thought of his father and his mother stopped him. They would be glad to take him back and smother him.

David crouched, swung the pack from his shoulder, and took out the metal detector. Sweeping it a few inches above the ground in front of him, he crawled forward on his hands and knees. It was slow going. There was something funny about the air: he didn't smell anything but field and earth—no people, no rubber, no gasoline. He eyed the nearest watchtower, where he knew infrared scanners swept the Median and automatic rifles nosed about incuriously. Whenever the light in his palm went red, David slid slowly to one side or the other and went on. Once he had to flatten himself suddenly to the earth as some object—animal or search mech—rustled through the dry grass not ten yards away. He waited for the bullet in his neck.

He came to the first line of barbed wire. It was rusty and overgrown. Weeds had used it for a trellis, and when David clipped through the wire the overgrowth held the gap closed. He had to tear the opening wider with his hands, and the cheap work gloves he wore were next to no protection.

He lay in the dark, sweating. He would never last at this rate. He decided to take the chance of moving ahead in short, crouching runs, ignoring the mines. For a while it seemed to ease the pressure, until his foot slipped on some metal object and he leapt away, crying aloud, waiting for the blast that didn't come. Crouched in the grass, panting, he saw that he had stepped on a hubcap.

David began to wonder why the machines hadn't spotted him yet. He was far beyond the point any right-thinking driver might pass. Then he realized that he could hear nothing of either Westbound or Eastbound. He had no idea how long it had been since he'd left the parking lot, but the gibbous moon was coming down through the clouds. David wondered what his mother had done after he'd taken the pack and left; he could imagine his father's drunken amazement as she told him. Maybe even Caroline was worried. He was far beyond them now. He was getting away, amazed at how easy it was, once you made up your mind, amazed at how few had the guts to try it. If they'd even told him the truth.

A perverse idea hit him: maybe the teachers and drivers, like sheep huddled in their trailer beds, had never tried to see what lay in the Median. Maybe all the servodefenses had rotted like the barbed wire, and it was only the pressure of their dead traditions that kept people glued to their westward course. Suddenly twelve lanes, which had seemed a whole world to him all his life, shrank to the merest thread. Who could say what Eastbound might be? Who could predict how much better men had done for themselves there? Maybe it was the Eastbounders who had built the roads, who had created the defenses and myths that kept them all penned in filthy Nashes, rolling west.

David laughed aloud. He stood up. He slung the pack over his shoulder again, and this time boldly struck out for the new world.

"Halt!"

A figure stood erect before him, and a blinding light shone from its head. The confidence drained from David instantly; he dropped to the ground.

"Please stand." David was pinned in the center of the search beam. He reached into the knapsack for the revolver. "This is a restricted area, intruder," the machine said. "Please return to your assigned role."

David blinked in the glare. He could see nothing of the thing's form. "Role?"

"I am sure that the first thing they taught you was that entry into this area is forbidden. Am I right?"

"What?" David had never heard this kind of talk from a machine.

"Your elders have said that you should not come here. That is one very good reason why you should not be here. I'm sure you'll agree. The requests of the society that, in a significant way, created us, if not unreasonable, ought to be given considerable thought before we reject them. This is the result of evolution. The men and women who went before you had to concern themselves with survival in order to live long enough to bear the children who eventually became the present generation. Their rules are engineering-tested. Such experience, let alone your intelligence working *within* the framework of evolution, ought not to be lightly discarded. We are not born into a vacuum. Am I right?"

David wasn't sure the gun was going to do him any good. "I guess so. I never thought about it."

"Precisely. Think about it."

David thought. "Wait a minute! How do I know *people* made the rules? I don't have any proof. I never see people making rules now."

"On the contrary, intruder, you see it every day. Every act a person performs is an act of definition. We create what we are from moment to moment. The future before us is merely the emptiness of time that does not exist without events to fill it.

The greatest of changes is possible: in theory you are just as likely to turn into an aimless collection of molecules in this next instant as you are to remain a human being. That is, unless you believe that human beings are fated and possess no free will. . . ."

"People have free will." David knew that, if he knew anything. "And they ought to use it."

"That's right." The machine's light was as steady as the sun. "You wouldn't be in a forbidden area if people did not have free will. You yourself, intruder, are a proof of mankind's freedom."

"Okay. Now let me go by—"

"So we have established that human beings have free will. We will assume that they follow rules. Now, having free will, and assuming that by some mischance one of these rules is distasteful to them—we leave aside for the moment who made the rule—then one would expect people to disobey it. They need not even have an active purpose to disobey; in the course of a long enough time many people will break this burdensome rule for the best—or worst—of reasons. The more unacceptable the rule, the greater the number of people who will discard it at one time or another. They will, as individuals or groups, consciously or unconsciously, create a new rule. This is change through human free will. So, even if the rules were not originated by humans, in time change would ensue given the merits of the 'system,' as we may call it, and the system will *become* human-created. My earlier evolutionary argument then follows as the night the day. Am I right?"

If a robot could sound triumphant, this one did.

"Ah—"

"So one good reason for doing only what you're told is that you have the free will to do otherwise. Another good reason is God."

"God?"

"The Supreme Being, the Life Force, that ineluctable, undefinable spiritual presence that lies—or perhaps lurks—within the substance of things. The Holy Father, the First—"

"What about him?"

"God doesn't want you to cross the Median."

"I bet he doesn't," David said sarcastically.

"Have you ever seen an automobile accident?"

The robot was going too fast, and the light made it hard for David to think. He closed his eyes and tried to fight back. "Everybody's seen accidents. People get killed. Don't go telling me God killed them because they did something wrong."

"Don't be absurd!" the robot said. "You must try to stretch your mind, intruder; this is not some game we're playing. This is real life. Not only do actions have consequences, but consequences are pregnant with Meaning.

"In the auto accident we have a peculiar sequence of events. The physicist tells us that heat and vibration cause a weakening of the molecular bonds between certain long-chain hydrocarbons that comprise the substance of the tire of a car traveling at sixty miles per hour. The tire blows. As a result of the sudden change in the moment of inertia of this wheel, certain complex analyzable oscillations occur. The car swerves to the left, rolls over six times, tossing its three passengers, a man and two women, about like tomatoes in a blender, and collides with a bridge abutment, exploding into flame. To the scientist, this is a simple cause-and-effect chain. The accident has a rational explanation: the tire blew."

David felt queasy. His hand, in the knapsack, clutched the gun.

"You see right away what's wrong with this explanation. It explains nothing. We know the rational explanation is inadequate without having to be able to say how we know. Such knowledge is the doing of God. God and His merciful Providence set the purpose behind the fact of our existence, and is it possible to believe that a sparrow can fall without His holy cognizance and will?"

"I don't believe in God."

"What does that matter, intruder?" The thing's voice now oozed angelic understanding. "Need you believe in gravity for it to be an inescapable fact of your existence? God does not demand your belief; He merely requests that you, of your own inviolate free will and through the undeserved gift of His grace, come to acknowledge and obey Him. Who can understand the mysteries of faith? Certainly not I, a humble mechanism. *Knowledge* is what matters, and if you open yourself to the currents that flow through the interstices of the material and immaterial universe, that knowledge will be vouchsafed *you*, intruder. You do not belong here. God knows who you are, and He saw what you did. Am I right?"

David was getting mad. "What has this got to do with car accidents?"

"The auto accident does not occur without the knowledge and permission of the Lord. This doesn't mean that He is responsible for it. He accepts the responsibility without accepting the Responsibility. This is a mystery."

"Bull!" David had heard enough talk. It was time to act.

"Be silent, intruder! Where were you when He laid the asphalt of Westbound? Who set up the mileage markers, and who painted the line upon it? On what foundation was its reinforced concrete sunk, and who made the komfy kabins, when the morning stars sang together, and all the droids and servos shouted for joy?"

It was his chance. The machine was still motionless, its mad light trained on him. A mist had sprung from the no-man's-land. Poison gas? He had no gas mask; speed was his only hope. He couldn't move. He hefted the gun. He felt dizzy, a little numb, steeling himself to move. He had to be stronger than the robot! It was just a machine!

"So that is the second good reason why you should not proceed with your ill-advised adventure," it droned on. "God is telling you to go back."

God. Rifles. He had to go! Now! Still he couldn't move. The fog grew, and its smell was strangely pungent. Once past the robot, who knew what he could find. But the machine's voice exuded self-confidence.

"A third and final good reason why you should return to your assigned role, intruder, is this:

"If you take another step, I will kill you."

David woke. He was cold, and he was being shaken by a sobbing man. It was his father.

"Not responsible! Park and lock it!" For the first time in as long as he could remember, David actually heard the crying of the loudspeakers in the parking lot. He struggled to sit up. His mouth tasted like a thousand miles of road grime.

George Baker held his shoulders and looked into his face. He didn't say anything. He stood up and went to stand by the car. Shakily, he lit a cigarette. David's mother crouched over him. "David—David, are you all right?"

"What happened?"

"Your father went after you. We didn't know what happened, and I was so afraid I'd lose both of you—and then he came back carrying you in his arms."

"Carrying me? That's ridiculous." George wasn't capable of carrying a wheel hub fifty yards. David looked at the potbellied man leaning against the front fender of their car. His father was staring off across the lot. Suddenly David felt ashamed of himself. He didn't know what it was in his chest striving to express itself, but sitting there in the parking lot at mile 1.375×10^{25}, looking at the middle-aged man who was his father, he began to cry.

George never said a word to David after that day about how he had managed to follow his son into the Median, about what a struggle it must have been to make himself do that, about how and where he had found the boy, and how he had managed to bring him back, or about what it all meant to him. David never told his father about the robot and what it had said. It was all a little unreal to him. The boy who had stood there, desperately trying to get somewhere else, and the words the robot had spoken, all seemed terribly remote, as if the whole incident were something he had read about. It was a fantasy that could not have occurred in the real world of pavement and gasoline.

Father and son did not speak about it. They didn't say any-thing much at first, as they tentatively felt out the boundaries of what seemed to be a new relationship. Even Caroline recognized that a change had taken place, and she didn't taunt David the way she had before. Unstated was the fact that David was no longer a boy.

A month later and many thousand miles farther along, George nervously broached the subject of buying David a car. It was a shock for David to hear that, and he knew they could hardly afford it, but he also knew there was a rightness to it. And so they found themselves in the lot of Gears MacDougal's New and Used Autos.

George was too loud, too jocular. "How about this Chevy, David? A Chevy's a good driving man's car." He looked embar-rassed.

David got down and felt a tire. "She's got good rubber on her."

The salesdroid was rolling up to greet them as George opened the hood of the Chevy. "Looks pretty clean," he said.

"They clean them all up."

"They sure do. You can't trust them as far as you'd . . . ah, hello."

"Good morning," the droid said, coming to rest beside them. "That's just the little thing for you. One owner, and between you and me, he didn't drive her too hard. He wasn't much of a driver."

George looked at the machine soberly. "Is that so."

"That is so, sir."

"My son's buying this car, not me," George said suddenly, loudly, as if shaking away the dust of his thoughts. "You should talk to him. And don't try to put anything over on him; he knows his stuff and . . . well, you just talk to him, not me, see?"

"Certainly, sir." The droid rolled between them and told David about the Chevy's V-8. David hardly listened. He watched his father step quietly to the side and light a cigarette. George stood with Polly and Caroline and looked ill at ease, quieter than David could ever remember. As the robot took David around the car, pointing out its extras, it came to him just what his father was: not a strong man, not a special man, not a particularly smart man. He was the same man he had been when David had sat on his lap years before; he was the same man who had taken him on his strolls around the rest stops so many times. He was the drunk who had slouched on the stool in Fast Ed's. He was a good driving man.

"I'll take it," David said, breaking off the salesdroid in mid-sentence.

"Righto," the machine said, its hard smile unvarying. It did not miss a beat. Within seconds a hard copy of the title had emerged from the slot in its chest. Within minutes the papers had been signed, the mileage validated and subtracted from George Baker's yearly total, and David stood beside his car. It was not a very good car to start out with, but many had started with less, and it was the best his father could do. Polly hugged him and cried. Caroline reached up and kissed him on the cheek; she cried too. George shook his hand, and did not seem to want to let go.

"Remember now, take it easy for the first thousand or so, until you get the feel of her. Check the oil, see if it burns oil. I don't think it will. It's got a good spare, doesn't it?"

"It does, Dad."

"Good. That's good." George stood silent for a moment, looking up at his son. The day was bright, and the breeze disarrayed the thinning hair he had combed over his bald spot. "Good-bye, David. Maybe we'll see you on the road?"

"Sure you will."

David got into the Chevy and turned the key in the ignition. The motor started immediately and breathed its low and steady rumble. The seat was very hot against his back. The windshield was spotless, and beyond the nose of the car stretched the access ramp to Westbound. The highway swarmed with the cars that were moving while they dawdled there still. David put the car in gear, stepped slowly on the accelerator, released the clutch, and moved smoothly down the ramp, gathering speed. He shifted up, moving faster, and then quickly once again. The force of the wind streaming in through the window increased from a breeze to a gale, and its sound became a continuous buffeting as it whipped his hair about his ear. Flicking the turn signal, David merged into the flow of traffic, the sunlight flashing off the hood ornament that led him on toward the distant horizon, just out of his reach, but attainable he knew, as he pressed his foot to the accelerator, hurrying on past mile 1.375×10^{25}.

GULLIVER AT HOME

No, Eliza, I did not wish your grandfather dead, though he swears that is what I said upon his return from his land of horses. What I said was that, given the neglect with which he has served us, and despite my Christian duties, even the best of wives might have wished him dead. The truth is, in the end, I love him.

"Seven months," he says, "were a sufficient time to correct every vice and folly to which Yahoos are subject, if their natures had been capable of the least disposition to virtue or wisdom."

There he sits every afternoon with the horses. He holds converse with them. Many a time have I stood outside that stable door and listened to him unburden his soul to a dumb beast. He tells them things he has never told me, except perhaps years ago during those hours in my father's garden. Yet when I close my eyes, his voice is just the same.

His lips were full, his voice low and assured. With it he conjured up a world larger, more alive than the stifling life of a hosier's youngest daughter.

"I had no knowledge of the deepest soul of man until I saw the evening light upon the Pyramids," he was saying. "The geometry of Euclid, the desire to transcend time. Riddles that have no answer. The Sphinx."

We sat in the garden of my father's house in Newgate Street. My father was away, on a trip to the continent purchasing fine holland, and Mother had retired to the sitting room to leave us some little privacy.

For three and a half years Lemuel had served as a surgeon on the merchantman *Swallow*. He painted for me an image of the Levant: the camels, the deserts, the dead salt sea, and the dry stones that Jesus Himself trod.

"Did you not long for England's green hills?" I asked him.

He smiled. Your grandfather was the comeliest man I had ever seen. The set of his jaw, his eyes. Long, thick hair, the chestnut brown of a young stallion. He seemed larger than any of my other suitors. "From my earliest days I have had a passion to see strange lands and people," he told me. "To know their customs and language. This world is indeed a fit habitation for gods. But it seems I am never as desirous for home as when I am far away from it, and from the gentle conversation of such as yourself."

My father was the most prudent of men. In place of a mind, he carried a purse. Lemuel was of another sort. As I sat there trying to grasp these wonders he took my hand and told me I had the grace of the Greek maidens, who wore no shoes and whose curls fell down round their shoulders in the bright sun. My eyes were the color, he said, of the Aegean Sea. I blushed. I was frightened that my mother might hear, but I cannot tell you how my heart raced. His light brown eyes grew distant as he climbed the structures of his fancy, and it did not occur to me that I might have difficulty getting him to return from those imaginings to see me sitting beside him.

You are coming to be a woman, Eliza. But you cannot know what it was like to feel the force of his desire. He had a passion to embrace all the world and make it his. Part of that world he hoped to embrace, I saw as I sat beside him in that garden, was me.

"Mistress Mary Burton," he said, "help me to become a perfect man. Let me be your husband."

Little Lemuel, the child of our middle age, is just nine. Of late he has ceased calling on his friends in town. I found him yesterday in the garden, playing with his lead soldiers. He had lined them up, in their bright red coats, outside a fort of sticks and pebbles. He stood inside the fort's walls, giving orders to his toys. "Get away, you miserable Yahoos! You can't come in this house! Don't vex me! Your smell is unredurable!"

The third of five sons, Lemuel hailed from Nottinghamshire, where his father held a small estate. He had attended Emanuel College in Cambridge and was apprenticed to Mr. James Bates, the eminent London surgeon. Anticipating the advantage that would be mine in such a match, my father agreed on a dowry of four hundred pounds.

Having got an education, it was up to Lemuel now to get a living as best he could. There was to be no help for us from his family; though they were prosperous they were not rich, and what estate they had went to Lemuel's eldest brother John.

My wedding dress? Foolish girl, what matters a wedding dress in this world?

My wedding dress was of Orient silk, silk brought to England on some ship on which Lemuel perhaps served. My mother had labored over it for three months. It was not so fine as that of my older sister Nancy, but it was fine enough for me to turn Lemuel's head as I walked up the aisle of St. Stephen's church.

We took a small house in the Old Jury. We were quite happy. Mr. Bates recommended Lemuel to his patients, and for a space we did well. In those first years I bore three children. The middle one, Robert, we buried before his third month. But God smiling, my Betty, your mother, and your uncle John did survive and grow.

But after Mr. Bates died, Lemuel's practice began to fail. He refused to imitate the bad practice of other doctors, pampering hypochondriacs, promising secret cures for fatal disease. We moved to Wapping, where Lemuel hoped to improve our fortune by doctoring to sailors, but there was scant money in that, and his practice declined further. We discussed the matter for some time, and he chose to go to sea.

He departed from Bristol on May 4, 1699, on the *Antelope*, as ship's surgeon, bound for the south seas, under Master William Prichard.

The *Antelope* should have returned by the following spring. Instead it never came back. Much later, after repeated inquiries, I received report that the ship had never made its call at Sumatra. She was last seen when she landed to take on water at the Cape of Good Hope, and it was assumed that she had been lost somewhere in the Indian Ocean.

Dearest granddaughter, I hope you never have cause to feel the distress I felt then. But I did not have time to grieve, because we were in danger of being left paupers.

What money Lemuel had left us, in expectation of his rapid return, had gone. Our landlord, a goodly Christian man, Mr. Henry Potts of Wapping, was under great hardship himself, as his trade had slackened during the late wars with France and he was dependent on the rent from his holdings. Betty was nine and Johnny seven, neither able to help out. My father sent us what money he could, but owing to reverses of his own he could do little. As the date of Lemuel's expected return receded Mr. Potts's wife and son were after Mr. Potts to put us out.

I took in sewing—thank God and my parents I was a master seamstress. We raised a few hens for meat and eggs. We ate many a meal of cabbage and potatoes. The neighbors helped. Mr. Potts forbore. But in the bitter February of 1702 he died, and his son, upon assuming his inheritance, threatened to put us into the street.

One April morning, at our darkest moment, some three years after he sailed on the *Antelope*, Lemuel returned.

The coach jounced and rattled over the Kent high road. "You won't believe me when I tell you, these minuscule people, not six inches high, had a war over which end of the egg to break."

Lemuel had been telling these tales for two weeks without stop. He'd hired the coach using money we did not have. I was vexed with the effort to force him to confront our penury.

"We haven't seen an egg here in two years!" I said. "Last fall came a pip that killed half the chickens. They staggered about with their little heads pointed down, like drunkards searching for coins on the street. They looked so sad. When it came time to market we left without a farthing."

Lemuel carefully balanced the box he carried on his knees. He peeked inside, to assure himself for the hundredth time that the tiny cattle and sheep it held were all right. We were on our way to the country estate of the Earl of Kent, who had summoned Lemuel when the rumors of the miniature creatures he'd brought back from Lilliput spread throughout the county. "Their empress almost had me beheaded. She didn't approve my method of dousing a fire that would have otherwise consumed her."

"In the midst of that, Betty almost died of the croup. I was up with her every night for a fortnight, cold compresses and bleeding."

"God knows I'd have given a hundred guineas for a cold compress when I burned with fever, a castaway on the shores of Lilliput."

"Once the novelty fades, cattle so tiny will be of no use. There's not a scrap of meat on them."

"True enough. I would eat thirty oxen at a meal." He sat silent, deep in thought. The coach lurched on. "I wonder if His Grace would lend me the money to take them on tour?"

"Lemuel, we owe Stephen Potts eleven pounds sixpence. To say nothing of the grocer. And if he is to have any chance at a profession, Johnny must be sent to school. We cannot even pay for his clothes."

"Lilliputian boys are dressed by men until four years of age, and then are obliged to dress themselves. They always go in the presence of a Professor, whereby they avoid those early impressions of vice and folly to which our children are subject. Would that you had done this for our John."

"Lemuel, we have no money! It was all I could do to keep him alive!"

He looked at me, and his brow furrowed. He tapped his fingers on the top of the cattle box. "I don't suppose I can blame her. It was a capital crime for any person whatsoever to make water within the precincts of the palace."

Last night your grandfather quarreled with your uncle John, who had just returned from the Temple. Johnny went out to the stables to speak with Lemuel concerning a suit for libel threatened by a nobleman who thinks himself the object of criticism in Lemuel's book. I followed.

Before Johnny could finish explaining the situation, Lemuel flew into a rage. "What use have I for attorneys? I had rather see them dropped to the deepest gulf of the sea."

In the violence of his gesture Lemuel nearly knocked over the lamp that stood on the wooden table. His long gray hair flew wildly as he stalked past the stall of the dappled mare he calls "Mistress Mary," to my everlasting dismay. I rushed forward to steady the lamp. Lemuel looked upon me with a gaze as blank as a brick.

"Father," Johnny said, "you may not care what this man does, but he is a cabinet minister, and a lawsuit could ruin us. It would be politic if you would publicly apologize for any slight your satire may have given."

Lemuel turned that pitiless gaze on our son. "I see you are no better than the other animals of this midden, and all my efforts to make something better of you are in vain. If you were capable of logic, I would ask you to explain to me how my report of events that occurred so many years ago, during another reign, and above five thousand leagues distant from this pathetic isle, might be applied to any of the Yahoos who today govern this herd. Yet in service of this idiocy you ask me to *say the thing that is not*. I had rather all your law books, and you immodest pleaders with them, were heaped into a bonfire in Smithfield for the entertainment of children."

I watched Johnny's face grow livid, but he mastered his rage and left the stable. Lemuel and I stood in silence. He would not look at me, and I thought for a moment he felt some regret at his intemperance. But he turned from me to calm the frightened horses. I put the lamp down on the table and ran back to the house.

Johnny was ten when Lemuel returned from Lilliput. He was overjoyed to see his father again, and worshiped him as a hero. When other of the townschildren mocked Lemuel, calling him a madman, Johnny fought them.

The Lilliputian cattle and sheep, despite my misgivings, brought us some advantage. Following the example of the Earl of Kent, Sir Humphrey Glover, Lord Sidwich, and other prominent men commanded Lemuel to show these creatures. Johnny prated on about the tiny animals all day, and it was all I could do to keep him from sleeping with them beneath his bedclothes, which would have gone the worse for them, as he was a restless child and in tossing at night would surely have crushed the life out of them. He built a little stable in the corner of his room. At first we fed them with biscuit, ground as fine as we could, and spring water. Johnny took great pains to keep the rats away.

It was his idea to build a pasture on the bowling green, where the grass was fine enough that they might eat and prosper. Lemuel basked in Johnny's enthusiasm. He charmed the boy with the tale of how he had captured the entire fleet of Blefescu using thread and fish-hooks, and towed it back to Lilliput. Johnny said that he would be a sea captain when he grew up.

As if in a dream, our fortunes turned. Lemuel's uncle John passed away, leaving him five hundred sterling and an estate in land near Epping that earned an income of about thirty pounds a year. Lemuel sold the Lilliputian cattle for six hundred pounds. He bought our big house in Redriff. After years of hardship, after I had lost hope, he had returned to save us.

We had been better served by bankruptcy if that would have kept him beside me in our bed.

*   *   *

You will find, Eliza, that a husband needs his wife in that way, and it can be a pleasant pastime. But it is different for them. Love is like a fire they cannot control, overwhelming, easily quenched, then as often as not forgotten, even regretted. Whenever Lemuel returned from these voyages he wanted me, and I do not hesitate to say, I him. Our bed was another country to which he would return, and explore for its mysteries. He embraced me with a fury that sought to extinguish all our time apart, and the leagues between us, in the heat of that moment. Spent, he would rest his head on my bosom, and I would stroke his hair. He was like a boy again, quiet and kind. He would whisper to me, in a voice of desperation, how I should never let him leave again.

Two months after his return, despite the comforts of my arms, he was gone again. His wild heart, he said, would not let him rest.

This time he left us well set. Fifteen hundred pounds, the house in Redriff, the land in Epping. He took a long lease on the Black Bull public house in Fetter Lane, which brought a regular income.

We traveled with him to Liverpool, where in June of 1702 he took ship aboard the *Adventure,* Captain John Nicholas commanding, bound for Surat.

It was a dreary day at the downs, the kind of blustery weather Liverpool has occasion for even in summer, low leaden clouds driven before a strong wind, the harbor rolling in swells and the ends of furled sails flapping above us. With tears in my eyes, I embraced him; he would not let me go. When I did pull away I saw that he wept as well. "Fare thee well, good heart," he whispered to me. "Forgive me my wandering soul."

Seeing the kindness and love in his gaze, the difficulty with which he tore himself from my bosom, I would have forgiven him anything. It occurred to me just how powerful a passion burned within him, driving him outside the circle of our hearth. Little Johnny shook his hand, very manly. Betty leapt into his arms, and he pressed her to his cheek, then set her down. Then he took up his canvas bag, turned and went aboard.

*   *   *

It is no easy matter being the wife of a man famous for his wild tales. The other day in town with Sarah to do the marketing, in the butcher's shop, I overheard Mrs. Boyle the butcher's wife arguing with a customer that the chicken was fresh. By its smell anyone past the age of two would know it was a week dead. But Mrs. Boyle insisted.

The shop was busy, and our neighbor Mr. Trent began to mock her, in a low voice, to some bystanders. He said, "Of course it is fresh. Mrs. Boyle insists it's fresh. It's as true as if Mr. Gulliver had said it."

All the people in the shop laughed. My face burned, and I left.

One June morning in 1706, three long years after Lemuel was due to return, I was attending to the boiling of some sheets in the kitchen when a cry came from Sarah, our housemaid. "God save me! Help!"

I rushed to the front door, there to see an uncouth spectacle. Sarah was staring at a man who had entered on all fours, peering up, his head canted to the side, so that his long hair brushed the ground (he wore no periwig) as he spied up at us. It was a moment before I recognized him as my Lemuel. My heart leapt within my breast as I went from widow to wife in a single instant.

When he came to the house, for which he had been forced to enquire, Sarah had opened the door. Lemuel bent down to go in, for fear of striking his head. He had been living among giants and fancied himself sixty feet tall. Sarah had never met Mr. Gulliver, and thought him a madman. When I tried to embrace him, he stooped to my knees until I was forced to get down on my own to kiss him.

When Betty, your mother, who was then sixteen, ran in, holding some needlework, Lemuel tried to pick her up by her waist, in one hand, as if she had been a doll. He complained that the children and I had starved ourselves, so that we were wasted away to nothing. It was some weeks before he regained his sense of proper proportion.

I told him it was the last time he should ever go to sea.

It wasn't ten days before a Cornish captain, William Robinson, under whom Lemuel had served on a trip to the Levant some years before we were married, called upon us. That visit was purely a social one, or so he avowed, but within a month he was importuning Lemuel to join him as ship's surgeon on another trip to the East Indies.

One night, as we prepared for bed, I accosted him. "Lemuel, are you considering taking up Robinson on this offer?"

"What matter if I did? I am the master of this house. You are well taken care of."

"Taken care of by servants, not my husband."

"He is offering twice the usual salary, a share of the profits, two mates and a surgeon under me. I shall be gone no more than a year, and you will see us comfortably off, so that I might never have to go to sea again."

"You don't have to go to sea now. We have a comfortable life."

He removed his leather jerkin and began to unbutton his shirt. "And our children? Betty is nearly of marriageable age. What dowry can we offer her? Johnny must go to Cambridge, and have money to establish himself in some honorable profession. I want to do more for him than my father did for me."

"The children mourn your absences." I touched his arm. The muscles were taut as cords. "When you disappeared on the *Antelope,* we suffered more from the thought that you were dead than from the penury we lived in. Give them a father in their home and let the distant world go."

"You are thinking like a woman. The distant world comes into the home. It is a place of greed, vice, and folly. I seek for some understanding I can give to cope with it."

"Lemuel, what is this desire for strange lands but a type of greed, this abandonment of your family but the height of folly? And your refusal to admit your true motives is the utmost dishonesty, to the woman who loves you, and whom you vowed to love."

Lemuel took up his coat, pulled on his shoes.

"Where are you going?"

"Out. I need to take some air. Perhaps I can determine my true motives for you."

He left.

A week later, on the fifth of August, 1706, he left England on the *Hope-Well*, bound for the Indies. I did not see him again for four years.

The only time I can coax him into the house is when he deigns to bathe. He is most fastidious, and insists that no one must remain on the same floor, let alone the same room, when he does.

I crept to the door last week and peeked in. He had finished, and dried himself, and now stood naked in front of the mirror, trembling. At first I thought he was cold, but the fire roared in the grate. Then he raised his hands from his sides, covered his eyes, and sobbed, and I understood that he was recoiling in horror from his own image.

When he left on the third voyage I was five-and-thirty years old. In the previous seven years he had spent a total of four months with me. I had no need to work, I was not an old woman, and my children had no father. When Lemuel did not return in the promised year, when that year stretched to two and the *Hope-Well* returned to Portsmouth without Lemuel aboard, I fell into despair. Captain Robinson came to the house in Redriff and told the tale. Stuck in the port of Tonquin awaiting the goods they were to ship back to England, Robinson hit on the plan of purchasing a sloop, giving command of it to Lemuel, and bidding him trade among the islands, returning in several months at which time, the *Hope-Well* being loaded, they might return. Lemuel set off on the sloop and was not heard from again. Robinson supposed that they might have been taken by the barbarous pirates of those islands, in which case Lemuel had undoubtedly been slain, as Christian mercy is a virtue unknown in those heathen lands.

I cannot say that I was surprised. I was angry, and I wept.

Being the wealthiest widow in the town, and by no means an old woman, I did not lack for suitors. Sir Robert Davies himself called on me more than once. It was all I could do to keep from having my head turned. "Marry me," he said. "I will be a father to your daughter, an example to your son."

"Johnny is about to go off to school, and Betty soon to be married," I told him. "One wedding is enough to worry about right now." Thus I put him off.

In truth I did lose myself in your mother's wedding; Betty was giddy with excitement, and your father, her betrothed, was about continually, helping put the house in order, traveling with Johnny to school. So it was I kept myself chaste.

The townspeople thought I was a fool. My mother commended me for my faithfulness, but I could tell she regretted the loss of a connection with nobility. Betty and Johnny stood by me. I don't need another father, Johnny said, I have one.

My reasons? Wherever he went Sir Robert carried a silver-headed cane, with which he would gently tap his footman's shoulder as he instructed him. I was mistress of my own home. I had given my heart once, and still treasured a hope of Lemuel's return. There are a hundred reasons, child, and there are things I cannot explain. Lemuel did return, and despite his ravings about a flying island and the curse of immortality, I felt that all my trouble had been justified. He seemed weary, but still my husband, the love of my youth come again. The joy of our meeting was great. Within three months he had got me with child.

Within five he had left again.

And so he came back, five years later, from the longest of his absences. He was aged five-and-fifty, I five-and-forty. He saw his son Lemuel for the first time. His daughter, married and a mother herself; his son, grown and an attorney. His wife, longing to hold him again.

No, I have not, Eliza. He shudders at my touch. He washes his hands. He accuses me of trying to seduce him.

"Are you ashamed of the touch that got you your sons and daughter?" I once asked him. "That got us poor Robert? That gave us young Lemuel, to be our comfort in our old age?

His face registered at first revulsion, and then, as he sat heavily in his chair, fatigue. "I can't regret our children if they be good, but I most certainly regret them if they be bad. There are Yahoos enough in the world."

We had long given him up for dead. I had made my peace, and held in my memory the man who had kissed me in my father's garden.

At first I thought that he had caught some foreign disease. As thin as a fence post, he stood in the doorway, his face a mask of dismay. It was the fifth of December, 1715. Three o'clock in the afternoon. I ran to him, kissed him. He fell into a swoon that lasted most of an hour. With difficulty we carried him to his bed. When he awoke, I put my hand to his face: he pulled away as if his skin had been flayed.

And so we live by these rules: "Save for the sabbath, you may not eat in the same room with me. You may not presume to touch my bread. You may not drink out of the same cup, or use my spoon or plate. You may not take me by the hand. That I might bear the reek of this house, fresh horse droppings shall be brought into my chambers each morning, and kept there in a special container I have had fashioned for that purpose."

My father's house, in Newgate Street, was not far from the prison. Outside, on the days of executions, straw was scattered on the street to muffle the wheels of passing wagons, in deference to the men being hanged inside. Here we scatter straw over the cobbled courtyard outside the stables because the noise of the wheels troubles him.

As a young man his heart was full of hope, but his heart has been beaten closed, not only by the sea and the storms and the mutinies and the pirates—but by some hard moral engine inside of him. He would rather be dead, I think, than to abide his flesh. Perhaps he soon will be. And I will have to go on living without him, as I have learned to do over these many years.

Might it have been different? I could say yes, but some thing I saw in his eyes that first afternoon in Newgate Street rises to stop me. He was a man who looked outward while the inward part of himself withered. He was drawn to the blank spaces outside the known world; we are too small to make a mark on his map. To Lemuel ordinary people are interesting only as we represent large things. He asked me to make him a perfect man. In seeking perfection he has gulled himself, and the postscript is that he spends four hours every day attempting to communicate with a horse, while his children, his grandchildren, his wife wait in his well-appointed home, the home they have prepared for him and labored to keep together in his absence, maintaining a place for him at every holiday table, praying for him at every service, treasuring him up in their hearts and memories, his portrait on the wall, his merest jottings pressed close in the book of memory, his boots in the wardrobe, maps in the cabinet, glass on the sideboard.

At Christmas, when we can coax him to eat with us, I sit at the other end of twelve feet of polished mahogany table and look across at a stranger who is yet the man I love.

During our conversation in the garden thirty years ago, Lemuel told me a story. The Greeks, he told me, believed that once there existed a creature that was complete and whole unto itself, perfect and without flaw. But in the beginning of time the gods split this being into two halves, and that is how man and woman came into the world. Each of us knows that we are not complete, and so we seek desperately after each other, yearning to possess our missing halves, pressing our bodies together in hope of becoming that one happy creature again. But of course we cannot do it, and so in frustration we turn away from each other, tearing ourselves apart all of our lives.

His book has been a great success. It is all they speak of in London. It has made us more money than his sixteen years of voyages.

He accuses us of enticing him into writing the wretched thing, and deems it a failure because it didn't immediately reform all of humanity. He told his story to the world in the hope that he would magically turn it into something perfect. I tell you mine,

Eliza . . . I tell you mine because . . . bless me, I believe I've burned my hand on this kettle. Fetch me the lard.

That's better.

Soon you'll come of age to choose a husband, if your parents give you leave to choose. I don't doubt you tremble at the prospect. But remember: it is the only choice a woman is given to make in her life, save for the choice of clothes for her funeral.

And now, help me carry this soup up to him; help me to cover him, and make sure he is warm for the night.

THE MIRACLE OF IVAR AVENUE

Inside the coat pocket of the dead man Corcoran found an eyepiece. "Looks like John Doe was a photographer," the pathologist said, gliding his rubber-gloved thumb over the lens. He handed it to Kinlaw.

While Corcoran continued to peel away the man's clothing, Kinlaw walked over to the morgue's only window, more to get away from the smell of the autopsy table than to examine the lens. He looked through the eyepiece at the parking lot. The device produced a rectangular frame around a man getting into a 1947 Packard. "This isn't from a camera," Kinlaw said. "It's a cinematographer's monocle."

"A what?"

"A movie cameraman uses it to frame a scene."

"You think our friend had something to do with the movies?"

Kinlaw thought about it. That morning a couple of sixth graders playing hooky had found the body on the beach in San Pedro. A man about fifty, big, over two hundred pounds, mustache, thick brown hair going gray. Wearing a beat-up tan double-breasted suit, silk shirt, cordovan shoes. Carrying no identification.

Corcoran hummed "Don't Get Around Much Anymore" while he examined the dead man's fingers. "Heavy smoker," he said. He poked in the corpse's nostrils, then opened the man's mouth and shone a light down his throat. "This doesn't look much like a drowning."

Kinlaw turned around. "Why not?"

"A drowning man goes through spasms, clutches at anything within his grasp; if nothing's there he'll usually have marks on his palms from his fingernails. Plus there's no foam in his trachea or nasal cavities."

"Don't you have to check for water in the lungs?"

"I'll cut him open, but that's not definitive anyway. Lots of drowning men don't get water in their lungs. It's the spasms, foam from mucus, and vomiting that does them in."

"You're saying this guy was murdered?"

"I'm saying he didn't drown. And he wasn't in the water more than twelve hours."

"Can you get some prints?"

Corcoran looked at the man's hand again. "No problem."

Kinlaw slipped the monocle into his pocket. "I'm going upstairs. Call me when you figure out the cause of death."

Corcoran began unbuttoning the dead man's shirt. "You know, he looks like that director, Sturges."

"Who?"

"Preston Sturges. He was pretty hot stuff a few years back. There was a big article in *Life*. Whoa. Got a major surgical scar here."

Kinlaw looked over Corcoran's shoulder. A long scar ran right to center across the dead man's abdomen. "Gunshot wound?"

Corcoran made a note on his clipboard. "Looks like appendectomy. Probably peritonitis, too. A long time ago—ten, twenty years."

Kinlaw took another look at the dead man. "What makes you think this is Preston Sturges?"

"I'm a fan. Plus, this dame I know pointed him out to me at the fights one Friday night during the war. Didn't you ever see *The Miracle of Morgan's Creek?*"

"We didn't get many movies in the Pacific." He took another look at the dead man's face.

When Corcoran hauled out his chest saw, Kinlaw spared his stomach and went back up to the detectives' staff room. He checked missing-persons reports, occasionally stopping to roll the cameraman's monocle back and forth on his desk blotter. There was a sailor two weeks missing from the Long Beach Naval Shipyard. A Mrs. Potter from Santa Monica had reported her husband missing the previous Thursday.

The swivel chair creaked as he leaned back, steepled his fingers and stared at the wall calendar from Free State Buick pinned up next to his desk. The weekend had brought a new month. Familiar April was a blonde in ski pants standing in front of a lodge in the snowy Sierras. He tore off the page: May's blonde wore white shorts and was climbing a ladder in an orange grove. He tried to remember what he had done over the weekend but it all seemed to dissolve into a series of moments connected only by the level of scotch in the glass by his reading chair. He found a pencil in his center drawer and drew a careful X through Sunday, May 1. Happy May Day. After the revolution they would do away with pinup calendars and anonymous dead men. Weekends would mean something and lives would have purpose.

An hour later the report came up from Corcoran: there was no water in the man's lungs. Probable cause of death: carbon monoxide poisoning. But bruises on his ankles suggested he'd had weights tied to them.

There was no answer at Mrs. Potter's home. Kinlaw dug out the L.A. phone book. *Sturges, Preston* was listed at 1917 Ivar Avenue. Probably where Ivar meandered into the Hollywood hills. A nice neighborhood, but nothing compared to Beverly Hills. Kinlaw dialed the number. A man answered the phone. "Yes?"

"I'd like to speak to Mr. Preston Sturges," Kinlaw said.

"May I ask who is calling, please?" The man had the trace of an accent; Kinlaw couldn't place it.

"This is Detective Lemoyne Kinlaw from the Los Angeles Police Department."

"Just a minute."

There was a long wait. Kinlaw watched the smoke curling up from Sapienza's cigarette in the tray on the adjoining desk. An inch of ash clung to the end. He was about to give up when another man's voice came onto the line.

"Detective Kinlaw. How may I help you?" The voice was a light baritone with some sort of high-class accent.

"You're Preston Sturges?"

"Last time I checked the mirror, I was."

"Mr. Sturges, the body of a man answering your description was found this morning washed up on the beach at San Pedro."

There was a long pause. "How grotesque."

"Yes, sir. I'm calling to see whether you are all right."

"As you can hear, I'm perfectly all right."

"Right," Kinlaw said. "Do you by any chance have a boat moored down in San Pedro?"

"I have a sailboat harbored in a marina there. But I didn't wash up on any beach last night, did I?"

"Yes, sir. Assuming you're Preston Sturges."

The man paused again. Kinlaw got ready for the explosion. Instead, Sturges said calmly, "I'm not going to be able to convince you who I am over the phone, right?"

"No, you're not."

"I'll tell you what. Come by the Players around eight tonight. You can put your finger through the wounds in my hands and feet. You'll find out I'm very much alive."

"I'll be there."

As soon as he hung up Kinlaw decided he must have been a lunatic to listen to Corcoran and his dames. He was just going to waste a day's pay on pricey drinks in a restaurant he couldn't afford. Then again, though Hollywood people kept funny hours, as he well knew from his marriage to Emily, what was a big-time director doing home in the middle of the day?

He spent the rest of the afternoon following up on missing persons. The sailor from Long Beach, it turned out, had no ring finger on his left hand. He finally got through to Mrs. Potter and discovered that Mr. Potter had turned up Sunday night after a drunken weekend in Palm Springs. He talked to Sapienza about recent mob activity and asked a snitch named Bunny Witcover to keep his ears open.

At four-thirty, Kinlaw called back down to the morgue. "Corcoran, do you remember when you saw that article? The one about the director?"

"I don't know. It was an old issue, at the dentist's office."

"Great." Kinlaw checked out of the office and headed down to the public library.

It was a Monday and the place was not busy. The mural that surrounded the rotunda, jam-packed with padres, Indians, Indian babies, gold miners, sheep, a mule, dancing señoritas, conquistadors, ships and flags, was busier than the room itself.

A librarian showed him to an index: the January 7, 1946 issue of *Life* listed a feature on Preston Sturges beginning on page 85. Kinlaw rummaged through the heaps of old magazines and finally tracked it down. He flipped to page 85 and sat there, hand resting on the large photograph. The man in the photograph, reclining on a sound stage, wearing a rumpled tan suit, was a dead ringer for the man lying on Corcoran's slab in the morgue.

Kinlaw's apartment stood on West Marathon at North Manhattan Place. The building, a four-story reinforced concrete box, had been considered a futuristic landmark when it was constructed in 1927, but its earnest European grimness, the regularity and density of the kid's-block structure, made it seem more like a penitentiary than a work of art. Kinlaw pulled the mail out of his box: an electric bill, a flyer from the PBA, and a letter from Emily. He unlocked the door to his apartment and, standing in the entry, tore open the envelope.

It was just a note, conversational, guarded. Her brother was out of the army. She was working for Metro on the makeup for a new Dana Andrews movie. And oh, by the way, did he know what happened to the photo album with all the pictures of Lucy? She didn't have a single one.

Kinlaw dropped the note on the coffee table, took off his jacket and got the watering can, sprayer and plant food. First he sprayed the hanging fern in front of the kitchen window, then moved through the plants in the living room: the African violets, ficus, and four varieties of coleus. Emily had never cared for plants, but he could tell she liked it that he did. It reassured her, told her something about his character that was not evident from looking at him. On the balcony he fed the big rhododendron and the planter full of day lilies. Then he put the sprayer back under the kitchen sink, poured himself a drink, and sat in the living room. He watched the late afternoon sun throw triangular shadows against the wall.

The *Life* article had painted Sturges as an eccentric genius, a man whose life had been a series of lucky accidents. His mother, a Europe-traipsing culture vulture, had been Isadora Duncan's best friend, his stepfather a prominent Chicago businessman. After their divorce Sturges's mother had dragged her son from opera in Bayreuth to dance recital in Vienna to private school in Paris. He came back to the U.S. and spent the twenties trying to make a go of it in her cosmetics business. In 1928 he almost died from a burst appendix; while recovering he wrote his first play; his *Strictly Dishonorable* was a smash Broadway hit in 1929. By the early thirties he had squandered the play's earnings and come to Hollywood, where he became Paramount's top screenwriter, and then the first writer-director of sound pictures. In four years he made eight movies, several of them big hits, before he quit to start a new film company with millionaire Howard Hughes. Besides writing and directing, Sturges owned an engineering company that manufactured diesel engines, and The Players, one of the most famous restaurants in the city.

Kinlaw noted the ruptured appendix, but there was little to set off his instincts except a passing reference to Sturges being "one of the most controversial figures in Hollywood." And the closing line of the article: "As for himself, he contemplates death constantly and finds it a soothing subject."

He fell asleep in his chair, woke up with his heart racing and his neck sweaty. It was seven o'clock. He washed and shaved, then put on a clean shirt.

The Players was an eccentric three-story building on the side of a hill at 8225 Sunset Boulevard, across Marmont Lane from the neo-gothic Chateau Marmont hotel. Above the ground-level entrance a big neon sign spelled out "The Players" in easy script. At the bottom-level drive-in, girls in green caps and jumpers waited on you in your car. Kinlaw had never been upstairs in the formal rooms. It was growing dark when he turned off Sunset onto Marmont and pulled his Hudson up the hill to the terrace-level lot. An attendant in a white coat with his name stitched in green on the pocket took the car.

Kinlaw loitered outside and finished his cigarette while he admired the lights of the houses spread across the hillside above the restaurant. Looking up at them, Kinlaw knew that he would never live in a house like those. There was a wall between some people and some ways of life. A lefty like the twenty-four-year-old YCL member he had been in 1938 would have called it money that kept him from affording such a home, and class that kept the people up there from wanting somebody like him for a neighbor, and principle that kept him from wanting to live there. But the thirty-five-year-old he was now knew it was something other than class, or money, or principle. It was something inside you. Maybe it was character. Maybe it was luck. Kinlaw laughed. You ought to be able to tell the difference between luck and character, for pity's sake. He ground out the butt in the lot and went inside.

At the dimly lit bar on the second floor he ordered a gin and tonic and inspected the room. The place was mostly empty. At one of the tables Kinlaw watched a man and a woman whisper at each other as they peered around the room, hoping, no doubt, to catch a glimpse of Van Johnson or Lizabeth Scott. The man wore a white shirt with a big collar and a white Panama hat with a pink hat band, the woman a yellow print dress. On the table they held two prudent drinks neatly in the center of prudent cocktail napkins, beside them a map of Beverly Hills folded open with bright red stars to indicate the homes of the famous. A couple of spaces down the bar a man was trying to pick up a blonde doing her best Lana Turner. She was mostly ignoring him but the man didn't seem to mind.

"So what do you think will happen in the next ten years?" he asked her.

"I expect I'll get some better parts. Eventually I want at least second leads."

"And you'll deserve them. But what happens when the Communists invade?"

"Communists schmomunists. That's the bunk."

"You're very prescient. The State Department should hire you, but they won't."

This was some of the more original pickup talk Kinlaw had ever heard. The man was a handsome fellow with an honest face, but his light brown hair and sideburns were too long. Maybe he was an actor working on some historical pic.

"You know, I think we should discuss the future in more detail. What do you say?"

"I say you should go away. I don't mean to be rude."

"Let me write this down for you, so if you change your mind . . ." The man took a coaster and wrote something on it. He pushed the coaster toward her with his index finger.

Good luck, buddy. Kinlaw scanned the room. Most of the clientele seemed to be tourists. At one end of the room, on the bandstand, a jazz quintet was playing a smoky version of "Stardust." When the bartender came back to ask about a refill, Kinlaw asked him if Sturges was in.

"Not yet. He usually shows up around nine or after."

"Will you point him out to me when he gets here?"

The bartender looked suspicious. "Who are you?"

"Does it matter?"

"You look like you might be from a collection agency."

"I thought this place was a hangout for movie stars."

"You're four years late, pal. Now it's a hangout for bill collectors."

"I'm not after money."

"That's good. Because just between you and me, I don't think Mr. Sturges has much."

"I thought he was one of the richest men in Hollywood."

"Was, past tense."

Kinlaw slid a five-dollar bill across the bar. "Do you know what he was doing yesterday afternoon?"

The bartender took the five note, folded it twice and stuck it into the breast pocket of his shirt. "Most of the afternoon he was sitting at that table over there looking for answers in the bottom of a glass of Black Label scotch."

"You're a mighty talkative employee."

"Manager's got us reusing the coasters to try to save a buck." He straightened a glass of swizzle sticks. "I paid for the privilege of talking. Mr. Sturges is into me for five hundred in back pay."

Down the end of the bar the blonde left. The man with the sideburns waved at the bartender, who went down to refill his drink.

Kinlaw decided he could afford a second gin and tonic. Midway through the third the bartender nodded toward a table on the mezzanine; there was Sturges, looking a lot healthier than the morning's dead man. He saw the bartender gesture and waved Kinlaw over to his table. Sturges stood as Kinlaw approached. He had thick, unkempt brown hair with a gray streak in the front, a square face, jug ears and narrow eyes that would have given him a nasty look were it not for his quirky smile. A big, soft body. His resemblance to the dead man was uncanny. Next to him sat a dark-haired, attractive woman in her late thirties, in a blue silk dress.

"Detective Kinlaw. This is my wife, Louise."

"How do you do."

As Kinlaw was sitting down, the waiter appeared and slid a fresh gin and tonic onto the table in front of him.

"You've eaten?" Sturges asked.

"No."

"Robert, a menu for Mr. Kinlaw."

"Mr. Sturges, I'm not sure we need to spend much time on this. Clearly, unless you have a twin, the identification we had was mistaken."

"That's all right. There are more than a few people in Hollywood who will be disappointed it wasn't me."

Louise Sturges watched her husband warily, as if she weren't too sure what he was going to say next, and wanted pretty hard to figure it out.

"When were you last on your boat?"

"Yesterday. On Saturday I went out to Catalina on the *Island Belle* with my friends, Dr. Bertrand Woolford and his wife. We stayed at anchor in a cove there over Saturday night, then sailed back Sunday. We must have got back around one P.M. I was back at home by three."

"You were with them, Mrs. Sturges?"

Louise looked from her husband to Kinlaw. "No."

"But you remember Mr. Sturges getting back when he says?"

"No. That is, I wasn't at home when he got there. I—"

"Louise and I haven't been living together for some time," Sturges said.

Kinlaw waited. Louise looked down at her hands. Sturges laughed.

"Come on, Louise, there's nothing for you to be ashamed of. I'm the one who was acting like a fool. Detective Kinlaw, we've been separated for more than a year. The divorce was final last November."

"One of those friendly Hollywood divorces."

"I wouldn't say that. But when I called her this morning, Louise was gracious enough to meet with me." He put his hand on his wife's. "I'm hoping she will give me the chance to prove to her I know what a huge mistake I made."

"Did anyone see you after you returned Sunday afternoon?"

"As I recall, I came by the restaurant and was here for some time. You can talk to Dominique, the bartender."

Eventually the dinner came and they ate. Or Kinlaw and
Louise ate; Sturges regaled them with stories about how his
mother had given Isadora the scarf that killed her, about his marriage to the heiress Eleanor Post Hutton, about an argument he'd
seen between Sam Goldwyn and a Hungarian choreographer, in
which he played both parts and put on elaborate accents.

Kinlaw couldn't help but like him. He had a sense of absurdity, and if he had a high opinion of his own genius, he seemed
to be able to back it up. Louise watched Sturges affectionately, as
if he were her son as much as her ex-husband. In the middle of
one of his stories he stopped to glance at her for her reaction,
then reached impulsively over to squeeze her hand, after which
he launched off into another tale, about the time, at a pool, he
boasted he was going to "dive into the water like an arrow,"
and his secretary said, "Yes, a Pierce-Arrow."

After a while Sturges wound down, and he and Louise left. At
the cloak room Sturges offered to help her on with her jacket,
and Kinlaw noticed a moment's skepticism cross Louise's face before she let him. Kinlaw went back over to talk with the bartender.

"I've got a couple more questions."

The bartender shrugged. "Getting late."

"This place won't close for hours."

"It's time for me to go home."

Kinlaw showed him his badge. "Do I have to get official, Dominique?"

Dominique got serious. "Robert heard you talking to Sturges.
Why didn't you let on earlier you were a cop? What's this
about?"

"Nothing you have to worry about, if you answer my questions." Kinlaw asked him about Sturges's actions the day before.

"I can't tell you about the morning, but the rest is pretty
much like he says," Dominique told him. "He came by here
about six. He was already drinking, and looked terrible. 'Look
at this,' he says to me, waving the L.A. *Times* in my face. They'd
panned his new movie. 'The studio dumps me and they still hang

this millstone around my neck.' He sat there, ordered dinner but didn't eat anything. Tossing back one scotch after another. His girlfriend must have heard something, she came in and tried to talk to him, but he wouldn't talk."

"His girlfriend?"

"Frances Ramsden, the model. They've been together since he broke with Louise. He just sat there like a stone, and eventually she left. Later, when business began to pick up, he got in his car and drove away. I remember thinking, I hope he doesn't get in a wreck. He was three sheets to the wind, and he's already had some accidents."

"What time was that?"

"About seven-thirty, eight. I thought that was the last I'd see of him, but then he came back later."

"What time?"

"After midnight. Look, can you tell me what this is about?"

Kinlaw watched him. "Somebody's dead."

"Dead?" Dominique looked a little shaken, nothing more.

"I think Sturges might know something. Anything you remember about when he came back? How was he acting?"

"Funny. He comes in and I almost don't recognize him. The place was clearing out then. Instead of the suit he'd had on earlier he was wearing slacks and a sweatshirt, deck shoes. He was completely sober. His eyes were clear, his hands didn't shake—he looked like a new man. They sat there and talked all night."

"They?"

"Mr. Sturges and this other guy he came in with. Friendly looking, light hair. He had a kind of accent—German, maybe? I figure he must be some Hollywood expatriate—they all used to hang out here—this was little Europe. Mr. Sturges would talk French with them. He loved to show off."

"Had you seen this man before?"

"Never. But Mr. Sturges seemed completely familiar with him. Here's the funny thing—he kept looking around as if he'd never seen the place."

"You just said he'd never been here before."

"Not the German. It was Sturges looked as if he hadn't seen The Players. 'Dominique,' he said to me, 'How have you been?' 'I've been fine,' I said.

"They sat up at Mr. Sturges's table there and talked all night. Sturges was full of energy. The bad review might as well have happened to somebody else. The German guy didn't say much, but he was drinking as hard as Mr. Sturges was earlier. It was like they'd changed places. Mr. Sturges stood him to an ocean of scotch. When we closed up they were still here."

"Have you seen this man since then?"

The bartender looked down the bar. "Didn't you see him? He was right here when you came in, trying to pick up some blonde."

"The guy with the funny haircut?"

"That's the one. Mr. Sturges said to let him run a tab. Guess he must've left. Wonder if he made her."

It was a woozy drive home with nothing to show for the evening except the prospect of a Tuesday morning hangover. He might as well do the thing right: back in the apartment Kinlaw got out the bottle of scotch, poured a glass, and sat in the dark listening to a couple of blues records. Scotch after gin, a deadly combination. After a while he gave up and went to bed. He was almost asleep when the phone rang.

"Hello?"

"Lee? This is Emily."

Her voice was brittle. "Hello," he said. "It's late." He remembered the nights near the end when he'd find her sitting in the kitchen after midnight with the lights out, the tip of her cigarette trembling in the dark.

"Did you get my letter?"

"What letter?"

"Lee, I've been looking for the photo album with the pictures of Lucy," she said. "I can't find it anywhere. Then I realized you must have taken it when you moved out."

"Don't blame me if you can't find it, Emily."

"You know, I used to be impressed by your decency."

"We both figured out I wasn't as strong as you thought I was, didn't we? Let's not stir all that up again."

"I'm not stirring up anything. I just want the photographs."

"All I've got is a wallet photo. I'm lucky I've got a wallet."

Instead of getting mad, Emily said, quietly, "Don't insult me, Lee." Her voice was tired.

"I'm sorry," he said. "I'll look around. I don't have them, though."

"I guess they're lost, then. I'm sorry I woke you." She'd lost the edge of hysteria; she sounded like the girl he'd first met at a Los Angeles Angels game in 1934. It stirred emotions he'd thought were dead, but before he could think what to say she hung up.

It took him another hour to get to sleep.

In the morning he showered, shaved, grabbed some ham and eggs at the Indian Head Diner and headed in to homicide. The fingerprint report was on his desk. If the dead guy was a mob button man, his prints showed up nowhere in any of their files. Kinlaw spent some time reviewing other missing persons reports. He kept thinking of the look on Louise Sturges's face when her husband held her coat for her. For a moment she looked as if she wasn't sure this was the same man she'd divorced. He wondered why Emily hadn't gotten mad when he'd insulted her over the phone. At one time it would have triggered an hour's argument, rife with accusations. Did people change that much?

He called the Ivar Avenue number.

"Mrs. Sturges? This is Lemoyne Kinlaw from the LAPD. I wondered if we might talk."

"Yes?"

"I hoped we might speak in person."

"What's this about?"

"I want to follow up on some things from last night."

She paused. "Preston's gone off to talk to his business manager. Can you come over right now?"

"I'll be there in a half an hour."

Kinlaw drove out to quiet Ivar Avenue and into the curving drive before 1917. The white-shingled house sat on the side of a hill, looking modest by Hollywood standards. Kinlaw rang the bell and the door was answered by a Filipino houseboy.

Once inside, Kinlaw saw that the modesty of the front was deceptive. The houseboy led him to a large room at the back that must have been sixty by thirty feet.

The walls were green and white, the floor dark hardwood. At one end of the room stood a massive pool table and brick inglenook fireplace. At the other end, a level up, surrounded by an iron balustrade, ran a bar upholstered in green leather, complete with a copper-topped nightclub table and stools. Shelves crowded with scripts, folders, and hundreds of books lined one long wall, and opposite them an expanse of French doors opened onto a kidney-shaped pool surrounded by hibiscus and fruit blossoms, Canary Island pines and ancient firs.

Louise Sturges, seated on a bench covered in pink velveteen, was talking to a towheaded boy of eight or nine. When Kinlaw entered she stood. "Mr. Kinlaw, this is our son, Mon. Mon, why don't you go outside for a while."

The boy raced out through the French doors. Louise wore a plum-colored cotton dress and black flats that did not hide her height. Her thick hair was brushed back over her ears. Poised as a *Vogue* model, she offered Kinlaw a seat. "Have you ever had children, Mr. Kinlaw?"

"A daughter."

"Preston very much wanted children, but Mon is the only one we are likely to have. At first I was sad, but after things started to go sour between us I was glad that we didn't have more."

"How sour were things?"

Louise smoothed her skirt. Her sophistication veiled a calmness that was nothing cheap or Hollywood. "Have you found out who that drowned man is?"

"No."

"What did you want to ask me about?"

"I couldn't help but get the impression last night that you were surprised at your husband's behavior."

"He's frequently surprised me."

"Has he been acting strangely?"

"I don't know. Well, when Preston called me yesterday I was pretty surprised. We haven't had much contact since before our separation. At the end we got so we'd communicate by leaving notes on the banister."

"But that changed?"

She watched him for a moment before answering. "When we met, Preston and I fell very much in love. He just swept me off my feet. He was so intense, funny. I couldn't imagine a more loving husband. Certainly he was an egotist, and totally involved in his work, but he was also such a charming and attentive man."

"What happened?"

"Well, he started directing, and that consumed all his energies. He would work into the evening at the studio, then spend the night at The Players. At first he wanted me totally involved in his career. He kept me by his side at the sound stage as the film was shot. Some of the crew came to resent me, but Preston didn't care. Eventually I complained, and Preston agreed that I didn't need to be there.

"Maybe that was a mistake. The less I was involved, the less he thought of me. After Mon was born he didn't have much time for us. He stopped seeing me as his wife and more as the mother of his son, then as his housekeeper and cook.

"Some time in there he started having affairs. After a while I couldn't put up with it anymore, so I moved out. When I filed for divorce, he seemed relieved."

Kinlaw worried the brim of his hat. He wondered what Sturges's version of the story would be.

"That's the way things were for the last two years," Louise continued. "Then he called me Sunday night. He has to see me, he needs to talk. I thought, he's in trouble; that's the only time he needs me. Back when the deal with Hughes fell through, he showed up at my apartment and slept on my bed, beside me, like a little boy needing comfort. I thought this would just be more of the same. So I met with him Monday morning. He was contrite. He looked more like the man I'd married than he'd seemed for years. He begged me to give him another chance. He realized his mistakes, he said. He's selling the restaurant. He wants to be a father to our son."

"You looked at him last night as if you doubted his sincerity."

"I don't know what to think. It's what I wanted for years, but—he seems so different. He's stopped drinking. He's stopped smoking."

"This may seem like a bizarre suggestion, Mrs. Sturges, but is there any chance this man might not be your husband?"

Louise laughed. "Oh, no—it's Preston all right. No one else has that ego."

Kinlaw laid his hat on the end table. "Okay. Would you mind if I took a look at your garage?"

"The garage? Why?"

"Humor me."

She led him through the kitchen to the attached garage. Inside, a red Austin convertible sat on a wooden disk set into the concrete floor.

"What's this?"

"That's a turntable," Louise said. "Instead of backing up, you can flip this switch and rotate the car so that it's pointing out. Preston loves gadgets. I think this one's the reason he bought this house."

Kinlaw inspected the garage door. It had a rubber flap along the bottom, and would be quite airtight. There was a dark patch on the interior of the door where the car's exhaust would blow, as if the car had been running for some time with the door closed.

They went back into the house. In the backyard the boy, laughing, chased a border collie around the pool. Lucy had wanted a dog. "Let me ask you one more question, and then I'll go. Does your husband have any distinguishing marks on his body?"

"He has a large scar on his abdomen. He had a ruptured appendix when he was a young man. It almost killed him."

"Does the man who's claiming to be your husband have such a scar?"

Louise hesitated, then said, "I wouldn't know."

"If you should find that he doesn't, could you let me know?"

"I'll consider it."

"One last thing. Do you have any object he's held recently—a cup or glass?"

She pointed to the bar. "He had a club soda last night. I think that was the glass."

Kinlaw got out his handkerchief and wrapped the glass in it, put it into his pocket. "We'll see what we will see. I doubt that anything will come of it, Mrs. Sturges. It's probably that he's just come to his senses. Some husbands do that."

"You don't know Preston. He's never been the sensible type."

Back at the office he sent the glass to the lab for prints. A note on his desk told him that while he had been out he'd received a call from someone named Nathan Lautermilk at Paramount.

He placed a call to Lautermilk. After running the gauntlet of the switchboard and Lautermilk's secretary, Kinlaw got him. "Mr. Lautermilk, this is Lee Kinlaw of the LAPD. What can I do for you?"

"Thank you for returning my call, Detective. A rumor going around here has it you're investigating the death of Preston Sturges. There's been nothing in the papers about him dying."

"Then he must not be dead."

Lautermilk had no answer. Kinlaw let the silence stretch until it became uncomfortable.

"I don't want to pry into police business, Detective, but if Preston was murdered, some folks around here might wonder if they were suspects."

"Including you, Mr. Lautermilk?"

"If I thought you might suspect me, I wouldn't draw attention to myself by calling. I'm an old friend of Preston's. I was assistant to Buddy DeSylva before Preston quit the studio."

"I'll tell you what, Mr. Lautermilk. Suppose I come out there and we have a talk."

Lautermilk tried to put him off, but Kinlaw persisted until he agreed to meet him.

An hour later Kinlaw pulled up to the famous Paramount arch, like the entrance to a Moorish palace. Through the curlicues of the iron gate the sun-washed soundstages hulked like pastel munitions warehouses. The guard had his name and told him where to park.

Lautermilk met him in the long low white building that housed the writers. He had an office on the ground floor, with a view across the lot to the sound stages but close enough so he could keep any recalcitrant writers in line.

Lautermilk seemed to like writers, though, a rare trait among studio executives. He was a short, bald, pop-eyed man with a Chicago accent and an explosive laugh. He made Kinlaw sit down and offered him a cigarette from a brass box on his desk. Kinlaw took one, and Lautermilk lit it with a lighter fashioned into the shape of a lion's head. The jaws popped open and a flame sprang out of the lion's tongue. "Louie B. Mayer gave it to me," Lautermilk said. "Only thing I ever got from him he didn't take back later." He laughed.

"I'm curious. Can you arrange a screening of one of Preston Sturges's movies?"

"I suppose so." Lautermilk picked up his phone. "Judy, see if you can track down a print of *Miracle of Morgan's Creek* and get it set up to show in one of the screening rooms. Call me when it's ready."

Kinlaw examined the lion lighter. "Did Sturges ever give you anything?"

"Gave me several pains in the neck. Gave the studio a couple of hit movies. On the whole I'd say we got the better of the deal."

"So why is he gone?"

"Buddy DeSylva didn't think he was worth the aggravation. Look what's happened since Sturges left. Give him his head, he goes too far."

"But he makes good movies."

"Granted. But he made some flops, too. And he offended too many people along the way. Didn't give you much credit for having any sense, corrected your grammar, made fun of people's accents and read H. L. Mencken to the cast over lunch. And if you crossed him he would make you remember it later."

"How?"

"Lots of ways. On *The Palm Beach Story* he got irritated with Claudette Colbert quitting right at five every day. Preston liked to work 'til eight or nine if it was going well, but Colbert was in her late thirties and insisted she was done at five. So he accommodated himself to her. But one morning, in front of all the cast and crew, Preston told her, 'You know, we've got to take your close-ups as early as possible. You look great in the morning, but by five o'clock you're beginning to sag.' "

"So you were glad to see him go."

"I hated to see it, actually. I liked him. He can be the most charming man in Hollywood. But I'd be lying if I didn't tell you that the studios are full of people just waiting to see him slip. Once you start to slip, even the waitresses in the commissary will cut you."

"Maybe there's some who'd like to help him along."

"By the looks of the reactions to his last couple of pictures, they won't need to. *Unfaithfully Yours* might have made money if it hadn't been for the Carole Landis mess. Hard to sell a comedy about a guy killing his wife when the star's girlfriend just committed suicide. But *Beautiful Blonde* is a cast iron bomb. Daryl Zanuck must be tearing his hair out. A lot of people are taking some quiet satisfaction tonight, though they'll cry crocodile tears in public."

"Maybe they won't have to take it. We found a body washed up on the beach in San Pedro answers to Sturges's description."

Lautermilk did not seem surprised. "No kidding."

"That's why I came out here. I wondered why you'd be calling the LAPD about some ex-director."

"I heard some talk in the commissary, one of the art directors who has a boat down in San Pedro heard some story. Preston was my friend. There have been rumors that he's been depressed. Anyone who's seen him in the last six months knows he's been having a hard time. It would be big news around here if he died."

"Well, you can calm down. He's alive and well. I just talked to him last night, in person, at his restaurant."

"I'm glad to hear it."

"So what do you make of this body we found?"

"Maybe you identified it wrong."

"Anybody ever suspect that Sturges had a twin?"

"A thing like that would have come out. He's always talking about his family."

Kinlaw put the cinematographer's monocle on Lautermilk's desk. "We found this in his pocket."

Lautermilk picked it up, examined it, put it down again. "Lots of these toys in Hollywood."

The intercom buzzed and the secretary reported that they could see the film in screening room D at any time. Lautermilk walked with Kinlaw over to another building, up a flight of stairs to a row of screening rooms. They entered a small room with about twenty theater-style seats, several of which had phones on tables next to them. "Have a seat," Lautermilk said. "Would you like a drink?"

Kinlaw was thirsty. "No, thanks."

Lautermilk used the phone next to his seat to call back to the projection booth. "Let her rip, Arthur."

"If you don't mind," he said to Kinlaw, "I'll leave after the first few minutes."

The room went dark. "One more thing, then," Kinlaw said. "All these people you say would like to see Sturges fail. Any of them like to see him dead?"

"I can't tell you what's in people's heads." Lautermilk settled back and lit a cigarette. The movie began to roll.

The Miracle of Morgan's Creek was a frenetic comedy. By twenty minutes in Kinlaw realized the real miracle was that they had gotten it past the Hays Office. A girl gets drunk at a going-away party for soldiers, marries one, gets pregnant, doesn't re-member the name of the father. All in one night. She sets her sights on marrying Norval Jones, a local yokel, but the yokel turns out to be so sincere she can't bring herself to do it. Norval tries to get the girl out of trouble. Everything they do only makes the situation worse. Rejection, disgrace, indictment, even suicide are all distinct possibilities. But at the last possible moment a miracle occurs to turn humiliation into triumph.

Kinlaw laughed despite himself, but after the lights came up the movie's somber undertone began to work on him. It looked like a rube comedy but it wasn't. The story mocked the notion of the rosy ending while allowing people who wanted one to have it. It implied a maker who was both a cruel cynic and dizzy optimist. In Sturges's absurd universe anything could happen at any time, and what people did or said didn't matter at all. Life was a cruel joke with a happy ending.

Blinking in the sunlight, he found his car, rolled down the windows to let out the heat, and drove back to homicide. When he got back the results of the fingerprint test were on his desk. From the tumbler they had made a good right thumb, index, and middle finger. The prints matched the right hand of the dead man exactly.

All that afternoon Kinlaw burned gas and shoe leather looking for Sturges. Louise had not seen him since he'd left the Ivar Avenue house in the morning, he was not with Frances Ramsden or the Woolfords, nobody had run into him at Fox, the restaurant manager claimed he'd not been in, and a long drive down to the San Pedro marina was fruitless: Sturges's boat rocked empty in its slip and the man in the office claimed he hadn't seen the director since Sunday.

It was early evening and Kinlaw was driving back to Central Homicide when he passed the MGM lot where Emily was working. He wondered if she was still fretting over the photo album. In some ways his problems were simpler than hers; all he had to do was catch the identical twin of a man who didn't have a twin. It had to be a better distraction than Emily's job. He remembered how, a week after he'd moved out, he'd found himself drunk one Friday night, coming back to the house to sit on the backyard swing and watch the darkened window to their bedroom, wondering whether she was sleeping any better than he. Fed up with her inability to cope, he'd known he didn't want to go inside and take up the pain again, but he could not bring himself to go away either. So he sat on the swing he had hung for Lucy and waited for something to release him. The galvanized chain links were still unrusted; they would last a long time.

A man watching a house, waiting for absolution. The memory sparked a hunch, and he turned around and drove to his apartment. He found the red Austin parked down the block. As he climbed the steps to his floor a shadow pulled back into the corner of the stairwell. Kinlaw drew his gun. "Come on out."

Sturges stepped out of the shadows.

"How long have you been waiting there?"

"Quite a while. You have a very boring apartment building. I like the bougainvillea, though."

Kinlaw waved Sturges ahead of him down the hall. "I bet you're an expert on bougainvillea."

"Yes. Some of the studio executives I've had to work with boast IQ's that rival that of the bougainvillea. The common bougainvillea, that is."

Kinlaw holstered the gun, unlocked his apartment door and gestured for Sturges to enter. "Do you have any opinion of the IQ of police detectives?"

"I know little about them."

Sturges stood stiffly in the middle of Kinlaw's living room. He looked at the print on the wall. He walked over to Kinlaw's record player and leafed through the albums.

Kinlaw got the bottle of scotch from the kitchen. Sturges put on Ellington's "Perfume Suite."

"How about a drink?" Kinlaw asked.

"I'd love one. But I can't."

Kinlaw blew the dust out of a tumbler and poured three fingers. "Right. Your wife says you're turning over a new leaf."

"I'm working on the whole forest."

Kinlaw sat down. Sturges kept standing, shifting from foot to foot. "I've been looking for you all afternoon," Kinlaw said.

"I've been driving around."

"Your wife is worried about you. After what she told me about your marriage, I can't figure why."

"Have you ever been married, Detective Kinlaw?"

"Divorced."

"Children?"

"No children."

"I have a son. I've neglected him. But I intend to do better. He's nine. It's not too late, is it? I never saw my own father much past the age of eight. But whenever I needed him he was always there, and I loved him deeply. Don't you think Mon can feel that way about me?"

"I don't know. Seems to me he can't feel that way about a stranger."

Sturges looked at the bottle of scotch. "I could use a drink."

"I saw one of your movies this afternoon. Nathan Lautermilk set it up. *The Miracle of Morgan's Creek.*"

"Yes. Everybody seems to like that one. Why I didn't win the Oscar for original screenplay is beyond me."

"Lautermilk said he was worried about you. Rumors are going around that you're dead. Did you ask him to call me?"

"Why would I do that?"

"To find out whether I thought you had anything to do with this dead man."

"Oh, I'm sure Nathan told you all about how he loves me. But where was he when I was fighting Buddy DeSylva every day? *Miracle* made more money than any other Paramount picture that year, after Buddy questioned my every decision making it." He was pacing the room now, his voice rising.

"I thought it was pretty funny."

"Funny? Tell me you didn't laugh until it hurt. No one's got such a performance out of Betty Hutton before or since. But I guess I can't expect a cop to see that."

"At Paramount they're not so impressed with your work since you left."

Sturges stopped pacing. He cradled a blossom from one of Kinlaw's spaths in his palm. "Neither am I, frankly. I've made a lot of bad decisions. I should have sold The Players two years ago. I hope to God I don't croak before I can get on my feet again."

Kinlaw remembered the line from the *Life* profile. He quoted it back at Sturges: " 'As for himself, he contemplates death constantly and finds it a soothing subject.' "

Sturges looked at him. He laughed. "What an ass I can be! Only a man who doesn't know what he's talking about could say such a stupid thing."

Could an impostor pick up a cue like that? The Ellington record reached the end of the first side. Kinlaw got up and flipped it over, to "Strange Feeling." A baritone sang the eerie lyric. "I forgot to tell you in the restaurant," Kinlaw said. "That dead man had a nice scar on his belly. Do you have a scar?"

"Yes. I do." When Kinlaw didn't say anything Sturges added, "You want me to show it to you?"

"Yes."

Sturges pulled out his shirt, tugged down his belt and showed Kinlaw his belly. A long scar ran across it from right to center. Kinlaw didn't say anything, and Sturges tucked the shirt in.

"You know we got some fingerprints off that dead man. And a set of yours, too."

Sturges poured himself a scotch, drank it off. He coughed. "I guess police detectives have pretty high IQ's after all," he said quietly.

"Not so high that I can figure out what's going on. Why don't you tell me?"

"I'm Preston Sturges."

"So, apparently, was that fellow who washed up on the beach at San Pedro."

"I don't see how that can be possible."

"Neither do I. You want to tell me?"

"I can't."

"Who's the German you've been hanging around with?"

"I don't know any Germans."

Kinlaw sighed. "Okay. So why not just tell me what you're doing here."

Sturges started pacing again. "I want to ask you to let it go. There are some things—some things in life just won't bear too much looking into."

"To a cop, that's not news. But it's not a good enough answer."

"It's the only answer I can give you."

"Then we'll just have to take it up with the district attorney."

"You have no way to connect me up with this dead man."

"Not yet. But you've been acting strangely. And you admit yourself you were on your boat at San Pedro this weekend."

"Detective Kinlaw, I'm asking you. Please let this go. I swear to you I had nothing to do with the death of that man."

"You don't sound entirely convinced yourself."

"He killed himself. Believe me, I'm not indifferent to his pain. He was at the end of his rope. He had what he thought were good reasons, but they were just cowardice and despair."

"You know a lot about him."

"I know all there is to know. I also know that I didn't kill him."

"I'm afraid that's not good enough."

Sturges stopped pacing and faced him. The record had reached the end and the needle was ticking repetitively over the center groove. When Kinlaw got out of his chair to change it, Sturges hit him on the head with the bottle of scotch.

Kinlaw came around bleeding from a cut behind his ear. It couldn't have been more than a few minutes. He pressed a wet dish towel against it until the bleeding stopped, found his hat and headed downstairs. The air hung hot as the vestibule of hell with the windows closed. Out in the street he climbed into his Hudson and set off up Western Avenue.

The mess with Sturges was a demonstration of what happened when you let yourself think you knew a man's character. Kinlaw had let himself like Sturges, forgetting that mild-mannered wives tested the carving knife out on their husbands and stone cold killers wept when their cats got worms.

An orange moon in its first quarter hung in the west as Kinlaw followed Sunset toward the Strip. When he reached The Players he parked in the upper lot. Down the end of one row was a red Austin; the hood was still warm. Head still throbbing, he went into the bar. Dominique was pouring brandy into a couple of glasses; he looked up and saw Kinlaw.

"What's your poison?"

"I'm looking for Sturges."

"Haven't seen him."

"Don't give me that. His car's in the lot."

Dominique set the brandies on a small tray and a waitress took them away. "If he came in, I didn't spot him. If I had, I would have had a thing or two to tell him. Rumor has it he's selling this place."

"Where's his office?"

The bartender pointed to a door, and Kinlaw checked it out. The room was empty; a stack of bills sat on the desk blotter. The one on the top was the third notice from a poultry dealer, for $442.16. PLEASE REMIT IMMEDIATELY was stamped in red across the top. Kinlaw poked around for a few minutes, then went back to the bar. "Have you seen anything of that German since we talked yesterday?"

"No."

Kinlaw remembered something. He went down to where the foreigner and the blonde had been sitting. A stack of cardboard coasters sat next to a glass of swizzle sticks. Kinlaw riffled through the coasters: on the edge of one was written "Suite 62."

He went out to the lot and crossed Marmont to the Chateau Marmont. The elegant concrete monstrosity was dramatically floodlit. Up at the top floors, the building was broken into steep roofs with elaborate chimneys and dormers surrounding a pointed central tower. Around it wide terraces with traceried balustrades and striped awnings marked the luxury suites. Kinlaw entered the hotel through a gothic arcade with ribbed vaulting, brick paving, and a fountain at the end.

"Six," he told the elevator operator, a wizened man who

stared straight ahead as if somewhere inside he was counting off the minutes until the end of his life.

Kinlaw listened at the door to Suite 62. Two men's voices, muffled to the point he could not make out any words. The door was locked.

Back in the tower opposite the elevator a tall window looked out over the hotel courtyard. Kinlaw leaned out: the ledge was at least a foot and a half wide. Ten feet to his right were the balustrade and awning of the sixth-floor terrace. He eased himself through the narrow window and carefully down the ledge; though there was a breeze up at this height, he felt his brow slick with sweat. His nose an inch from the masonry, he could hear the traffic on the boulevard below.

He reached the terrace, threw his leg over the rail. The French doors were open and through them he could hear the voices more clearly. One of them was Sturges and the other was the man who'd answered the phone that first afternoon at the Ivar house.

"You've got to help me out of this."

"Got to? Not in my vocabulary, Preston."

"This police detective is measuring me for a noose."

"Only one way out then. I can fire up my magic suitcase and take us back."

"No."

"Then don't go postal. There's nothing he can do to prove that you aren't you."

"We should never have dumped that body in the water."

"What do I know about disposing of bodies? I'm a talent scout, not an executive producer."

"That's easy for you to say. You won't be here to deal with the consequences."

"If you insist, I'm willing to try an unburned moment-universe. Next time we can bury the body in your basement. But really, I don't want to go through all this rumpus again. My advice is to tough it out."

"And once you leave and I'm in the soup, it will never matter to you."

"Preston, you are lucky I brought you back in the first place. It cost every dollar you made to get the studio to let us command the device. There are no guarantees. Use the creative imagination you're always talking about."

Sturges seemed to sober. "All right. But Kinlaw is looking for you, too. Maybe you ought to leave as soon as you can."

The other man laughed. "And cut short my holiday? That doesn't seem fair."

Sturges sat down. "I'm going to miss you. If it weren't for you I'd be the dead man right now."

"I don't mean to upset you, but in some real sense you are."

"Very funny. I should write a script based on all this."

"*The Miracle of Ivar Avenue?* Too fantastic, even for you."

"And I don't even know how the story comes out. Back here I'm still up to my ears in debt, and nobody in Hollywood would trust me to direct a wedding rehearsal."

"You are resourceful. You'll figure it out. You've seen the future."

"Which is why I'm back in the past."

"Meanwhile, I have a date tonight. A young woman, they tell me, who bears a striking resemblance to Veronica Lake. Since you couldn't introduce me to the real thing."

"Believe me," Sturges said. "The real thing is nothing but trouble."

"You know how much I enjoy a little trouble."

"Sure. Trouble is fun when you've got the perfect escape hatch. Which I don't have."

While they continued talking, Kinlaw sidled past the wrought iron terrace furniture to the next set of French doors, off the suite's bedroom. He slipped inside. The bedclothes were rumpled and the place smelled of whiskey. A bottle of Paul Jones and a couple of glasses stood on the bedside table along with a glass ashtray filled with butts; one of the glasses was smeared with lipstick. Some of the butts were hand-rolled reefer. On the dresser Kinlaw found a handful of change, a couple of twenties, a hotel key, a list of names:

Jeanne d'Arc		Carole Lombard	x
Claire Bloom		Germaine Greer	x
Anne Boleyn	x	Vanessa Redgrave	
Eva Braun	x	Alice Roosevelt	x
Louise Brooks	x	Christina Rossetti	
Charlotte Buff	x	Anne Rutledge	
Marie Duplessis		George Sand	x
Veronica Lake			

Brooks had been a hot number when Kinlaw was a kid, everybody knew Hitler's pal Eva, and Alice Roosevelt was old Teddy's aging socialite daughter. But who was Vanessa Redgrave? And how had someone named George gotten himself into this company?

At the foot of the bed lay an open suitcase full of clothes; Kinlaw rifled through it but found nothing that looked magic. Beside the dresser was a companion piece, a much smaller case in matching brown leather. He lifted it. It was much heavier than he'd anticipated. When he shook it there was no hint of anything moving inside. It felt more like a portable radio than a piece of luggage.

He carried it out to the terrace and, while Sturges and the stranger talked, knelt and snapped open the latches. The bottom half held a dull gray metal panel with switches, what looked something like a typewriter keyboard, and a small flat glass screen. In the corner of the screen glowed green figures: 23:27:46 PDT 3 May 1949. The numbers pulsed and advanced as he watched . . . 47 . . . 48 . . . 49 . . . Some of the typewriter keys had letters, others numbers. The keys in the top row were Greek letters. Folded into the top of the case was a long finger-thick cable, matte gray, made out of some braided material that wasn't metal and wasn't fabric.

"You have never seen anything like it, right?"

It was the stranger. He stood in the door from the living room.

Kinlaw snapped the case shut, picked it up and backed a step away. He reached into his jacket and pulled out his pistol.

The man swayed a little. "You're the detective," he said.

"I am. Where's Sturges?"

"He left. You don't need the gun."

"I'll figure that out myself. Who are you?"

"Detlev Gruber." He held out his hand. "Pleased to meet you." Kinlaw backed another step.

"What's the matter? Don't tell me this is not the appropriate social gesture for the mid-twentieth. I know better."

On impulse, Kinlaw held the case out over the edge of the terrace, six stories above the courtyard.

"So!" Gruber said. "What is it you say? The plot thickens?"

"Suppose you tell me what's going on here? And you better make it quick; this thing is heavier than it looks."

"All right. Just put down the case. Then I'll tell you everything you want to know."

Kinlaw rested his back against the balustrade, letting the machine hang from his hand over the edge. He kept his gun trained on Gruber. "What is this thing?"

"You want the truth, or a story you'll believe?"

"Pick one and see if I can tell the difference."

"It's a transmogrifier. A device that can change anyone into anyone else. I can change General MacArthur into President Truman, Shirley Temple into Marilyn Monroe."

"Who's Marilyn Monroe?"

"You will eventually find out."

"So you changed somebody into Preston Sturges?"

Gruber smiled. "Don't be so gullible. That's impossible. That case isn't a transmogrifier, it's a time machine."

"And I bet it will ring when it hits the pavement."

"Not a clock. A machine that lets you travel from the future into the past, and back again."

"This is the truth, or the story?"

"I'm from about a hundred years from now. 2043, to be precise."

"And who was the dead man in San Pedro? Buck Rogers?"

"It was Preston Sturges."

"And the man who was just here pretending to be him?"

"He was not pretending. He's Preston Sturges, too."

"You know, I'm losing my grip on this thing."

"I am chagrined. Once again, the truth fails to convince."

"I think the transmogrifier made more sense."

"Nevertheless. I'm a talent scout. I work for the future equiv-alent of a film studio, a big company that makes entertainment. In the future, Hollywood is still the heart of the industry."

"That's a nice touch."

"We have time machines in which we go back into the past. The studios hire people like me to recruit those from the past we think might appeal to our audience. I come back and persuade historicals to come to the future.

"Preston was one of my more successful finds. Sometimes the actor or director or writer can't make the transition, but Pre-ston seems to have an intuitive grasp of the future. Cynicism combined with repression. In two years he was the hit of the in-teractive fiber optic lines. But apparently it didn't agree with him. The future was too easy, he said, he didn't stand out enough, he wanted to go back to a time where he was an exception, not the rule. So he took all the money he made and paid the studio to send him back for another chance at his old life."

"How can you bring him back if he's dead?"

"Very good! You can spot a contradiction. What I've told you so far isn't exactly true. This isn't the same world I took him from. I recruited him from another version of history. I showed up in his garage just as he was about to turn on the ignition and gas himself. In your version, nobody stopped him. So see, I bring back my live Sturges to the home of your dying one. We arrive a half hour after your Sturges is defunct. You should have seen us trying to get the body out of the car and onto the boat. What a comedy of errors. This stray dog comes barking down the pier. Preston was already a madman, carrying around his own still-warm corpse. The dog sniffs his crotch, Preston drops his end of the body. Pure slapstick.

"So we manhandle the ex-Sturges onto the boat and sail out

past the breakwall. Dump the body overboard with window counterweights tied to its ankles, come back and my Sturges takes his place, a few years older and a lot wiser. He's had the benefit of some modern medicine; he's kicked the booze and cigarettes and now he's ready to step back into the place that he escaped earlier and try to straighten things out. He's got a second chance."

"You're right. That's a pretty good story."

"You like it?"

"But if you've done your job, why are you still here?"

"How about this: I'm actually a scholar, and I'm taking the opportunity to study your culture. My dissertation is on the effects of your Second World War on Hotel Tipping Habits. I can give you a lot of tips. How would you like to know who wins the Rose Bowl next year?"

"How'd you like to be trapped in 1949?"

Gruber sat down on one of the wrought iron chairs. "I probably would come to regret it. But you'd be amazed at the things you have here that you can't hardly get in 2043. T-bone steak. Cigarettes with real nicotine. Sex with guilt."

"I still don't understand how you can steal somebody out of your own past and not have it affect your present."

"It's not my past, it's yours. This is a separate historical stream from my own. Every moment in time gives rise to a completely separate history. They're like branches splitting off from the same tree trunk. If I come out to lop a twig off your branch, it doesn't affect the branch I come from."

"You're not changing the future?"

"I'm changing your future. In my past, as a result of personal and professional failures, Preston Sturges committed suicide by carbon monoxide poisoning on the evening of May 1, 1949. But now there are two other versions. In one Sturges disappeared on the afternoon of May 1, never to be seen again. In yours, Sturges committed suicide that evening, but then I and the Sturges from that other universe showed up, dropped his body in the ocean off San Pedro, and set up this new Sturges in his place—if you go along."

"Why should I?"

"For the game! It's interesting, isn't it? What will he do? How will it work out?"

"Will you come back to check on him?"

"I already have. I saved him from his suicide, showed him what a difference he's made to this town, and now he's going to have a wonderful life. All his friends are going to get together and give him enough money to pay his debts and start over again."

"I saw that movie. Jimmy Stewart, Donna Reed."

Gruber slapped his knee. "And they wonder why I delight in the twentieth century. You're right, Detective. I lied again. I have no idea how it will work out. Once I visit a time stream, I can't come back to the same one again. It's burned. A quantum effect; 137.04 moment-universes are packed into every second. The probability of hitting the same M-U twice is vanishingly small."

"Look, I don't know how much of this is malarkey, but I know somebody's been murdered."

"No, no, there is no murder. The man I brought back really is Preston Sturges, with all the memories and experiences of the man who killed himself. He's exactly the man Louise Sturges married, who made all those films, who fathered his son and screwed up his life. But he's had the advantage of a couple of years in the twenty-first century, and he's determined not to make the same mistakes again. For the sake of his son and family and all the others who've come to care about him, why not give him that chance?"

"If I drop this box, you're stuck here. You don't seem too worried."

"Well, I wouldn't be in this profession if I didn't like risk. What is life but risk? We've got a nice transaction going here, who knows how it will play out? Who knows whether Preston will straighten out his life or dismantle it in some familiar way?"

"In my experience, if a man is a foul ball, he's a foul ball. Doesn't matter how many chances you give him. His character tells."

"That's the other way to look at it. 'The fault, dear Brutus, is not in our stars, but in ourselves. . . .' But I'm skeptical. That's why I like Preston. He talks as if he believes that character tells, but down deep he knows it's all out of control. You could turn my time machine into futuristic scrap, or you could give it to me and let me go back. Up to you. Or the random collision of atoms in your brain. You don't seem to me like an arbitrary man, Detective Kinlaw, but even if you are, basically I don't give a fuck."

Gruber sat back as cool as a Christian holding four aces. Kinlaw was tempted to drop the machine just to see how he would react. The whole story was too fantastic.

But there was no way around those identical fingerprints. And if it were true—if a man could be saved and given a second chance—then Kinlaw was holding a miracle in his hand, with no better plan than to dash it to pieces on the courtyard below.

His mouth was dry. "Tell you what," he said. "I'll let you have your magic box back, but you have to do something for me first."

"I aim to please, Detective. What is it?"

"I had a daughter. She died of polio three years ago. If this thing really is a time machine, I want you to take me back so I can get her before she dies."

"Can't do it."

"What do you mean you can't? You saved Sturges."

"Not in this universe. His body ended up on the beach, remember? Your daughter gets polio and dies in all the branches."

"Unless we get her before she gets sick."

"Yes. But then the version of you in that other M-U has a kidnapped daughter who disappears and is never heard from again. Do you want to do that to a man who is essentially yourself? How is that any better than having her die?"

"At least *I'd* have her."

"Plus, we can never come back to this M-U. After we leave, it's burned. I'd have to take you to still a third branch, where you'd have to replace yet another version of yourself if you want to take up your life again. Only, since he won't be conveniently dead, you'll have to dispose of him."

"Dispose of him?"

"Yes."

Kinlaw's shoulder ached. His head was spinning trying to keep up with all these possibilities. He pulled the case in and set it down on the terrace. He holstered his .38 and rubbed his shoulder. "Show me how it works, first. Send a piece of furniture into the future."

Gruber watched him meditatively, then stepped forward and picked up the device. He went back into the living room, pushed aside the sofa, opened the case and set it in the center of the room. He unpacked the woven cable from the top and ran it in a circle of about ten feet in diameter around an armchair, ends plugged into the base of the machine. He stepped outside the circle, crouched and began typing a series of characters into the keyboard.

Kinlaw went into the bedroom, got the bottle of scotch and a glass from the bathroom and poured himself a drink. When he got back Gruber was finishing up with the keyboard. "How much of all this gas you gave me is true?"

Gruber straightened. His face was open as a child's. He smiled. "Some. A lot. Not all." He touched a switch on the case and stepped over the cable into the circle. He sat in the armchair.

The center of the room, in a sphere centered on Gruber and limited by the cable, grew brighter and brighter. Then the space inside suddenly collapsed, as if everything in it was shrinking from all directions toward the center. Gruber went from a man sitting in front of Kinlaw to a doll, to a speck, to nothing. The light grew very intense, then vanished.

When Kinlaw's eyes adjusted the room was empty.

Wednesday morning Kinlaw was sitting at his desk trying to figure out what to do with the case folder when his phone rang. It was Preston Sturges.

"I haven't slept all night," Sturges said. "I expected to wake up in jail. Why haven't you arrested me yet?"

"I still could. You assaulted a police officer."

"If that were the worst of it I'd be there in ten minutes. Last night you were talking about murder."

"Since then I had a conversation with a friend of yours at the Marmont."

"You—what did he tell you?" Sturges sounded rattled.

"Enough for me to think this case will end up unsolved."

Sturges was silent for a moment. "Thank you, Detective."

"Why? Because a miracle happened? You just get back to making movies."

"I have an interview with Larry Weingarten at MGM this afternoon. They want me to write a script for Clark Gable. I'm going to write them the best script they ever saw."

"Good. Sell the restaurant."

"You too? If I have to, I will."

After he hung up, Kinlaw rolled the cinematographer's monocle across his desk top. He thought of the body down in the morgue cooler, bound for an anonymous grave. If Gruber was telling the truth, the determined man he'd just spoken with was the same man who had killed himself in the garage on Ivar Avenue. Today he was eager to go forward; Kinlaw wondered how long that would last. He could easily fall back into his old ways, alienate whatever friends he had left. Or a stroke of bad luck like the Carole Landis suicide could sink him.

But it had to be something Sturges knew already. His movies were full of it. That absurd universe, the characters' futile attempts to control it. At the end of *Morgan's Creek* the bemused Norval is hauled out of jail, thrust into a national guard officer's uniform, and rushed to the hospital to meet his wife and children for the first time—a wife he isn't married to, children that aren't even his. He deliriously protests this miracle, a product of the hypocrisy of the town that a day earlier wanted to lock him up and throw away the key.

Then again, Norval had never given up hope, had done his best throughout to make things come out right. His character was stronger than anyone had ever given him credit for.

Kinlaw remembered the first time he'd seen his daughter, when they called him into the room after Emily had given birth. She was so tiny, swaddled tightly in a blanket: her little face, eyes clamped shut, the tiniest of eyelashes, mouth set in a soft line.

How tentatively he had held her. How he'd grinned like an idiot at the doctor, at the nurse, at Emily. Emily, exhausted, face pale, had smiled back. None of them had realized they were as much at the mercy of fate as Sturges's manic grotesques.

He looked up at the calendar, got the pencil out and crossed off Monday and Tuesday. He got the telephone and dialed Emily's number. She answered the phone, voice clouded with sleep. "Hello?"

"Emily," he said. "I have the photo album. I've had it all along. I keep it on a shelf in the closet, take it out and look at the pictures and cry. I don't know what to do with it. Come help me, please."

AUTHOR'S NOTE

I grew up loving the science fiction short story before I loved the novel, and I still get a kick out of stories that I never get from longer works. I hope to write a few more before I'm done.

The original idea was to reprint my Arkham House collection *Meeting in Infinity.* But then my editor Beth Meacham and I talked it over, and we pretty quickly decided it would be more interesting to do this book. *The Pure Product* is a collection of stories that do not also exist as portions of either *Freedom Beach* or *Good News from Outer Space.* Nine of these stories appeared in *Meeting in Infinity,* another eight did not, and the two poems are an indulgence I hope you will forgive. "Faustfeathers: A Comedy," though based on an earlier story, has never appeared before, and "Gulliver at Home" is also new. So what you've got here is, with the exception of "Another Orphan," my idea of my best work in independent short fiction.

Thanks to everyone who helped me write and publish these over the years, especially Jim Kelly and Sue Hall.

—JOHN KESSEL
Raleigh, North Carolina
11 June 1997